VULKAN
ВУЛКАН

A novel by

David Shirreff

Vulkan
Вулкан

By David Shirreff

Published in 2015 by Crunch Books, 22 Ellison Road, London
SW13 0AD
www.crunchbooks.org

A CIP record for this book is available from the British Library

ISBN: 978-0-9932969-0-1

For all victims of terror

DISCLAIMER

All characters, apart from well-known historical figures, are an invention of the author. Any similarity that might be found with actual persons living or dead is purely unintentional.

CHAPTER ONE

Leningrad, Winter 1984

He ran his hand over the bronze hull. It was the colour of the murky Baltic Sea. The shape was like every schoolboy's dream of a mechanical fish - pointed snout, tail, propeller, a squat conning tower with small blind windows and a screw-down hatch.

It was about three metres long and the height of a man. Displayed around it were relics of the Russian imperial navy, models of Peter the Great's men o'war, paintings of sea battles, models of early ironclad warships with shiny brass cannon and propellers. Full-size torpedoes lay like sharks on the wooden floor, their deadly gyro mechanisms exposed.

But for György the centrepiece was this small, clumsy shape - the embodiment in solid copper and iron of man's longing to share the deep with fish and other sea creatures. He patted its fat belly.

"Niet!" A voice rang through what used to be the St Petersburg stock exchange, now the maritime museum of Leningrad. A square Russian woman with a mop and pail advanced towards him. "Do not touch."

"Excuse me," said György in his bad Russian. He walked round to the pointed bronze snout and the piggy eyes. A label described the exhibit: he could read only the date - 1881.

So this was Swordfish. He dreamed of its dark, sweaty descent to 15 metres; the tin-can warping of the hull; the stale air shared with guttering lanterns; the soiled white uniform of Commander Grigory Tallin as he emerged a hero. A group of sea cadets brushed rudely past, and he came to.

György walked out of the museum, his hands thrust deep into his pockets. A bitter wind gusted off the Neva and slammed into the museum's Corinthian facade. Across the river lay the long wedding cake of the Winter Palace, its chandeliers already winking in the twilight.

Over the road his driver gunned the engine of black Volga and came over to pick him up. His driver was silent. György suspected he hated Hungarians, especially Hungarians who hadn't bothered to learn Russian, the lingua franca of the socialist bloc.

They drove in silence over the Dvortsovy Bridge and turned right toward the docks. Queues of hunched figures stood outside food shops waiting to fight for delicacies behind the steamed-up windows; more queues stood at bus stops waiting to go home. It was rush hour, but in Leningrad it was always rush hour. The palaces and cathedrals, planted on marshland by Peter the Great and his descendants, were now the offices and apartment blocks of the masses; and the masses plied at all hours from workplace, to shop, to decaying dwelling place.

What had happened to the great Russian people whose princes had brought home the best of European art and whose peasants had thrown out the war machines of Hitler and Napoleon? Beneath the rabbit fur and the tatty overcoats were they still the same?

He had seen them in the cathedral of St Nicholas in

their scores, kissing icons, trembling before smoking candles, whispering to bearded patriarchs. He had seen them drinking in crowded restaurants, pouring down vodka in a frenzy worthy of a Dostoyevsky hero. And he had seen them surge like ants along the Nevsky Prospekt, stripping the meagre shops of bargains - anything new to splurge their hoarded roubles on.

The car passed the squeaking wheels of a tram, metal on metal. The streetcar shone like a pale lantern in the gathering dark, swaying across the cobbles. They passed the floodlit gold spire of the Admiralty, once the focus of Russia's maritime greatness. Now the focus had moved, to a rock-hewn submarine park in the arctic wastes.

They came to the first checkpoint at the naval dockyard and the driver showed a pass. One of the sentries bent down to examine the passenger. Cold eye met cold eye. Soviet steel, György told himself: show no emotion - a race apart from the icon-kissers and vodka drinkers. Or maybe not. Maybe the steel face was just a mask, covering a raging, vodka-quaffing, icon-smothering mortal within.

He would never know. The Volga swept on to the next checkpoint. Top security. A red and white barrier discoloured in the sodium glare. This time he had to wait for clearance. The sentry beckoned him from the car. As he got out the icy blast invaded his clothes and tore away precious pockets of warm air. The sentry frisked him, robbing him of further warmth, and sent him back to the Volga's plastic seat, which was already cold.

They drove along the hard, past the hulks of grey warships, with yellow gangways leading to cosy wardrooms. György was in awe of these phantom shapes, perhaps, he reflected, because he had grown up in a land-locked country. Until he was eighteen the sum total of his maritime experience had been spotting barges on the Danube and rowing on Lake Balaton. Here were the warships of the second most powerful navy in the world - *Potemkin*, *V I Lenin*, *Ukraina*. His eyes snatched at the giant Cyrillic letters as they passed.

More security as they entered the submarine basin. The big hitters of the Soviet sub fleet were mostly at sea, but there were berthing facilities at Leningrad for official visits. György looked, but the four slipways were empty. They stopped at a long, single-storey building. György stumbled in from the cold.

"You're late, Dr Matthäus." There were three men in the laboratory, two in naval uniform and one in a white coat, Starchenko, the man who had spoken. He used English - the simplest common language.

"I was paying my respects to Commander Tallin."

"We haven't much time," said Starchenko. "They want an answer now."

"What's the hurry?" asked György. Starchenko glanced at the two naval officers.

"They're always in a hurry," he said. The uniformed men shuffled their feet. They had their orders, thought György. They had superiors breathing down their necks, and those in turn had their superiors, and so on in one frozen, Stalinist pyramid. György had the views expected of a man whose country had been invaded by the Russians as recently as 1956.

"Let's get started," he said, grinning broadly at his hosts. Starchenko led him to a workbench. There was György's baby, an aluminium box about the size and shape of a car silencer. He picked it up and caught the whiff of scorched copper. He knew at once what had happened.

"You've used this at the wrong voltage. I can't guarantee it will work at the specified range of temperature and pressure if you don't feed it the right voltage."

"The batteries we're using are very powerful, but they tend to surge," said Starchenko. "We haven't mastered that yet."

"Then install a regulator."

"There's no space and there's no time."

"If you don't do something this will happen again and again; maybe someone will get killed. The filter needs another three months of development in Budapest if we have to cope with your surges."

Starchenko gestured impatiently his hands. "Three months?" he said. "We haven't got three minutes." He took György by the arm and led him along the workbench. "These jackals have been here for two days, pacing up and down, waiting for that part to be flown in. They haven't left me for a moment, even to go to the bathroom. Okay, they have a job to do. But the only way to get them off my back is to give them something to satisfy their masters. A little modification to keep them happy for a month or so until you've got the real answer."

"You're asking me to risk someone's life. One of your own people. You're crazy," said György.

"I'm asking you to get these hyenas off my back. Someone has stepped up the pressure. Maybe Tikov, maybe Mikhailov. Who knows? But this has become vitally important to them. More important than one puny life."

"Maybe more than one, maybe a whole string of lives."

"More important than that. Believe me, these guys are making waves."

"You Russians spend your time beating the shit out of each other."

"Shh!" Starchenko glanced nervously behind him. "Do this for me, my friend." György turned and marched back to the burnt-out filter.

Maybe if he made the filter bath smaller the filter would use less power and so ride out the surges better. But that would endanger the purity of the filtered air. Poisons could creep in and even be recycled through the system. What the hell. They were only lousy Russians. One or two more or less would make no difference. But György was a kind of humanist.

"I can't do it," he said firmly.

"You have professional scruples, I see," said Starchenko. "I got over those a long time ago. Tell us what you think might work and we'll do it ourselves. I'll say it was my idea." György rested his hands on the workbench and lowered his head. "There'll be no repercussions," said Starchenko. "This thing is much bigger than you imagine."

"Why?" György didn't want to know. So many innocent inventions had been grabbed and perverted by the military. This was simply another one - but he wanted no part of it. He wanted to go home to his wife and kids in Szemlohegy and forget about the whole thing.

"It's a Delta category defence project."

György sighed. "I didn't think it was for finding mermaids."

"Have you ever heard of Nautilus?" whispered Starchenko. György shouted in protest.

"I don't want to hear!" This man was the worst kind of ally, the compulsive informer. He was dangerous. He'd have them both arrested and carted off to Siberia. "Look," he said. "Change the filter bath. Make it smaller and maybe the bloody thing will work. But keep your damned secrets to yourself. I want to get out of here." Starchenko smiled: he had read the Hungarian like an open book.

Starchenko dismissed the men in uniform. "We can manage alone now," he said. György took a sketch pad and began to draw the modifications. Under his breath he let out a stream of Hungarian oaths.

Starchenko offered him a cigarette, which he took without protest, although he hated them. He gasped at the first puff of Caucasian leaf.

"Even more horrible than I expected," said György. "Haven't you any Marlboro?" For György, a whiff of Marlboro was a whiff of the decadent West - he longed for the taste, mingled with a smell of whisky, horse sweat, camp fires, and the great outdoors.

But he settled down to his drawing and smoked the cigarette anyway. After half an hour they brought him tea which stood at his elbow and grew cold. Starchenko knew better than to breathe down his neck. He paced the laboratory, now and then throwing a glance at the engineer. He jumped when György shouted at him:

"A calculator! Do you have one?" Starchenko looked along the benches. "A slide rule, then." György began to scour the benches too. They found an abacus. György grabbed it and for a time Starchenko listened with admiration to the clicking of the beads. But then he heard the abacus crash against the wall.

"I need a calculator," said György again. "Even better, an IBM PC. Maybe one of the ships has one," he said, laying on the irony. It was infuriating to think that this super-power was run on a shoestring, relying on extraordinary and involuntary sacrifices by its people and its satellites.

Why couldn't they do their own dirty work? He was staggered by the gigantic hopelessness of the Soviet system. And he felt sorry for Starchenko. He felt sorry for the navy. Why should he feel sorry for them?

"Can your engineers work from drawings or do they need me to hold their hand?" he asked.

"It would be better if you were there, my dear friend," said Starchenko. "Let's go to the workshop."

Another sortie into the cold wind; the stars rode unmoved above the radar tower. The Volga took them to a workshop ringing with shouts and hammer blows, and filled with the roar of a gas turbine, belching flames to take the edge off the cold. Not a place for precision work, reflected György.

But he was surprised to find in one corner an oasis of competence. He could tell by the layout of the place that here were some real engineers. There was even a calculator.

How easy it is to misjudge these people, he thought. But they spoke no English. He mimed his way through the modifications he had devised.

The engineers showed him drawings of the complete air filter cycle. He tried not to look. He wanted to learn nothing that might be confidential. But the shape of the system intrigued him. It was extremely cramped and the ducts had been forced into drastic contortions. Now he saw a hundred other reasons why the system could suffer overload. But that was their problem. I'll do what they ask, he told himself. I'll get on the plane and make sure I never come back.

The Soviet engineers were good at their job. With no trouble they fashioned a new filter bath from aluminium. It looked rather better than the Hungarian original. The bath was filled, a new coil was installed and the filter was tested to several atmospheres.

"Can I go now?" György asked Starchenko. He didn't want to suggest testing the part with a surging battery and the connecting ducts twisted to damnation - they would find out soon enough, and he wanted to be on that plane before they did.

"It seems to work," said Starchenko. "I'll take you to your hotel."

CHAPTER TWO

The Volga glided through the streets of Leningrad. The city was asleep. Lights no longer illuminated the dome of St Isaac's cathedral, the Admiralty, the Winter Palace. A few cars moved like beetles through the dark streets.

György leaned back in the plastic seat. "Are there any nightclubs, any real bars in this town?" he asked. Starchenko laughed.

"You Hungarians," he said, "you're all the same. One night away from home and the first thing you want is a piece of arse."

"I didn't mean that. I want a drink. Aren't you supposed to have everything here, stashed away?"

"We have everything." Starchenko spoke to the driver. The car swung south, down a narrow street and then west alongside a quiet canal. György caught sight of houses with magnificent façades picked out by the headlights. There were lions guarding porches, caryatids under balconies, and classical friezes beneath mansard roofs. Through windows he saw chandeliers lit like cities, reflected in full-length mirrors. The car stopped by a house with a lion's head door-knocker.

"A moment, please." Starchenko climbed out and knocked. Warm light poured across the street. Starchenko beckoned and György dived into the warmth. They were in a cavernous hallway. Starchenko led the way up three flights of stairs worn into concave shapes. The noise of music and voices grew louder then burst out as Starchenko opened an apartment door.

It was like the entrance to another world. A room with a tall ceiling, full of people - older men in suits, youths in roll-neck sweaters, some women devastatingly chic, others scruffily casual. There was champagne, whisky, vodka and caviar, both red and black. Waiters in white jackets kept the glasses filled.

"What the hell is this?" asked György.

"These are members of the Kirov ballet," said Starchenko. "There's the French consul talking to the blonde girl, and the man by the fireplace is an Italian banker. Enjoy yourself." Starchenko, as if wearied by all this celebration, withdrew. György stood for a moment, sizing up the scene, then launched himself towards the drinks table. He asked for a mixture of vodka and Georgian champagne - fifty-fifty. After a first refreshing draught he turned and surveyed the company.

He was tired and felt shabby in his rumpled suit, but he wasn't a bad-looking guy. Maybe some of these ballerinas spoke English. György chose a knot of people by the fireplace and sailed in.

"Hallo," he said. A few heads turned. "Does anyone speak English?" The heads turned back. But he heard a woman's voice behind him call softly:

"Hallo, stranger." He turned to see a tall woman in her thirties, her body hugged to the calves by a dress of black wool, and draped in a black shawl. She smiled at him. If this was a set-up then he was happy to walk into it. "Are you alone?" she asked.

"Not any more," said György. "Are you with the Kirov ballet?" The woman blew smoke into the air and laughed.

"Do I have ten kilos on each thigh?" György couldn't prevent himself from looking at the wide hips and the slender legs.

"They look okay from here," he said. She looked him up and down critically.

"You're not British, are you?" she said. "Or American?"

"No."

"Let me guess." György stared into her deep grey eyes as they searched for clues. He felt they knew the answer already - the ill-cut suit, the thick-soled shoes were a giveaway. But the tie: it was pure silk, from Italy.

The grey eyes narrowed.

"You might be French or Swiss," she said. György moved uncomfortably. He knew she was playing a game with him, but he didn't want to break the illusion.

"Let's say I'm not Russian," he said.

"Nor me. I had a Polish grandfather and a German grandmother. That's why I'm different. I'm not cold and I'm not, how do you say, xenophobic." She put her hand on his shoulder and murmured: "I'm cosmopolitan. Call me Nadia."

It got through to him. She was a whore - well dressed, well-educated, a high-class tart. Well, he wasn't proud and he'd had a lousy day: Starchenko had read him right. He gulped down his vodka and champagne.

"Get you another drink, Nadia?" he asked.

"I don't think so. I have an apartment near here. It's very comfortable." She smiled at him. "These parties bore me." György looked longingly at the drinks table.

"Do you have vodka there, or brandy?"

"Everything."

"Let's go." Nadia went to get her coat and György looked at the guests, wondering which had spotted his conversation with the whore. No one appeared to notice. The consul had his arm round the blonde, and the Italian banker was holding court, like one of the Medici, surrounded by a tableau of dancers in affected poses.

They walked down the stairway and into the street. György saw the Volga parked by the canal.

"I have a car," he said.

"We'll walk," said Nadia. He felt the cold fur yield as she took his arm. The wind had dropped and they walked by the mirror-still canal, listening to the quiet roar of a city that never slept.

"I think this is your first time in St Petersburg," said Nadia. "I like to call it by its old name. We long for the old days, the old furniture, aristocratic society, concerts, exhibitions, banquets for a thousand people." György didn't want to contradict her, but he thought of the thousands of serfs who would have supplied such banquets, the terror of the secret police which hung over the intelligentsia, the sudden arrests at dawn, and political prisoners languishing in the Fortress of Peter and Paul. Things hadn't been much better then for people who thought; in fact, they were probably worse.

György heard the cough of a car engine. The Volga was following them, its lights doused.

"Don't worry about him," said Nadia. "He's only doing his job." She led him through an archway into a courtyard. They walked up one flight and she opened the door of a first-floor apartment. The lights were ablaze inside. There were rugs and cushions on the floor, icons and candlesticks by the fireplace, sweeping velvet curtains. Outside, György heard the Volga draw up and the engine cut. Nadia turned to him and smiled.

"All this will cost you fifty dollars. Have a drink." She pulled back a curtain to reveal a shelf of drinks - Beefeater,

White Horse, Courvoisier. György registered the names without reading them. Fifty dollars, he thought. He had ten, scraped together to buy some Marlboro in the beriozka hard-currency shop. Apart from that he had some unwanted roubles and equally worthless Hungarian forints. When should he tell her? Now - or later? György was a gentleman.

"I have only ten dollars," he said. Nadia was taking off her coat. She shrugged and advanced towards him.

"Give me the ten dollars," she said. He handed it over and for a moment she examined the wigged head of George Washington. "Now get out." György looked at her.

"What about my drink?" he said. The grey eyes stared unblinking; the face was hard, suddenly lined and old.

"You thought you could buy me with this?" she waved the note at him, her voice rising: "I'm not a cheap girl off the street."

"It's relative," said György. "In New York fifty dollars is cheap." But he could see he was losing. Now he wouldn't even enjoy the drink. She had turned from sex idol to harridan in an instant.

"I'm only a poor Hungarian with forints in my pocket," he explained.

"I know, and you're probably Jewish," she spat. He backed towards the door.

"Sorry for the trouble," he said and shut the door on a torrent of Russian abuse.

Down in the street the Volga was waiting. György got in and said, "Hotel - gastinitsa."

"Bistro!" said the driver and roared with laughter. Once or twice he said 'bistro' and exploded with mirth again.

In his overheated hotel room György twisted and turned. He had a raging thirst but didn't dare drink the tap water which was notoriously contaminated. His thoughts raced through anger and frustration but settled, in a wakeful hour before dawn, on that drawing of the air filter system. It was intriguing. He could remember it as if he had it in front of him - the perfect lucidity of a true hallucination. What had been in that drink? He fell asleep.

György flew out that day, via Warsaw to Budapest. When he got home and had greeted his family, he locked himself in the bedroom. He took out some airmail paper which he had carefully saved, smoothed it out on a book and began to draw.

He remembered the curves of the ducts very clearly. Half closing his eyes he could see again how they bent inside the shape of a small cabin. He drew fluently but tried to embellish nothing. Taking the scale from the size of the filter it looked as though there was room for only one person - two at a pinch. What had Starchenko called it?

György finished his drawing and wrote underneath it 'Nautilus'.

CHAPTER THREE

Simpnäs, Sweden

Across the Baltic Sea from Leningrad, a summer swell heaved on the Swedish shore. It was four in the morning but already light. A body lay beyond the breakers, clad in a wetsuit. A few hundred metres down the coast a fat lozenge, the size of a saloon car, rolled in the foam with water dripping from a hatchway.

Out to sea a black inflatable with four men aboard charged through the swell. Boris Tikov crouched in the bows trying to steady his binoculars and scan the shore. Surely it was too early for anyone, even a Swede, to be up and about. Maybe the odd fisherman, but this coast was barren; there wasn't a village for miles.

But he did see a man, picking his way over the rocks and lichen towards the cove. Tikov stabbed the lenses further into his eyes. "Damnation!" he said.

The man stood for a moment by the breakers then waded in and dragged the body out of the water. Tikov could see him pitch his weight onto the lifeless chest, again and again. Then the man looked up and gazed towards him, into his very eyes.

The inflatable was close now and Tikov's mind raced. He had to decide fast what to do with this potentially embarrassing witness. His orders left no room for doubt - this man had to be killed. But, although he had reached the rank of brigadier, he'd never before been faced with taking a human life.

Tikov nudged Zholobov beside him and pointed to the human on the shore. "Shoot," he said, trying to show calm as a cold sickness hit him in the stomach. Zholobov raised his weapon. "Wait," said Tikov.

When the inflatable reached the shallows Zholobov slipped overboard, sought a foothold, and took aim. The automatic rifle cracked twice and the man went down.

The helmsman had cut the engine and for a moment the four Russians paused in the water, aghast at what they had done.

"Bring the bodies on board," said Tikov calmly. They picked up the bodies and swung them into the bilges, covering them with oil-cloth. Then the inflatable nosed round to the helpless lozenge rolling in the foam. Zholobov closed the dripping hatch and attached a tow-rope. It needed all four men to right the clumsy craft and push it into deep water where it pitched and rolled, half full of water. The rubber boat towed it slowly towards the horizon.

A second witness watched the boat through a telephoto lens. He fought to hold the camera steady but he was trembling. He had heard the shots and seen his friend carted lifeless out to sea. Now he shot frame after frame as if emptying a rifle magazine at the departing convoy.

But in the arctic dawn he noticed the light-metre hadn't registered and he flung the camera down in despair. After several minutes, when the two craft were a speck on the horizon, he rose to his feet and staggered drunkenly down to the shore. There was nothing. Foam seethed on the pebbles of the little cove. He climbed over the rocks to where the canister, or whatever it was, had been. A few scratch marks on the rocks, some torn seaweed, but otherwise nothing. The raiding party and his friend might never have existed.

Dimock couldn't think straight. For a long time he stared out to sea with tears in his eyes. If John wasn't dead already he soon would be. He imagined his blood pumping unchecked into the bilges of the boat. Even if it had been an accident, even if they cared, they obviously had no medical equipment. Who the hell were they? Pirates? Terrorists? Soviets?

Tikov looked down at the two corpses in the heaving boat - Karpov's white, crinkled face jutting from the glistening rubber - and the other man fresh-faced, as if death had hardly touched him. There wasn't much blood.

Zholobov searched his jacket and found a wallet and some car keys. Tikov took the wallet and went through the separate pockets. There were credit cards and some Swedish currency, also two £20 sterling notes. Tikov read the name on one of the credit cards - John A Stallybrass. He was an Englishman!

What the hell had he been doing on the Swedish shore? Had he been spying on them? Unlikely. He would have been more circumspect. Then was it just a chance encounter? Englishmen don't travel alone, he thought.

Tikov seized the binoculars and scanned the distant shore. Of course there was nothing. Damnation! His mind raced through possibilities. Perhaps they should go back and send out a shore party. Then he relaxed again. What was done, was done.

They winched the crippled Nautilus onto the deck of the fishing boat and camouflaged it with nets and tarpaulins. The crew hoisted the two bodies out of the rubber dinghy. Karpov was taken below for a post-mortem. The Englishman was laid on deck in preparation for a sea burial. They measured his height and photographed his face; then they attached some spare fishing weights and threw him overboard.

Tikov muttered a quiet prayer. "His death will be all over the papers. The best detectives from Scotland Yard will swarm over Sweden studying the case of the missing Mr John Stallybrass. Dies irae, dies illa." He radioed the master on the bridge: "We'll head for Ainazi." A Swedish spotter plane appeared from the coast circled the vessel and returned. "Just in time," thought Tikov. He'd enjoyed the last three months, testing the Nautilus to its limits in a hostile environment but he hated the idea of it ending in failure. This was failure - a submariner drowned because of some inexplicable malfunction and a murder to stop the exposure of the entire five-year project. And who would take the blame? Boris Alexeivich Tikov, former cosmonaut and hero of the Soviet Union, fighting to preserve himself from an early retirement which would have ended the way it did for Gagarin - in daredevilry and sudden death. Yuri Gagarin, the Soviet Union's first man in space, had become a victim of his own celebrity. One day in 1967 he took a supersonic MiG fighter on a joyride and dashed himself into the Urals at 1,025 kilometres an hour.

Tikov had agreed to head this project because he wanted to prove that his cosmonauts, Lebedyev, Volkov, Demirkan and Cheung, and others in the back-up crew of the famous Apollo-Soyuz link-up mission in 1975, were the finest bunch of operators in the world, a team of elite, adaptable human beings - his idea of modern renaissance man. Of course, he knew he was wrong. Lebedyev had cracked up twice after a prolonged sub-surface mission. Demirkan was inclined to be hot-headed; Kardali was more of an artist than a scientist. Tikov himself was soft-headed, sentimental; he was the first to admit it. He didn't like to lose people and he shied away from tough decisions. His worst moment, which he re-lived on dark nights, had been to let a man die, spinning out of control in a space capsule, rather than risk two more lives on a rescue mission. "You're not tough enough for this job, Boris," Mikhailov had told him. Mikhailov was the party member on the Kremlin's committee for clandestine warfare, GEKO - a man of no rank and yet of supreme rank, an éminence grise whom they all hated and were polite to. He was the mouthpiece of many orders and decisions though it was difficult to tell whether they had come from him or from some higher authority. The empirical fact was that an order from him had never yet been countermanded.

Mikhailov called this operation Vulkan. Tikov had come to think of Mikhailov himself as Vulkan, a dark, malformed creature forging Zeus's thunderbolts deep under the earth. It was only later that he learned how deadly accurate his analogy was.

When they got back to Ainazi, he'd have another argument with Mikhailov. They had to investigate what went wrong, modify the design and do more tests. That should mean modifying all the prototypes in operation - there were four or five now as far as he knew. Mikhailov was in a hurry, driven either by personal ambition or by the whips held over him by his superiors. He would never allow a three- or four-month delay on Vulkan. It was too damned important. That meant other men, Tikov's men, might die.

Tikov went below to the boardroom. On this converted fishing boat there was a pretence of a military pecking order. He, his second-in-command Major Lebedyev, the captain and the mate shared a small but well-furnished boardroom. Lebedyev was there, tucking into black bread and a plate of beans. The vodka bottle was already on the table although it was only 8.30am.

"You think that'll help you forget Karpov?" said Boris.

"I'm honouring the dead," said Lebedyev. "A martyr in the cause of Soviet world domination." Tikov laughed without smiling. "He was a good comrade. He had technical flair. And he was a bloody good —" Lebedyev searched for the word, "hunter. But he wasn't quite —".

"One of us," offered Tikov.

"Exactly." Karpov wasn't a cosmonaut; he was a submariner - one of Mikhailov's blue-eyed boys, drafted in from the navy. It was decided that he would do most of the early tests on Nautilus while the cosmonauts adapted to the new medium. As the programme advanced Karpov continued to hog most of the diving time, as a selfish motorist will hog the driving. Tikov and Lebedyev looked on cynically, but with some curiosity, as he appeared to take greater and greater risks testing the sluggish vehicle to its limits. In the end Karpov had literally blown it. They still had to find out exactly why, and offer Mikhailov a credible explanation.

"My bet is those Hungarian filters," said Lebedyev."The Magyars look flashy but they never get things quite right."

"I think he ran out of air," said Tikov. "He'd been under for more than 17 hours without using the snorkel. Then he panicked and blew the hatch." Tikov imagined his oxygen-starved limbs fighting madly to reach the surface while the brain slipped into unconsciousness, and as the hands clawed, the lungs gratefully inhaled lethal doses of the Baltic Sea. By the time they got there, the half-submerged craft was being dashed among rock pools and Karpov lay dead half a kilometre along the coast.

Tikov poured himself a small vodka for breakfast. "In New York we had Canadian ham with eggs easy over, orange juice from Florida and the most delicious, pure American coffee," Tikov reminded Lebedyev. "Cup after cup, as much as you wanted." He looked at the tray of herrings in vinegar and the samovar crowned with its pot of lukewarm tea concentrate. In New York they had been garlanded like homecoming heroes and had the garish honour of a ticker-tape parade, a Broadway show and then a reception in Washington at the White House, all on television. Anywhere else in the world it would have been plain vulgar; there it was vulgar but magnificently American. Tikov had loved every minute of it as if it were a trip not into the enemy camp but to the archaic grandeur of ancient Rome - the language, the simplicity and the naive self-confidence of it all were just like the snatches of Roman history he'd studied at school. Hail to the Chief - Hail Caesar!

The fishing boat reached Ainazi a small port near Riga. Tikov saw the black Zil saloon on the quayside. It took him to the nearest airfield and he was flown to Moscow. Mikhailov was at the foot of the gangway, waiting like an impatient lover, except that he was flanked by two bodyguards. From that angle he looked smaller and more hunched than usual in his well-made dark suit. While Tikov greeted him, his mind recalled the punch-line of one of Demirkan's awful jokes: "I've no idea what's wrong with him - but he's got a good tailor." Mikhailov's bushy eyebrows knitted as he forced a smile: "Ustinov's expecting us," he said.

In the back of the big limousine, Mikhailov's seat of power, he turned to Tikov and started talking rapidly about the next phase of project Vulkan.

"But what about the Swedish incident?" interrupted Tikov.

"Forget it," said Mikhailov, brushing the notion away as if it were a fly. "We've no time to lose. The Americans are going ahead with their Star Wars programme and this is our only answer to it." Tikov tried to work that out by himself. He didn't like to ask too many questions but it was certainly a brain teaser - how could a miniature submarine be the answer to Star Wars? Star Wars was the name given to the American defence system that when developed would shoot down any nuclear missile thrown at the United States from anywhere in the world. It was a goal beset with enormous technological obstacles - even if the theory worked on paper. If it had been anything other than a defence project it would have been thrown out months ago as the hare-brained scheme of a madman. But the Egyptian pharaohs built their pyramids, mediaeval archbishops built their cathedrals, and President Reagan was going to have his Star Wars system, a monument to American imperialism. It couldn't be relied on not to work - every human and technological resource would be thrown at it. Half of the exercise was to intimidate America's enemies. It was clear the Soviet Union's system of SS 20 intercontinental ballistic missiles wouldn't be enough. Mikhailov and his masters wanted to deploy another system under its shadow - a system so secret that the Soviet defence ministry itself wouldn't know about it. Like Vulcan's thunderbolts they would be forged and kept underground. Jupiter wouldn't ever lay his hands on them - he wouldn't know they existed.

"What's the payload of the ZX-B?" asked Mikhailov.

"About 2,000 kilogrammes," said Tikov, "excluding the pilot."

"Just the right size for a strategic nuclear device."

"Strategic! That's enough room for a 50 megaton bomb."

"Precisely."

"But wait a minute. The Nautilus isn't designed to carry a bomb, let alone deliver it."

"It isn't and it wouldn't. The Nautilus will be the bomb."

"And the pilot?"

Mikhailov smiled. "You've heard of the suicide bombers in Lebanon. Or Japan's kamikaze pilots. They're very effective."

"That's preposterous. The whole idea's monstrous!" There was a cascade of laughter from Mikhailov: "My dear Boris Alexeivich, I was teasing you. Of course the pilot will have a chance of escape. We Russians aren't pigs and fanatics. We have a deep respect for the sanctity of human life, even that of a lousy cosmonaut."

Tikov was not amused. "But the bomb will be carried." Mikhailov laid a hairy hand on Tikov's knee. Tikov was repelled by the sudden warmth. "That is a secret between you and me."

"What authority do you have for re-directing this project?" asked Tikov rather bravely.

"The very highest - Ustinov."

"And if I refuse."

"God help your family and God help Mother Russia," said Mikhailov.

VULKAN

CHAPTER FOUR

Moscow

They had reached the outskirts of Moscow - rank upon rank of grey, cracking apartment blocks - but the trees were in full leaf and clutches of brightly-clad children were playing in the sun, something Tikov hadn't seen for many months. His heart warmed at the thought of his homeland and seeing his family even if it was for only a few days.

"Who knows about this project?" asked Tikov.

"The beauty of this project," said Mikhailov now in his element, "is that many people will think they know about it, hear rumours about Nautilus, may even get a glimpse of it. The Hungarians are as leaky as hell. But few will conceive that the Nautilus, by its quietness and stealth, can render the hundreds of billions of dollars that Mr Reagan is spending on Star Wars completely useless. You see it's an economic weapon just as much as a military one."

Tikov, in spite of his horror at the thought of his toy submarine becoming a bomb, began to be tickled by the idea. It would be a deterrent thousands of times cheaper than lasers in space. Just another move and a very economical one in the nuclear chess game. He wondered where this bomb would be deployed.

"New York, London, Tokyo are the most obvious places. They're by the sea," said Mikhailov, "but it's remarkable how many of the world's major cities can be reached secretly, underwater, by a small, bottom-crawling submarine."

"The Nautilus's batteries wouldn't carry it far up the River Seine. You'd need enormous back-up."

"That's your problem. I've dreamt up the broad scheme, you're going to put it into action."

"It's madness," said Tikov. "Why not just build a bomb secretly in a Manhattan basement?"

"No, no."

"And then call up Reagan and say "I've got you by the balls."?"

"It wouldn't work. It's too risky."

"Too risky!" Tikov had to laugh "Would you mind telling me why it's any more risky than crawling up the bottom of the Hudson River?"

"It's a question of control," Mikhailov almost shouted. "There would be too much dependence on external factors, too many contact men and technicians involved. With Nautilus you need only one, carefully selected, highly trained, dedicated individual."

"You mean one of my cosmonauts. And what will he do - spend his life at the bottom of the Thames or the Hudson waiting for the order that never comes?"

"Once the bomb, the Nautilus, is in place he won't have to be inside, except for routine visits."

"The thing's bound to be discovered - by trawlers, dredgers, boys fishing or other submarines. I bet they search every inch of New York harbour."

"That's your problem, Boris Alexeivich. I've painted the canvas, you fill in the detail."

The limousine glided into Red Square and turned towards the high walls of the Kremlin. It hardly hesitated at the gate before sweeping past three security checks into an inner courtyard. The two men entered a high portico and ascended a broad staircase to the first floor. They were shown through high double doors into an ante-room and then into a well-lit panelled gallery. Sitting at a desk at the end was Marshall Dmitri Ustinov, supreme commander of the Soviet armed forces. He rose as they entered. As Tikov advanced he was able to distinguish some of the array of medals on the general's chest, but he was drawn more strongly by the sagging, weary face of the commander-politician who should have retired long ago. Ustinov asked one question.

"Can you do it, Comrade Tikov?"

"Yes, Comrade General." Ustinov nodded. The interview was over. The two men were shown the door. In the corridor Mikhailov put a friendly claw on Tikov's shoulder.

"Well, I expect you have missed your family," he said. "We'll meet again soon." Mikhailov lurched towards his own department. Tikov watched him go, with some disgust and even a little pity. Was it inevitable that a twisted mind should inhabit such a twisted body?

Tikov dismissed the black Volga waiting for him downstairs. He wanted to walk and clear his head of the unnatural pressures it had suffered over the last three months. He walked for a while in the pine-clad Kremlin gardens, and stared down at the jumble of roofs across the Moscow river. It was great to be home, even though home meant the start of another battle with Natasha about when he would next go away.

"You've done your heroics," she was in the habit of saying. "What more do you have to prove? Your children are growing up around me like wild animals; they need their father." Alexei was thirteen, Sonya was ten and Yuri three.

They were nice kids, but he hardly knew them. The two eldest weren't interested in sport, astronomy or science - things which had monopolised his attention since early childhood. Alexei buried his nose in books endlessly, devouring the classics of Russian literature, and the forbidden poets; Tikov found them too harrowing and too right-wing for his taste. Sonya was into punk dress, the only thing she seemed to care about, apart from English pop music - the more vicious and cacophonic the better.

Well, there were no record shops on the Baltic sea bed. For once the cold warrior had returned without an armful of peace offerings. Tikov looked at his watch. It was 4.30pm, just time to do some defensive shopping. He couldn't go home empty-handed.

He joined the throng of Kremlin visitors leaving by the public entrance through the Kutafya tower. The militia on the gate saluted his weather-beaten uniform. Tikov crossed Karl Marx Prospekt towards Arbatskaya. Perhaps in one of the bookshops he could find something new to interest Alexei, and perhaps a record for Sonya. Yellowing sunlight was already gilding the dirty windows on the highest buildings and picking out the giant letters of the rooftop slogans: 'Kommunism pobedit' and 'Leninism-Nashe ziama'. But no one, except a returning cold warrior, looked up that high. There were too many tough grannies and determined mothers barging along at pavement level.

Tikov boarded a trolleybus which took him along Kalinin Prospekt towards the bookshop. The bus was full, too full for him to throw his five kopeks into the machine and take his ticket. What the hell. In spite of his uniform he felt comfortable using public transport. He liked the feeling of community. Even if the system is decrepit we're all part of it, it seemed to tell him. He was himself again, no different from the young student at Moscow University twenty-five years ago, except that every molecule in his body had replaced itself since then - but he was essentially the same: enquiring, stubborn and a little bit brave.

The doors hissed and Tikov descended from the bus. Crowds poured into the bookshop and poured out again. They besieged the cashiers, they besieged the serving counters. Tikov fought his way along the shelves to some of the modern writers. What had Lebedyev been reading on the fishing boat? Favori? He said it was good, but who the hell had written it? There was no one to ask. How about the new life of Pushkin? You couldn't go wrong with him, but then he remembered what Alexei had called Russia's greatest poet during their last attempt at a literary discussion - 'an Ethiopian half-wit'. Tikov squeezed through to the record department and browsed among Moscow's fashionable teenagers gyrating to heavy rock music. His adventures with pop music had stopped with the Beatles and their Russian imitators in the 1960s. This was hopeless. It was simpler to give his children the money and let them buy what they wanted. At least little Yuri, the three-year-old, was easier.

Tikov bought a record and a book at random and came out into the street for air. Darkness covered all but a pale glow on the horizon. At the entrance to the shop, unmistakeable, he saw the bulk of two KGB men, leather coats, felt hats. Poor bastards, thought Tikov, tailing some dissident, or waiting to spot proscribed books changing hands.

With his two presents, Tikov walked down to the river, past the stark tower of the Comecon headquarters and across the Kalininsky Bridge under the shadow of that Stalinist wedding cake, the Ukraine Hotel. It was a crude attempt to imitate and outshine the Gothic skyscrapers of Manhattan; it was splendid, though - a battery of lights shone from windows set deep into decorated walls. In the next block was a toyshop, Dom Igrushki, allegedly the best in Moscow. It was more crowded than the bookshop.

Frenzied parents fought for the counter-girls' attention, waving tickets and cash receipts, and using their shoulders and elbows. Tikov found himself elbowed towards a self-service section where toys in cardboard boxes could be taken straight to a cash desk.

"At last," he thought, "something for Yuri." He looked at the piles of sagging cardboard, model-kits of planes, boats, even the great Vostok space craft which he himself had flown. But the models were crude and wretched, the materials cheap and nasty. Sadness hit him in the stomach. Was there nothing he could waste his roubles on? Wait a minute! He felt in his pocket - he remembered he had some stray dollars. Illegal, but he was carrying some as a contingency, in case he landed on some foreign shore. Across the street was a beriozka - a foreign currency shop where tourists could buy souvenirs. Tikov dodged the traffic on the busy highway. As he reached the far pavement he heard a screech of tyres. The cause of it wasn't him. Caught in the traffic halfway across the street was a figure in a long coat and hat. And on the opposite pavement, running for the pedestrian underpass, was another. Tikov walked to the beriozka. As he opened the door and half turned he saw the second figure emerge from the underpass and join the first - two fellow shoppers, he thought, one with traffic sense, one without, like him. But he caught a glint of shiny leather in the lamplight. It was the KGB, thought Tikov, they're everywhere. He entered the shop. But they never run like that, he reflected; a KGB man is all style. He wouldn't be seen dead running. Tikov looked at the neat rows of Russian dolls, the wooden spoons, the crystal glass, hats and coats of mink, sable and karakul. Here it was all different, no rush, no fighting, because the buyers who came in here had weight in their wallets, real currency: dollars, Deutschmarks and, better still, plastic money, American Express cards.

They never run like that, thought Tikov, unless they're hunting someone and afraid of losing him. Christ, he was slow! What did they want him for? He peered out of the brightly lit window but saw only his own reflection. Tikov bought a wooden toy for Yuri and a bottle of Stolichnaya for himself, slid all his purchases into a plastic bag and went into the street.

Best to make sure, he told himself. He took a well-worn path between apartment blocks towards the Kievskaya railway station. They were after him alright, more furtive than before, but not stealthy, not with the invisible art of the true tail-man. Tikov felt his anger rising. Nobody hunted down a brigadier, cosmonaut and hero of the Soviet Union, especially not on a private shopping expedition. Tikov quickened his step. He would teach the KGB a thing or two.

The Gothic form of the Kiev railway terminal rose out of the darkness. Commuters, beetle-like, scurried around its base seeking bus and metro connections. Queues at kiosks waited to buy cigarettes or an evening paper. Tikov wove through the crowds and dived down the stairway to the metro station. He fed in his five kopeks at the barrier and joined a surge of people at the head of the escalator. Temporary metal hurdles manned by policemen guided the rush hour travellers towards the moving staircase. Tikov shuffled forward patiently, aware that his height would make him easily visible to his pursuers. As he journeyed down the deep escalator he thought of vaulting across to the ascending staircase - but it would have been undignified and awkward carrying his shopping, especially the vodka.

Tikov reached the platform and waited for his train. A red digital display at the end of the platform showed the time in seconds since the last train had departed. It was over two minutes, so the next one was due any moment; even now the beam of its headlights lit the curve of the tunnel. It arrived and the doors slid open. Tikov boarded a carriage. He saw the two sleuths enter at the other end. The commuters made space for the men in leather as if they were lepers. Tikov began to move. He forced his way along the crowded carriage pulling the beriozka bag behind him. The standing passengers, silently and grudgingly gave way.

One of the KGB men caught Tikov's eye and hurriedly looked away. He nudged his companion who observed Tikov's reflection in the carriage window as he advanced in their direction. The train glided into Smolenskaya station and a loudspeaker announced the next stop. The shorter KGB man pulled at the other's sleeve and started to make for the open door, but his companion stood his ground. "Got you," muttered Tikov under his breath and continued his advance.

The KGB men were getting nervous, the shorter one continually hissing at the other through clenched teeth. Tikov hailed them:

"Ah ha! Oblomov, Skolkov, fancy meeting you here." The two men looked at each other. "It's a small world." Silence. "Do you always hunt in pairs?" There was a titter from the usually silent Russian commuters. Oblomov, the larger one, brushed past Tikov and started barging his way up the carriage. Skolkov followed. "Wait," yelled Tikov. "Don't leave without me." He squirmed after them. "It's dark out there." He hated this exhibitionism, but they were hating it more.

The train stopped at another station and the doors opened. "Are you getting out here?" asked Tikov. The two men moved to the open door, Oblomov stepped onto the platform, Skolkov stayed on board: good KGB tactics. About half the people, not wanting to be involved, left the carriage. A handful entered followed by Oblomov, and the doors closed. Tikov moved closer to Oblomov, he was the more inert one. "Let's clear the carriage; then we can talk," he whispered. Oblomov raised an eyebrow.

"Talk here," said Oblomov in strange, thick Russian.

"Why are you following me?"

"Orders." Skolkov closed in on the other side. Tikov didn't fancy a fight, particularly on account of the shopping. Oblomov was heavy, Skolkov was fast. Eighty-five kilogrammes of cosmonaut couldn't defeat them both, although they looked flat-footed.

"Whose orders?"

"Official. For your own good." This wasn't native Russian. But he'd heard that accent many times. It was Slav and heavy, maybe Slovak or Bulgarian. Had the KGB started recruiting in Plovdiv?

"Who are you working for?" asked Tikov. Oblomov ignored the question.

"Can we talk?" he asked, nodding towards the carriage door. The train was slowing for the next station. Tikov looked both men in the eye and they stared back as the three of them stepped off the train. It was a busy platform but they stood in a knot waiting for the train to leave. Oblomov took out a packet of Troika cigarettes, jerked them in Tikov's direction then lit one for himself. The stench of low-grade tobacco rose as the train rattled away. Oblomov spoke:

"We're trying to protect you and your operation, although we hardly know what it is."

"I don't need protection. What do you think you're protecting me from?" Oblomov smiled:

"Mainly from the KGB," he said.

"You mean you're not the KGB? You do a good imitation."

"We're keeping those jackals away."

"Why?"

"Mikhailov doesn't trust them, they're too leaky." At Mikhailov's name the hairs prickled at the back of Tikov's neck. These guys were deeper than he thought, but who the hell were they?

"I apologise for the performance on the train," said Tikov. Oblomov smiled.

"You gave us an awkward moment," he said. His face became serious, almost confiding. "We hoped you could help us with a small security problem. The missing Englishman." Tikov stared at him in alarm. How much did this man know?

"I can't say anything," he said. "You must excuse me." He wanted to get home.

"There was a second Englishman," said Oblomov. "Our people are tracking him down in London."

"Good," said Tikov, "but I doubt he saw much."

"We'll find out." Tikov didn't like the man's cold confidence. His tone said that more killing would be done.

"Getting rid of him will just attract attention," said Tikov.

"We're more subtle than that, Boris Alexeivich." The two men stared at each other for some time. Who was this Bulgar? "You could help us by giving some details of what happened there in Sweden."

"First, I'm going to check you out," said Tikov. "Meanwhile, get off my back. I can deal with the KGB myself." He turned to leave. Oblomov held onto his shoulder:

"Remember, my friend, that we're on the same side." Skolkov grinned. Tikov left the platform, conscious that four eyes were still following him.

He was back in the centre of Moscow, Revolution Square. He hurried past the life-size bronze nudes which decorated the underground walkways of the metro station, up the escalator to ground level, and stepped out through square columns of black granite into the square. At the other end was the Bolshoi Theatre, its classical facade and four bronze horses bathed in yellow light. Rush hour pedestrians surged through underpasses and halted in battalions at traffic lights before charging across the highways. Tikov joined them. If the Bulgars were still following they would need to stick to him like limpets. He dived into another metro station, Prospekt Marx, and caught the train home.

Tikov lived in Frunze, in one of the tall apartment blocks built at the turn of the century for the Czar's cavalry officers. The rooms were large with high ceilings, but the fin-de-siècle elegance had disappeared long since. Plaster mouldings were buried under layers of thick gloss paint, fireplaces had vanished to make way for brutal radiators. Natasha always talked of restoring the furnishings, as some of her neighbours had done. But with three children, there wasn't time. And there was always the threat of a move back to the cosmodrome at Baikonur.

Tikov pressed the buzzer three times. He heard the stamp of feet to the door, which was flung open to reveal his whole family. Alex wore spectacles; they were new. Sonya was dressed elf-like in a short skirt and woollen tights, and Natasha stood in the background, looking tired, with little Yuri peeping between her legs.

"You knew I was coming," said Tikov as he stood there, slightly embarrassed.

"You had a telephone call," said Natasha.

"They had no business ringing me here."

"It was Sergei. He wants to meet you tonight." This was Sergei Lebedyev. They'd parted only that morning after three months at sea.

"Didn't you ask him round?"

"Look at me," said Natasha throwing up her hands. "I haven't got a thing in the house."

"He wouldn't expect anything."

"Nonsense. You need to celebrate on your first night home. Go on you boys, go out and enjoy yourselves." Tikov could see the tears brimming in her eyes.

"Look," he said. "I got some tinned ham at the beriozka. He can come here." Natasha took the tin and walked to the kitchen.

"Borushka, this Polish stuff is disgusting." She put it down and threw her arms around him. The children had followed them into the kitchen, the centre of the household. Tikov looked at them over Natasha's shoulder; they were silent and shy. This had to be sorted out. He would take some leave. Maybe they could go for a week to their small dacha outside Moscow. The telephone rang and Natasha answered. It was Sergei again and she handed the telephone to Tikov.

"I have to talk to you," said Lebedyev.

"Can't you come here?"

"Privately, if you don't mind."

"Okay," said Tikov. "I'll meet you at the National."

"I've done better than that," said Lebedyev. "We'll meet at Aragvi. It won't take long. Then we can enjoy ourselves. Demirkan said he might look in." These men are like children, thought Tikov; they can't keep away from each other. Still, they're my children. He looked across at his three quiet offspring. There would be time to make friends with them again. Tikov took Natasha by the hands.

"It's just for this evening," he said. "Then we can be together. We can go to the country." They clung to each other for a moment. "I must get out of this uniform." He went to the bedroom. There were his suits hanging in the cupboard, smelling of mothballs.

Tikov took the metro back into town. He walked up Gorky Street mingling with the late-night shoppers and put his nose into the great food hall of Gastronome One. The furnishings rivalled Fortnum & Mason in London but the goods were always the same, apart from the occasional load of fresh fish from the Baltic or the Caspian. Tikov could tell at a glance there were no such bargains tonight.

As he continued up Gorky Street it started to rain. If Oblomov and Co. were following, they were being more discreet. Tikov turned right at a war memorial into a small square. On the right a crowd had gathered by a closed door. This was Aragvi, the best Georgian restaurant outside Tbilisi, and the crowd was trying to get in. The place was always booked weeks in advance by dollar-wielding tourists and Moscow's gilded youth. To get a table on the day of his return Lebedyev must have some good connections, thought Tikov.

"The best," said Lebedyev as he guided Tikov past the fierce doorman. "My mother was a Georgian princess." They found themselves in a low hallway. To the left was a vaulted cellar with a table set along its length. "That's for the tourists," said Lebedyev. "We go this way." He led Tikov into a high hall, decorated with murals of Georgian horsemen. At the end was a gallery where a band played amplified Caucasian music. "No one can eavesdrop here," shouted Lebedyev above the din. They sat at a small table under the gallery.

The room held no more than thirty or forty people crammed together at small tables. But Lebedyev's table was somewhat apart and private. The head waiter, a rotund, sad-looking man, immediately attended them.

"We'll have some vodka and Georgian champagne," said Lebedyev. "The driest you've got."

"There's only sweet champagne."

"Sweet, then." There was food already on the table, salads, pickles and warm pastries stuffed with cheese and meat. They helped themselves and ordered grilled chicken. After two swift shots of vodka they toasted each other in the sickly-sweet champagne. Tikov looked round the room. At the centre was a table of foreigners (Australian diplomats - "We couldn't refuse them", the head waiter confided). There was a young couple treating two portly parents to a night out; a table of Georgian businessmen already awash with vodka, and nearest to them a pair of elegant women in clothes that wouldn't disgrace a Paris couturier; but they were obviously Russians, living well on the ballet or the black market. There was no Oblomov and no Skolkov. In the gallery the band, led by a moustachioed Georgian, began to play.

"Right, we can talk," said Tikov. Lebedyev looked at him with an almost paternal smile.

"I've decided to quit," he said. "I thought you should be the first to know."

"What changed your mind since this morning?" Lebedyev looked at his plate.

"I had a shock when I got home. Marishka is three months pregnant."

"That's happened before. She's not even your wife."

"This is different," said Lebedyev violently. "When Katya had our two children I could hardly bring myself to touch them, especially the boy. But I was young. I was terrified of childbirth, that monster which seized Katya and gored her like an animal. It affected our whole marriage. But with Marishka, we know what we're doing. Everything will be alright. I want to be there at the birth - that was our big mistake last time."

"So you're giving up your career."

"It's not just that. You know it isn't." Lebedyev laid his hand on Tikov's clenched fist. "I've been thinking about this for some time. I want out. This mucking about underwater isn't for me. It lacks dignity, it lacks imagination."

"So does pissing into a catheter at zero gravity." They both laughed.

"I'll drink to that." Lebedyev's face became serious again.

"What is this game? Haven't you pissed about in the Baltic long enough? What's in it for you, Boris Alexeivich?

Surely not promotion." Tikov looked around the room and leaned in closer.

"It's big, Sergei. Maybe the biggest thing we've done." He leaned even more. "Listen. Are we soldiers or are we cosmonauts?"

"Cosmonauts, of course," said Lebedyev, dead-pan.

"I'll ask the question again, you priceless buffoon," said Tikov.

"Soldiers."

"Very good, Sergei Ivanovich. And what do soldiers do?"

"Defend their country."

"Exactly." Tikov took a gulp of champagne and tossed a ball of pastry into his mouth. He forked some salad onto his plate. "We are about to defend our country in a unique - at least I believe it's unique - and bizarre way." Tikov ate some more; Lebedyev watched him glumly. Tikov continued: "Mikhailov is mad. We're agreed on that. But he is fronting a brilliant scheme which could throw nuclear defence technology as we know it out of the window."

"What's that got to do with us?"

"Wait!" Tikov almost stabbed Lebedyev with his fork. "Nautilus." Tikov lowered his voice. "Nautilus carries the payload."

"What!" Lebedyev could hardly hear. Tikov grinned and whispered in his ear. The band struck up a fast folkloric tune and two dancers whirled into the hall between the packed chairs and tables. The diners applauded and asked for more. By the time the dancers had left, the truth had sunk into Lebedyev. It was also the moment that Demirkan chose to arrive.

He had already been drinking. Demirkan was an Uzbek, large, round-faced and a collector of bad jokes. He saluted Tikov and Lebedyev and sat down as the head waiter slid a chair under him.

"Civilization," said Demirkan. A German tourist leaned in the archway swigging from a half-empty vodka bottle and shouting at the band. He wanted the Radetsky March. After a while someone led him away.

Tikov knew Lebedyev wouldn't quit. Together they were like the three musketeers, all for one and one for all. It didn't matter what crazy system they got their orders from - somehow they would stick together and enjoy themselves. Tikov leaned over to Demirkan.

"Are you turning chicken too?" Demirkan laughed and flapped the question away with his hand.

"Where would I run?" Demirkan had come through selection panels at the Baikonur space centre because of one thing - determination. He was overweight, he smoked too much, he came from the wrong republic and he had the wrong creed - Islam. But in tests for resistance to stress and mental agility, and in the flight simulator, he was the best - highly competitive. Only in live situations, Tikov later realized, he had to be handled right. But the cosmonaut existence was his life and he'd abandoned his family and home to follow it. Only his religion he kept under wraps as a souvenir of childhood.

The three men drank toasts to each other in the sweet champagne. Tikov seized Demirkan's forearm and drew him close.

"Sergei wants to have a baby. But I need him. I need you both. This entire planet is crawling with babies. It's complete madness to want to produce one more, let alone stay home and gloat over the result, while you could be out there with us making the world a better place."

"Is that what we're doing?" asked Demirkan. Tikov prodded him with his finger.

"We, the Soviet Union, are going to shock the world out of its nuclear impasse," he said.

"You think our precious Nautilus is going to do all that? Listen." Demirkan filled his mouth with cheese and chewed for a moment. "The Israelis might do it, the Japanese might. But it's way beyond poor old Mother Russia. We can build bombs and doomsday machines on a grand scale but we're hopeless at miniatures. Look at the Tretiakov gallery." Tikov was astonished by Demirkan's remark.

"Who said anything about doomsday machines?"

"Nobody," said Demirkan. "I've suspected it for some time." He shrugged, and the corners of his mouth went down. "Why else would such resources and human talent be lavished on a tiny one-man bubble?" Tikov laughed. They both knew Nautilus was being run on a shoestring, without any back-up or support staff. It had been conceived and developed in an administrative vacuum. That had made them all uncomfortable. But Tikov was uncomfortable no longer.

"I've had my orders from the top," he said. "As high as you can go. They know what they want. We just have to get the mechanics right. That's why I need you - the cream of the cream." Demirkan looked into his glass.

"We're yesterday's men," he said. "Our names were written in the stars." He drained his champagne glass and filled it with vodka. "Now they're going to drown us in obscurity under the sea."

"My god, the Turk's getting morbid," said Tikov. "He's coming to grips with his own mortality."

"We're all going to die," said Lebedyev suddenly, "but some of us prefer to die surrounded by our grandchildren."

"Listen!" said Tikov. "To me you're both already dead. Why? Because you've forgotten that the life we chose always came very close to being a game. We're a special case. We carried our childhood fantasies almost intact into adult life. We live for the game. If we give it up we're as good as dead." Demirkan was giggling.

"You've completely lost your head," he said. "You're nearly fifty. The solar rays have addled your brain."

"The game's the thing," insisted Tikov. "Remember when the Americans first confronted us with the idea of the space walk. They had done it, but without style, without finesse. That was a challenge and together we solved it. We sent Borodin soaring into space without wires, without a safety net."

"Borodin's dead," said Demirkan.

"That happened two years later," said Tikov impatiently. "But think of the walk. What was the purpose of it? There wasn't one. But we'd won the game. We showed ourselves and the world that it could be done."

"Is Nautilus a game?" asked Lebedyev. Tikov looked around for the waiter.

"Let's get out of here," he said. "Let's get some fresh air." Tikov looked at the bill and put forty roubles on the table. The three men got their coats and rolled into the night air. It had stopped raining. There were even a few stars winking above the dark war memorial. They strolled slowly up Gorky Street towards Pushkinskaya. "The game is this," continued Tikov. "We have to find a way of planting these vehicles undetected in every major city in the world. London, Tokyo, New York, Sydney, Hong Kong, San Francisco, Shanghai, Istanbul, anywhere where there's water. We choose the target, we set up a base, we send a man in. It's a watertight operation. No hangers on, no passengers, no mission control back in Moscow. To me it's a challenge - one of the biggest in my life. As for morality, I don't think about it - let the others work it out. I'm a simple cosmonaut doing my job."

"You're kidding yourself," said Lebedyev. "Your conscience runs deeper than that."

"I believe in staying ahead," said Tikov. "If we're ahead then neither side does something stupid." Demirkan belched.

"Stick to sardine cans," said Demirkan. "They suit you better."

"I'm going to do this thing," said Tikov, "alone if I have to. But I just have to remind you of one thing. Nobody leaves this project and goes back to a normal life. You back off and you go to Gorky or Ufa for the duration - you're a top security risk."

They walked in silence for some time. The three men had come to another square where a statue of Pushkin gazed over Gorky Street's homebound traffic.

"It looks like you have us over a barrel," said Demirkan.

"Look on the bright side," said Tikov. "We're in this together. We can choose how to run the show. Within reason we can choose where and how we deploy the craft." Lebedyev and Demirkan maintained a glum silence. "Let's put it this way," continued Tikov. "We need a test bed for the project, a site picked at random to try out deployment and concealment of Nautilus. Where should it be?" Silence. "If I asked you to choose where you would like to spend your next holiday would it be Amsterdam, Alicante, Athens?"

"Sydney, Rio, San Francisco," said Lebedyev.

"Zurich," said Demirkan firmly.

"But that's inland," said Lebedyev.

"It's got a lake," said Demirkan.

"How the hell would you get the thing there? Drop in by parachute?" asked Lebedyev.

"That's the game, your precious game," said Demirkan triumphantly. "You wanted a test bed. If you can get it into Zurich you can get it anywhere."

"Touché," said Tikov. The three of them began to fight, swinging great bear-cuffs at each other until they collapsed at the feet of Pushkin.

VULKAN

48

CHAPTER FIVE

London

Richards hated the damp Chelsea basement with the embossed wallpaper peeling off the walls and the spluttering gas fire. But he needed Pike, because Pike, world-weary and scruffy with great bags under his eyes, was the greatest living authority in London on obscure pieces of weaponry and the arsenal of funny tricks that from time to time have been devised by the CIA, KGB, MI6, BOSS, Mossad, Savak, and the defence forces of the Western and Eastern hemispheres.

Pike, surprisingly, hadn't sold his soul to any one of these organizations. He brought to this nasty little world the noblest tradition of academic detachment and scholarship. His mind was open. He liked gadgets, whichever ideological brand name had been painted on them.

This one, represented in a dozen hazy photographs, was no exception.

"Ah, yes," said Pike, "you call it the Spyfish but it's really the Nautilus ZX-B. It's a bottom-crawling miniature submarine. What a beauty! I've never seen a picture of one before, even a bad one like this. It lies on the sea bed like a sting-ray and buries itself in the mud where it's virtually undetectable. They've been testing one up on the Swedish coast - much to the annoyance of the Swedish navy."

"That's where this one ran aground."

"Probably got into trouble and beached itself. And here they are towing it off. Who took these photographs - one of your embassy guys? The definition's very poor."

"It was a young botanist from London University. They'd just shot his friend and taken his body with them. Luckily they didn't spot him."

"No witnesses, eh? This thing must be damned important."

"Or they were just over-cautious."

"My god!" said Pike, "these photographs may be bad but look at that face. It's familiar."

"They all look the same to me."

"Let's blow it up on the screen, life-size." Pike fiddled excitedly with his document projector. "It's Tikov - Boris Tikov."

"Who's he when he's at home?"

"He did that spectacular docking with Apollo. His face was televised all over the world. He's a Soviet cosmonaut."

"Doesn't mean anything to me. But then I'm not space-mad like you."

"What the hell's he doing towing a miniature submarine in the Baltic?"

"The plot thickens."

"It certainly does," said Pike. "I can see you're not taking this very seriously, but to me it suggests it's a major project. You know Tikov's a brigadier?"

"And I'm only a captain," said Richards. "That makes me feel very small." Richards was a staff captain in the war office. He'd been there for three months after tours of duty in Northern Ireland, Germany and two glorious years in Hong Kong. He felt he'd been grounded although his war office posting was supposed to be a step up. He was what is usually called a high flyer. He also had an ability to step outside the narrow world of the officer's mess and the wonderful preciseness of the average military brain. His friendship or rather acquaintance with Pike was a good example. He just happened to bump into Pike at a cocktail party three doors down the street. He learned that Pike published a small, highly specialized magazine on military hardware. The acquaintance seemed useful and stuck. Richards was able to use Pike as a sounding board, and a counter-balance to the extraordinarily nutty views and ideas of his fellow officers. Pike found Richards was a source of peripheral information, such as these photographs which were top secret and should never have been allowed out of Whitehall.

"I should follow up the Tikov lead if I were you," said Pike, nursing his injured pride somewhat.

"I suppose driving a submarine is much like riding in a space capsule. A lot of the training's probably the same."

"What are you getting at?"

"Well, if you're over the hill as an astronaut then maybe they offer you deep sea diving as a sinecure."

"I say, do you mind if I keep one of these, one with Tikov in it?"

"It's most irregular, you know."

"Say it was such a bad print it was a waste of time."

"I'll say I accidentally put it in the shredder." Richards drained his glass of sherry. "Well, I must be going."

"Keep in touch," said Pike as he closed the front door. He went back to the projector and studied the picture again, then picked up the telephone.

"Laszlo, it's William. I've got something quite interesting to show you."

"What sort of thing, William my friend?"

"Can you come over? It concerns Captain Nemo." Laszlo was a Hungarian doctor practising in Bayswater. He had a large house there, in which he and his wife entertained a stream of interesting friends, artists, musicians, collectors, doctors, scientists, bankers, many of them with Hungarian or Austro-Hungarian connections. It was Laszlo who first told Pike about the Nautilus. He'd seen a primitive drawing provided by a friend of a friend who worked for a Budapest-based engineering firm. It was drawn from memory by an engineer on his return from a visit to Leningrad. Laszlo, who believed that knowing what the other side is doing is the best deterrent for war, passed the information to his friend William.

Laszlo parked his Mercedes, waited a few minutes to satisfy himself he wasn't being followed then made for Pike's basement flat. He didn't like this cloak and dagger stuff, nor did he like Pike's stuffy little basement. He preferred the elegant game of international intrigue that he played from his salon in Bayswater.

Pike poured him a sherry. "I've seen some photographs of the Nautilus," he said, "taken by an English botanist just after his friend had been shot and dragged off to a watery grave."

"Did he bring them to you?"

"No, let's say a mutual friend brought them. He carelessly left one behind. Look at that picture."

"It's riding a bit low in the water to see anything."

"But look in the open boat. Have you seen that face before?"

"Can't say I have. But we must find this botanist."

"It's Tikov."

"Who?"

"Boris Tikov, the Soviet cosmonaut who led the link up with Apollo 17."

"Can't say I remember him. Is he important?"

"I think so, very. I don't suppose any of your contacts could help find out what they're up to?"

"We can try," Laszlo winced as he sipped his sherry. "What about this botanist? Can we get in touch?"

"All I know is he's English, he's at London University and he was in Sweden a couple of weeks ago. Oh, and his friend didn't come back."

"Shouldn't be too difficult."

54

CHAPTER SIX

The black ball struck just above the sounding board. It was a perfect drop shot destined to die quickly on the side wall. But Dimock was there. His long legs and simian arms reached magically across the court and his wrist flicked the ball to a sudden death in the corner.

"Seven - one," grunted Fortescue. He was about to lose his fourth game in a row. His face had acquired a blotchy crimson, showing that his thermostat was now fully out of control. His breath came in long gasps and the T-shirt clung to his back like a wet cloth.

Dimock served again. His coiled frame lashed suddenly. Fortescue chased the ball into the corner behind him, lunged and flicked it back into play. But Dimock was perfectly placed to tap it away to the far left. Eight - one. There was hardly a sign of fatigue on his body, although his face betrayed some colour above the curly beard.

"Good shot," groaned Fortescue. On the next service he managed a better return, sending the ball high behind Dimock's head. Dimock's shot skimmed the side wall. Fortescue threw himself desperately after it, managed a stroke but left his rear dangerously exposed. Dimock dispatched him without mercy.

"How about another?" said Fortescue. But he hung from the hips, his tongue lolling, whooping for breath. Dimock studied him with a trace of sadism.

"We'd better call it a day," he said. Fortescue collected his keys from the corner and they left the court.

"I'm supposed to be fit," he protested.

"It's a game for brains, not brawn," said Dimock.

"We're meant to have both in my job." Fortescue was attached to the Foreign and Commonwealth Office. Since Dimock's adventure in Sweden, Fortescue had been keeping an eye on him, a kind of part-time minder, checking that the Soviets weren't on his tail. As the months dragged on and nothing happened, Fortescue's minding role had shrunk to a weekly game of squash in Kensington. Even though Fortescue was regularly beaten he came back for more.

Dimock was amused by this weekly appointment with Fortescue. He teased him about his job as mercilessly as he beat him on the squash court.

"I'll buy you a drink," he said. They went to the bar, away from the kerthud of squash balls and the squeak of rubber soles. Armed with two pints of shandy, they sought out a quiet corner. Dimock continued:

"I enjoy beating the hell out of you, Fortescue, but when are you guys going to get off my back? It's been five months now. You've really cramped my style, did you know that?"

"Ruined your squash you mean?"

"No. Just my whole life. There's nothing like a babysitter to keep you on the straight and narrow. I mean, when did I last visit a brothel, or do a nice bit of breaking-and-entering or even fuck someone who wasn't Anna Stallybrass?"

"She's a great girl; you're lucky to have her."

"You would think so, wouldn't you, Fortescue? Just your type - the major's daughter. I heard about your little episode with the major down in Hampshire."

Anna Stallybrass was the sister of John, who had died in Sweden. She was like John, tall, blond, and sensible. She was also beautiful, with the effortless grace that came with taking her looks for granted. Dimock's greatest worry had been breaking the news to her when he got home.

But he needn't have worried. She took it on the chin. She simply transferred all the love and affection she had felt for John onto him. Like brother and sister they travelled from London to Hampshire to tell the major.

At the family home in Hampshire Major Stallybrass was mowing the lawn. It took some time to persuade him to shut off the engine and dismount. When he heard the news he walked down to the greenhouse by himself along the narrow strip of grass between the beans and the asparagus, beside the tall yew hedge.

Mrs Stallybrass came back from Fordingbridge with the afternoon shopping. She ran to greet her daughter then saw her red eyes and stopped. It was three days before the family were surprised by a sudden joke at the dinner table and laughed.

Major Stallybrass wasn't satisfied by Dimock's account of his son's death. He rang the embassy in Stockholm. "According to our files your son is only missing, not dead," replied the consular official. The major prepared to fly to Stockholm and organize a search party. Then one afternoon a visitor came to the house in Hampshire in a Reliant Scimitar - a tall young man wearing a brown trilby. It was Fortescue.

"It's about your son," he told Major Stallybrass. "He quite innocently stumbled on something the Russians wanted to keep quiet and they… eliminated him."

"In Sweden?"

"The Cold War blows very hot up there, I'm afraid. The thing is we can't tell you any more and we'd rather the whole incident died a quiet death, if you'll forgive the expression."

"I still don't understand."

"He wasn't working for us, if that's what you're thinking. Um, and of course he wasn't working for anyone else either. That is, as far as we know."

"Shut up. And get out." That was the last Major Stallybrass heard of his son.

"Typical piece of Foreign Office tact," said Dimock, "telling an old soldier to keep his mouth shut and forget about his son."

"We were only doing what's in the national interest," protested Fortescue, his mouth rimmed with beery foam.

"Like those two old aunties I saw in Sweden," said Dimock. "What were their names? Gabittas and - no, Webster and Tring."

"Shh!" Fortescue looked round furtively. "Don't mention names in here."

"A right pair of poofdas they were." Dimock took a deep draught and finished his pint. Fortescue dutifully got up to buy refills.

Webster and Tring, one tall, the other fat, had come scuttling out of the embassy in Stockholm to see Dimock, stranded without car keys, in a small Swedish village up the coast.

On the telephone that morning, still shaking a bit with fear and rage, he had rung the embassy. The duty officer seemed uninterested until Dimock described the tin can in the water, whatever it was. That got him through to Webster, the military attaché.

"Stay where you are," Webster said. "We'll be with you in three hours."

They arrived in style - Tring, the information officer, and Major Webster, the attaché. Besides the embassy Rover there were two police cars and two white armoured personnel carriers. Dimock got into the Rover and took the motorcade to the site on the coast.

There was the Volvo he and John had hired. A hundred yards away, their tent, snug among the rocks and lichen. Four hundred yards farther on was their site - a patch of bare earth.

"What the hell were you doing here?" asked Tring.

"This is our experiment," said Dimock. "We were studying the recuperation rate of contaminated soil. This one has Cesium-137 in it."

From the site Dimock could see how John would have noticed the stranded diver and the submarine. Obviously he ran down to help. He remembered the crack of gunfire.

"Show us exactly where the vessel was," said Webster. The tide had gone out a little, revealing more ripped seaweed where the hull had been dragged. Webster crouched down.

"This is our little friend alright," said Webster. "What we and the Swedes call Spyfish One." Behind them the troops from the two personnel carriers had spread in a thin line. They were examining every inch of the ground. Dimock had drawn his own conclusions: if they were so excited they must be dealing with the enemy: the Spyfish had to be Russian. Tring strolled towards him, hands thrust into the pockets of his sheepskin.

"So," he said smiling. "It seems you have stumbled on something. Sorry about your friend."

"What happens now?" asked Dimock.

"You know the next of kin?"

"Yes, I'll tell them. But I assume there'll be an official protest. The Russians can't get away with murder." Webster looked at Tring.

"Actually we'd rather play it down at the moment," said Tring. "Things are rather delicate. We don't want the Americans to know about this. They're dying to come into

Sweden - which as you know is a neutral country - and play hunt-the-thimble with the Russians in Swedish waters. We, the British and the Swedes, don't want that. We're lucky you and your friend weren't Yanks."

Fortescue put two dripping pints on the small table.

"Is that one of the conditions of entry?" asked Dimock, "being a poofda?"

"Entry to what?" asked Fortescue guardedly.

"MI6." Dimock leaned forward. "Military intelligence." Fortescue scanned the bar hurriedly.

"I wish you wouldn't..."

"I suppose it helps," mused Dimock. "All boys together, eh?"

"That's a typical media comment," spat Fortescue, refusing to be drawn as he had been in the past. They finished their drinks and prepared to leave. As usual, Fortescue descended to the street first to make sure the coast was clear. Dimock found the procedure comic.

"I'm going to Anna's," said Dimock. "At least, that's the official story. Can I give you a lift?"

"No thanks, I'll walk." Fortescue lived in Earl's Court. As Dimock kicked his sports car into life and pulled out of the car park he saw the lean figure of Fortescue, in his college scarf, lope down the rain-sodden street.

Dimock had picked up the threads of his life at the university. But his heart wasn't in it. Inside he felt a deep anger at the murder of John, and at the conspiracy to cover it up.

A few days later he met Matyas. Matyas sat next to him at lunch one day in the Imperial College canteen. He was dark-haired with a thin face and two days' growth of beard.

"Mind if I sit here?" he asked and put down his tray of Wienerschnitzel and spaghetti. He wore the student's uniform of jeans, pullover and checked shirt, but there was something about him that was too self-assured, Dimock reflected later. Their initial conversation was limited.

"Could you pass the salt?" the man asked. Having eaten a third of the Wienerschnitzel he resumed: "I think I've seen you in the earth sciences department."

"Possibly," said Dimock. The man forked through some spaghetti.

"It's an interesting subject," he said. "Plenty of opportunity to get back to nature." Dimock didn't reply; he was trying to place the man's accent which sounded foreign, or could it just be Jewish? But he felt he was being rude:

"Most of it's hard work in the lab, like every other science - ninety per cent perspiration."

"But you must go on some spectacular field trips, to collect specimens."

"Everyone thinks we spend our summers hunting for rare orchids up the Amazon."

"Or studying the flora in Sweden."

"That's a good guess. I was there this summer as a matter of fact, but I was looking at bare patches of earth; very boring."

"On the contrary; I think you had quite an exciting time, Mr Dimock, rather too exciting." Dimock looked at the man, hoping he didn't mean anything more than John's death.

"Oh, you've heard about that, have you? If you'll forgive me I don't much like talking about it."

"I understand. But I'm afraid we must talk about it. I'm here to help you. You see, we know there are some people in London determined to find out how much you know."

"About what?"

"About certain things which move under the sea."

"I don't know what you're talking about."

"You may lie, but your camera doesn't." The photographs. He'd forgotten completely about them, hoping they hadn't come out. He had given Webster and Tring his roll of film, almost as an afterthought.

"I'll get us some coffee," said the man. He threaded his way between the tables with the same assurance. Who the hell was he? If he knew about the photographs he must be from MI6 or something. But did they employ foreigners? He sounded foreign, middle European. Dimock was sure of it. He could just as easily be working for the Russians - trying to lure him into his confidence. But if the man was trying to protect him - his mind was confused, he needed to think. Ivan, he'd already christened him Ivan, returned with the coffee.

"I didn't know whether you took sugar, so I put some in the saucer."

"Thank you." They stirred their coffee. Ivan looked at him expectantly. "OK, who are you?" asked Dimock.

"I'm a friend." Ivan touched him on the wrist. "I'm not one of your British intelligence agents, or Smersh, or the KGB. I'm a Hungarian citizen." Then Ivan wouldn't do, thought Dimock; he'd have to call him Tibor. "There are quite a few of us in London - some are political refugees, others are just sitting on the fence."

"What's that got to do with me?"

"We like to think that we have a view from both sides. You will protest that we are signatories of the Warsaw Pact, but to the average Hungarian citizen, even to a soldier, that means nothing. The spirit of 1956 isn't dead; we're just biding our time, trying to limit the military adventurism of the superpowers. We hope that reason will finally prevail over aggression." Tibor's a bit of a loony, thought Dimock.

"My name is Matyas," said the Hungarian.

"Ah."

"We think some people at the Russian embassy are interested in you. They were requested by Moscow to make sure that Stallybrass didn't have a colleague with him in Sweden, another witness you understand. When they read nothing in the newspapers about his disappearance, they became suspicious. Very suspicious."

"I'll tell you for nothing. If it wasn't for the funnies and their silly games this would have been splashed all over the newspapers, I would have seen to that. The Russians, or whoever they are, are guilty of cold-blooded murder."

Matyas twisted his face as if in pain. "Don't start talking like that. You don't know what you're up against. There's no law for these people. They're dangerous and they could kill you too, like that." He snapped his fingers.

"What do they want from me? I didn't see anything. You tell them from me they're wasting their time."

"You took some photographs."

"How do they know that?"

"They don't."

"Unless you told them," Matyas laughed.

"Why should we do that? That isn't our style at all. We are passive observers. Except," he touched Dimock's wrist again, "when we think someone is in danger."

"What am I supposed to do?"

"Disappear for a few weeks. Take a holiday. Maybe Anna can go with you."

"I suppose you've been following her as well."

"Please! Don't get angry. Anger clouds the judgment and you need all the judgment you've got. Call Anna this afternoon and see if she can take some time off, but don't mention on the telephone where you might go, and don't tell your friends."

"You want me to drop everything and get involved in your little game of hide-and-seek."

"It's a bit more serious than that. Your friend has been killed. That is just the hors d'oeuvre." Matyas paused for effect. "If there's any trouble, call this number - nine three zero, zero one eight six. It's a doctor's surgery - ask for Doctor Felix. Good luck." The Hungarian rose and left through the throng of students by the canteen door.

On an impulse, Dimock followed him. He dived through the students to see Matyas striding across the lawn towards Exhibition Road. Dimock waited for him to walk through the college gates then jogged after him. By the time he rounded the gates Matyas was well down Exhibition Road, walking towards South Kensington underground station. It was a broad two-lane avenue with cars parked on each side and down the central division.

Dimock kept a line of cars between himself and his quarry but he didn't notice two men talking by a parked car. As Matyas passed they grabbed him. The car door opened and they bundled him in. Dimock hardly registered what had happened until he heard the car rev fiercely and come down the road towards him. He waved his hands but the vehicle sped past and turned left down Prince Consort road.

Dimock was shaking. He tried to remember things about the car - the number - TWV, something, something; colour - beige; make - nondescript, a Ford or a Vauxhall. How many people in the car? Three - and Matyas. What were they like? Well-built, pasty. What did he do now? Call Fortescue and ask for protection? Somehow he didn't trust Fortescue. Call the police? He didn't have much faith in them after what he'd seen at demonstrations: they'd arrested him once already. He could call Doctor Felix. What was the number? Nine three zero - zero one eight six or was it zero eight one six? He found a red telephone box and dialled the first number. A girl answered.

"Doctor Felix?" There was a pause then a man's voice.

"I didn't expect to hear from you so soon."

"I'm afraid your colleague's had an accident." There was a pause.

"Can you meet me right away? At the Grosvenor House Hotel. In the coffee room. I'll be reading the *New Yorker*." Dimock waved down a taxi.

"Grosvenor House Hotel. Can you drive around a bit, and make sure no one's tailing me?" The cabbie grinned.

"Hold onto your seat, mate." He drove to Hyde Park Corner and circled it three times, mixing with groups of identical black taxis. "Never fails," he said.

Laszlo thumbed through his *New Yorker*, but without taking anything in. He was nervous. What the hell could have happened to Matyas? When the waiter came he absent-mindedly ordered a coffee. An accident? He loved Matyas like a son. The Englishman, Dimock, looked furtive as he crossed the lounge and slid into an armchair beside him.

"Dr Felix?"

"You can call me by my real name which is Tomar. Tell me about this accident."

"Matyas has been kidnapped, I think." Dimock told him what he had seen.

"There's nothing we can do," said Laszlo. "They'll either kill him or release him in a few days after interrogation. They've done it before."

"Who's 'they'?"

"It's better you don't know."

"They're Russians, aren't they?"

"Yes, but which Russians?" Laszlo needed to establish whether these were regular embassy staff, clearing up some loose ends of an old project, or whether they were a new team, embarking on something he hadn't heard about. Was it anything to do with Nautilus and this man beside him?

"Let's assume this was completely unrelated to you. They tailed him to the college and jumped on him as he came out. They weren't interested in you at all. But I think you should lie low. Go to the country. The average KGB agent, if he does follow you, makes himself ludicrously conspicuous in the country. If anything happens, call me. By the way, you are Dr Felix. It's your code name, not mine."

Dimock telephoned Anna from the lobby. She was in a meeting. He decided to clear his head by walking across

Hyde Park to his flat. It was a hot afternoon in early October. Cyclists with naked torsos pedalled round the track and women sun-bathed beside neat piles of clothes, drinking in the last juices of the Indian summer. He and Anna would go to Scotland or the Lake District. There would be no one around and they would enjoy that heavy season before the sun paled and the leaves turned gold. But at the same time he felt he was running away. Shouldn't he stay and resist bastards who shot and kidnapped people in broad daylight in other people's countries? Hadn't he demonstrated in his youth against violence and oppression of all kinds? Wasn't this just as bad as Polaris missiles and the Establishment's computer files?

He walked past a children's Punch and Judy show in the corner of the park, under the shadow of the Soviet embassy. He joined the Bayswater Road and turned right into Kensington Park Road. His flat was at the top of a terraced house near the Portobello Road, in a street that lay in a limbo between restoration and dereliction. He collected his mail on the ground floor and took the stairs two at a time, up three flights. The door of his flat was ajar: the Yale lock had been forced open.

CHAPTER SEVEN

It wasn't a complete ransacking but the drawers of his desk and the filing cabinet had been rifled through. Papers littered the floor and his box files lay about like decapitated soldiers. He looked immediately for the material from his Swedish trip; he didn't see it. The box file was gone and the folder from the filing cabinet. "Good luck to them," he thought. "They won't find anything."

This was a police matter. They couldn't be kept out any longer. He picked up the telephone and dialled 999. He didn't care if the telephone was bugged. The police said that since the burglar was no longer there they would send someone from the CID next morning.

"I won't be here," said Dimock. "Besides this isn't an ordinary burglary: they've stolen some important papers, to do with my research."

"We'll have someone round in half an hour, sir." Dimock went down two floors to Mrs Steinitz. She hadn't heard anything but offered to make him a cup of tea. He rang all the doorbells in the building. The man on the ground floor, who was on a night shift, said he had heard someone run down the stairs at about midday.

"But he was whistling just like you, I thought it was you," he said to Dimock. Dimock had left around nine.

Two policemen arrived and looked over the flat. They examined the door and traced the mark of a running shoe. It was size 11 or 12. Dimock then found that his camera and lenses were missing. At least they were insured.

The telephone rang. It was Anna.

"I got your message," she said. "I'm taking ten days off, will that do?"

"Okay for a start," said Dimock. He described the scene at his flat.

"You'd better stay for couple of days and sort things out," said Anna.

"No. We'll go tonight. I'll pick you up at seven."

"What's the big hurry?"

"Just do it," he yelled and slammed down the receiver.

"Are you alright, sir?" Dimock looked at the policeman, considering the effect of what he was about to say.

"You won't believe this, but I think the intruder was a foreign agent."

"I see, sir. Now what makes you think that?" Dimock explained the events of the day.

"We haven't heard of a kidnapping."

"It hasn't been reported."

"Why didn't you report it, sir?"

"Because I thought the man's friends could handle it."

"Who are his friends?"

"I can't say."

"Who is the man?"

"I can't say that either."

"Now let's take this one thing at a time. You've reported a burglary. Now you want to report a kidnapping. But you can't give us the subject's name or any other details."

"I'm just saying that this burglary might be connected with a kidnapping."

"I'm sorry, sir, but unless we have some firm evidence to go on..."

"I realize that, but you could help me trace the car. The number was TWV something, something, six, X. Can you check to see if it was stolen?"

The policeman took out his radio. He called up the station which, in turn, checked with the police computer. Voices crackled and half a minute later there was an answer.

"There are about 20 cars with that combination of letters and numbers," said the policeman. "Not one of them has been reported stolen."

"Okay, forget it," said Dimock, "forget the whole thing." His mind was working on another tack. The police obviously weren't equipped to deal with matters that weren't strictly felonious. "Please let me know if any of my things turn up."

The policemen left. Dimock packed a suitcase, screwed the Yale lock back onto the doorframe as best he could and cancelled the milk and the newspapers.

At about 6.30 he loaded his car. He drove a few blocks and stopped to use a phone box. First, he called Tomar.

"This is Dr Felix," he said. "Your friends have paid me a visit."

"Leave it to me," said Laszlo. "We'll send someone round right away."

" I called the police." There was a pause at the other end.

"That was most unwise," said Laszlo.

"This cloak and dagger stuff has gone too far."

"What did you tell them?"

"I asked them to check on the car. Nothing."

"Listen to me," said Laszlo. "Take that piece of advice I gave you. Leave town." He hung up. Why did these

Hungarians want him out of the way? Dimock was becoming suspicious.

He dialled another number - Fortescue's. He knew Fortescue would fly into a panic.

"Stay where you are," said Fortescue. "We'll send round protection."

"Thank you but I can look after myself," said Dimock. "I'll ring you in ten days. Book a court for the seventeenth."

He climbed into his car and took a tortuous route to Anna's flat, mixing with the early evening traffic. He parked his car round the corner, waited a few minutes and got out.

Dimock walked to the corner of the street and waited again. All seemed quiet. He walked up the mansion steps and rang Anna's doorbell.

Anna was ready. But she was also in a fuming rage. Her eyes burned blue-grey as she let him in and kicked the door shut.

"What the hell did you mean by slamming the phone down?"

"Sorry!" Dimock threw up his meat-cleaver hands and met her glare head-on. "Come here a second," he said. She stood her ground. "Okay, I'll tell you." He crash-landed into a deep sofa. "Things are starting to happen," he said.

"What do you mean?"

"Somebody thinks I know something - about what happened in Sweden. Somebody else tried to warn me - and got himself kidnapped. Somebody broke into my flat - and was looking for something."

"Who are these people?"

"Russians, Hungarians, something to do with the Eastern bloc."

"Can't you just tell them you know nothing?"

"Ah, but I do know something." Dimock smiled cynically. "Apparently I took some very good photographs. Everyone seems to know about them except me."

"Who's got them?"

"The British? The Hungarians? I don't know."

"I thought the Hungarians were on the same side as the Russians."

"Not in London, apparently. The Hungarians, the Russians and the British are all playing silly games, for each other and against each other; it doesn't really matter. That's why you and I are leaving. We'll let them fight it out between themselves." Dimock got up and pulled Anna close to him.

"You great, brawny bearded ape," said Anna, "you're running away."

"Too bloody right. I'm not sticking around to get myself kidnapped or killed. And I won't let them get their maulers on you either. We'll find a bolt-hole in the Welsh hills." Anna rested her head on his broad shoulder.

"Why don't we stay the night here and go first thing in the morning?"

"No," said Dimock. "We leave right away." He went into the kitchen, turned out the light, and looked into the street below. "All clear," he said. He looked at Anna's two suitcases. "You're not bringing all this clobber are you? Christ!" He picked up the biggest one and took it down the stairs. Anna locked up.

"I didn't know where we were going," she said. Dimock squeezed one of the cases into the boot and the other behind the bucket seats. He started the engine and switched on the radio.

"Let's go!" he yelled, as if it were a battle cry, over the deafening music.

Dimock headed west out of London. He took the M40 motorway towards Oxford, weaving in and out of the congested traffic to make doubly sure of losing any pursuers, as dusk fell and headlights snapped on. As they came into Oxford at about 9.30 they were looking for a place to have a drink and maybe a bite to eat. Dimock drove down Headington Hill and stopped at some traffic lights. In the driving mirror, the shape of the car behind him caught his attention. It was hanging back at a distance of about 25 yards. It wasn't a remarkable car but the shapes of the driver and passengers were somehow familiar - well-built, thick-set.

"Don't look round but see if you can read the number of that car," said Dimock. Anna half turned. It was difficult in the soft sodium glow of the street lights. "TWV 906X," she said.

"How the hell did they follow us here?" exclaimed Dimock.

"Is that them?"

"Perhaps they've put a homing device on the car." The lights changed. "I'm going to try and shake them off."

"Why don't we just go to the police?"

"That won't do any good." Dimock cruised towards the city centre. He suddenly swung left down a side street and accelerated away, taking the next right-hander. Then he turned left and hit the Cowley Road. The headlights of the other car obstinately followed.

"Dimock, you'll never get away. They do this for a living. We'll have an accident."

"Shut up," said Dimock. His heart was pounding. He accelerated out into the path of another car and turned right towards the city again. "OK, we'll see if they know Oxford." He accelerated over Magdalen Bridge and turned right into a narrow lane. His only hope he thought was to get into north Oxford, a maze of residential roads. Turning into a main road he built up a small lead then dived right, down a leafy avenue. He took the first left, then a right, entered the first driveway and killed the lights and the engine. "Hide!" he shouted and they put their heads down. The beige car sped past and took the next corner. They waited five minutes, ten minutes. "Let's have that drink," said Dimock. He eased the car back into the main road. But a light-coloured car came from the right and joined the traffic behind them.

"It's them," said Anna. A cold fury possessed Dimock. He changed gear and kicked his foot down to the floor, pulling out to overtake everything despite the stream of oncoming traffic, and despite protests from Anna. He was determined to shake these bastards off. The screaming sports car shot over the first roundabout without decelerating, and headed for the ring road. Then Dimock saw blue lights flashing behind him. A police motorcycle overtook him and forced him to slow down and stop.

Dimock switched off the engine. He saw the beige car flash past pursued by another police bike. The policeman walked slowly over to Dimock's car. He knocked on the window and Dimock wound it down.

"Been drinking have we, sir? I'll have those keys if you don't mind," said the policeman. Dimock climbed out of the car and looked down from his great height at the policeman. But the officer wasn't intimidated. He demanded Dimock's driving licence and asked him to blow into a green bag.

The test was negative. "I see, just having a dice with death, then. Do you realize you nearly knocked me off my bike back there? I don't suppose you even noticed me."

Dimock apologized. He'd been in the wrong, he said, and would face the consequences. The policeman took out his notebook and began to take particulars. He walked round to the front of the car and wrote down the number. Dimock stood in silence, wondering whether the beige car would return, gunfire pumping from a lowered window. The radio crackled on the policeman's motorbike and he closed his notebook and stepped over to it. After a minute he came back.

"You're a lucky bastard. I would've pinched you for dangerous driving, but my colleague's called me away. He's found himself with a carload of Bulgarian diplomats." He tossed Dimock the car keys and roared off on his bike.

CHAPTER EIGHT

Lake Maggiore, Italy

Lebedyev saw the small guiding light from the boat on the surface above him. He forced more water from the ballast tanks and the tiny craft rose from the lake bottom. With a touch on the rudder and hardly any forward speed he manoeuvred the Nautilus under the hull of the cabin cruiser. This was the trickiest part of the operation. It was all very well in the experimental tank in Riga but the surface of Lake Maggiore wasn't still. A force four wind was gusting from shore to shore and the cabin cruiser, the Flying Finn, was pitching clumsily. A big segment of its hull below the water line had been lowered to offer a platform onto which the Nautilus would dock. With the Nautilus docked home the bottom of the cruiser would close again, taking the miniature submarine into its womb. The Nautilus then rested in the bilges, taking up a great deal of cabin space and lowering the trim of the Flying Finn considerably. But apart from a certain sluggishness she looked and behaved like an ordinary pleasure cruiser.

Lebedyev concentrated on aligning the Nautilus with the docking light. Bent almost double in the tiny cockpit, he felt the sweat collecting above his eyebrows. He knew that sooner or later the dam would break and the grimy sweat would pour into his eyes. The Nautilus lurched under the pressure of the surface swell and the Flying Finn danced the same crazy tango. But the nose made contact and Lebedyev quickly powered the electromagnets to keep the Nautilus in place as it was levered into the belly of the mother ship.

When the hull was back as one piece and watertight, the deck and cabin air seals were released. These seals made the upper half of the boat airtight to keep it buoyant like an inverted cup, while the hull was open. Without them, and with the weight of the Nautilus, the Flying Finn would have sunk like a stone.

Lebedyev threw back the submarine hatch. "Give me docking in deep space any day," he said.

"Well, it worked," said Demirkan, who had the job of piloting the Flying Finn. "Now we have the Volvo link-up, but not till morning." The lights of Locarno burned steadily on the lake's northern shore while above the hulks of the mountains the less steady lights of the stars were warped by the wind. Demirkan and Lebedyev were now in Swiss waters. The Flying Finn had gone through regular customs procedures while Nautilus had traversed the underwater hillsides of the lake.

"Better get some sleep," said Demirkan. Lebedyev looked at the stars. He traced the flight of a man-made satellite until it sank behind the Alps. Despite the assignment in Switzerland he felt unhappy. He wouldn't see his daughter for months, even years. This skulking around under water was the very opposite of the glamour and fanfare of space travel. Whoever decided cosmonauts could double up as submariners had made a profound psychological error.

"Are you about to lay an egg"?" asked Demirkan. "Look on this as a holiday," he continued. "No logs to fill, no progress reports, no aptitude tests to ruin your taste for drink, eh?"

"What about that thing in there?" Lebedyev indicated the Nautilus.

"Oh that. Listen, my friend. It's never going to happen. At least, not in a little place like Switzerland. It's just to scare the Yanks and their mad president."

"How can they be scared when they don't even know about it?"

"They will, Vladimir Petrovitch. We'll let them know when the time comes. Before it's too late." The Nautilus was now a self-propelled, self-arming nuclear bomb. It was one of several prototypes being carefully deployed in what Mikhailov judged to be the nerve centres of the non-communist world.

They were not large nuclear bombs, but they were enough to rip the heart out of Downtown Manhattan, London's Square Mile or Tokyo Harbour if correctly positioned, and to contaminate those areas for years. The exercise, as much intellectual as strategic, was to deploy these devices so that they would be undetectable, independent of human qualms and foibles, and usable at the push of a button in Moscow. Mikhailov realized that there were potential weaknesses in the chain of command at the deployment stage. But he was relying on the team spirit of Tikov's cosmonauts to overcome that. They would regard it as a challenge, a kind of terrestrial jeu sans frontières, to deploy these tiny craft undetected. He told Tikov to start with Zurich as much for emotional as for strategic reasons. Zurich was where Lenin had developed his revolutionary ideas; it was the birthplace of Bolshevism. But it was also the centre of the world's gold trade and after New York the biggest physical depot of gold bullion in the world. The yellow metal would boil nicely in a thermo-nuclear blast, he reflected.

Squeezing a nuclear device into the confines of the Nautilus was a miracle of engineering. The Hungarians had had to redesign the air filter system. The pilot now had little room to move once he had shoe-horned himself into the driving position. For, planted solidly at the craft's centre of gravity, was the implosion chamber of the nuclear device with its heavy lead walls. In theory, the pilot was protected from radiation but it was unlikely that a human body could come unscathed through such a bombardment while sitting in such proximity. Lebedyev didn't think so much about that. After all, he'd probably had a debilitating dose of cosmic rays already, in space. The worry he felt was of being rolled towards an outstanding moral question: when did he drop loyalty to Mother Russia in favour of loyalty to himself? Tikov and he had never discussed this question. Tikov was too jovial, too keen to maintain the spirit of '75.

The first plan for Switzerland had been marvellously simple.

"You load the Nautilus into a container," said Tikov, "and drive it in as part of the diplomatic bag, claiming customs immunity. It'll slay 'em." Unfortunately the imagination of the Swiss authorities couldn't accommodate a 90 cubic metre container within the term diplomatic bag. The truck was turned away at the frontier.

The next plan was more elaborate. The pleasure craft Flying Finn was designed and built in Finland, to Tikov's specifications. It was sailed to Riga, pulled apart, its deck and cabin given airtight seals and was given its drop-bottom hull. Then the Flying Finn was sailed by Demirkan to the Mediterranean. Nautilus, still in its container, was driven to the Black Sea, loaded on a Soviet trawler and shipped down the Bosphorus to the Eastern Mediterranean.

Demirkan sailed the Flying Finn to a yacht marina near Brindisi in southern Italy and went through customs formalities. The Russian trawler, avoiding the American Sixth Fleet and the Italian guardia di finanza, released Lebedyev in his Nautilus near the Italian shore. At a night-time rendez-vous five kilometres offshore the Flying Finn picked up the Nautilus. It was Lebedyev's first live docking, an experience he was happy to forget even though there was a flat calm. Back at the marina, Flying Finn and its cargo were hauled from the water and driven on a trailer the length of Italy to Stresa on Lake Maggiore. Once water-borne, the Flying Finn released Nautilus and sailed into Switzerland. Nautilus followed at nightfall for its starlit rendez-vous.

Lebedyev sought sleep in a corner of the cabin not filled by the grey, dripping Nautilus. When he awoke they were in the marina at Locarno. A Volvo truck was already backing its trailer down the slipway to receive the Flying Finn. "You're missing all the fun," Demirkan shouted down the hatchway. Lebedyev rose and sealed the cabin's smoked glass windows. Then he went on deck and locked the hatch. The Nautilus was invisible from outside.

Demirkan nosed the Flying Finn onto the submerged trailer and cut the engine. The hull, with its heavy load, creaked as the trailer left the water. It had been reinforced by Soviet engineers.

"The driver will take it to the marina in Zurich," said Demirkan, "and we go by train." They took a taxi to Bellinzona and caught the Ticino express to Zurich. Both men were travelling on Danish passports, trusting that they wouldn't meet someone who spoke the language. In Zurich it would be easier; they could act as Soviet diplomatic staff. They went to the restaurant car and drank schnapps with their grilled steak and rösti. "The Danes always get drunk," said Demirkan, "even at eleven in the morning." Lebedyev ordered a bottle of red wine. It was quite smooth and drinkable, so they ordered another. By the time they reached Zurich Hauptbahnhof their breathing was a little heavy.

"A toast to Brigadier Tikov," said Lebedyev.

"And his whoremaster Mikhailov," added Demirkan. Arm in arm they sailed out of the station across the path of taxis and trams and into the Bahnhofstrasse.

"We want a number 10," said Demirkan, indicating a tram.

"Is this the Bahnhofstrasse? I don't see any banks," said Lebedyev, having heard it was the Swiss equivalent of Wall Street. "They're down the other end," said Demirkan. He had been in Zurich three weeks on reconnaissance. They bought tickets from the machine and boarded a number 10 tram. It took them past the country's biggest bank, the Union Bank of Switzerland, then swung into the Paradeplatz. Ahead of them was the Zurich branch of Swiss Bank Corporation and on their right the head office of Credit Suisse. "This is the heart of European capitalism," said Demirkan. "Think of all the gold in those underground vaults." But Lebedyev was looking at the lace curtains of a café, behind which he thought he could see elegant ladies in furs having afternoon coffee and cake. The tram continued. Lebedyev was overwhelmed by the tidiness of the streets, despite the age of the houses. On the right, steep streets rose up a wooded hillside; it all looked highly civilized. The tram nosed past well-kept parks, following the strand of Lake Zurich.

"Out we get," said Demirkan. "I'll show you the house." On a dull, rather busy road they walked along the narrow pavement. Demirkan was scanning the house numbers. "Here it is, number 417." It was a large grey town house with a grey door and grey shutters which may once have been elegant but whose paint was now cracked and flaking. Demirkan rang the bell. A young man in black trousers and waistcoat opened the door. Demirkan led the way in. Lebedyev followed and asked quietly, "Is he Russian?"

"Estonian. It's alright, this house is ours. Everything and everyone in it is totally trustworthy." Everywhere had an air of decayed elegance - worn carpets, unrepaired chandeliers, smoke and aged-stained silk wallpaper, furniture mottled with damp. "This bit will interest you," said Demirkan. He opened French windows onto a terrace. The view was straight onto Lake Zurich, where sailing craft and ferryboats drew complicated patterns on the choppy water. Below the terrace was an overgrown garden and on the water's edge an old wooden boathouse. "There's the Nautilus's new home," said Demirkan.

"Is it burglar-proof?" asked Lebedyev.

"It's everything proof." They walked down through the tall grass. Demirkan took a key out of his pocket and applied it to a new-looking lock. The boathouse was simple: a concrete quay on three sides and a slatted gate at the end allowing strips of light to fall on the flashing water.

"We'll have to make that gate more solid," said Lebedyev.

"We have to put in power cables too," said Demirkan, "to charge the battery - and the telephone link."

"You think of everything." Lebedyev imagined the boathouse in its heyday, harbouring perhaps a skiff for early morning rowing and a graceful steam launch for afternoon excursions with the ladies. Now it would be the den of one of the most destructive weapons in history. He had a half hopeful feeling that, like the house itself, the project was doomed to superannuation and decay.

Demirkan looked at his watch. "We must go to the marina," he said. They left the house and walked a further kilometre up the Seestrasse. Turning left onto the shore they came to a well-organized marina with ranks of sailing craft moored in lagoons of wooden jetties. At one end was a circular clubhouse and restaurant built on its own peninsula. The Volvo was waiting there with its precious load. When the Russians had arrived and identified themselves the Flying Finn was lowered into the water. Demirkan had already joined the yacht club.

"A fine craft," said the club secretary, looking at the boat doubtfully as it settled in the water with a slight list to starboard.

"Some of the ballast must have shifted on the journey, we'll soon put it right," said Demirkan. He and Lebedyev stepped aboard. Demirkan started the engine and the Flying Finn limped to a temporary mooring. "We'll have to drop the Nautilus tonight," he said. "She's handling very badly. I don't think she'd ride out a storm."

"So much for Tikov's fabulous calculations." From the clubhouse Demirkan called a taxi and they rode into the centre of Zurich. "How about a coffee in one of those wonderful cafés?" suggested Lebedyev.

"First I've got to introduce you to your new boss." The taxi swung into the Schützengasse. There stood one of the more ugly buildings in Zurich, a triangular wedge clad in 1950s plate glass and in plain lettering next to a symbol of the globe, the legend Wozchod Bank. They used the side entrance and took the lift to the fifth floor. A secretary received them.

"Mr Giger is very busy but he can see you for a few moments." The balding man behind the desk looked at them with obvious distaste. He stood up and shook each of them by the hand. "I understand it's my duty to welcome another employee to the bank," he said in heavily accented Russian - Mr Giger was a mandatory Swiss member of the management board - "but I think, in fact I hope, we will be seeing very little of each other. I am trying to run a profitable bank, gentlemen, not an asylum for down-and-outs, refugees and spies. That's all I have to say." Giger sat down again and bent himself to his work leaving the Russians hovering. Demirkan signalled Lebedyev to follow him and they tiptoed to the door, snorting with laughter when they had closed it behind them. "Humourless gnome," declared Demirkan. "Now we'll meet your real boss." He walked down the corridor and came to an unmarked door. He punched a code into the digital keyboard beside it and the door clicked open. In the room, Reuters machines and other wire services were chattering. There were several television screens and keyboards. "This is where the second-by-second, minute-by-minute gold trading strategy of the Soviet Union is formulated," said Demirkan. "What goes on downstairs is just a front, chicken feed. The market sees us dealing as Wozchod Bank in petty amounts, but here, the dealing is done quietly, in vast amounts in the name of the State Bank of the Soviet Union. We deal in confidence with only fifteen of the world's major banks and central banks, in co-operation with the world's other major gold producer South Africa. That's just background," said Demirkan, "but I thought you'd like to know." He flung open a door to the adjoining room. "Sergei, you leather-faced loon," he shouted. "I've brought Vladimir to see you."

Sergei was indeed leather-faced. Lebedyev had never seen a physiognomy so creased, wrinkled and tanned by the elements as the one now breaking into a smile before him. He couldn't tell whether the smile was for him or simply caused by attempts to draw the last evil from a dying cigarette. A hand shot out to greet him causing the sleeve of the cheap leather jacket to squeak under the strain. "Sergei Ivanovich Nesterov," mumbled a leather voice.

Was this anarchy, thought Lebedyev. What kind of outfit were they running here? Could they really be handling a large part of the Soviet Union's reserves from this room, with this man at the helm? A squawk-box on Nesterov's desk crackled.

"UBS Geneva wants to do 500 kilos at three hundred and twelve, private buyer," it said.

"OK," said Nesterov. He lit a fresh cigarette. "This is the only way we can beat the American futures markets," he said. "It's our defence against a nation of gamblers."

"Central Bank of Kuwait selling a quarter tonne at three ten," announced the voice-box. Nesterov glanced at his screen.

"No," he said. Nesterov stood up and wheeled his arms, throwing a few punches at Demirkan. He turned to Lebedyev. "I used to be a chess player, but I found it too political. This is a much better game." He glanced at his watch. "New York's going to lunch, why don't we have a drink somewhere?"

"Vladimir wants to visit a Bahnhofstrasse café and find a classy dame with a mink coat."

"Okay, we can drink there too," said Nesterov. He pressed the intercom and said: "Toni, I'm going out." The three Russians squeezed into the narrow lift and burst forth into the gathering dusk in the Schützengasse. Nesterov led them through the cobbled streets of old Zurich by the Limmat River, past St Peter's Church and the cathedral, the Fraumünster. In a courtyard between the Paradeplatz and the river they found a first floor café. Lebedyev had a can of coffee and several cakes stuffed with rich cream, the others drank brandy.

"Na, what about the women?" teased Demirkan. Lebedyev looked up with the cream adorning his mouth.

"We're too old. And they seem too interested in food." They drank some more brandy.

"Let's go somewhere more interesting," said Nesterov. They paid the bill and ducked through an archway into the Börsenstrasse. A sharp wind was blowing off Lake Zurich. It sobered Lebedyev and Demirkan in an instant.

"Mother of God, we must be going," said Demirkan. He embraced Nesterov who stood swaying gently as the two newcomers ran for a taxi.

At the marina the water was slapping against the quay and the wind smacked halyards against metal masts. Lebedyev and Demirkan leapt aboard the Flying Finn. Lebedyev cast off while the Uzbek started the engine. Demirkan lit no lights. Nothing but ferries would be mad enough to be out on a night like this. The Flying Finn, belying its name, lurched between the strong gusts of wind. Lebedyev checked the deck and cabin air seals. He sealed the deck hatch behind him and climbed into the cockpit of the Nautilus. He hadn't time to put on his wet suit. "We're near the house now," said Demirkan through the intercom. "I'll drop you then berth the Flying Finn. Don't try to get into the boathouse until I've raised the gate and lit an underwater light." Demirkan flooded the bilges slightly and lowered the hull bottom. Lebedyev switched on the electromagnets and felt the Nautilus tilt downwards. He opened the valves to flood the buoyancy tanks then, achieving negative buoyancy, shut off the magnets. The Nautilus slid gently from the mother ship. It was pitch black. Lebedyev heard the engine of the Flying Finn recede into the distance. He kept Nautilus at a depth of five metres, nosing against the slight current. The battery levels were low. There had been no opportunity to charge them since leaving the trawler five days ago. A ferryboat thundered half a kilometre behind him. Nervously he put the Nautilus into a dive. "May as well rest on the bottom," he told himself, "play the game."

Demirkan guided the Flying Finn to its berth. There was a reception party - a car on the jetty and three men in uniform. "Guten Abend, Polizei," said a voice as Demirkan stepped ashore. "Sind Sie der Eigentümer dieses Boots?"

"I'm sorry, I speak only English," said Demirkan.

"Are you the owner of this boat?"

"Of course. I have the papers here." The policeman looked at them by torchlight.

"You are a diplomat?" he asked.

"Yes."

"You were sailing without lights."

"I couldn't find the switch."

"It's hardly the weather for a pleasure cruise."

"I was impatient," said Demirkan. "You see my baby girl only arrived today from Italy. I couldn't wait to sail her."

"Have you been drinking?"

"Only a little," said Demirkan. "Is that against the law?"

"I must ask you to come with us," said the policeman. Demirkan began to protest, but thought better of it. The Swiss didn't like a fuss, he told himself. But what about Lebedyev? He would be waiting, frantic.

At the police station Demirkan was allowed to call the embassy in Berne. That was at 9.30. The embassy lawyer claimed diplomatic immunity. He demanded that Demirkan be released and said he would be in Zurich the next day to sort the matter out. Demirkan was kept for two more hours to dictate a statement, to be photographed, fingerprinted and then released. He immediately took a taxi to Seestrasse 417, unlocked the door, shouted for a torch and a plastic bag and headed for the garden. Meanwhile he cursed himself: "If I'd wanted to blow my cover sky high, I couldn't have done better. I hope the Swiss are as dumb as the Russians."

He found some rope and tied the lighted torch inside the plastic bag, then lowered it into the water. If he'd had the time and leisure he would have brought the guidelight and a small radio beacon from the boat, but this would have to do.

The torch was burning underwater but the wind and waves lashed the creaking boathouse. Demirkan wound the handle which raised the gate and waited. He hoped there was no skiff, or no police launch lurking out there. He stared out into the turbulent lake. A noise behind him made him jump; a monster rising up in the sheltered water. It was Nautilus. Lebedyev threw open the hatch and tossed Demirkan a rope. He closed the hatch and leapt ashore.

"What the hell went wrong?" he hissed. "You kept me waiting nearly four hours. The battery is just about dead and I almost had to abandon ship."

"A little trouble with the police," said Demirkan weakly. "I was picked up on the jetty." Lebedyev looked at Demirkan for a moment, then slapped him on the shoulder and laughed.

"Son of a bitch," he said.

VULKAN

CHAPTER NINE

After the dismantling of the British Empire the great port of London, the busiest in the world, became a backwater lined with idle cranes and empty warehouses. But in the 1980s with the growth of the City as a financial centre the surging price of property drove the developers east into empty dockland. Old Billingsgate fish market and Hay's Wharf became the sites of ambitious office development. Farther east the tall, forbidding warehouses were gutted and converted into luxury apartments overlooking the idle Thames. Only a few ugly lighters and oil barges now plied where fifty or a hundred years before the water teemed with sailing barges, ferryboats and pleasure steamers, majestic tea clippers and freighters from all over the world. Gun Wharf at Wapping, on the north bank of the Thames, was one such luxury conversion. The outer façade with its wooden loading platforms at each window was preserved. Seven of the twelve apartments on each floor had French windows giving onto these wooden balconies. By the spring of 1985 most of them had been sold for between £55,000 and £200,000.

Zilin was a latecomer. But he'd no sooner seen the building than he realized it was exactly what he needed. He sent a message to Moscow: "I need £101,000 cash, on the nail." The cash was paid through Moscow Narodny Bank.

Zilin walked into the estate agent's office with a briefcase full of money. The formalities took a little longer but within a month Zilin moved into one of the first floor flats, empty apart from curtains and wall-to-wall carpet. He opened the French window and stepped onto the wooden balcony. "Excellent," he said. He looked down at the shiny Thames mud, exposed as the river shrank, revealing the black piles along the bank and the growth-strewn legs of numerous jetties. He'd spent many days walking on the mud, measuring the flows of the tide and the time-lag between high water at Wapping and official high water at London Bridge, as published each day in *The Times*. Zilin leaned over the guard rail and ran his eye down the weathered brickwork to the concrete foundations and the wooden piles covered with mud and green slime. How easily could he disguise the line of a power cable down the brickwork? His eye caught sight of a drainpipe five metres to the right. If he could camouflage the cable that far he was home and dry.

He worked with the USSR Trade Delegation in Highgate. He was a minor official, but involved in the purchase of high technology equipment - what little of it wasn't embargoed by the United States. His work wasn't arduous but it took him out every weekday, either to Highgate by underground, or into the City on foot. Before long he bought himself a bicycle with ten gears and cut down his journey to Highgate by 20 minutes. The bicycle also allowed him to take sinuous routes through London, to ships chandlers, electrical shops, and do-it-yourself stores. In the evenings his real work began.

First, at low tide, he took a narrow alley which ended in a flight of steps onto the Thames mud. Then he walked until he was standing beneath Gun Wharf. The river bottom there was firmer, covered with rubble and broken bricks from recent rebuilding work. The concrete foundations were smooth and the brickwork had been repointed. There were few irregularities that would disguise the line of a power cable. He walked to the western edge of the building and he saw the solution. A copper lightning conductor ran from the top of the building to the bottom. At intervals it was secured by brackets to the wall. But there was a gap between the wall and the copper, wide enough to squeeze in a cable and a telephone wire. The cable could then run on a small horizontal ledge from the conductor to his apartment. Far better than the drainpipe whose bottom would be exposed at low tide.

On one of his shopping expeditions Zilin bought the cable, 200 metres of it, three waterproof junctions, and a small bag of cement. From now on he took care not to be seen. He worked outside only at night, when it was low tide and there was enough wind to whisk away the sound of his workmanship and his feet on the water-soaked rubble. The lightning conductor was a godsend. The length of cable and the telephone wire were soon in place behind it. Then, on a stormy night, applying his skill as a mountaineer, he laid the horizontal stretch across to his apartment, covering the cable with a thin layer of cement.

At one of the lowest spring tides of the year, Zilin completed the third and final stage. He laid a cable from the foot of the lightning conductor to a pleasure boat jetty 150 metres away, Woods River Services. He dug a trench and buried the cable where it would otherwise be visible at low tide, then diving to the slimy feet of jetty he anchored the cable with its waterproof socket well below low water mark.

Zilin was ready. Next day at work he telephoned Moscow.

"We're waiting for the consignment from Riga," he said.

Tikov himself had decided to undertake the next stage. He was already in a trawler which was pretending to fish in the North Sea. There was little room in the hold for the embarrassing haul of cod and whiting caught in their net and they had to tip much of it back overboard. Nautilus 3, already primed with its nuclear device, was taking up a large part of the refrigerated hold. Off Goodwin Sands on a blustery night in May the Nautilus was lowered into the sea with Tikov inside. On the still bottom, away from the swell rising onto the shallows, Tikov took his bearings and directed Nautilus towards the Thames estuary. His plan was to reach the new Thames barrier, just as the tide was in full flood and ride in on the current to Wapping. Unassisted by currents he had a range of 30 kilometres before the batteries ran down - and 12 hours of air. For some of the time he would have to use the snorkel if he was to stay submerged until the next nightfall.

Tikov was cramped. He was unusually tall and had to bend his head forward permanently to fit around the central nuclear core. "If only the Americans had designed this thing," he thought wryly. "They would have a Coca Cola machine in one corner and a shower in the other. We always do things on a shoestring." The Nautilus moved forward, beneath the rumbling of the Gravesend passenger ferry, over the rumbling of the Dartford Tunnel. It rose to within two metres of the surface and put up its snorkel. There was little chance of detection and it was more efficient than crawling along the sea bottom. For a moment Tikov surfaced and took in the bleak waste of the Thames estuary, punctuated by a few twinkling lights and crossed by an occasional freighter. The tide was still on the ebb but it was slowing. He passed the Thames barrier, looming concave shapes in the approaching daylight. It was time to sink close to the river bottom and tumble forward under very light power with the force of the tide. Visibility was bad because of the rolling billows of mud. Tikov had to rely on staying with the main stream of the current and the compass was no good because the river often coiled through 180 degrees. If the groundspeed indicator slowed he headed left or right until it picked up again. He longed for the deep clear void of space rather than this murky hell.

Perhaps it would have been better to wait until nightfall and float on the surface like a piece of driftwood. This was far worse than any Nordic fjord. Occasionally he risked a peep with a small periscope which ruffled the surface no more than a twig. He passed the Woolwich Ferry, East India Dock and the Blackwall Tunnel where the Thames suddenly narrowed. At the next bend was Greenwich, and his periscope showed him the tall masts of the tea clipper Cutty Sark, distorted by the fisheye lens. It was nearly 11 am. The tide was beginning to turn. He would have to find a place to lie low, below the low water mark, and wait for darkness 10 hours ahead. As he concentrated on this and put Nautilus into a shallow dive the thump thump of a marine engine came deafeningly close. A tugboat hit Nautilus from behind, only a glancing blow, but enough to send it slewing on its side. Tikov cursed his inattention, blew the buoyancy tanks and sent the sub to the bottom in an emergency dive. He hardly breathed, listening for signs of damage, the tell-tale hiss of water forcing itself in. There was nothing. The tugboat went on. Maybe the impact had sounded to those on board like hitting driftwood, Tikov thought. He waited. He couldn't tell now whether he was below the low water mark. Too bad. He couldn't risk using the dying battery to pump out ballast. Blowing the tanks had also cost him some precious air. He would have to lie still and consume as little oxygen as possible until nightfall. To save energy he didn't even swear.

Six hours later, at low tide, he was able to put up the periscope. He judged he was somewhere near the middle of the river. Could he risk the snorkel? Probably. But his childlike desire to see this project succeed allowed him to take no risks. He lay there slowly suffocating, aware that if the carbon dioxide level got too high he would go to sleep and never wake up. He pinched himself, bit the inside of his cheek until the blood flowed freely, filling his mouth with its salty taste. Then as the sun set and an evening breeze ruffled the water he blew the tanks. The sub righted itself and swung towards the surface. With almost no forward turn on the propeller he raised the snorkel and gulped in lungfuls of damp Thames air, coughing uncontrollably. Then he dropped the snorkel again and cruised under minimal power with the rising tide.

In darkness, through the periscope, Tikov identified the pier that Zilin had described to him. The lights of Gun Wharf played on the surface as he drew closer. At the east end of the pier he released air and allowed Nautilus to sink gently to the bottom. It came to rest at a slight angle but seemed secure. Tikov pressed a switch which extended four grappling claws. Then he squeezed himself into the tiny airlock in the conning tower. As the chamber filled with water he continued to breathe through a face mask. Taking a final gasp he opened the hatch and swam to the surface. It was high tide.

Tikov had arrived in England with no possessions besides his black, drip-dry jump suit and some documents and money in a waterproof bag. He climbed onto the pier of Woods River Services and listened in the darkness. The tall shape of Gun Wharf rose above him patched with soft light from curtained windows. First floor, second from the left, was Zilin's. Tikov swept as many drops as he could from his drip-dry clothes; he emptied the water from his shoes and ran his fingers through his hair. Then he walked quietly along the pier, scaled a door topped with barbed wire and descended the alley into Wapping High Street. The name was a hangover from busier times: there was no one in sight. Tikov walked quickly to the door of Gun Wharf, pressed Zilin's bell, grunted, and was let in. On the first floor the door to Zilin's flat was open. He pushed it, entered, and closed it quietly behind him. There was a smell of cabbage. "You Russians," said Tikov. "You can always make a place smell like home."

VULKAN

CHAPTER TEN

The body of Matyas Nagy fell from the upholstery of a sofa as it was lifted onto a Thames barge. The sofa had been deposited at a West London rubbish dump. Police examining the decomposed body found lacerations consistent with torture and electric shock. But the circumstances of his death and the motive were a mystery. Laszlo heard from the consulate. He wanted revenge. The only witness who might link his fellow Hungarian's death with the Bulgarian thugs was Dimock Torrence who had disappeared with his girlfriend Anna in October. It was now June.

He called Torrence's London flat off and on for three days. On the third day, a voice answered.

"Dr Torrence?"

"Yes."

"Dr Tomar. How are you? How is Anna?" Dimock took some time to reply.

"Fine."

"I'm having a small party at my house this evening. Just a few friends. Would you and Anna like to come? Shall we say around nine o'clock at 7 Albion Mews."

"I'll think about it," said Dimock. He hadn't forgotten Anna but they seldom met these days. Four nervous weeks in a cottage in Wales had seen to that. But Dimock telephoned her at work. "Come here for a drink and we can go on to Laszlo's."

By 9.30, after some quiet drinking, they were drawn out of curiosity to visit the Hungarian's party. For a converted mews, the house was sumptuous. Antique carpets and mediaeval carvings hung on white walls, and more rugs adorned the floors of polished wood. Laszlo's wife was an interpreter, a fifty-year-old, kept glamorous by hair and face treatments. There were only three other guests - a musician, a painter and an Englishman called Pike, introduced as a publisher. Drinks were mixed. From upright armchairs the conversation flowed artificially, touching on the art relics still to be found in Hungary - Turkish carpets, Chinese screens - the recital that Malik had just given in the Purcell Room. The painter, long-haired and sensitive-looking, flirted with Anna. Mrs Laszlo re-focussed the evening by bringing in a huge cream-filled cake and dispensing slices. Drinks were replenished several times. Then the discussion became serious. Laszlo spoke:

"They found the body of Matyas Nagy three days ago; he'd been missing for nearly eight months. Dimock, you were the last person to see him alive."

"I thought you said they would let him go after a few hours," said Dimock.

"Who?"

"The Bulgarians."

"Do you know they were Bulgarians?"

"The same car followed us out of London. They were stopped by the police - Bulgarian diplomats." For Laszlo it was all fitting into place.

"Would you remember the car?"

"TWV 906X."

"Very good. Do you think you could go to the police and tell them you saw the kidnapping?"

"I told them once. They wouldn't believe me."

"But they've got a body, an unsolved crime. The police don't like such things. They'll jump at the chance to tidy the case up."

"Look," he said, "I've had a quiet six months. My flat was broken into. We were chased across the country. Do we need to go into all that again?"

"We'll make sure it's all done quietly," said Laszlo. "We won't go to the police; we'll go to the foreign office. After all, no one's going to be prosecuted. The culprits have diplomatic immunity."

"What are you aiming at, then?"

"The expulsion of three or four Bulgarian diplomats. The embarrassment, the confusion in their chain of command. That will be enough."

"They'll just be replaced by another bunch of thugs. It won't make any difference."

"Dimock, I think you should help," said Anna. "This is all linked to John's death. We owe it to him."

"Those weren't Bulgarians they were Russians," retorted Dimock.

"It's all the same," said Laszlo. "The Ruskies and the Bulgars are like that." He rubbed his two index fingers together. "The Bulgars do all the dirty work. They murder embarrassing political exiles with poisoned umbrellas. You must remember George Markov, who was killed on Waterloo Bridge as he was walking to the BBC. Then there was the plot to shoot the Pope. Moscow wanted to stop him visiting Poland, so they got the Bulgars and a crazy Turk to do it for them."

Pike moved uncomfortably. He didn't believe in the conspiracy theory of history. He believed more in cock-ups that became conspiracies and in conspiracies that turned into cock-ups.

"Do you have friends in the foreign office?" asked Dimock. "I thought you were part of the Warsaw Pact." Laszlo smiled.

"We Hungarians always take a middle road."

"Only a Hungarian," said the musician suddenly, "can enter a revolving door behind you and come out in front of you. That's what they say."

"That didn't help poor old Matyas," said the painter.

"Who do you know at the foreign office?" asked Dimock. He was curious. Didn't they know about Fortescue and their weekly game of squash? Perhaps Fortescue's lot and Laszlo's lot didn't communicate.

"Someone in MI5, counter-intelligence," said Laszlo. "Leave it to me. All it needs is a short private interview and I'm sure you can forget the whole thing for the rest of your life."

"However long that is," said the musician laughing.

"Well, I think we should be going now," said Dimock, standing up. Anna clutched his arm.

"Say you'll do it," she said. All eyes were on Dimock, the tall, obstinate, Englishman. He looked at them: they were like children waiting to be let out of school.

"I refuse to become part of some private squabble between two Balkan countries."

"You're right, of course," said Laszlo. "It must look like that to an outsider. But our motives are not quite as petty as they seem. We're not just trying to avenge a murder. The Russians and the Bulgarians are up to something, we know that. A new operation. We're piecing the evidence together. Whatever it is the time has come to give them a shock and expose some of the loose ends. You can help us, Dimock." Dimock thought a moment.

"Okay," he said. He slung his jacket over his shoulder and prepared to leave. Laszlo rose and shook him by the hand.

"I'll call you tomorrow," he said. "It will be a very short meeting."

Dimock drove Anna home. As he stopped the car she put her arms round his neck.

"Won't you come in?" she said.

"No. I've got to think." He watched her let herself in through the front door, then nosed his car homeward.

Pike stayed with Laszlo until early that morning. He listened to the Hungarian map out his plan of campaign. The musician and the painter went home; Mrs Laszlo retired to bed. As the first feelers of dawn crept over London Pike shook Laszlo by the hand and walked home across Hyde Park.

The foliage on the trees was just turning from monochrome to green, the dawn chorus had ceased. There was a thick dew which wettened but didn't penetrate his black brogues. Pike walked down Exhibition Road which he had learned was the scene of Matyas Nagy's kidnapping. He was still unsure how to link that event with the Nautilus, the shooting of an Englishman in Sweden, and the photographs of Boris Tikov - if it really was Tikov. He was beginning to have doubts.

CHAPTER ELEVEN

Pike reached home and slept for three hours. When he awoke, light from the day he had already greeted was streaming through half-drawn curtains. He pulled the sleeve of his crumpled shirt and studied his watch - twenty-five to seven or was it eight? He got up anyway. It was time to catch Richards at home before he left for Whitehall.

"Bit early isn't it?" protested Richards down the telephone.

"How about dinner tonight. Our numismatic venue, at around 8.30?"

"OK. If you're buying." Pike's cryptic reference meant Coin Street, near Waterloo Station. It was a restaurant used by theatre-goers and concert-goers at London's South Bank, so in the early evening it was quiet. Pike chose a table upstairs next to a window overlooking one of London's bleak parking lots. While waiting for Richards he ordered a kir and studied the menu which was hand-written in French.

Richards had grown a moustache since Pike had last seen him, probably as a protest at his office-bound existence. He sat down and looked about him.

"Isn't this a bit public?"

"The waiters are all fancy boys or actors; they're not interested in our kind of conversation."

"I don't remember it being so empty."

"It'll fill up. Now what will you have?" They ordered fish mousse with raspberry vinegar, followed by guinea fowl cooked with black cherries, and a bottle of Fleurie.

"How's Emma?" asked Pike.

"Fine. How are your spy ships? I notice you haven't mentioned them in your publication recently."

"We haven't got any more information. I don't suppose you have either."

"No. They seem to have gone to earth, if that's the right expression. Anyway you haven't got me here to talk about schoolboy fantasies."

"No, but there may be a connection. You remember that lad who took the photographs? Eight months ago he was approached by a Hungarian student and warned about something. Minutes later the Hungarian was kidnapped almost before his eyes. Then his flat was broken into—"

"I know about that."

"—the same day. And that night he and his girlfriend were chased all the way to Oxford by the very car used in the kidnapping. He took the number."

"Very rum."

"Luckily for us, and him, the car was flagged down by the police before any real damage was done. And lo and behold who steps out of the car but three Bulgarian diplomats."

"Moscow's rude mechanicals."

"But wait. Three, no four days ago, a crane operator at Wandsworth municipal rubbish dump had the fright of his life when he saw a body in the jaws of his mechanical grab. It had been stitched into the upholstery of an old settee, but obviously not very well. It turned out to be the unfortunate young Hungarian."

"So you think the Bulgarians killed him."

"It's obvious, isn't it?"

"Wouldn't stand up in court."

"It doesn't have to, Ian. Don't you think our friends the funnies would rather resent having this sort of thing going on under their very noses, on English soil?"

"Ah, but do they know it's going on?"

"They bloody well ought to."

"And if they don't, your friends the Hungarian exiles will wise them up, is that what you're telling me?"

"That's what they intend to do, but I think they're reading it all wrong."

"Let them. If they're lucky they'll get three or four Bulgarians expelled. A small victory for the spirit of '56." For a moment Pike attacked his guinea fowl, wrenched off a leg and sucked it clean.

"My feeling is this is a bit more serious than Comecon fun and games," he said. "There's been a six-month lull. I think it would be a mistake to stir things up again now when we should be trying to find out what these people are up to."

"We should? That's not like you, Bill. I thought you had a policy of strict neutrality."

"I do, I do. But I like to know what's going on. Until I do, I don't like to see things stirred up by too much impetuous action."

"So you want to enlist my support, or rather my department's support, to rein in the FCO. Anything we say to those prima donnas over there is likely to be counter-productive."

I was thinking of something subtle," said Pike, filling both their glasses. "Not a bad little Fleurie, don't you think?" He took a draught and continued. "Your military attaché in Moscow, Walker I think."

"What about him?"

Pike grinned. "Shall we order another bottle?"

"Not for me."

"Anything as dramatic as the expulsion of three Warsaw Pact diplomats is likely to be met with some form of retaliation, isn't it? If you could persuade your friends that Walker is onto something big in Moscow, but that any ripples caused in the diplomatic pond…"

"Would make his future a little dicey?"

"I think you catch my drift."

"But he isn't onto something big. Slade-Walker is a first-class idiot. He was posted to Moscow because they couldn't stand him in the office."

"Tell them he's close to finding out who's behind the spy ship project, and what it all means."

"But he's nowhere near that level of sophistication."

"The most unlikely people can find themselves approached by the other side, by disgruntled dissidents or conscientious objectors."

"You know who's behind the project, don't you?"

"My Hungarian friends think they do."

"And you might tell us, if we go soft on the Bulgarians. Sometimes I suspect your motives, Bill. I think you might be working for the other side."

"Waiter, another bottle of this excellent Fleurie." Pike was smiling, out of pain, because he knew that his motives would always be suspect. Unlike Ian he was never identified with a particular side, he wore no uniform apart from his shabby suit. He was British, culturally and emotionally. Despite his better judgment his heart had stirred a little at news of British victories in the Falklands War and the success of the Harrier jump jet. Perhaps, if pressed, he would come out in favour of a Western style of democracy. But for him the real world was divided into economic, political and military power groups within and between which various degrees of injustice and cruelty prevailed. The fact that at home in his Hampshire village he could enjoy almost total physical security and freedom of thought was an accident of history from which he wouldn't generalize - there was no other place on earth where that was so; the chances of it occurring elsewhere were as remote as those of finding intelligent life on another planet. Pike smiled.

"I'm on the side of common sense," he said. "And I don't want this planet blown up before I've lived out my three-score years and ten."

"And do you seriously think that anything you or I can do will affect the outcome by one atom?"

"I'm surprised you don't."

"I suppose I believe in doing my bit, otherwise I wouldn't be in the army. But that's the official view. My decision to join I put down largely to social and economic pressures."

"I'm in the communications and common-sense business. My view is that it's better to interfere a bit and fail than not to interfere at all. Otherwise I'd probably still be at Cambridge teaching law."

"One thing has always puzzled me," said Richards. "Why are you, such a sensitive and apparently gentle person, so deeply involved with weapons and instruments of death?" Pike smiled his tortured smile again.

"Family business." He paid the bill with cash and they walked out into the sultry South Bank air. Richards was heading for Waterloo Station and Pike for Charing Cross. They stood at the foot of Hungerford Bridge for a few last words.

"By the way," said Richards, "I was remembering your interest in Soviet cosmonauts. One was spotted in Zurich the other day, drunk in charge of a cabin cruiser. His name is Demirkan."

"An Uzbek. One of the class of '75." While Pike was still reflecting on this, Richards had vanished. Pike climbed the steps to the bridge slowly and walked even more ponderously on the wooden boards spanning the Thames.

They made a reassuring sound as he tried to work out the full implication of that news. Did that mean they had a Nautilus in Zurich? What the hell for - to spy on the ferry boats? To neutralize the world-famous Swiss navy? It didn't make sense, except that Switzerland, like Sweden, was a neutral country. The NATO powers didn't have listening posts there which meant that it could be a kind of lab experiment. But how the hell did they get the Nautilus in there? Then he remembered the incident, reported in the press, of the Soviet embassy's container refused entry as part of the diplomatic bag. They must have found some other way. Pike found himself under the arches of the bridge walking past a summer collection of tramps with their bundles of plastic bags and bottles of vermouth, their seasonal tipple. He bought a ticket for the underground and boarded a Circle Line train. As the harshly lit carriage rattled to Sloane Square his fantasy was forming a plan of action. He would go to Zurich and investigate. His heartbeat raced with the daring of it all. He would need an accomplice. Not Richards, he was too conspicuous, but what about that young Englishman, Dimock? Was he as hostile as he seemed?

Dimock walked across the courtyard of the Foreign and Commonwealth Office with a card marked "visitor" clipped to his lapel. He and his escort took a creaking lift to the third floor and he followed the old man dressed like a zoo keeper to an unmarked door. There was Fortescue with three other men and one woman standing in the room. One man was behind a desk.

"Ah, Dr Torrence," he said, "my name's Brand. We haven't met before and we're unlikely to again. I think it's better if my colleagues remain anonymous, don't you? We'd like to ask you some questions, just a formality you understand. Do sit down." Dimock sat down and so did Brand. The others remained standing because there was only one free chair. "Parsons, where's the file?" asked Brand, and was handed it instantly. So much for anonymity, thought Dimock. "Now according to one of our highly confidential sources…"

"You mean the Hungarian," said Dimock. Brand glared at him.

"According to one of our sources you witnessed the kidnapping of Mr Matyas Nagy. Why didn't you report it at the time?"

"I was scared. He'd just warned me that I was on their list."

"Whose list?"

"The Russians or the Bulgarians - what's the difference?"

"You must try to be precise."

"I think he said the Russians."

"So what did you do about this kidnapping?"

"I phoned Laszlo, the Hungarian. He said do nothing. Later my flat was broken into."

"Yes, yes, wc know all about that."

"When the police came I asked them to check out the car used in the kidnapping. They only said it hadn't been stolen."

"Let's move on to the incident in Oxford," said Brand. "According to our report you led this car in a wild chase from Headington to the Banbury Road. What did you think they were going to do to you?"

"I didn't want to find out." There were sniggers from Dimock's audience.

"Had they threatened you in any way?"

"For Christ's sake. I'd seen them kidnap someone in front of my very eyes. Then they broke into my flat and stole my Swedish notes. They had murdered my friend in Sweden."

"Now keep calm, Dr Torrence. You're confusing Russians and Bulgarians. Would you say the Bulgarians had menaced you in any way?"

"They followed me in a menacing way, certainly."

"With weapons?"

"They put a bug on my car. I found it the next day.

"What we are trying to establish, Dr Torrence, is whether these Bulgarians were in some way threatening the security of the nation. You are well aware I think that they cannot be prosecuted in a court of law for either civil or criminal offences."

"They were certainly threatening the security of two of this country's citizens."

"Of course, the rights of the individual are highly important in this country but that's not quite the same thing. Naturally now we know about this the strongest protest will be made to the Bulgarian ambassador. But we're trying to decide what retaliatory action if any should be taken against the Bulgarian mission. It's rather like a game of chess," said Brand and he broke into a smile for the first time.

"I'd rather you didn't use me as a pawn."

"Thank you; we won't be bothering you again. Show Dr Torrence out would you, Fortescue?" Fortescue led Dimock down three flights of stairs. As they crossed the courtyard he said,

"I remember going down to see your friend's father, Major Stallybrass. Rather bitter he was."

"I don't suppose you were very tactful."

"I was doing my job."

"Not much of a job, telling people to shut up when their sons have been murdered."

"I'm sorry you see it that way. We rely on support from people like you, loyal British subjects."

"Goodbye, Fortescue," said Dimock, thinking 'It's people like you who make me long to be Peruvian, or Bulgarian.' But he kept his thoughts to himself.

From Whitehall he knew he could walk four miles over parkland to Notting Hill Gate and home. It would take him about an hour. Under the midday sun he slung his jacket over one shoulder and walked over the undulating grass avoiding the dog turds. A tramp slept peacefully on a grassy bank. A girl lay bare-breasted beneath a huge beech tree. Dimock walked on deep in thought, depressed by his inability to affect the world around him or to say what he felt. 'Why didn't I tell them to get stuffed? Bloody mandarins playing their phoney games of chess! People are dying and the world's destroying itself while they play games. History doesn't change anything.' He strode on under Waterloo Place and through subways into Hyde Park. He began to think of Anna. She was about their level, part of the Establishment. That would never change, however good she was in bed. By the time Dimock got home it would be fair to say he was in a state of depression. He threw himself into an armchair and gazed at the pattern of his Turkish carpet. The telephone rang. He answered.

"This is Pike, William Pike," a voice said breathlessly. "We met at Laszlo's two nights ago. I've been trying to get hold of you all day."

"I wish you people would leave me alone." Pike wasn't a salesman, but he needed help.

"There's something I feel you should know."

"About what?"

"About this whole affair. But I can't tell you over the telephone."

"I don't want to know any more."

"I can't tell you how important this is. Bear with me this once, then I promise you I'll never trouble you again."

"Just like the foreign office."

"I am not the foreign office," said Pike emphatically. "Look, there's a phone box at the end of your street. Be there in three minutes and we'll arrange a place to meet. Don't worry, I've got the number." Canny bastard, thought Dimock. Curiosity got the better of him. He hung up, pocketed his key and slipped out of the flat. It was about one o'clock; there were few people about and he didn't think they would be watching him any more. At the street corner the telephone was occupied by a fat West Indian lady. Immediately she had finished and pushed open the kiosk door, the telephone rang. Dimock forced his way past her: "It's for me," he said.

"Christ, I thought something had happened to you," said Pike.

"You're jumpy."

"Can you come to my flat in Chelsea, 39A Redburn Street, at about six thirty? We can grab a bite to eat later, if you like."

"OK." Dimock hung up. More than ever he felt like a pawn in an elaborate chess game, with the difference that here various grand masters took it in turn to make the moves. And the sides weren't obviously black and white, more a murky grey.

Like many before him he was repelled by Pike's flat, a dark basement in an otherwise well-tended street. But there was a small conservatory at the back.

"Ah. Helleborus petiolaris," he exclaimed, looking at a small plant struggling out of a pot onto two cane sticks. "It looks pretty sick. Very difficult to grow in this country."

"My sister gave it to me. She's got an elaborate greenhouse in Essex. I don't think it gets enough sun here."

"You'd think botanists had green fingers, but I don't. Plants only have to look at me and they start dying."

Pike offered Dimock a drink - white wine rather than the usual sherry. "It's a Mersault," said Pike, "one of the few pleasures I allow myself."

Dimock gulped the tangy liquid down. "I'm getting confused," he said. "Whose side are you on?" Pike told him about his publishing business and his specialist knowledge of informal weaponry.

"I don't comment, I don't moralize, I don't take sides. I simply report what I think to be the facts as they become available to me."

"That sounds a bit feeble. You can't be neutral about napalm or nerve gas."

"Don't get me wrong," said Pike anxiously. "It doesn't mean I don't abhor instruments of death and destruction in every form. I do. But by an accident of birth to start with - my publication's a family business - and now in the light of experience I feel it's important to know about these things. The more we know about them, the less likely they are to be used."

"So you have contacts with people like Laszlo."

"I have contacts with everyone."

"It must be quite dangerous."

"Very rarely. Once I get hold of information it's usually available to the public. What I do is piece it together in digestible form. That's what people pay for. It's erroneously called intelligence." Pike got up and disappeared into the adjoining room. He returned, carrying an envelope. "These are a couple of your photographs. Have you seen them?"

"No. How the hell did you get hold of them?" Pike smiled.

"It was very cool-headed of you, to snap away even though your friend had just been shot."

"I was scared as hell. My hands were shaking."

"Nevertheless the shots aren't bad. Look at this one for instance. I was able to recognize the gentleman's face."

"Who is he?"

"A Soviet cosmonaut. Now that struck me as pretty significant. Until then I thought Nautilus was just any old experimental project. But this Tikov, he's a big fish. Since last July I've been thinking very hard, wondering what the devil they can be up to. There's one thing I now know, which nobody else will think of any significance at all." Dimock was interested, in spite of his determination to be disgusted by this grim side of the world. "Some months ago another cosmonaut was spotted in Zurich. He was arrested last March by the Swiss police for being drunk in charge of a cabin cruiser on Lake Zurich. It was a filthy stormy night too. He flashed a Soviet diplomatic passport and was released immediately but the oddness of it all must eventually have penetrated even the thick hide of British intelligence in Berne. I heard about it a few days ago."

"You think he's something to do with the Nautilus project?"

"I intend to find out."

"How?"

"By going to Zurich."

"Why do you think this is so important?"

"It scares the hell out of me. Shall I tell you why? Because of the potential. I was quite amused by the stories of Soviet miniature submarines playing hide and seek with the Swedish navy until I realized what a deadly weapon a miniature submarine could be if it were virtually undetectable. Almost every major city in the world is accessible by water. Something underwater is invisible and undetectable as long as it makes no sound, sends no signals, and doesn't present too solid a mass of metal." Outside in the garden the shade was deepening while the sun caught the chimneypots against a saffron sky. "Have some more vino," said Pike, and continued.

"Now. For several years I have seen signs that the Soviets are dropping hopelessly behind in the arms race on all levels, nuclear, conventional land forces, navy, air force, missile systems. They don't have the constant flow of entrepreneurial innovation that the Americans get from their private sector, they're losing whatever grip they ever had on their Warsaw Pact allies and, worst of all, because of the failure of their monolithic economic system they can't afford massive defence expenditure. So what are they doing? They're bluffing. Matching dummy missile systems to everything the Americans deploy, stalling at the SALT talks and the Geneva disarmament conference. For internal and external consumption they don't dare to do anything else." Pike took a large gulp of his wine.

"So what do they do?" He laughed. "Sometimes I feel it's so crazy it's more like science fiction. But I suppose that's in keeping with the Star Wars programme and all that weaponry still on the drawing board, lasers, rail guns and the like. At least the Nautilus exists, or we assume it does." Pike studied Dimock in the half-light as if sizing him up for the next assault on his credulity.

"Given this scenario, and the strategic disadvantage not to say desperation of the Soviets, is it surprising that they would look for a cheap alternative - something like Dr Strangelove's doomsday machine?"

"You mean the Nautilus?" asked Dimock.

"The first nuclear bombs dropped on Hiroshima and Nagasaki were huge affairs, nearly the size of a car. Nowadays they've slimmed down a lot. A 20 kilotonne device, that's as powerful as the two dropped in Japan combined, along with the trigger and arming mechanism, could now fit comfortably into a large suitcase. Of course you'd need about ten people to lift it, so you couldn't carry one through the green channel at Heathrow. But you can stuff it in the nose cone of a missile, or build it into a rather slower but more stealthy form of transport - the Nautilus submarine." Dimock laughed.

"I'm not a military strategist," he said, "but the Nautilus would seem to have rather limited battlefield capability in the event of a nuclear holocaust."

"You're right," said Pike. "It's a no-hope device. One you wouldn't use unless all other avenues had failed. But that's its subtlety. It would be there. While all Reagan's missiles are pointed at Soviet cities and dummy Soviet missile bases, and all his lasers are searching the skies, the Nautilus will be there, in place, ready to cut swathes through the office blocks and shopping centres of the world's major cities. And just to make the point the bombs wouldn't be your nice clean neutron variety but a thoroughly dirty breed pushing out acres of iodine 131 and strontium 90."

"How can you be so sure about this? You're making it all up…"

"Man's real genius, I have come to the conclusion, lies in inventing machines for his own destruction. In every age brilliant men with trivial minds have busied themselves with the very short-term goal of refining ways to kill their own species, with the minimum of danger to themselves. Only a small percentage of these schemes leave the drawing board, of those most become obsolete before they're used, and a very, very few are ever used in the theatre of war. Ideas are quickly born, tested and rejected. I've seen the Nautilus project, or something very like it, propounded in a paper by a Yugoslav military strategist in 1973. Of course this young warmonger was thinking in terms of the Yugoslav navy and Slavic or Serbian world domination. He was laughed off the rostrum. But a year later he was whisked off to Moscow on a research fellowship. All copies of his paper were collected up, except one which fell into my hands ten years later along with piles of other Serbo-Croat rubbish…" Pike's monologue tailed off. He looked embarrassed as if he'd committed a social indiscretion. "It's not conclusive. Of course it isn't. I must sound like one of those weirdoes who tell you that Stonehenge was built as a launch-pad for flying saucers."

"I don't mind hearing you out," said Dimock. He was warming to this diffident, pathetic man who nevertheless might have his finger on something literally earth-shattering. "I haven't got much on this evening."

"What about your girlfriend? I should have asked her too."

"No, no. That's all over."

"I'm sorry. She looked nice. Well," continued Pike, "having read Jankovich's paper, he's the Yugoslav, I couldn't help asking myself more questions. Could you build a nuclear bomb that small? Wouldn't its effect just be cushioned by the water? Who would arm it and detonate it? Would it be a suicide pilot inside the machine or could you do it by remote control? Who could possibly be trusted to keep the devices operational around the world, deep in enemy territory? Then, on the other hand, wouldn't it be easy to detect such a thing - with underwater listening devices, submarine nets, metal detectors and geiger counters. Well I've gone into all that and the answer, as far as I can see, is that there is no watertight system in any seaboard city in the world that would guard against such a super stealthy device."

"You mean there might be one in London at the moment?"

"At this very moment."

"I find that incredible. I mean it's theoretically possible, I grant you, if the technology is there. But I can't believe any nation would base its defences on a product like that. It's so Heath Robinson." Pike guffawed with glee.

"Quite right," he said, "but remember the first lunar module covered with crinkly silver paper, or the first lunar buggy with its little sun umbrella - did you ever see anything more Heath Robinson than NASA's moon-shot programme? That was the cutting edge of technology."

"I'm not thinking of the technology but of the operators, the human factor."

"Precisely," said Pike. "That's the weak link. But, if my theory's correct, they've tried to solve that in the most romantic way. If you wanted an operator who was loyal, technically highly trained, cool-headed, physically fit, with a proven track record, where would you look?"

"I know you want me to say space crew."

"When I saw that face of Brigadier Tikov I thought my mind was playing tricks. You see I was looking out for something like that. It was too good to be true - perhaps I was just imagining his features in that blurred image. Perhaps that's all it is. But Demirkan in Zurich. No one could have dreamt up that crazy episode. Look, look at this." Pike sprang up and dived again into the gloom of the house where Dimock could hear him rummaging among files. He emerged, clutching an old newspaper cutting. There was a rank of yellowing, half-smiling faces across the page. "The school of 1975. Soviet cosmonauts involved in the Salyut programme - Tikov, Lebedyev, Demirkan, Volkov, etcetera."

"If your theory's correct," said Dimock, "all you would have to do is seek out these characters in the various cities of the world where they've deployed Nautilus, put a tail on each one of them and eventually they should lead you to the weapon."

"Not bad but a) once in place they may not have to go near their weapon for months and b) you'd need a whole army of secret agents."

"If you told MI5 or the CIA they'd do that for you."

"They wouldn't buy it."

"How do you know?"

"I have my contacts. I know their mentality. They've already written me off as an eccentric old loon. Sometimes I think I am."

"So you're going to Zurich to prove it all yourself."

"Has it occurred to you why I'm telling you this?" Dimock saw Pike's anxious, baggy eyes quizzing him for any sign of pity or sympathy.

"No," he said. The thought came to him again as it did when he first stepped into the house. Was this man a homosexual? Was he going to make a pass?

"I think I'll need help in Zurich," said Pike. "Tracking down Demirkan. Maybe driving a cabin cruiser. Frankly, I need someone younger and stronger than me." Dimock laughed. "You wouldn't have to worry about money. I can pay your expenses and maybe something on top. I don't think it would take long, but it's a terribly important step. If it fails then my whole Nautilus theory falls to the ground. If it doesn't then the thing will be out of our hands."

"I'm not sure I'm the right guy," said Dimock, "and I've got commitments here."

"Nothing's impossible," said Pike and he got up briskly. "We need some supper." He guided Dimock through the gloomy basement and up the stairs into the street. "There's a great restaurant in Milner Street, run by some friends of mine. Real old English grub."

Dimock woke at 7.30. The sunlight was streaming through his bedroom window. His head felt a little heavy, but he remembered the wine had been good. That made him feel better. He savoured his mild hangover, something he'd seldom experienced since his student days. "Pike, bon viveur and madman," he said to himself.

Dimock went to the bathroom, elbowed himself into a shirt and jeans, shuffled on some beach shoes and left the flat. Automatically he looked around for pursuers - there were none. The sun was already melting away the haze. It was one of those fresh English mornings with a promise of great heat - a day to be walking on Scafell Pike, he thought, with two oranges and a litre of water.

Ten minutes later, dry-mouthed, with his head throbbing, he was at his favourite breakfast place. The newspaper rustled and flashed in the sun, the glass of orange juice was beaded with condensation, his coffee steamed from an octagonal cup. This could be the south of France, he thought. Or Switzerland.

Suddenly, he had an urge to travel, not necessarily a desire to be in another place, but to be in transit, sipping coffee anonymously at a roadside café, watching an old woman take in washing, someone he would never see or hear of again. It was a longing which almost hurt, like the couple of months he'd been in love with Anna. He needed a break. His heart pounded as he finished his coffee and paid the bill. Dimock hurried to the nearby tube station. In a telephone kiosk reeking of urine he called Pike.

"I'm coming," he said.

"Blast. I've just got myself a train ticket. You couldn't nip down to Victoria and buy another, could you?"

"I thought we'd be flying."

"It's more anonymous this way. The boat train to Basel leaves at 11.00 tonight. See you there."

CHAPTER TWELVE

New York

She wasn't a classic Chinese beauty like some of the hostesses on Cathay Pacific. She had fuller lips and coarser, wavy hair. Her figure too wasn't languid but taut and solid. In fact, she was Mongolian. Tikov had chosen her for the New York assignment, he told Mikhailov, because of her qualities as a cosmonaut, her fierce dedication to the Soviet cause, and her cool command of American English. He also chose her on a personal whim. He was conducting his own private war with Comrade Irena Angur.

Irena had arrived in New York, posing as the secretary of a Hong Kong businessman, Mike Chew. She took an apartment on the upper west side of Manhattan near the Dakota Building where John Lennon had been murdered. A kilometre away, on the shore of the Hudson River was the 79th Street yacht marina, a ramshackle network of jetties packed with yachts and cabin cruisers, some smart and expensive, others warped and blistered, incapable of rising from their couch of mud. The waiting list for a berth was two and a half years. But it was possible to acquire a berth by buying the boat that lay in it. Irena paid a visit. There were three boats for sale. She chose the one berthed farthest out into the Hudson River. It was a cabin cruiser, old and untidy. But it had power and a telephone link, although the lines were apt to go down in bad weather, the broker told her.

Irena paid cash - $55,000. The bilges were full of water. At flood tide the stern heaved itself off the mud while the bows dug themselves in deeper. But the Mary Jane was perfect. Irena installed a battery charger. She stocked the cruiser with drink, cleaned the kitchen and made the cabin as comfortable as a Mongolian yurt.

One night, Tikov arrived. Not in a conventional way but from the bed of the Hudson River, where he had anchored Nautilus 4. He swung himself dripping onto the deck of the Mary Jane. Irena was waiting. Tikov peeled off his wetsuit and entered the cabin. She had some towels and a suit of clothes.

"Very cosy," said Tikov. "Just like a space capsule. All we need are Demirkan's farts and his foul humour." Irena's face didn't flicker.

"I'll go outside and let you change," she said.

"I've had a murderous trip," said Tikov. In the lamplight he looked haggard and grey. "You can't stretch your legs in those things; you can't even turn your head."

"That sounds very tough."

"It's alright for you…but a great hulk like me? I'll get even with Mikhailov."

"And how will you do that, Comrade Brigadier?" Tikov screwed up his face in thought.

"Maybe by stringing him up by the balls." Irena went to the small galley and brought out a plate of cooked meat and some dark rye bread.

She set it before Tikov then opened a cabinet above his head. She put a bottle of Stolichnaya vodka and a glass in front of him. Tikov's eyes followed her, taking in her grace and economy of movement. She was wearing all black, as she always did. "She wouldn't disgrace the Bolshoi," Tikov thought. "This is magnificent," he said aloud, "but what I'd really like is some Jack Daniels whiskey." She took the vodka bottle, opened the cabinet again and drew out a square bottle of Jack Daniels. Tikov poured himself a slug and drank it in two gulps then refilled his glass. "That's better. When in Rome..." and he tore off a handful of bread and fell on the plate of meat. Fifteen minutes later he picked up his half-filled glass, reclined on the cushions behind him and belched.

Irena went onto the deck. The hum of Manhattan drifted across Riverside Park. An orange glow hung over the dark shapes of the trees, which hid the high buildings of mid-town. Two miles across the river, the lights of New Jersey winked and stared. Only a few of the boats were lived in this late in the summer. Only a few windows glowed faintly, two hours after midnight. Irena inhaled the night air. She heard a step beside her and the voice of Tikov, speaking in English now.

"You know, I've been six weeks at sea. A man gets damn lonely at sea. I've hardly seen my wife for seven months." Irena stiffened. Tikov went on: "I always thought you and I had something in common. As if, all those months at the centre, and all those weeks above the earth, we shared a secret. We had a private plan, which of course we couldn't put into action."

"Funny. I didn't feel like that."

"It was too public. We had a job to do. But here, on board our little yacht, what is there to stop us finally coming to grips with our little secret?"

"Mr Harrison," said Irena, "I don't think we're on the same wavelength." Tikov laughed.

"We are," he said softly, "but you don't realize it. You won't admit it to yourself." He put his hand on her shoulder. Irena was ready for him. With the deftness of one well drilled in the martial arts she snatched the errant hand downwards and pitched Tikov over the side. To his credit he went in without a murmur. He climbed out dripping, as he had done once before that night and dried himself below, in silence. Irena glared at him and pointed to a small bunk no bigger than a sail locker, in the bows. "Pax," said Tikov, waving a placatory hand, and he climbed into the bunk. He slept for 16 hours.

When he awoke it was already evening. Barges puttered down the Hudson River. He felt stiff but refreshed. Tikov stretched and looked in the refrigerator for some food. He took a carton of orange juice and drank a mouthful. There was some bacon and the cold meat and some tomatoes. His appetite was bigger than that. "Irena!" he shouted. She wasn't there. So he made himself some coffee, shaved at the cramped wash-basin, then he poured himself another Jack Daniels and sat on the deck. A little girl was running down the jetty, chasing a cat. When she saw Tikov, she stopped.

"Who're you? I haven't seen you before."

"I'm staying with Irena, you know, the beautiful lady."

"She's not beautiful; she's Chinese, isn't she?" The cat had come back and caressed her legs. She picked it up. "My mother's beautiful. We live on that boat out there." She pointed to a yacht anchored a hundred yards from the marina. I'm Nancy. This is Sugar." She stroked the cat. "Are you married to her?" she asked.

"In a manner of speaking."

"She's very quiet." Tikov laughed. Irena was walking down the jetty. When she was in earshot Tikov said:

"She keeps herself to herself." Irena was carrying some large packages. She went below without a word.

"Is she mad at you?" asked Nancy.

"No, she's in love with me." Nancy shrugged.

"I have to go," she said and she ran back down the jetty. Later, Tikov saw Nancy and her cat being rowed to the anchored yacht. As dusk fell and a flat calm lay on the Hudson River, Tikov went below.

"I could eat a horse," he said.

"We have work to do, Comrade Tikov," said Irena. She was crouched over a voltage rectifier. Tikov had a strong urge to squeeze her buttocks. "I'll get into my suit," he said. Tikov took his wet suit from a locker. With it were a face mask and a small aqualung. Irena had also bought a diver's torch. Thus equipped, Tikov slipped over the side and tugged himself down the anchor chain to the river bed. The Nautilus was only 15 metres away, hull down, compact on the muddy bottom. Tikov swam round with the torch making sure the craft was firmly rooted to the seabed. He opened the airlock hatch and unclipped a length of cable. This was Nautilus's lifeline. He attached it to terminals on the hull then payed it out as he swam back to the Mary Jane. He climbed aboard then fed the cable through the port for the anchor chain. By the time he had gone below and peeled off his wet suit Irena had already connected the cable. "The telephone is linked up and Nautilus's batteries are on charge," she said.

"Good, we must celebrate," said Tikov. "Did you get me some smart clothes?" Irena pointed to a locker behind the bench. Tikov drew out a button-down shirt, cotton trousers, leather shoes and a silk jacket. He whistled. "You have taste, Irena Elenovna Angur." He put them on, and the silk tie he found in the pocket. He strutted up and down the cabin. "Tell me I look a million dollars," he said. Irena didn't look up.

"Two hundred and fifty-five, to be precise," she said. "The receipts are in the inside pocket." Tikov drained his glass of whiskey.

"Come on," he said. "I'm starving."

"Give me a few minutes," she said, nodding at the hatchway. Tikov took the hint and went on deck. He strutted about, conscious of the sound of his new shoes on the planking. He stared into the black water at the stern following the line of the newly-laid cable, imagining the Nautilus down there snug on the mud, a squat machine capable of ripping apart a quarter of Manhattan Island.

Irena came out of the darkened cabin. He couldn't see much but noticed she'd put on a long jacket and tied it with a belt. She also carried a hint of expensive perfume. They walked in silence up the jetty, crossed Riverside Park, and hailed a cab. Within minutes they were in the thick of midtown Manhattan. As the cab swung down Park Avenue Tikov felt some reverence for the nation that had thrown up such buildings, crazy totems reaching for the sky from Manhattan bedrock. The broad avenues, the broad cars, the garish yellow cabs, the potholes, and the people waiting at crossroads, his enemies, relaxed, at home, in this vertical jungle. He imagined part of it flattened by one small thermo-nuclear blast. The screams, the sirens, the silence. Tikov closed his eyes. He was paid not to think that way.

"Here we are," he said, and flung open the door. They were on East 49th Street. Tikov was hungry and he meant to slake his hunger in an American way. They walked upstairs to the bar, passing a fair imitation of Goya's Maya, the nude version. Tikov ordered two glasses of the house red, which was French Merlot, full and fruity. Then they moved to a table and ordered prawns and sirloin steak for two. No Russian would have seen so much meat in two months. They drank some more wine and finished the meal with blueberries soft, sweet-sour and mouth-staining. Irena laughed briefly as she found it difficult to rise from the table. They staggered into the heavy night air and caught a cab.

"West 79th," said Tikov, but Irena corrected him.

"West 74th." Irena stopped the cab outside a brownstone house. Tikov paid the driver and followed Irena into the house and up to the first floor. She led the way to a three-room apartment, well-furnished with modern-paintings on the walls. This was the official New York residence of Mr Michael Chew.

Irena walked through to the bedroom. Tikov hovered, then looked for the drinks cabinet. He found it behind a dummy bookshelf and poured himself a malt whisky. Then he noticed Irena in the bedroom doorway. "Well, Comrade Brigadier," she said, "are you going to finish the evening properly?" She lay down on the bed. Tikov followed. He felt gauche, almost superfluous, but this was an opportunity not to be missed. He took off his jacket and stood over her, uncertain where to begin. This was the culmination of a long campaign which had begun with the tantalizing brush of space suit against space suit 90 kilometres above the earth. "I'm getting impatient, Boris Alexeivich," said Irena, untying her loose jacket and shrugging out her bare shoulders. The brutal vaccination marks on her left arm were part of her attraction. Tikov knew her armpits would harbour the rankness of a wild animal. He had caught a whiff of them before in the space capsule, a savage smell which filled his stomach with desire. It had been a long wait. Now he was so free to gaze at her face, it seemed pitted and discoloured, even ugly, but he knew he wanted her. He put his hand to her warm neck and ran it over her body, as if checking her contours. His hand slid along the flat of her stomach under the black trousers and found her pubic hair. She bit and scratched him like a tiger but held his hand there, forcing his fingers hard into the wet opening. He tore at her clothes with his free hand, trying to expose more flesh, her back, her breasts, small and firm. He grabbed her hair and forced her to lie back on the bed, holding her there with a fierce kiss on the lips. She relaxed for a moment and he slid both hands behind her shoulders, but with a twist of her thighs she kicked him across the room. Irena glared at him and tore off the remains of her clothes. He got up and did the same. They were eyeing each other like boxers between rounds.

Freed from his clothes Tikov moved into her territory again, warily, touching her upper body with his fingertips. She threw him onto the bed and bestrode him, her powerful thighs around his waist. She pulled his head and rammed it between her legs, forcing him to taste her juices. Her rings and her sharp fingernails scored his back, drawing blood. Tikov twisted sideways and pinned her down, fighting to force his body on top of hers. Irena locked her legs around his thighs and he felt the hot mat of her pubic hair close to him. As he forced himself closer they slid to the floor. On the hard, rush matting beside the bed he entered her. For a moment they were calm, like a ship entering port after a storm, but then the tempest surged again. Irena fought him fiercely, resisting the thrust of the enemy inside her, twisting, pulling, strangling with powerful sinews, until the duel ended in sudden death.

Tikov had tamed the beast, he thought. But she used him mercilessly that night, and demanded him again and again until, as dawn peered through the window, she turned her back on him and slept. Like a discarded garment, he slid to the floor, lay there for an hour then dressed, longing for his bunk on the Mary Jane and some real sleep.

Tikov had allowed a week to make Nautilus operational in New York. It had taken two days. He longed to recapture the atmosphere of his first days in America ten years before: the ticker-tape parade, the visit to the White House, the crowds, the big bands. He thought more and more of his friend Tom - Tom Stafford, the Apollo astronaut with whom in the course of a few days he had struck up a blood friendship. Tom lived in Houston. They'd even corresponded a little and vowed to see each other again when detente had gone far enough to allow it. Well, since Afghanistan, detente had frozen over, but here he was, incognito, with time on his hands. He could visit Tom, pop up from nowhere, shake him by the hand and vanish again without a trace. As Irena sat on top of him in the cramped cabin on the Mary Jane, coaxing out more than he had ever given, he still thought about that visit to Tom.

On day three he boarded a Greyhound bus for Houston. He called Stafford's number and heard his voice answer. That was enough for him. The journey took nearly two days. At Houston he hired a car in the name of Cardew and drove out to the Stafford ranch. Stafford had retired early but still worked as consultant on the NASA programme.

He might be at work. Tikov parked the car in the driveway. He stepped over a fence into a field containing a pair of horses. From 200 metres he saw Mary Stafford at the kitchen window. Tom appeared in the kitchen then reappeared on the terrace carrying a tray. Tikov worked his way along the fence then followed a hedge up to the garden, close to the edge of the terrace. By this time Tom had disappeared inside the house again. He was laying lunch for two. Tikov sprang into a hanging seat at the edge of the terrace and swung himself nonchalantly to and fro.

Tom came out again.

"Well, son-of-a-bitch, it's Boris!" he exclaimed, still holding the tray. "Have you defected?"

"This is a private visit. I was in the States on business so I just had to come and see my old co-pilot." Tom put down the tray.

"Hey, Mary, it's our old friend the Amerussian. D'you remember him? Let's do this the Russian way." And the two friends embraced. "Son-of-a-bitch," said Tom. Mary came out and embraced Tikov too. They sat and enjoyed the Texan sunshine and drank Californian wine. They played old tunes on the tape deck and danced, sometimes two, sometimes all three together.

Tom and Mary's two children were away. After dinner Tom got out a bottle of Jim Beam whiskey.

"Come on, Boris," he said. "Don't give me all this crap about a business trip. A guy like you doesn't go into business, not a hero of the Soviet Union." Tikov looked down as he twirled the whiskey around the base of his glass.

"OK, Tom, I'll tell you. You've been good to me and you can keep a secret. I'm on a kind of peace mission, a mission that I hope will bring an end to the arms race as we know it and all nuclear war, even Star Wars."

"No one's fooled by Star Wars except the Pentagon press department," said Tom. "Everyone else knows it's just an excuse to spend more money and shower contracts on the private sector. Jobs for the boys, good Republican politics."

"I thought the bidding was international. Who knows they might even give some of the work to firms in Poland or Hungary."

"That would be the ultimate absurdity. Don't tell me you're here touting for business."

"No, I'm not," said Tikov firmly. "Tom, you know we love each other like brothers." The Russian was becoming Russian, Tom thought. Tikov continued: "We love our own countries. Well, I want to tell you that there may come a time when one of us thinks what is going on in his country is not quite right. I'm not talking about human rights, that's something else. If such a time should come we should be ready to trust each other absolutely and respond to a cry for help. If for instance your telephone should ring in the middle of the night and a voice should say 'It's me - Boris' you should be prepared to do everything that voice says. I'm not talking about spying, passing petty information, NATO secrets, anything like that. I'm talking about an emergency which would involve us equally because it would affect the future of the entire human race." Tom was silent. Boris went on.

"You know, Tom. This is difficult for me to say. I'm a loyal Russian and tomorrow I will go back. But sometimes there are people in charge of this thing who aren't the right people." At that moment Tikov felt Mikhailov's warm hand on his knee. "They may do something quite mad."

"Hey, snap out of it, Boris," said Tom jovially. "You're a real party pooper, did you know that? But I'll tell you something, we've got our crazy guys too, quite bananas. They make Al Haig look like Saint Francis of Assisi." He filled the morose Tikov's glass. "Don't you worry, Boris, we'll keep the world on the right track, you and me."

Tikov slept in the Staffords' son's room. The boy was now at college reading pure mathematics, but around the room were all the paraphernalia of an American childhood - baseball glove, skateboard, posters of Middle Earth and Michael Jackson, a mask of Darth Vader, a desk, a blackboard and a teddy bear. Tikov imagined the kind of American he might have been himself, very like Tom, perhaps, or more like Al Haig.

In their bedroom the Staffords were arguing in low voices. "It's a question of national security," said Mary. "We should at least call security at NASA."

"But he's a good friend, Mary. He trusts us, otherwise he wouldn't have come. He's a good human being. Fuck security."

"Think of your reputation, think of your own security clearance if this ever gets out."

"To hell with that. If one decent human being can't have faith in another..."

"Then think of your family." Mary began to weep. Tom knew it was just a device. He turned over on his side.

"Let's sleep on it, eh pal?" he said. Mary lay awake, blinking at the ceiling. Nightmares were running through her mind. She knew the generosity of Tom, but sometimes he needed protection from it. For the sake of sanity, if someone must be cast in the role of betrayer, then it must be her, not Tom. Towards 3.30 she crept downstairs to the living room. Quietly she picked up the telephone and punched up NASA security.

"Hello, Matt, this is Mary Stafford. No everything's fine, but we have a tricky situation here. A surprise visit from one of our old friends - Boris Tikov, the Soviet cosmonaut. Remember him? No, he hasn't defected, he says he's here on business. I, Tom and I, thought we should tell you in case of any, you know, security implications. No, no he's sleeping peacefully, we gave him a lot to drink. Thank you. You know what's best."

Tikov heard the murmur of Mary's voice downstairs. A sudden nausea hit his stomach and sweat froze on his legs and brow. It was betrayal, he thought, denunciation. It happened every day at home, brother against brother, son against father. He slid out of bed and onto the landing. There was silence now downstairs but the light was on. He went down the stairs and saw Mary in the living room sitting frozen like a statue, staring ahead of her. He retreated upstairs. His heart was pounding now and inwardly he was cursing himself over and over again. He jumped into his trousers and shoes, grabbed his jacket and small travelling bag. The window was open. He looked down at the drop to the lawn, about eight feet if he hung from the window ledge. He swung down, pulled his bag through the window, hit the ground and began running. When he reached the hedge he turned round. If Mary had heard him she wasn't making a song and dance about it.

Tikov's car was still halfway down the drive. The engine purred quietly when he started it. He turned round without using the lights and coasted down to the highway.

If Mary had raised a hue and cry, they would soon have a photograph of him circulated to every police force and border post in the country. That was the penalty for being a famous cosmonaut. The public might have forgotten his face but newspapers, libraries and archives didn't. He could dash for the Mexican border, only two hours' drive away. But that was too obvious. There was a risk of playing right into their hands. His escape had to be 100% certain, or the Nautilus project could be blown apart.

In New York there was an escape route already planned for him. But that lay 2,000 kilometres across enemy territory. The solution that first occurred to him had one tragic flaw. It involved murder.

That was distasteful to Tikov who prided himself on his humanity, despite his military rank. The plan was to stop at a motel and hi-jack a truck as the driver was climbing into the cab, probably killing the driver, then drive like hell for New York. But it was risky. The driver might kill him. Tikov gunned the car along the highway as he racked his brains. New Orleans wasn't far, maybe 200 or 300 miles. He could lose himself there, but then how could he get to New York?

Tikov was back in Houston and headed out on the New Orleans road. He reckoned he had until daylight before they started checking the highways. It was just after four o'clock. Tikov nudged the speed up to 85, 90 miles an hour. That was acceptable in Texas but he wasn't sure how firmly they would enforce the 55 mile-an-hour speed limit once he crossed into Louisiana.

Matt Brinsley, head of NASA security, was laying the groundwork for a dawn raid on the Stafford ranch. He'd called the Texas state police purely as back-up, since he expected to arrest a peacefully sleeping man. Then at 4.15 he had a second phone call from Mary Stafford. She had peeped in to look at the innocent object of her betrayal, and he'd gone. "We know he's driving a white sedan," said Mary, "but we don't know the licence plate, or where he's heading. I didn't warn him, you have to believe me, I wouldn't do a thing like that." She was shaking. Tom paced up and down in his pyjamas. They were heading for the biggest storm in their 25 years of marriage.

Brinsley put down the telephone, picked it up again and dialled the police chief in Houston. "Charlie," he said, "we now have an escapee, six foot, male, Caucasian driving a white sedan licence plates unknown, could be headed anywhere. What do you suggest?"

"How important is this guy?" asked Charlie.

"Former cosmonaut, hero of the Soviet Union, but he's also a serving officer in the Soviet armed forces, therefore considered an active enemy agent. However, we want him alive."

"We can put out road blocks, but they'll take some time to organize. If he's headed for Mexico we'll probably catch him, unless he goes cross country. If he's headed for New Orleans he may get into Louisiana."

"Can we bring in Louisiana?"

"I imagine this is a federal matter. He ain't just speeding out there. I'll call Louisiana."

Charlie had forgotten one thing about Louisiana: Hurricane Elena. The storm had been threatening the Gulf coastline for days. Hundred mile-an-hour winds were expected. In some places there was forcible evacuation to avoid loss of life. Every policeman in Louisiana was on overtime, but pre-occupied with the menace to the south. Tikov, by choosing New Orleans, was unwittingly driving into the teeth of the storm.

As he crossed the state border he began to notice the stream of vehicles pouring west, heavily laden. The wind was gusting across the highway but he kept up his high speed, trusting that all the time he was ahead of his pursuers. In three more hours Tikov was at the airport. It was chaos but shuttles were flying to Memphis, St Louis, and New York. Being a single passenger with no baggage he was able to squeeze onto a flight to JFK airport, New York, as James Harrison. By the time he'd landed at New York, FBI agents had found the car in New Orleans, but it was too late. Tikov had escaped the net.

For two days he lay low in the 74th street apartment. He was afraid to go to the Mary Jane at the Marina, in case he was recognized. He watched television, but there was nothing on the news about a Soviet agent at large. Irena bought the newspapers - nothing. It appeared the FBI wanted no witch hunt. Maybe he'd imagined the whole thing. Maybe Mary had been telephoning a friend.

Tikov didn't tell Irena the truth. She would have despised him for his weakness if not denounced him secretly to Mikhailov. As far as she was concerned his absence had been part of a mission so secret that she wasn't to know about it.

A day later than scheduled Tikov took a Finnair flight to Helsinki. From there it was an easy hop home. His last act before boarding the plane to Moscow was to telephone Tom Stafford in Houston.

"Hi Tom," he said, "no hard feelings," and rang off.

VULKAN

CHAPTER THIRTEEN

Zurich, Switzerland

Pike and his friend Dimock arrived in Zurich by train at 3pm the same day. They booked into the Gasthaus Kindli, close to the centre in the old part of the city, halfway down a cobbled street leading to the Limmat River. Pike had already planned his first move. At 4.30 after a bath and a change of clothes he set off for the headquarters of the Zurich Yacht Club. He knew the name of the boat he was looking for - a cabin cruiser called the Flying Finn. If they didn't have it on their books they'd know how to track it down.

At the clubhouse in the Zurich suburb of Zollikon he ran into the very friendly Commodore Rudi Ganz. He established that the Flying Finn had been registered in March. She was a company craft used for recreation by the directors of Wozchod Trading Bank, being berthed at Wollishofen on the west side of the Lake. The named directors were Friedrich Giger, Sergei Nesterov and Korkut Demirkan.

"Thank you, Herr Commodore," said Pike.

"Are they friends of yours?"

"Not exactly, although we do share some interests. I'm a banker myself. We met last year in the Mediterranean but all I could remember was the name of the boat." Pike felt he had talked enough. He took a tram back to the hotel where Dimock was waiting, already beginning to worry that Pike had fallen into a trap.

"Tomorrow we stake out Wozchod Bank," said Pike. "That's where Demirkan's supposed to be working."

Staking out a bank in Zurich is not so easy for two foreigners unfamiliar with the craft of espionage. There were no useful restaurants or cafés overlooking the entrance. There were no empty offices to be rented or broken into, even if either of them had had lock-picking skills. They couldn't get hold of a delivery van and, even if they could, it would have been moved on swiftly by the traffic police.

Pike sent in Dimock at 8.00 the next morning. He stood there clutching his briefcase and a *Neue Zürcher Zeitung*, pretending to be waiting for someone. Every now and then he glanced at his watch. He looked up and down the street, hoping that William would come and relieve him. At 9.30 he gave up and took a roundabout route back to the hotel. Nobody waits for someone that long, he thought.

Pike had been to the marina on the western shore.

"I've seen the Flying Finn," he said. "It's a big boat, quite capable of carrying a Nautilus, except that there doesn't seem any way of opening up the deck enough to lower it in." Pike didn't seem upset that Dimock had left his post. "We'll try again this evening."

At 4.30 they were both in place, Dimock a long way down the street towards the Bahnhofstrasse, and Pike in a hired car at the street corner occupied by the Wozchod Bank. It was a quiet backstreet, but very close to the elegant shops at the north end of Bahnhofstrasse. Pike wore a chauffeur's cap. He had insisted on this disguise even though the car was only a Fiat. "Not all the Swiss like to flaunt their wealth even though they have a chauffeur," he protested.

At 5.00 people began to leave the bank. They all looked Swiss, none of the flabby, pasty-complexioned Slavonic features that Pike associated with Russians abroad. Still, Demirkan wasn't really a Russian; he was an Uzbek and looked more like a Turk.

There he was, unmistakably. Pike's heart raced. He wasn't used to this cloak and dagger stuff. With relief he saw that Demirkan was heading towards the Bahnhofstrasse and would be Dimock's responsibility. But would Dimock recognize him?

Pike couldn't drive his Fiat into the Bahnhofstrasse. The street was closed to all but trams and taxis. He got out, threw his chauffeur's cap into the car and hurried after the disappearing cosmonaut.

Dimock hadn't spotted Demirkan but he saw Pike striding towards him. Then he saw Demirkan at the tram-stop. "Get on the tram," said Pike out of the corner of his mouth as he passed Dimock. Both Englishmen stepped into the queue. They followed Demirkan as he boarded a number 10 tram. Pike and Dimock were pretending not to know each other. The tram stopped at the Paradeplatz and more people climbed on. "What do we do about tickets?" hissed Dimock.

"Someone will come round," said Pike. Sure enough a man in a cap stepped on at the next halt and did a tour of the passengers. But he was inspecting tickets not selling them. "He's an inspector," whispered Dimock. They felt like two naughty schoolboys caught in the act.

"Haben Sie keine Fahrkarten?" asked the inspector.

"I'm sorry, we're English," said Pike. "In England we buy tickets on the bus." Nearby passengers looked at the English couple incuriously. Luckily Demirkan was at the other end of the tram.

"Where are you going?" asked the inspector.

"Along the lake," said Pike. "We want to see Lake Zurich."

"Two francs twenty," said the conductor. "Next time you buy the ticket at the machine. Yes." He pointed to a notice. "Strafe," said the conductor, "one hundred francs. I am a nice man." The Englishmen grinned contritely.

They were skirting Lake Zurich but it was obscured by buildings and greenery. Pike judged they must be heading for the marina which he'd visited that morning. Two stops later Demirkan alighted and so did the Englishmen. They looked about them as the tram drove on. Demirkan was walking down a road which forked towards the lake.

"I don't think he's seen us," said Pike. "Let's follow." The road went downhill until it joined with another main road, heavy with traffic coming from the city centre. Demirkan had already crossed it and was following this new road, which ran close to the lake. He came to a large grey house, walked up some steps and entered. "Walk on," said Pike. "We mustn't act suspiciously." But as they were about to pass the house they saw a small road to the left which led right down to the lake. The two men turned down the road and came to a small park with views across the lake and down the western shore. "That's the marina," said Pike, pointing to a cluster of masts and white hulls about a mile away. But what interested them more was the rear view of the big grey house and the structure at the bottom of the garden. "A boathouse!" exclaimed Pike. "Of course."

"You think the Nautilus is in there?" asked Dimock.

"It has to be." Pike was getting nervous. "We'd better not stay here too long. Maybe we can come back after dark."

"Perhaps we can hire a pedalo," said Dimock, spotting a few pedal craft far out on the lake. Pike looked at Dimock. "Have you done any scuba diving?"

"No."

"Damn." Pike had never been an athlete,, and the thought of physical exertion was repugnant to him. But it seemed an expedition by stealth was needed to get a closer look at the boathouse. He couldn't ask Dimock to do something so dangerous. This was his show. It was his responsibility.

They took the tram back into town and retrieved the Fiat, which had collected a parking fine. That night, in Pike's hotel room, they devised a plan. All they needed was to get a look inside the boathouse through the slatted gateway. A few seconds with a powerful torch should be enough. It wouldn't need sophisticated diving equipment. A snorkel and mask would be enough.

"I think I should do it," said Dimock.

"You keep out of it," said Pike fiercely. "If anyone gets killed I want it to be me."

The next morning they went shopping. Pike bought himself a snorkel and mask, a wetsuit for his top half and a pair of flippers.

"I feel a complete idiot," he confessed to Dimock as he tried on the suit. They also bought an inflatable boat and a waterproof torch.

That afternoon they drove 40 kilometres along the shore of Lake Zurich and put the equipment to the test. Dimock took out a foot pump and inflated the rubber boat. Pike peeled off his city suit and laid it carefully over the front seat of the Fiat. Occasionally he caught sight of his white, flabby legs. He squeezed himself into the wetsuit top, pressing in the flesh of his stomach as he pulled up the zip. He felt the taut rubber suiting press his body into a better shape, like armour, boosting his confidence. Perhaps he was cut out for this cloak-and-dagger-stuff after all.

They launched the little craft and stepped in, trying not to get wet. For a time they went round in circles trying to use the paddles as silently as possible, without a splash or a ripple. Then Pike put on his flippers, took the torch and slipped over the side. It was a shock to the system, and his heart pounded. It was years since he'd forced himself to take any more exercise than a brisk walk to a country pub. He had to cling to the boat immediately and take off the mask, gulping in fresh air. "This is hopeless," he told himself. "Pull yourself together." He put back the mask, grimaced at Dimock and launched himself across the water. The flippers took him in easy strides across the surface. That was better; he was breathing more easily and began to take an interest in the water below. Pike detached the torch from his belt and shone it downwards, seeing slabs of green rock coated with slime and algae. He tried a dive but at first found he was too buoyant. "Too much fat," he told himself. But then he managed several passes under the boat, peering with his torch into the murky depths, and suddenly he felt free, like one of those great walruses in the zoo, flabby and crippled on land, but majestic in the water, propelled along effortlessly by a flick of their mighty tails. "I am a Pike," he thought.

That night they drove to the Marina where the Flying Finn was berthed. It was around 11.30 and a few people were still drinking in the distant clubhouse.

It was a clear night with a fresh wind, causing enough ripples to mask the sound of their paddles. They stayed close to the shore. Few of the houses backing onto the water appeared to be lived in. They paddled from boathouse to boathouse hardly concerned that they would be seen.

As they drew closer to 417 Seestrasse, Pike began to sweat under the wetsuit. He wasn't sure how he'd react at the moment of danger. They had various emergency procedures if things went wrong. The place looked unguarded but they had no way of being sure. Dimock touched his arm and held out a flask of schnapps, but Pike shook his head. He had an idea alcohol and snorkelling didn't mix. They saw the dark hulk of the boathouse.

Behind it the only lights shining were on the top floor of the main house.

It was tempting to risk simply paddling up to the gates of the boathouse and shining a light in. But it was most likely that the Nautilus would be submerged. And Pike didn't want Dimock to come too close in the boat. He felt responsible for this innocent who had been drawn into a game in which life could be snuffed out without a moment's thought.

Pike slipped over the side without a splash. Take it easy, he told himself. He was two or three hundred yards from the boathouse and he had all night ahead of him to ascertain one thing: was a Nautilus lurking in there? Would they have a sentry, he wondered. What kind of alarm system did they have? He turned onto his back and rested for a moment. The stars mocked him from above, reminding him how small he was and how futile his efforts to keep civilization on its course.

There was the boathouse. He approached it from the side, lifted off his facemask and listened. The lights on the top floor had gone out. With any luck they were asleep in there. Pike put back the mask. His breathing sounded thunderous. He could see the grill of the gate, but decided he mustn't touch it in case it was attached to an alarm. He had to submerge, approach the gate, shine his torch and then retreat in the space of a minute, the maximum that he could hold his breath.

Pike submerged. He was no longer the lithe walrus he had been in the daytime. A thousand fearful shapes appeared to close around him and it was difficult to keep a sense of direction. He decided to risk the torch. There was the gate ahead of him, its great spikes descending into the water like a portcullis. But from that distance he couldn't see beyond. He kicked with his feet, his torch peering through the grill. Was that a hull-shape beyond? He started rising and clung to the gate to stop his ascent. "Hell," he thought, but used his new leverage to get a good look through the bars. There was the unmistakeable squat, grey outline of the Nautilus, almost as he had imagined it, but it looked bigger from this distance. The hull appeared not metallic but rubbery, rounded and soft. "Is that how it beats sonar?" he wondered.

By this time his heart and lungs were fighting for air. He had to get away. He swam quickly to the side of the boathouse and up to the surface. If I could touch it, I would discover more, he thought. How can they leave it there so poorly guarded? Pike rested, then dived again.

Inside the house the alarm signal woke Demirkan from a sleep assisted by good Swiss wine. "Lebedyev," he shouted, "it's your bloody alarm system again." Lebedyev grunted. Since he'd installed the system in the boathouse some weeks before it had tormented them with its oversensitivity, calling them out at all hours of the day and night. Each time, they came to the conclusion that it had been triggered by something very small, a fish, a piece of driftwood, or a tin can. Once during a storm they'd had to switch it off altogether as it responded to every high wave driven across from the eastern shore. "Why don't you check it out?" said Lebedyev. "It's your turn." But after a few more minutes Lebedyev shuffled into his slippers, pulled on his dressing gown, slipped a pistol into the pocket and stumbled into the garden. He unlocked the boathouse, turned on the lights and switched off the alarm.

Pike was under the gate when the light came on. He doused the torch and froze, fighting back his lungs' urge to blast out carbon dioxide. Lebedyev stood and listened. He walked to the mouth of the boathouse and checked it for flotsam. There was nothing. "It must have been a fish," he told himself. He turned round, reset the alarm, turned off the light and went back to bed. Pike had already kicked himself towards the surface. His first gasp for air was an uncontrolled explosion. He lay back in the water terrified he'd been heard. But he heard the door of the house slam. A minute later the light on the top floor went out.

Dimock, meanwhile, had gone through his own panic, having seen the light come on. He decided the worst had happened and that Pike had been discovered or even killed. The light went out again. He paddled ashore to the adjoining garden and waited. He heard the slam of a door and then nothing. His fingernails cut into the palms of his hands as he waited.

He tried to remind himself what fall-back procedures they had discussed. The first was to meet at a point round the next headland, the small park from which they'd first observed the boathouse. Dimock paddled off, describing a huge arc to avoid the boathouse. When he landed at the park Pike was there, shivering in his wetsuit. "Where on earth have you been?" he whispered.

"I'm sorry," said Dimock. "I thought you'd copped it. I thought they'd caught you in there."

"They nearly did. I think I set off an alarm."

"Have some of this." Dimock proffered the schnaps and Pike took several gulps.

"Firewater," he said. He felt privately elated. He'd come through a physical test and the whole tenuous theory hatched in his mind had become real.

"Was it in there?" asked Dimock.

"Yes. The same as the one in Sweden."

They watched the house and waited, surprised it hadn't reacted like a hornet's nest. After an hour they paddled in another wide arc back to the marina, deflated the boat and returned to their hotel. They were debating what to do. If they told the Swiss they would treat it as a local problem, raid the house and send the Russians packing, impounding the Nautilus. But what about the other Nautili which Pike was sure would soon be in place in the major capitals of the free world? A search for them all would have to be co-ordinated - without if possible triggering any more alarms.

Pike didn't have a high opinion of the British intelligence services, but at least he had contacts there. Dimock suggested Greenpeace, which had had some spectacular successes against western nuclear tests in the Pacific, against nuclear waste dumpers and the Russian whaling fleet.

"Too risky," said Pike. "Whoever does this has to be highly disciplined and not squeamish."

For economy and to keep a low profile they took the train back to London next day. They stood outside Victoria Station, shaking hands awkwardly in the din of traffic.

"I'll give you a call," said Pike.

Dimock walked to his bus. Could he now slide back into an anonymous life in Notting Hill? Was that what he wanted? To be an innocent doctor of botany again, steadying the pace of his life to the growth of plants and the pop of corks in the stripped-pine kitchens of his mates? He would leave the heroics to the others like Pike, who were weary of life.

Pike saw Richards at a safe house in Barnes. Richards had brought some wine and cheese.

"No reason why we should starve," he said, drawing the cork on a bottle of Burgundy. They found some glasses and sat at a large, dusty kitchen table.

"Rather young," said Pike as he eyed the fizzy purple liquid. Richards cut up some cheese and they ate and drank while the afternoon sun blazed a square on the kitchen floor.

"Remember your tip about Demirkan," said Pike. "Well, we tracked him down in Zurich. He works for the Foreign Trade Bank of the USSR, Zurich branch. The bank stopped trading under the Wozchod name after that gold fraud last year. One day we followed him home. He lives in a sodding great house smack on the shore of Lake Zurich, with its own boathouse."

"So," said Richards," I suppose you're going to tell me he keeps a small submarine at the bottom of his garden."

"I saw it. I saw it with my own eyes. We went in late one night by boat and I took a look at it with a torch. The point is, Ian, it's a Nautilus with a cosmonaut in place, just as I predicted."

"But why Zurich? What the hell do they want with a spy ship in Switzerland? Hardly to track the Swiss navy. Maybe it's to tunnel into bank vaults in the Bahnhofstrasse and extract gold."

Richards paused. "How did they smuggle it into Switzerland anyway?"

"The cabin cruiser," said Pike. "You remember Demirkan was found driving one about Lake Zurich late at night. It's my theory that the Nautilus was smuggled in, in the hold of the Flying Finn."

"OK," said Richards, "let's accept all your theories so far. Why Zurich?"

"I can think of two reasons. First, this is a pilot project. Sweden was a pilot project. What do the two places have in common? They're non-NATO. If anything goes wrong the Russians aren't going to be faced with the entire alliance falling on them like a pack of hounds. But that doesn't apply any more because I believe they've already started deploying these things throughout the Western world."

"You mean there might be one here in London?"

"Very likely."

"But what for? It's a funny way to collect military intelligence."

"Aha. You intelligence guys have fallen into your own trap. You call it a spy ship, but it isn't a spy ship at all. It's called Nautilus. Captain Nemo, what was he after? He was cocking a snook at the world. The Soviet plan is to do the same - to opt out of the arms race yet keep a jump ahead of the Americans. You see I've come to the conclusion, and you will have to test it, that these Nautili are small, mobile nuclear bombs. Each one of them is hidden in an important

Western city and can be detonated at will, either for strategic initiative or in defence if anything is thrown at the Eastern bloc." Richards thought for a moment. He needed ammunition to shoot down such a preposterous idea.

"It's absurd to think that the Soviets would build something like that into their defence strategy. It's too footloose, it's Bohemian. The Soviets go for the big picture, the grand stratagem. This is fiddly. It depends on drunks in charge of cabin cruisers and dilapidated Zurich mansions. Positively fin de siècle." He took a gulp of wine. Pike was angry at his indifference.

"Well, I'm handing it to you on a plate. If you don't like it, I'll take it to someone else, the Americans maybe, or the Israelis. Why not go down to Zurich and see for yourself? It wouldn't cost very much." Richards smiled. He darted a glance at Pike.

"Help yourself to cheese," he said taking a big mouthful. "By the way, continuing the saga of grounded Soviet cosmonauts, we have strange reports about your friend Tikov. It seems he flipped his lid and went to see an old space chum in Houston, one of the Apollo crew, Tom Stafford. Turned up out of the blue, said he was on a business trip, then vanished as mysteriously as he had come. Stafford's wife tipped off security but they were too slow."

"When did that happen?" asked Pike.

"Last week."

"That means another Nautilus may already be in place."

"Where?"

"In Cape Canaveral, New Orleans, New York, San Francisco - God knows. Can't you see how devastating this plan is? One may be found, perhaps two, but there will always be one more. And none of your early warning systems or spy satellites can track them down."

"C'est magnifique, Guillaume, mais ce n'est pas la guerre. It disobeys one of the first rules of the battlefield:

don't overextend your lines of communication. It's fine for spying or subversive activity, but as a part of the Soviets' nuclear strike force, I don't buy it."

"It's an alternative," said Pike. "A back-up system. It's an antidote to the madness of the arms race. Who knows, if it came to the crunch it could be just as effective as firing 1,000 ICBMs and seeing four of them get through."

Richards got up and put the empty bottle and the glasses in the sink.

"Mrs Spencer comes in tomorrow," he said. "I'll drop you in Chelsea."

VULKAN

CHAPTER FOURTEEN

Moscow

News of Tikov's escapade in Houston reached Moscow before he did. A staff car collected him from the airport and drove him directly to Mikhailov's department. He was summoned into Mikhailov's presence but was kept waiting while Mikhailov finished a long telephone call apparently to his mistress. Tikov found it disgusting. He felt it had been stage-managed for his benefit, to impress on him that his rank and status now meant nothing. The hunched, black-clad figure of Mikhailov occasionally swung to face him and an eye winked or a hand waved in mock exasperation. Finally he held the receiver at arm's length for a second then slammed it down in the cradle.

"Women," he said, and smiled at Tikov. "Back so soon? We thought you were planning to linger on in the United States, to unwind a little before coming back to face the rigours of socialism."

"Well I—".

"In fact we were beginning to think you might stay there indefinitely." Tikov wanted to assure him that the Nautilus programme was safe and that whatever risks he had taken would not have endangered the project, however irregular they had been. But he realized it was no good. Mikhailov's oratory was in full flight. "But you mustn't think," continued Mikhailov, "that you caused us too much anxiety. It's clear that the mounting of the Nautilus programme has put tremendous demands on you, as it would on any ordinary man. You've done a terrific job and it's time you passed the burden of responsibility onto somebody else's shoulders."

"Whose?" asked Tikov.

"A simple co-ordinator. The groundwork's been done. All I need now is a communications expert, not a highly qualified officer and a hero of the Soviet Union."

"But what about my people in the field? They need encouragement, they need careful handling."

"They're superfluous. They're the icing on the cake. The system needed people to put it in place but it's now totally manageable from here."

"As long as Demirkan, Zilin and co keep paying their telephone bills. If there are any technical hitches, if any faults develop, then you're back to people again, and you have to maintain their alertness and their motivation. I know that. I've run space programmes. It's the same."

"Don't talk to me about motivation," said Mikhailov, and his face lost any semblance of humour. "What did you tell that American, Stafford? Why did you go and see him?"

"He's a friend. He's a nice, boring, solid American friend. We've shared experiences in space and on the ground. That's all it was."

"You called him from Helsinki. Why?"

"Just to tell him there were no hard feelings. His wife blew the whistle on me. It's understandable. I just wanted to show him that I understood."

"Well, you're off the Nautilus project. You're a security risk. Only your past exploits have saved you from exile or worse. At least you'll be spending plenty of time with your family." Tikov knew what that meant. It was house arrest. Virtual incarceration of his family, probably in their dacha outside Moscow. It was pleasant enough for a short while but soon the lack of certainty became a torture.

"How about Japan?" protested Tikov. "I haven't checked that out yet."

"Japan's under control. It's all been taken care of. You can relax, Boris Alexeivich. I assure you that from now on Nautilus has as much a psychological as a technical function. It's an instrument of terror. Imagine the panic when we announce that we have the power to touch off a 20-kilotonne blast at any population centre on earth, for the price of a telephone call. And the beauty of it is, we are doing this to end war and to eliminate the nightmare of an all-out nuclear holocaust in which no side is the winner."

"Do you think the Americans are going to give up without a fight? Their idea of defence is to strike first. So they'll call your bluff and throw everything at us, in megatons not kilotonnes. Moscow, Leningrad, Kirov, Omsk, Vladivostok. Then what do we do?"

"You're talking in ultimatums. Successful terrorists don't talk in ultimatums, they deal in reality. It will be a reality the Americans are faced with, long before it comes to lobbing ICBMs. For instance, we will ask them, on behalf of all humanity, to dismantle the Star Wars project, since that is a clear escalation of the arms race in both destructive and economic terms. The billions of dollars spent on Star Wars would better be spent on food and assistance in the Sahel and other hardship centres of the world, even on their own farmers. For once, even in the eyes of the West, we will have the moral argument on our side. And this will be achieved by holding hostage a few cities dotted about the world.

"And let's suppose the worst happens and Nautilus is discovered, thanks to you, in New York, or London. Only one cell in the network will be wiped out, the rest will continue to function. And we can build more, and more, until they are planted like amoeba in the guts of every major city in the world - dormant but potentially lethal."

"You forget that it wouldn't take the Americans very long to develop the same thing once they've discovered it. And knowing them they'd do it much more efficiently."

"Ah Tikov," said Mikhailov grinning, "full of praise for the Americans. But for them it wouldn't work. There are fundamental differences between our two countries. One is bounded by ice and hostile wastes, the other by warm water. One is open to all the bums and subversives of the world, the other is a tightly-run authoritarian regime - we may not like it but for this purpose it works. Lastly, the old cliché, we are a people used to suffering and sacrifice. How many died in the last war - five million, six million? Our greatest weapon at such moments of sacrifice is propaganda, the ability to control information. We have it. The Americans don't. Despite their fire-power that makes them the flabbiest nation on earth."

"Do you think it's right..." began Tikov then broke off. "Never mind."

"No, go on," said Mikhailov indulgently, "shooting down your objections is good exercise."

"Is it right that the Soviet Union, the second most powerful nation on earth, should resort to the tactics of international terrorism along with Palestinians, Islamic fundamentalists and the IRA?"

"This is terrorism only in the sense that it's dealing in fear. But it's not the angry backlash of a lost cause; it's a deliberate calculated device to lower the cost of conflict both in human and economic terms - de-escalation to use an American expression. Nor is it cloak-and-dagger work along the lines of the CIA, Mossad, MI6 or even our own boys at the KGB. It's more like...it's exactly like a space programme in the best traditions, pushing back the frontiers of human endeavour in an attempt to create better understanding and a better world." Mikhailov leaned back in his chair, obviously pleased with his own rhetoric.

"If one of the Nautilus weapons is ever used," said Tikov, "it will defeat its own purpose. Russia will be blamed for having lowered the nuclear threshold, justifying the West in slinging all its remaining hardware at us, and letting in a nuclear winter."

"Tactical nuclear weapons and neutron bombs have already done that," said Mikhailov. "They have reduced the shock and horror of nuclear weaponry to the scale of toys and cut back the theatre of war to the size of a sports field. Nautilus doesn't commit that act of hypocrisy. Nautilus brings nuclear horror closer to the urban citizen than ever before. Our soldiers can no longer be paid to do the job of dying for us; in fact they'll be better protected than the man in the street. The horrors of war won't be viewed from in front of a television set. They'll be inside the home. The American people will be faced with a value judgment - are the president and his aggressive policies worth half a city or several cities? With Star Wars protection they might think they have a sporting chance of zero casualties. With Nautilus, there won't be that luxury."

"Very persuasive," said Tikov, "assuming that American decision-making is totally rational. I don't have so much faith in US democracy."

"But that's another of the beauties of this weapon. They will have plenty of time to decide. The truth will not be presented to them in one violent act; it will dawn on them slowly as they piece together the evidence. They will be totally in my power as surely as a man who has swallowed poison to which only I have the antidote."

As Tikov gazed at the man in front of him, Mikhailov's head appeared to shrink in size and float away from his crippled shoulders, the disembodiment of evil. This was absurd. Behind Mikhailov was the full grandeur of the Soviet military machine with all its built-in checks and balances. No man could step outside that machine and retain his authority, let alone pervert it for his own use. Yet at this moment, and on occasions before, Tikov was driven to this extraordinary view of Mikhailov - as someone beating and arrogating the Soviet machine; a Vulcan forging thunderbolts not for Jupiter, but for himself.

The moment passed. A door opened at the end of the long office. Mikhailov had pressed a bell to signal the end of the interview. Tikov got up and left. As he walked down to the car he was followed at a distance by his escort, a pair of men in raincoats. There was no other sign that he was under arrest.

CHAPTER FIFTEEN

Zurich

There were six men in the Range Rover. Fortescue, long and lean in a woollen cap and green anorak, was driving. Richards, sporting three days' growth of beard, sat next to him; Fatty Williams, not fat at all but 220 pounds of Welsh Rugby forward, was on the left. In the second row was Bondi with a full beard and spectacles - nicknamed the Boffin. Next to him sat Mitchell, only five foot five. And behind the driver, Smythe, the radio operator.

Their destination was Zurich where, if conditions allowed, they would go ahead with Operation Water Rat. It was a long, dull drive from Ostend down the motorway network of Europe to Basel and Zurich. Richards advised them to get some sleep but only Mitchell obliged, hunched against the Boffin's shoulder.

In the back and on the roof were various items indicating a climbing and caving expedition - tents, ropes, inflatable boats, diving gear, even a couple of harpoon guns. Customs inspectors would have discovered no illegal weaponry. That aspect was being looked after by Rudi in Thalwil.

Rudi was an agent, an arms broker in the true sense of the word. He took orders to buy and he took orders to sell with no names asked. Delivery within Switzerland was no problem. Delivery outside required a complicated charade with weigh bills and end-user certificates but in this case it was, as he told the caller from Amsterdam, "a doddle". He had orders, as soon as the money reached his account at the Cantonal Bank of Zurich, to deliver some high quality merchandise at a certain map reference, a wood outside Zurich, at three o'clock one morning.

The Range Rover was waiting when the delivery van arrived. Richards and Fatty Williams watched two men unload three crates and place them beside a pile of logs. They waited until the two men departed in the van and the sound of its engine merged with the hum of Zurich 700 metres below. Then they drove up and lifted the crates on board. "Mad Mitch" Mitchell watched from the cover of the trees and rejoined the Range Rover as it drove away. The car descended the Uetliberg and returned to the Campingplatz Seebucht right on the shore of the Lake by the Zurich suburb of Wollishofen. This was next to the marina where the Flying Finn was berthed, only a kilometre along the shore from Seestrasse 417.

The British climbers had pitched their tents. No one was particularly curious when three of them came back singing at 3.45 in the morning. By daylight inside the main tent they inspected the weaponry - grenades, gas, stun bombs, three Heckler & Koch automatic pistols and three Beretta hand guns with silencers. "With luck we won't have to use them," said Fortescue.

Towards dusk Fortescue went out on his first reconnaissance mission, taking Mitch and his diving equipment in one of the inflatable boats. With the help of a sketch provided by Pike they spotted the boathouse. There were some lights on in the house, but all looked peaceful.

Mitch dived. He took a flashlight and a waterproofed Polaroid camera.

Mitch took care not to cross the boathouse entrance and set off the alarm. He ran his flashlight over the grey bulk of the Nautilus and took some snaps. After 15 minutes he surfaced by the inflatable. "It's there alright, as large as life," he said. They hauled Mitch on board and paddled for the campsite.

"Of course we never doubted old Pike for a moment," said Fortescue.

"Of course not," said Mitch.

Meanwhile, Richards and Williams investigated the land approaches to Seestrasse 417. There was an open driveway to the rear of the house. The first floor windows were accessible from a porch above the back door and the door itself didn't look too secure. They watched the house for three hours trying to assess how many people lived there and where they slept. They could see only three men. The man they spotted in the kitchen retired at 22.00 to a room in the basement. They called him Boris. Another, whom they dubbed Ivan, sat in the living room smoking and reading magazines while Demirkan, whom they recognized, spent some time playing an untuned grand piano in a room with no furniture. At around midnight Demirkan and Ivan retired to adjacent rooms on the first floor.

On the assumption that the Nautilus was there, Richards was beginning to formulate a plan.. They would take over the house in the morning, after Demirkan and perhaps his companion had gone to work. That would mean overpowering only one man. Then they could look over the Nautilus in broad daylight measuring and photographing. If either Russian came back to the house he would walk into a trap.

Depending on what Bondi, the Boffin, found in the Nautilus they would decide whether to leave it in place, destroy it or steal it. Stealing it would be difficult and would probably need the co-operation of the Swiss. At the moment the Swiss had been told nothing about Water Rat, nor had the British Embassy. It was a totally illegal operation. At that time Richards was acutely aware how these illegal ventures can come unstuck. Only a month before, the French DGSE had made a hopeless mess of sinking the Greenpeace vessel Rainbow Warrior in Auckland Harbour, New Zealand. Result: One Spanish photographer killed, two agents in a New Zealand jail and a grand government scandal in France. Operation Water Rat must either be a success or sink without trace.

At the campsite they made plans for the following day. Fortescue and Williams would make the assault on the house as soon as Ivan and Demirkan left for work. The four others would be waiting offshore in the inflatable. A bleep on the short-wave radio would tell Richards and the Boffin it was safe to move into the boathouse. They would approach and enter underwater, trusting that Fortescue had neutralized the alarm. Mitch and Smythe would be offshore to pick up the divers on their return.

The next morning, Demirkan opened his bedroom window and filled his lungs with free Swiss air. Lake Zurich glinted in the morning sun. A kilometre offshore he saw an inflatable craft and four men. They looked like divers. For a moment he had the chilling thought that they might be an assault commando. He took his binoculars from the chest of drawers and brought the boat into focus. He was reassured. Two of them wore silly hats. They were waving fishing rods and pushing each other about. He could see hands holding cans of beer. No assault commando behaves like that.

Ten minutes later, he and Lebedyev left the house. Romanov, the servant, returned to the kitchen at the back of the house. He turned on the radio. The Swiss Romande Orchestra was playing a Rossini overture and he sang the melody as he washed the dishes. There was a knock on the door. He stiffened, turned down the radio and listened. There was another knock.

"Was wollen Sie?" he asked in poor German.

"Telefondienst," said Fortescue in equally poor German. Romanov had been told on no account to let anyone into the house, especially not telephone engineers.

"Nein danke. Alles in Ordnung," he said firmly.

Fortescue had been told to keep bloodshed to a minimum.

"Nicht alles in Ordnung," he shouted. Meanwhile Fatty Williams, far from inagile, had climbed up one of the pillars of the porch with the aid of a grapple. It was an easy hop through Demirkan's open window. He listened to the Germanic utterances below and trod lightly down the staircase. Romanov still had a tea towel in his hand when he heard the command "Hände hoch!" and swung round to face the muzzle of a beretta.

Williams opened the door for Fortescue. They gagged Romanov, took him to the basement and tied him to a chair. Fortescue went to the first floor window, took out his short-wave radio and signalled a short bleep to Richards. Shortly afterwards through Demirkan's binoculars he saw that four heads in the inflatable had become two.

While Williams watched the surroundings of the house Fortescue made a search. He found the alarm buzzer in Lebedyev's bedroom and disconnected it. Downstairs he examined the telephone system. There was one conventional telephone set and beside it the cradle of a portable telephone. The hand-held receiver was missing. He looked for numbers on the two instruments, but they had been erased.

Next, Fortescue went through all papers and possessions he could find, looking for messages, codes, instructions of any kind. Apart from a couple of pistols and some ammunition there was nothing. Towards 10.30 the telephone rang. Williams and Fortescue didn't answer it.

"If that's Demirkan, he's likely to be suspicious," said Fortescue. "We'd better warn the others." But on second thoughts he didn't warn them. He wanted to give them more time. If Demirkan and Ivan came back they'd enter the house first. He and Williams would be ready for them.

Richards and the Boffin examined every nut and bolt of the Nautilus. They opened the hatch, learned how to operate the airlock, and Bondi crept inside. He examined with interest the heavy container just behind the craft's centre of gravity, about the size of a large suitcase. The wiring to it and the casing showed that it was undoubtedly a nuclear device. Locked onto it was a simple radio telephone handset. Bondi whistled. He looked at the instrument panel, read the dials. "Very primitive," he observed to himself, "but effective. My god, it's all here." He decided to disarm the weapon at once. It wouldn't take long to make a real mess of it.

Richards measured the outside, the approximate weight and strength of the hull. He saw that its surface was very smooth and not metallic at all but covered with a rubbery substance. He followed the wire connections from the hull and discovered and disabled the photosensitive alarm system. Richards decided they would have to take the Nautilus with them. It was too valuable a prize to be left here, and it would be dynamite in any future arms negotiations with the Russians, especially if they could keep it secret.

It was Lebedyev who became suspicious. At the bank he called Demirkan on an internal line. "I can't raise Romanov," he said. "He didn't answer my call at 10.30."

"He was probably sitting on the pan. That foul mincemeat has taken its revenge," said Demirkan. But then he remembered the inflatable boat. "Come on, let's go," he said.

They flagged down a taxi. "I know they're in there," said Demirkan. "What do we do?" Their only weapons were in the house, and that was presumably under enemy control. "Who the hell are they, anyway?"

"The Swiss, the Americans, who knows," said Lebedyev as the taxi sped to Seestrasse.

"I've got it," said Demirkan. "There's a Very pistol on the Flying Finn, then maybe we can do some damage." His main thought was to protect the Nautilus and get it out of prying hands. The taxi was diverted to the marina. As Demirkan dived on board the Flying Finn he glanced at the lake. He saw the inflatable boat and only two heads. Armed with the pistol and a box of flares he returned to the taxi. "Seestrasse," he said. He stopped the taxi just beyond number 417, by the little road which ran down to the lake. He and Lebedyev climbed out. With luck they hadn't been seen from the house. They crept close to the grassy shore grateful for the cover of tall trees which blocked the view from the house. Demirkan was able to get to the wooden wall of the boathouse. He kicked off his shoes and slid out of his jacket, holding the loaded pistol pirate-like between his teeth. The two men in the inflatable were still there, one kilometre out. He had to risk being spotted.

Demirkan waded into the water and worked his way round to the mouth of the boathouse, clinging to the wooden weatherboarding then slipping under the gate. Looking into the comparative gloom he saw that the hatch of the Nautilus had broken the surface. He could make out one man crouched by the charging equipment, not a very good target. He tried to heave himself noiselessly onto the wooden planking, but Richards spun round. Demirkan fired. A bright fireball blazed into Richards' chest and sent him reeling backwards. Demirkan fired again as he ran towards Richards. The flare missed and lodged itself in the woodwork.

Demirkan saw that the man was either unconscious or dead. He grabbed his flashlight and scanned the half-submerged Nautilus. The other man must be inside. He dived through the hatch. The airlock was open and below him he saw a pair of legs. With the advantage of surprise he fell on Bondi and hit his head with the Very pistol, until he sank back. There was no time to dispose of the body. Demirkan closed the hatch. He noticed that flames were crackling along one side of the boathouse. Throwing Nautilus's electric motor into reverse he put it into a shallow rearward dive and headed out into Lake Zurich.

Lebedyev heard the shots and saw Nautilus leave. He waited in cover, watching the house. Williams appeared at a first floor window. He noticed smoke rising from the boathouse. Very soon, he and Fortescue were running for the boathouse door. Lebedyev waited a moment then walked round to the front of the house and entered. He ran to get his pistol. It had gone; so had Demirkan's. He telephoned the police and the fire brigade then took up position at a first floor window.

Williams and Fortescue burst into the boathouse. They rushed to pull Richards away from the fire. The treated timber was blazing merrily and dropping firebrands of melted tar. Nautilus had gone and so had Bondi.

"I'll get the car, you bring Ian," said Fortescue. It was a risk. The fire must already have been seen and people would be gathering. The car was half a mile away. Williams examined Richards. It looked as though he had been badly hit in the ribs, but not fatally. He saw ugly burn-marks as he lifted a flap of the rubber wet suit. Richards opened his eyes.

"Can you walk?" Williams asked. Richards tried to get to his feet. Williams helped him. "Chas is bringing the car," he said. They stumbled towards the driveway. Within five minutes the Range Rover burst through a small crowd gathered on the pavement and wheeled round to the back of the house. Richards was bundled into the back seat. A policeman walked up but Fortescue shouted "Privat! Privat!" and scattered him along with the rest of the crowd. As the Range Rover left the scene, the fire engines were arriving.

Mitch and Smythe watched helplessly from the inflatable. They saw the flash of the Very pistol in the boathouse and the retreating figure of Lebedyev. They saw smoke then flames billow from the timberwork.

"What the hell's going on?" said Mitch.

"Shouldn't we go and help?" asked Smythe.

"We just stay put," said Mitch and kept his binoculars trained on the boathouse. He caught a glimpse of the hatch as the Nautilus broke out of the gateway. "The beastie's got out. We must track it if we can."

"How do we know who's driving it. One of theirs or one of ours?"

"We don't." Mitch put on his face mask and flippers. He dropped over the side. Visibility was about 30 metres through the green, hazy water. He heard a light buzzing, a tickling of the ears. For a moment, way below him, he saw the Nautilus at full power moving at around 10 knots, too fast to follow. He swam after it for a time, but each time he listened the sound had become fainter.

Demirkan followed the contours of the lake down to 100, 150 metres, shallow enough to give him a sporting chance to get out alive. He was looking for a place to bury the Nautilus for ever, a crack or a hole in the rock where sonar scanners wouldn't find her. He found the perfect place, a deep fissure with an overhanging ledge. Taking the Nautilus round in a circle he rammed it at speed into the gap. The craft shuddered and twisted sideways into the deep hole, deeper than he expected and the lights went out. He switched on the emergency circuit. The man against whose leg he was leaning was beginning to stir. Demirkan was faced with the prospect of killing him now in cold blood. In this confined space he couldn't do it. If he let him out of the hatch he'd probably die in the ascent anyway, in his condition. Better give him a human chance. He patted the man on the cheek.

"Hello, are you American, British, Swiss?"

"Greenpeace," said Bondi. "We're against nuclear arms." Demirkan grunted.

"I might have guessed," he said. "A do-gooder. Look where it's got you, eh? A hundred metres down in a crazy submarine, and only one parachute." He pointed to an aqualung. "What do you know about nuclear war, anyway?"

"I know that we're sitting on a bomb as powerful as the one used on Hiroshima," said Bondi. "Have you got any water?"

"Plenty out there." Demirkan opened a valve and a jet of water splashed onto his hand. He cupped both hands and gave Bondi a drink.

"Well, Mr Greenpeace, we have to get out of here, or this beautiful bomb will be our grave."

"From 100 metres?"

"It's possible, if we keep our heads and breathe out slowly as we come up." Demirkan explained. He would leave the Nautilus first, taking the aqualung, since the airlock could take only one man at a time. He would wait until Bondi had also used the airlock, then they would ascend together. Demirkan was taking a severe risk, since using an oxygen cylinder at that pressure produced a narcotic effect after two or three breaths, but he felt he had to stay around to encourage the helpless Englishman. "Provided we keep breathing out as the air expands in our lungs on the way up," said Demirkan, "we'll make it."

Demirkan curled himself into the escape hatch with the aqualung. He filled the chamber with water, undid the hatch bolts and pushed. The hatch cover wouldn't budge. He pushed again. It opened half a centimetre but no more. For two minutes he pushed then gave up and refastened the bolts, pumped out the water and returned to Bondi. His head was reeling after the effect of the pressurized oxygen.

"It's stuck," he said. "The hatch is rammed against rock." He threw the engine into reverse. The propeller whirred but the craft was wedged solid. "Mother of God," said Demirkan. For the first time he was afraid.

"What do we do now?" asked Bondi.

"Do?" shouted Demirkan. "There's nothing we can do, you damn fool Englishman. Why did you have to stick your nose in?" He hammered one huge fist against the hatch cover. Bondi was thinking.

"If we flooded the whole Nautilus isn't it possible it would alter its attitude and uncover the hatch?" Demirkan's tortured face broke into a smile.

"Brilliant Englishman, I love you. If it doesn't work we're dead men, you understand that."

"If we don't try it we're dead anyway," said Bondi. Demirkan opened the cocks and the water poured in slowly, as if they were running a bath. Periodically he released air pressure, hoping that the bubbles wouldn't be spotted on the surface. He regretted his recent outburst of anger.

"I'm sorry I called you a damn fool Englishman," he said. "For a moment I forgot myself."

"Is it easier to face death in space, Captain Demirkan?"

Demirkan smiled. "You've done your homework. We were bullied into this, Tikov, Volkov, Lebedyev, the whole crew. What kind of life is this for a cosmonaut? And do you know why? Because they couldn't trust any of their own people to do the job, the KGB, GRU, Spetsnaz, Z corps, they're all up to their necks in politics. They shouldn't have trusted us either. When we get up there I'll blow this whole thing into the sky. I'll tell you everything."

The water was around their shoulders. Demirkan handed Bondi the aqualung mouthpiece. "Here, have some practice," he said. The Nautilus shifted slightly. Demirkan undid the bolts on the hatch. As the pressure equalized he took a lungful of air from the mouthpiece and pushed upwards. The hatch wouldn't budge. He pushed again. He pushed until Bondi was a lifeless corpse next to him and the oxygen in both bottles was exhausted. And then he died.

Richards was in pain. Williams gave him a shot of painkiller as Fortescue packed up the tents at the campsite. Mitch and Smythe paddled ashore. They hadn't seen Bondi, but had watched fire hoses spray the boathouse, to no avail, and had been questioned by police in a launch. They had no idea how the fire started, they had said, perhaps some vandals.

Richards needed treatment but they also had to get rid of the Range Rover. It was too distinctive now that it had been at the scene of the crime. Fortescue took a tram into town to hire a car. The others cleared the campsite, paid the bill and drove out of Zurich to another forest rendez-vous. Half-an-hour later Fortescue arrived in a white Mercedes. They transferred Richards, drove him some way down the track, then Mitch and Williams scuppered the Range Rover with the help of a gallon of petrol. All distinguishing marks had been eliminated including the numbers on the chassis and engine block. They drove back to Zurich. Mitch and Smythe were dropped at the station to make their own way back to London. Fortescue and Williams planned to drive north, to take Richards to a US military hospital at Ulm in West Germany. "We have an arrangement there," said Fortescue.

Lebedyev searched the house and found Romanov bound and gagged in the basement. He released him then went outside to meet the police. "An accident," he said. "My handyman was smoking in the boathouse; I don't allow him to smoke in the house. He's full of remorse." The police were sceptical.

"What about the Range Rover? Those three men. One of them was wounded."

"I know nothing about it. If they are saboteurs or arsonists why pick on a boathouse? There was nothing in there. And in broad daylight. Really, I have no idea. You're welcome to search the boathouse for any little clue." They would find wires, a charging rectifier, thought Lebedyev, but it wouldn't add up to a submarine. They searched the carcass of the boathouse, the garden and even obtained a warrant to search the house. The Swiss police found nothing. Even to the question "Where is your radio telephone?" Lebedyev was able to reply: "Romanov took it down to the boathouse. It must have been burned in the fire."

CHAPTER SIXTEEN

London

Pike dined alone at The English House. He was restless and dissatisfied. He had no idea what was going on in Switzerland and it now seemed irrelevant, a side show. Blowing the Swiss operation wouldn't help them protect the most important centres, London and the United States. For those the hunt would have to start afresh. He cursed himself now for having sent Richards on a wild goose chase. He was alone in London with no back-up.

Pike telephoned Laszlo; maybe he could help. Laszlo had some guests but invited him round. He arrived at 7 Albion Mews at about 10.30. Malik, the musician, was there, and a man called Thomas whom Laszlo introduced as a writer. They were drinking whisky and talking about an exhibition of African artefacts. Pike waited impatiently for the guests to leave. At about midnight Laszlo showed them to the door. He turned to Pike.

"I think you have an apology to make," he said. They went back to the living room. "It seems you've joined MI6."

Pike protested but Laszlo went on. "We've certain information regarding an irresponsible jaunt in Switzerland. If it goes wrong - or even if it goes right - it's likely to upset some very delicate work we're doing here. Any early warning and the slug is going to draw in its horns."

"What are you working on?"

"After your recent exhibition I'm not sure I should tell you."

"Then let me tell you something," said Pike. "We've got to find this thing in London, forget about Switzerland. This is too important to let petty jealousies get in the way. There's a device somewhere along the Thames which could rip London apart at the touch of a telephone in Moscow."

"Do you have any evidence?"

"I've got no evidence. Only a process of deduction. That's why I've come to you. You've got manpower, you're close to the Russians, and you won't trip over your own bureaucracy."

"We've got something going already," said Laszlo. "We've run a check on all Soviet officials in this country. Their background, where they work. Not one of them is a cosmonaut, I'm afraid."

"What about where they live?"

"That's a bit more difficult. We'd have to follow each one home. That's about 200 tailing jobs to be done."

"We have to find out which of them lives by the river, then it's easy."

"How do you know he'll be a regular Soviet official? He's much more likely to be an illegal."

"I don't think so. You said yourself this isn't a KGB operation. If he was illegal he'd be run by the KGB. It's much more likely they put in someone new under normal diplomatic or trade mission cover to do this job."

"Then we can eliminate some of those 200," said Laszlo. "The seasoned guys and the known KGB agents.

Talking of which, our job will be made a whole lot simpler in a few days."

"Why?"

"Because our East German friends have uncovered a mole in the Soviet embassy here. Very embarrassing. Mr Tiedge, the head of counter-espionage in Bonn, tipped them off when he defected the other day. Apparently this mole is high up in the KGB. He'll have to go public, and there'll be expulsions from Britain, presumably all KGB."

"That should narrow the field."

"Maybe." Laszlo ate some peanuts from a silver bowl. He passed them to Pike. "Have some." Pike was thinking, sunk in an armchair, pressing his fingertips against his nose.

"Look," he said, "how many people can you spare?"

"What for?"

"Operation Mudlark."

"Mudlark?"

"This thing has got to be in the Thames. It has at least two links with the outside world: a power source to charge its batteries and a telephone to keep its detonator in touch with Moscow."

"It could have a radio telephone," objected Laszlo.

"It could but they're unreliable, and even then it has to be a number registered with the Post Office. A telephone wire leading from a riverside residence is most likely."

"It sounds most unlikely that Moscow would rely on British Telecom to provide its strategic defence link."

"This whole thing is crazy," said Pike impatiently, "but it exists. What I need is a team able to go over the whole riverside at low tide from Woolwich to Richmond Lock - that's about 24 miles. They'll inspect everything from bits of string, old cables, chains, pipes, abandoned bedsteads looking for any possible link between a submarine and the shore. I don't think it would take long. We could start with the most obvious places first, the ones near riverside houses." Laszlo shook his head and heaved with laughter.

"My dear William, I think you've finally flipped. But it will be done. After all, we have no other leads. We'll start tomorrow."

"Thanks. It's low tide at London Bridge at around 12.45pm. I think it would be sensible to start about an hour and a half before that, say 11.15, and go on for three hours. Depending on how many people you have we can divide the river into several sectors."

"I can give you two, possibly three. Any more and it's going to look like an invasion."

In the event Laszlo raised four of his Hungarian students in exile. Two of them took the north bank of the Thames and worked east and west of Albert Bridge; two took the south bank and worked east and west of Blackfriars Bridge. Janos had earphones and a metal detector. He looked like an enthusiast searching for Roman and mediaeval coins. Adam was dressed as a tramp, scavenging for scrap metal. The two others had theodolites and wore collar and tie, anoraks and Wellington boots, the uniform of the council surveyor. At 11.10 Pike strolled from his flat in Redburn Street down to the river. He witnessed the first moments of Operation Mudlark. On the first day each team covered eight miles of river, sixteen miles in all. They inspected dripping girders beneath bridges, sweating wooden piers and piles, jumbles of wires leading to houseboats and riverside lighting, drainpipes, sewerage outlets and subterranean streams. Each returned with nothing to report. When Pike went over the charts that evening with Laszlo they reckoned it would take three more days to cover Woolwich to Richmond.

Zilin had by now established his lifestyle. He was the proud owner of a Kawasaki motorbike and at weekends enjoyed outings to venues such as Clacton, Brighton and Southend-on-Sea to join the flocks of Hell's Angels clad like himself in black leather. The money he got for his job, and for contingencies, was good. He was keen to spend it. Against regulations he found himself a girlfriend, Cynthia, blonde and quiet, a loyal disciple. He judged she was dumb enough to take back to his flat by the river. She made him coffee, cooked him eggs and bacon and submitted to his urgent love-making with hardly a murmur, sometimes a tear.

One day, shortly after the fiasco in Zurich, he received a message. It was a blue alert. It meant that the Nautilus project was now known to the West. Zilin could expect them to come looking. He knew that meant an immediate end to his life as a trade delegate and Hell's Angel. He would have to leave his flat, his job, his bike and his girlfriend.

Zilin had already prepared his escape route. It was just a question of putting the plan into action, and it would take a little time.

That night he told Cynthia he was going away. He gave her a present, a gold chain, and they made love on and off until morning. He threw her out at around 8.00. He had work to do.

Taking his pedal bike he crossed the river at Tower Bridge and rode west through Southwark to Waterloo. Between Waterloo and the river is the South Bank, a jumble of modern buildings including the National Theatre, three concert halls, an art gallery and the UK headquarters of Royal Dutch/Shell. Outside the Shell headquarters in Belvedere Road stands a string of combi wagons and VW campers sometimes twenty, sometimes forty in number and never fewer than three or four. It is the market where Australians and a few others who have bought campers and toured Europe come to sell their vehicles before flying home. The peak season is August and September before the grand migration to the Australian summer.

Zilin propped his bike against a wall. He strolled up and down the collection of 20 or so vehicles looking for a suitable one. It had to be smart, anonymous, well-equipped for a long sojourn. He particularly liked one with heavy curtains on the windows. A hand-written notice said it was for sale at £2,500, negotiable. He knocked on the driver's window. The rear door opened and a big Australian with a moustache climbed out. Farther inside Zilin saw a girl reading a newspaper.

"Can I look her over?" asked Zilin.

"She's in beaut condition, only done 10,000 miles," said the Australian. Zilin drove up and down Belvedere Road, enjoying the distinctive air-cooled thrum of the VW engine.

"It's more than I wanted to pay," said Zilin, "but I'll give you £2,000 for her."

"Do us a favour. D'you know how much this thing cost new, with stereo, air-conditioning?"

"That's all I've got," said Zilin, enjoying a good haggle.

"How are you paying?" asked the Australian suspiciously.

"Cash," said Zilin and took out a wad of £50 notes. "Take it or leave it." The Australian liked the look of the money. They shook hands. Zilin put his bike inside and drove away, leaving the Australian, his girlfriend and two suitcases standing in Belvedere Road. He drove back to Gun Wharf and parked the van half a mile from his flat, returning there by bicycle. The rest of the day he spent cleaning the place up, packing essentials into two suitcases and throwing the rest away. Those essentials included the latest technology from British Telecom, a portable cellular telephone for which he had paid £1,515, and a year's rental in advance.

Throughout the day he was fascinated by the news bulletins on BBC radio. A top counsellor at the Soviet embassy, Oleg Gordievsky, had defected claiming to be the head of KGB operations in Britain. Gordievsky had been talking to the British and the Danes since 1966. The British government was to expel 25 Soviet officials denounced by him as KGB agents and more were likely to follow. Zilin felt safe; after all, he wasn't a KGB agent. His fears mounted, however, as it occurred to him that Gordievsky's denunciations could be false. His name could as easily come up as anyone else's. He decided to risk a call to the embassy. The telephone in his flat which had never rung or been dialled from, but which sat there as a detonator, might as well be used for this simple local call. After all, by this evening, Nautilus would have moved on, with a new communications link. Zilin lifted the receiver and punched up the embassy.

"Soviet Embassy, good afternoon."

"This is Zilin. Put me through to Nikolayev." Nikolayev's secretary answered.

"This is Zilin. Tell me one thing for my own peace of mind. Is my name on the list?"

"Not yet."

"What do you mean, not yet?"

"There are likely to be more reprisals. 'Tit-for-tat'," she said in English, and laughed.

"When?"

"Tomorrow or the next day."

"Thank you." Zilin hung up. He only needed until tomorrow. While he waited for it to get dark he sipped Pernod, looking from his balcony across the oily brownness of the Thames. A small tanker slipped down on the tide from the BP terminal at Fulham. Some river buses plied from Westminster to Greenwich. Apart from that, little disturbed the sleek surface. That was to his advantage. Tomorrow he'd be down there feeling his way through the murky deep. As the shapes of buildings merged with the sky across the river he extinguished his last cigarette and left the flat. He fetched the van and loaded the bicycle and the two cases, shutting the flat door for the last time. The embassy would take the flat over, or sell it.

Downstairs across the street he saw a movement - a change of shape among the shadows thrown by the sodium glare of the street lamp. Were they onto him already? Damn, he thought. His night glasses were in the van. He waited in the doorway, his mind racing through possibilities. The priority had to be the Nautilus. He could dive from the balcony, swim down and let himself in. He heard a girl's voice, quiet and pleading:

"Alex." It was Cynthia. That was better, but it wasn't good. He saw her blonde hair next to the dark brickwork. This break had to be a clean one. Otherwise whoever tailed him to Gun Wharf would pick up the trail again. Zilin trembled as he realized what he had to do. He whispered across the street. "Come here." And as she drew near to him, "I won't bite you." He opened the passenger door. "We're going for a ride," he said. She climbed in and he swung into the driver's seat, laughing. "Where shall we go?" he asked, starting the engine.

"Let's go to the Cat's Whiskers. Kev's playing tonight."

"I have a better idea," said Zilin. "We'll have our own party." He turned the radio onto a pop channel; the sound was good. "I've got some vodka in the bus."

"I don't like vodka."

"You will tonight." He rummaged in a bag behind him and fished out a bottle of Stolichnaya. "Open it." The girl unscrewed the top. "Now drink," said Zilin as he guided the van over Tower Bridge. "We have to celebrate my promotion."

"You got a new job?"

"I have become a non-person. Captain Nemo." Zilin laughed loudly at his own joke. Cynthia took another swig and giggled.

"Aye aye, skipper," she said. All the time his eyes were looking down side streets for somewhere suitable.

Anywhere would do, as long as it was dark and out of the way.

"Give me the bottle," he said. He needed Dutch courage. To do this he had to become somebody else. He couldn't do it as Igor Alexeivich Zilin. The car veered into the middle of the road.

"Steady, you'll get us killed," she screamed. Zilin saw what he wanted and lurched into a street marked as a dead-end. The van glided over bumpy tarmac; it was beginning to rain.

"Here. What are you doing?" asked Cynthia. Zilin put on his mock-serious face.

"I have this sudden urge," he said, and smiled at her. "I haven't made love for at least fourteen hours."

"You randy old bastard. What sort of girl d'you take me for?" He killed the engine and the music and they sat listening, while the rain fell and the engine clicked as it cooled. Zilin slid his arm round the shoulder of her leather jacket. It squeaked. "Not here," she said and looked down.

"OK," he rallied, "I know a great place." He started the engine and turned the van round.

"Can't we go to the flat?" she asked.

"No," he said emphatically.

"Why not?"

"Because I'm a non-person. I don't exist."

"You're one of those KGB agents, aren't you? The ones that they're sending back."

"That's right."

"I'll come back with you. I don't mind. Secretly I've always fancied living in Russia. Russian men can be really dishy, like Nureyev, or you, you look like Nureyev." She ran her hands over his ribs and downward. "And your bulge is just as big as his." Zilin pulled onto the South Circular Road. His feet played lightly on the clutch and accelerator as she undid his trousers and felt his organ swell under her hand. She played and rummaged, kissed and sighed as he drove along. For Zilin it was both ecstasy and agony. His loins prepared for an explosion then suddenly his limbs were frozen, cold sweat clung to his thighs and stomach as he felt he was falling from a great height into a cold sea.

"What's the matter?" she asked.

"Nothing." She started again, coaxing, blowing, persuading, as his legs drove on and his eyes stared through the windscreen swept clean at each stroke but filling again with the flashing rain. Again she brought him close to orgasm and again the cold sea spread out below him. "More vodka," he said. He drank, she drank as they rolled westwards. He turned right, over a railway bridge, and across a heath of trees and long grasses. One more set of traffic lights. The Volkswagen rolled across the lights and after 100 metres turned right down a tree-lined avenue. On the left were tennis courts and a children's playground, beyond it an empty car park. Zilin knew this place. Behind it was an open, neglected graveyard with Victorian tombs and broken columns rotting under yew and beech. He killed the engine. Cynthia was onto him in a flash, tearing at his clothes and devouring his exposed flesh. Zilin played along. Despite his horrifying task he was aroused now and tore at her clothes to reach the warm, soft skin. They dragged each other into the back of the van and Zilin was gentle with her, unbuttoning her long skirt and pulling the tights over her pale, vulnerable thighs.

"I'm cold," she said. He massaged the white flesh while she held his organ reverently between her hands, then she introduced it slowly into her.

"You brute," she said. "You lovely, great, tongue-tied Russian brute." He lay on top of her, pressing her buttocks onto the cold floor, and coaxed her into a single mass of moaning, yielding flesh. He was there. She was his entirely. Gently, he moved his hands around her neck.

CHAPTER SEVENTEEN

Zilin wanted to strangle her as they reached orgasm. He felt
somehow she would mind dying less that way. But it didn't
work. It was a botched job. The bitch got wise to his
intentions before the event and scrambled for the door. She
screamed and bit, forcing him to hit her on the head, twice,
three times with his heavy fist against the temple. He
pressed his hands to her throat and felt the life ebb out. He
was embarrassed. His masters in Moscow would have
sneered at the inefficiency and lack of style, and his testicles
ached.

Zilin sat listening. He wound down the window and
heard the rain tapping on all sides through the foliage. Cars
swished past on the main road 100 metres away. He listened
for footsteps but heard none, only the pat-pat of the leaves.

He had a plan for the body. For a long time he
couldn't stir himself from his reverie, but he had a deal of
work to do. It would help to get back to his main task and
the less squalid goal of serving his country. Zilin made up
one of the berths and laid Cynthia flat, as if she were
sleeping, covering all but her hair with a blanket. It was 11
o'clock.

Zilin stripped and put on his wet suit. Over that he pulled a black track suit and gym shoes. In a small rucksack he put diving goggles and an aqualung with one small oxygen bottle. He swung into the driver's seat and drove back towards town. He parked the car in Albert Bridge Road on the west side of Battersea Park.

Battersea Park lies beside the Thames south of Chelsea. Its waterfront has a high wall to keep out the Thames in flood. Behind it are tall beech and horse chestnut trees. The only building, halfway along, is a pagoda built in 1985 by Buddhist monks from Japan. When the wind blows, the horse chestnuts sigh and the hanging bells on the pagoda jingle their prayers. After dark not a soul goes there except perhaps a solitary jogger scaling the fence to do a late circuit of the park. There is a landing stage on the waterfront, a long wooden jetty guarded at its extremity by two solid wooden piers sunk deep into the Thames mud. Each is marked by a pair of red lights to warn off passing river traffic. The jetty is seldom used and the public are kept out by tall gates.

Zilin slung the rucksack on his back. He took the bicycle out of the van and locked the doors. As he rode over Albert Bridge he looked across at the four red lights on the wooden piers. Beneath them would be the Nautilus's new home. During one short summer night at low tide he had already grafted a junction onto the wire that powered one pair of red lights. That was to provide Nautilus with power to charge its batteries slowly each night. He had also attached a small, almost invisible wire to one of the piers, above the high tide mark, to serve as an aerial for Nautilus's new cellular telephone. He had only to fetch Nautilus and link it up to its new terminals. It would then be a weapon independent of outside maintenance, nestling in the Thames mud, virtually undetectable unless the river was drained. Yet it could be detonated by dialling 13 digits from Moscow.

Zilin pedalled along the embankment still gazing at the two red lights. It was warm work enclosed in a rubber suit. After half an hour he was at Wapping. He chained the bicycle to some railings, intending to collect it one day. Taking the rucksack he ducked into the alley by Gun Wharf and scaled the wire fence that guarded Woods River Services. Zilin waited ten minutes, listening. He took out the aqualung and air bottle. Then he took off his tracksuit and stuffed it into the rucksack, which was watertight. Zilin waited again. It was midnight. It would be high tide in an hour and a half.

By two o'clock it would be impossible for Nautilus to make headway against the ebbing tide. He would have to move fast. Zilin moved catlike down the wooden jetty and climbed down to water level. He wetted the goggles and put them on, and felt the torch in his pocket which he would use only in an emergency. Then he dived, keeping contact with the wooden pile which he knew would lead him to Nautilus. There it was. He felt the firm, moulded hull, a comfort among all the slime and mud. Why couldn't the English have a decent river like the Volga or the Don, broad, clean and majestic, instead of this muddy creek? Zilin disconnected the telephone and power terminals. He opened the hatch and crawled inside the air lock. Compressed air blew out the water and he let himself into the cold cramped space below. But it was home. It was his lair; it even smelled of him. He sniffed the stale air as if checking for intruders. Then he set to work.

The grappling feet of the Nautilus were retracted. Water was pumped out for more buoyancy. The tide caught the little craft and freed it from its berth. Zilin felt the hull scrape on the compacted mud and rubble. He pointed the nose westward and carefully rose close to the surface. He raised the snorkel and the periscope. Rain was still puckering the surface making it easy for him to proceed under power. If it had been too calm he could only have drifted on the tide.

It was six miles to Battersea. He estimated the tide was flowing at around two knots. He would do the first hour under full power then hope to drift into his berth with minimum disturbance. There was nothing on the river. If it had been ebb tide he might have seen an empty tanker scudding under the bridges hurrying to burst into the open sea. He might have heard the thump of disco music and seen the warm lights of a pleasure boat, but it was too late for that. Zilin settled into the familiar cramped posture, his legs each side of the Nautilus's sinister payload - equivalent to 20,000 tonnes of TNT. Every few seconds he glanced through the periscope, keeping himself in the centre of the tidal stream. He felt hungry. He promised himself a huge breakfast when this was over.

Within an hour and a half he saw the red lights of the Battersea jetty. Behind it was the Buddhist pagoda with a statue of the huge fat god in gold looking at him over the water. Zilin mused whimsically whether the power of prayer could ever neutralize the instrument of destruction that would be lodged so close to it. One thing was certain: if it didn't, and the device was detonated, the Buddha and his temple would be atomized in less than 2/100ths of a second. The thought amused him. He put Nautilus into a shallow dive. The tide was slack now and was beginning to drift the other way. He counted the seconds to judge his approach to the two piers. Then he risked illumination, a scattered infra-red light which bounced an enhanced image onto his screen.

Zilin berthed the Nautilus in the gap between the two piers to protect it from the tide. He deployed the grappling feet and ensured they were firmly in place. He checked again that the cellular telephone was connected to the external aerial. Then he left his watery lair, connected Nautilus to the aerial and power lines on the pier, and swam, below the surface, 200 metres along the shore to Chelsea Bridge. With hardly a ripple he broke the surface and eased himself onto a flight of steps which ran up from the water. Zilin waited. It was 2am. In a niche under the bridge he peeled off his wetsuit, dried himself with a towel and put on his track suit and gym shoes. He leaped over the park fence into Chelsea Bridge Road. If anyone saw him he would look like any late night jogger.

Zilin jogged round the three sides of Battersea Park. The load in his rucksack cramped his style, but the running did him good. The rain had stopped. He drew in lungfuls of the fresh, damp air, pushing at the pavement with long, springy strides. As the Volkswagen came in sight he shortened his stride and marked time. He stopped. A spasm of revulsion heaved up from his stomach. He remembered he would be sharing a bed with a corpse.

Zilin strode purposefully to the van, opened the door, slung in his rucksack and started up the engine. It was at that moment he expected the floodlights to snap on and the megaphone to bark: "Mr Zilin, you are surrounded by police officers. There is no escape." Or worse still he would hear the popping and smashing of glass about him as machine guns opened up. But nothing happened. His fantasies were drowned by the VW engine.

Zilin drove back to where his van would be least conspicuous, outside the Shell building in Belvedere Road. He crawled into the back of the vehicle, made up the second berth and fell asleep where he lay.

Five hours later his eyes snapped open. There was a small washbasin in which he managed to shave. Then he dressed in a jacket which he had never worn and walked across Waterloo Bridge for breakfast at the Savoy. On the way he bought the papers. As he munched through toast and quails' eggs he read about the game of tit-for-tat between London and Moscow. Six more officials had been expelled by both sides. He was glad to see his name wasn't among them. Nor was there any report of his having gone missing. Immigration officials at Heathrow would have recorded that Igor Alexeivich Zilin had left the country yesterday after a stay of only six months. Zilin belched quietly to himself. He paid cash and strolled back over the bridge.

His next task was to get rid of the body. After that his life would be relatively simple; keeping his head low, staying inconspicuous, checking periodically on Nautilus and keeping in touch as rarely as possible with his masters. With a regular cash flow he could settle into an acceptable lifestyle.

At 12.15 the same day, Laszlo's B team, Janos and Adam, were at Gun Wharf in Wapping. Janos spotted Zilin's wires running between the copper lightning conductor and the wall. He dug with his boot a few centimetres into the river bed and saw a continuation. It was enough. Janos shambled off the mud in his tramp's clothes and made a telephone call to Laszlo. Laszlo called Pike.

"Why the hell didn't he cut the wire there and then?" fumed Pike.

"I'm sorry. We employed him on a need-to-know basis. He doesn't appreciate what the wire is for. We'll fix it this evening before we move in."

"Do we know who the man is?"

"Not yet, but we'll find out through the landlord, or the gas board or something. Be patient. This thing's probably been operational for months; it's not going to go off today."

"Do you plan to tell you-know-who?" Pike meant MI5.

"We'll tell them tomorrow," said Laszlo. "This is our show, William, yours and mine." Laszlo hung up.

Pike was nervous and excited. He felt sick with indigestion and left the office to take some fresh air. Involuntarily he was drawn towards the river, down Chancery Lane, across Fleet Street into the Temple and through a wrought iron gateway to the embankment. No word had come back on the Swiss operation. They had been away nearly five days. Something must have gone wrong; perhaps Demirkan had got wind of it. But Pike had scoured the English and Swiss papers: there wasn't a hint of funny business on or under Lake Zurich. Would it turn out after all that they would get to the London Nautilus before the Swiss Nautilus had been blown? He hoped so. For him and for everyone except the Swiss it was much more important. Pike looked at the span of three bridges between him and the Houses of Parliament, the mother of parliaments. Wordsworth was wrong; there were plenty of sights fairer than the constellation of buildings on this stretch of the Thames. But emotionally he was right, thought Pike. The vision of all this being destroyed by one nihilistic brainwave from Moscow suddenly made him determined that not a stone of it should be changed, not even the rotting concrete slabs of the South Bank, a monument to the cheap functionalism of the 1960s. It must be preserved at all costs. Pike now found, added to his nervousness and nausea, a tear in the corner of his eye and a lump in his throat. How could his body perform so many contradictory functions at the same time? It disgusted him.

Laszlo's emotions were rather different. From his Bayswater surgery he was beginning to set in motion an operation that might be the crowning point of his career, even if it also spelt the end of it. Five telephone calls established the plan. He wanted a raid on the flat in Gun Wharf. He also wanted the Nautilus as a prize, hostage or bargaining counter for himself. Money wasn't something he needed to flesh out his lifestyle but since the age of thirty-five he had nurtured one expensive ambition: to set up his own museum of primitive artefacts - statues and carvings from the cradles of civilization in the Middle East and Africa, the Americas and Australasia. He wanted to set side by side for comparison the relics of past centuries and the best of today's aboriginal and primitive art. That was beyond the pocket of most West End doctors.

Janos, back in civilian clothes, called at Laszlo's surgery.

"Zilin," he said, "Igor Alexeivich Zilin. Born Riga, 1949. Member of the Soviet trade mission, specialising in computers and other high-tech products. He arrived in February this year and bought Flat 9, Gun Wharf in March, paying cash, most unusual. He's not KGB at least not on Gordievsky's list. By the way, what's all this about?"

"We go into the flat tonight," said Laszlo, "but first we have to cut those wires - that's top priority. Then at dawn we can send in the divers."

"Divers? Has he got something submerged down there?"

"Something we'd like to get hold of. A miniature submarine." Janos' face lit up.

"It's like a James Bond movie," he said.

"No it isn't," said Laszlo. "It's dull, dangerous and real, and you don't have nine lives. I don't want any heroics. You get this guy Zilin and you take him to the house at Marlow, right?"

"Right, boss." Janos made a half-salute and left.

By mid-afternoon they had a watch on Gun Wharf, two men patrolling the high street and an observer across the river. By 7.30 there was still no sign of Zilin. It was nearly dark and the tide was beginning to flow in again. Very soon it would be difficult to cut the wires. Janos climbed down broken wooden steps onto the river bed. He took out a pair of pliers and cut the cable at the base of the lightning conductor. There was no sigh, there was no protest. He looked up at that moment and saw a light in flat number nine. Zilin must be back.

Janos swung up the broken steps and into the deserted high street. He heard the improbable hoot of an owl. It was Adam with his brother, Peter.

"We're going in," said Janos. "Remember Matyas." Matyas had been kidnapped and killed by the Bulgarians. This was their revenge. As the three of them breasted the first floor landing they found, incredibly, that Zilin's door was open. They saw Zilin in the room with a suitcase in one hand and a portable radio in the other, apparently about to leave. He would hardly have time to reach for a gun. The three men stormed in. Janos hit the light switch to add to the confusion and the four of them ended in a heap on the floor. Zilin was gagged and pinned down. Janos switched on the lights and searched the flat. There was almost nothing there, no furniture to speak of and some unwashed, evil-smelling saucepans in the kitchen.

"These Russians live like pigs," said Janos. "Take him away." In a corner by the telephone he saw the extension lead carefully fed back behind the skirting board and onto the wooden balcony. He saw the two wires disappear under a fresh finish of cement along to the lightning conductor. "Hardly visible, unless you know what to look for," he noted.

Adam and Peter took Zilin down to the car. They made it clear in Russian that resistance meant death. He only grunted in reply. Janos switched out the lights and shut the door. He took the key which was still in the lock and slipped it into his pocket.

In the traffic, still light before the theatres closed, the car sped through the City and the West End to the M4 motorway. From there it was less than an hour's drive to the house in Marlow. Adam drove and Peter sat in silence in the back with their guest, poking a gun unimaginatively into his ribs.

Janos stayed in London. He had to co-ordinate the next operation, the capture of the Nautilus. Sitting in Laszlo's house at 10.30 he received a telephone call from Marlow. The man they had caught was not Zilin.

"Our man left England yesterday," said Adam. "It seems his friend just came to pick up a few things from his flat. He's a driver at the trade delegation and knows nothing. Either that or he's a bloody good actor."

Laszlo had lost his patrician poise and some of his sun tan, not because they had missed Zilin but because they were now exposed to an innocent man, a layman. There was only one sure way to silence him and it infringed the Hippocratic Oath.

"Tell them they know what to do," said Laszlo.

CHAPTER EIGHTEEN

Zilin had a good day. He was determined to keep calm and to play himself into his role as a visiting Polish American, preparing to tour Europe in his camper caravan. He bought provisions for a month, tins of corned beef, Mexican beans, packets of soup, condensed milk, tea and Nescafé. He bought several pounds of chocolate, fresh and preserved fruit in a proliferation never seen in Moscow's supermarkets. All the time, his 'wife' was asleep in the back of the van. He bought a spade, useful for digging latrines, and a dark canvas tarpaulin.

Towards evening Zilin left Hammersmith, where he had done most of his shopping, and drove onto the M4 motorway, heading west. It was a bright evening, with a high cirrus cloud flecked orange by the hidden sun. Zilin drove the van steadily on the inside lane. He mused on the sheer normality of what he was doing, spending a couple of days in the country testing out his equipment and catching the tail end of summer before the days drew in and a shirt was no longer enough protection against the moist blasts of wind. He was going on holiday but, before he was free, he had one small chore to perform.

Zilin was particularly interested in the bridges which spanned the motorway. He admired the graceful lines of precast concrete, the way in which they appeared to grow out of the motorway embankments, and the way in which vegetation had completely closed up the scars of construction - tough, tummocky grasses burying an upheaval of stones, earth and clay. On his map, the area between exits 10 and 11 had looked most promising. He noted three possible bridges, then at exit 11 he left the motorway and headed back east through a network of country lanes. The sky was now dark, apart from a faint glow behind him and the bright point of the planet Venus, the evening star, ahead. Zilin stopped the van in a gateway. He got out and stood with his hands in his pockets, sniffing the dew in the night air and listening. In the distance was the dull, perpetual roar of the motorway, sometimes louder, sometimes quieter but never completely absent. Nearer at hand a wash of wind over the landscape, a rustle in the hedgerow and the squeak of an owl. He had four hours before moonrise.

Zilin stepped into the van again and drove gently towards the motorway bridge. Twenty metres short of it there was another gateway, on the left. He drew into it and cut the engine. Again he got out, sniffed the air and listened. According to his map there were no houses within a mile. The country was forest and mixed farmland, large fields under plough. There was little danger of being disturbed.

Ahead of him the car headlights came and went on their set paths, hurtling into the blackness before them. Zilin was relying on the hypnotic quality of those light beams, directing the driver's gaze firmly at the pool ahead, never to the side, entranced by the dancing red pinpoints of the car in front.

He opened the side door and took out the tarpaulin and spade, dumping them over the fence. Then he took up

Cynthia, limp and cold after 24 hours and let her gently over the top of the fence. He locked the van and climbed over the fence, then took Cynthia towards the motorway embankment.

Zilin had never dug a grave before, but he knew from accounts of murders that the graves of victims are frequently found by citizens out for a walk with their dog. The dog finds an interesting smell. He digs, and before long his master comes up and sees the earth around it has been disturbed. They find a watch, a trace of cloth or worse still a hand protruding from its shallow, hastily dug resting place. But citizens don't walk their dogs on motorway embankments. The no-mans-land of the motorway is left to become a playground for Mother Nature. If he dug deep and carefully enough the grave would never be discovered, except perhaps by foxes.

Zilin selected a site close to the left side of the bridge, masked from the lights of westbound cars. He was confident that the eastbound drivers would see nothing, dazzled by the glare of oncoming lights. He set to work. He spread the tarpaulin beside the site then, with the spade, dug into the tummocky grass.

It was hard to cut through the fibres and the roots, but he carefully lifted each turf and laid it on the tarpaulin. Having opened up a Cynthia-sized area he began to dig down. It was stony: topsoil mixed with rubble from the roadworks and the bridge-building. After 20 minutes Zilin was sweating like a pig and cursing his choice of site. But he was committed to it, even if it took him beyond moonrise. He hacked and heaved at the stones, carefully transferring every crumb to the tarpaulin. He'd promised himself to dig a metre and a half into the embankment. Under the ever-changing glare of the motorway headlights he had to keep telling himself he was invisible, yet his imagination played with him. It told him he'd been spotted, a police car had sidled next to the van and they were watching him, waiting to catch him at the moment of heaving in the body. He planned his escape, a dart like a toreador between the headlights under a hail of bullets. Broken glass and the squeal of brakes as innocent motorists were caught in the crossfire, and then away into the woods on the other side, to be hunted by tracker dogs, living on nuts and berries through the long English winter.

Zilin needed a drink. Remembering the vodka, he stumbled back to the van and felt the broken blisters weeping on his sore hands. He found the vodka, two-thirds empty, and stood with his back to the van, swallowing the liquid. After two gulps the stupidity of drinking it got through to him. He searched for the washbasin in the darkness and bent down to suck at a thin jet of water from the tap. Another sound rose above the motorway noise, the noise of one engine. A light beam picked out the hedges at the end of the country road. Zilin turned off the tap and closed the van door. The light beam bobbed towards him, flashing on the uneven road. The engine lowered its pitch and ran past the van at little more than walking pace. The car stopped right in the middle of the bridge, but the engine ran on and the lights stayed up.

"What the hell is he doing?" thought Zilin. The minutes ticked by and the car sat there, apparently mesmerized by the charge of the car lights underneath. Zilin crouched like a caged animal on the floor of the van. His haunches ached. "Move on, you bastard!" After ten minutes the car moved on. He breathed normally again. After another ten he ventured out of the van and went back to his task.

It took him 40 more minutes to dig the grave to a satisfactory depth. Even then the base of the hole was uneven but he fancied he could fit Cynthia's contours into it. As he put Cynthia in he remembered the gold chain, failed to undo it and tugged it off her neck. Then carefully, in reverse order, he shovelled the earth back into the hole, compacting it as he went. There was some left over. Zilin reconstructed the jigsaw of turfs level with the surrounding grasses. With his fingers he kneaded the knots of grass together between the turves. By such attention to detail he hoped to camouflage the grave completely. He gathered up the tarpaulin around the remaining earth and took it back to the van. Then visiting the grave again he massaged the grass that had been flattened by the tarpaulin, to make it stand up again. Although he was trembling slightly, either through fear or guilt or simply the chill of his sweat, he felt some satisfaction at his ingenuity.

Having loaded everything into the van, Zilin took off his shoes, laid them on the tarpaulin and put on the new pair he had bought that afternoon. He climbed into the driving seat, and drove back to the motorway by another route. He headed west towards Wales. It took him three hours to reach the heart of the Welsh hills and the sort of seclusion he needed. As dawn broke he took the tarpaulin to a rushing mountain torrent, pitched its contents into the river and washed the fabric clean. He washed his shoes and the spade and the inside of the van until he was certain that all trace of Cynthia and the method of her disposal had been rinsed away. Only the broken chain sat in his pocket. He couldn't bear to part with the gold.

The operation to snatch the Nautilus from its berth in Wapping was planned for 1.30am - high tide. Two barges in tandem came upriver from Gravesend. The plan was to fasten hawsers to the Nautilus and for the barges to snatch them up as they sailed past. The submarine would then be winched close to the barges' stern and towed to a safe haven downriver for further inspection. When the barges reached Wapping they slowed down and performed a quiet turning manoeuvre. But instead of the small fishing float the crew had been expecting to see, bobbing in the water close to the jetty of Woods River Services, the hand of a frogman rose from the water, then his mask. Janos and Tibor pulled him on board.

"Nothing," said the frogman. "The Nautilus isn't there."

"What do you mean not there? We found the cable." said Janos.

"I followed the cable along its length," said the frogman. "Down to the terminals. There was nothing. I used my torch. There were marks in the mud as if something big had been pulled up, maybe yesterday, maybe the day before."

"Buggeration," said Janos, "they knew. They got wind of something."

Pike, sitting in Laszlo's drawing room, had his own interpretation.

"Either they saw us combing the riverbank, or something happened in Switzerland. Our friend Zilin must have been warned."

"But he left the country yesterday," said Laszlo.

"Then someone must have taken over, or," he stroked his chin, "Zilin is still here, and he's gone underground."

"Underwater," said Laszlo, relieved to find something to laugh at.

Later that day Pike learned about the Swiss expedition. Fortescue called him at home. He'd just arrived from Ulm having left Richards to recuperate there. Pike had promised to tell Dimock the result of the Swiss venture. They met for a late breakfast at a café in the King's Road. Pike told Dimock how both Nautiluses in Zurich and London had been lost.

"A nuclear scientist may be dead, and a top operator is in hospital in Ulm," said Pike. "We're near enough back to square one. No leads."

"You've been right twice. Isn't that a pretty good record? It must be time to make the thing public and show these Russians where to get off. Public opinion would force them to abandon the whole scheme."

"That's Greenpeace talking again. Tell me, what the hell have Greenpeace, CND or Greenham Common ever achieved in terms of strategic arms limitation?" Dimock didn't rise to the bait.

"We could make it clear to the Russians that what they're doing will alienate the entire human race."

"Since when did that give them sleepless nights? Think of Afghanistan, Hungary, Czechoslovakia. Western public opinion didn't stop them."

"That's different. Holding hostage part of a country's civilian population must be abhorrent to every nation on earth."

"That didn't stop the Nazis rounding up Jews in Europe or invading Poland and Czechoslovakia. One thing the study of conflict has taught me over the years: human nature doesn't get any better. It stays about the same, that is, capable of almost any conceivable atrocity against its own kind, if the circumstances are right." Pike poured them both some more coffee. "Now," he continued, "having established that any lethal weapon or hostile act, whatever its nature, is just as evil, from the point of view of its victim or victims, as any other lethal weapon or hostile act - why shouldn't the Soviets argue that Star Wars is just as evil as the Nautilus project, if not more so? The Americans argue that Star Wars is a defence mechanism. But even if your defence mechanism is 100% effective and it stops a Soviet first strike, are you going to sit there and wait for them to hurl the next lot of rockets? Certainly not. You hit back, and someone's going to get hurt, unless of course, which is preposterous, the Soviet defence line is perfect too and nothing of yours gets through. You end up playing a kind of nuclear tennis until someone misses the ball - then 'boom'."

"At least that's according to the rules accepted by both sides."

"What rules?" Pike stood up. He was angry now, or rather he was too excited to sit down any longer. "What do you know about rules, you young puppy! Waiter!" Pike signalled for the bill but then remembered he had to pay at the door. "You have no idea what belligerence means," he muttered under his breath as he waited for his change. They went out into the street. "It's a licence to throw out all existing rules and the ones that strategists will go on to invent." Pike said goodbye and walked home. As he walked he wondered whether Dimock was a security risk and, if he was, what should be done about it.

CHAPTER NINETEEN

Moscow

The Soviet machine was preparing for a summit conference between its new leader Mikhail Gorbachev and US president Ronald Reagan. It was the same Stalinist Soviet machine as ever but it was moving to a different tempo. Brezhnev was dead, Andropov and Chernenko were dead. This was the fourth Soviet leader in two years. A lot of the old, fossilized wood in the Politburo had been purged. Andrei Gromyko, long-serving Soviet foreign minister, had been promoted to non-executive president. There were strong signs, to those who could read them, that change was beginning to sweep the Kremlin. New ideas not born of fear, and decisions not hampered by guilt and caution, were finding their way through the corridors into fresh air. Already it was clear to insiders that the November 20th summit, and the disarmament talks due to open in Geneva two months before, were not being treated as a routine pageant and puppet show.

Soviet strategists had watched the excitement - and greed - flourish around Reagan's personal propaganda stunt, Star Wars. Military planners were called in and admitted that they had no answer to a high-technology American defence barrier.

"Then we must smash it," said Gorbachev, "with diplomacy." Feelers were put out at pre-Geneva talks in New York. The Americans responded coldly. On September 18 Reagan went on the record, rejecting any Soviet bargains to reduce the Star Wars programme. The Russians, uncharacteristically, kept their counsel. The new Soviet foreign minister Edouard Shevardnadze addressed the United Nations general assembly on September 23 calling for peace and arms reduction. He met his American counterpart George Shultz and coined a new phrase, 'Star Peace'. During a week of discussions they sparred over the agenda for the November summit. Shevardnadze was frank about the Soviet fear of Star Wars - franker than any Soviet negotiator since the darkest days of World War Two. But the Americans were adamant, as reluctant to discuss compromise as a boy with a new water pistol. The Soviet negotiators withdrew to their corner.

On September 29 Shevardnadze came out with his bombshell - a proposal to reduce long-range Soviet missiles by 50%, along with US reductions, provided Star Wars was abandoned. "Fifty per cent of what?" scoffed the cynics. But even allowing for the hyperbole, it was a generous offer. If the Americans didn't respond in some way they would look mean, both to the rest of the world and to their NATO allies.

The Americans didn't respond. At Geneva, Soviet negotiator Viktor Karpov made the same offer, in a relaxed fashion, in English, to journalists outside the US Arms Control Agency Building. Behaviour unheard of for a Russian official. Another propaganda coup.

Reagan tried to gather his forces. He called for a pre-summit meeting in New York of the six biggest Western industrial powers, scheduled for October 24. All but one accepted - France's President Mitterrand. French chauvinism forbad such an obedient response to the American summons, especially as Mitterrand was about to play host in Paris to Mr and Mrs Gorbachev. The Russian pair came on October 2. Gorbachev gave press conferences in English, Mrs Gorbachev visited fashion shops in the rue de Rivoli. Gorbachev approached each of the European leaders in turn, Mitterrand, Thatcher, Kohl, proposing separate European treaties in the face of American intransigence. But even Mitterrand drew a line at such overt attempts to split the Western alliance. The Russian bear, cuddly though he now seemed, was sent back to his corner.

Against this background of public negotiation and shadow detente, a fiercer, less compromising battle was being fought. Details of it were unknown to the two leaders, Reagan and Gorbachev. It was a battle far too important to be left to the politicians, both sides agreed on that.

The British, that is, a small branch of the British intelligence service, knew about the Nautilus project. They were reluctant to tell the Americans. Their first concern was to get the Nautilus out of the Thames and anywhere else in the British Isles, and then perhaps to negotiate on behalf of themselves and their allies.

On the Russian side, the Nautilus wasn't yet classified as a strategic weapon; it was an experimental project known fully only to two officials, Ustinov and Mikhailov. Apart from those involved who knew what they needed to, a handful of people had an inkling of what was going on but they had no proof. During preparations for the summit, Ustinov was asked how far his project had got. "Still in the experimental stage," he replied. "It's of no practical use."

Ustinov was weary of war. He'd been a young colonel at the siege of Leningrad. He'd eaten rats and watched his men die one by one. He'd seen thousands die during the Stalin purges. He wanted an end to war, but with dignity - an admission on both sides that belligerence was not the answer. With Nautilus he saw that chance, if the timing was right, and the correct amount of fear was injected into Russia's supposed enemies.

But he couldn't use the normal channels - the embassy defence attachés and the KGB agents in the West - whose cover was now suspect anyway since the unmasking of Gordievsky.

The fiasco in Switzerland and the loss of Demirkan and one Nautilus made the situation more urgent. Someone was onto Nautilus, but it wasn't clear who. Lebedyev and Romanov in Zurich thought they detected a British style but they weren't sure. Certainly the Americans would have used more people; the Swiss would have made a public fuss. Everything pointed to a team from outside, experienced, but also keen to keep their knowledge to themselves. How in hell had they got onto Nautilus? There was the Swedish accident; there was the Hungarian, Matyas Nagy, but he had been dealt with; there was the lapse of Tikov in Texas. But none of these added up to the exposure of the Nautilus project. Unless Tikov or one of his team had cracked.

After the news came from Switzerland, Mikhailov recalled Tikov from house arrest and interrogated him personally, using a full range of chemical and psychological techniques. Tikov withheld nothing, since he had no reason to. Even Mikhailov was sure he hadn't been the source of betrayal. That tempted Mikhailov to the conclusion, obvious to one of his arrogance, that he was faced on the other side by a detective, a master of deduction of the same calibre as himself - a worthy opponent. But who was he? What were his characteristics?

More evidence came in. Within a day of Zilin in London being warned to go underground, Zilin's flat had been raided and a driver called Suslov had gone missing.

Mikhailov had to assume that Zilin was safe and that the Nautilus was fully wired up in its new location. But there was no way of testing it from Moscow. Dialling the telephone number was dangerous, since it would betray the position of Nautilus and its radio telephone. For the first time, Mikhailov saw the difficulty of running this operation. Too much had to be taken on trust. And where had it landed him? One Nautilus missing and one that couldn't be relied on, even if it was operational.

However, he argued to himself, the presence of Nautilus in London was enough, even if it wouldn't detonate, provided Zilin wasn't found. Zilin was his agent, his trusted companion from the ballistics school at Rostov. Although Mikhailov was now in a position of almost supreme power, they kept in touch, they were kindred spirits. Zilin was the clown, he the dark, cynical dwarf. They had kept each other amused during long winters at the range in the Ural mountains. No one else had shared their particular sense of humour. Mikhailov grinned at the thought of it. If there was one person he could trust it was Zilin.

Then there were New York and Tokyo. New York was functioning perfectly as far as he could tell. Comrade Irena seemed equal to the task, despite his early reservations. Tikov had slept with her - that much had come out in the interrogations. So what? It had probably done her personality some good. Tikov was a handsome fellow; he would have slept with him too if he'd had the chance. Mikhailov read a telex and threw it into the shredding basket.

Tokyo. That seemed to have gone like clockwork. Even if there were alarm bells in Europe he felt it unnecessary to alert Garski in Hatchobori. He was so remote. There was surely no liaison between the European and Japanese intelligence services. Neither side would trust the other an inch. Yet he noted with amusement that Reagan's pre-summit meeting in New York would include Japan, but not NATO allies Belgium and Holland. One thing was certain. They weren't meeting to talk about

Nautilus. They had no idea about Nautilus. But they soon would, if Mikhailov had anything to do with it.

Mikhailov sent a message to the British Embassy requesting an interview with the military attaché. He knew Major Slade-Walker was a fool; that's why he hadn't been purged along with 30 other British diplomats last month But he was a credulous fool, and he would only be acting as a messenger boy.

Slade-Walker came, carrying himself with self-conscious ceremony. "Get in touch with your people," said Mikhailov. "Tell them to send to Moscow someone sensitive and intelligent who they can trust. Tell them he will have 48 hours' safe conduct."

"Which people do you mean?" asked Walker.

"Military intelligence, counter-terrorist department," said Mikhailov vaguely. "Isn't there a man called Brand?"

"Dr Brand, yes."

"Get in touch with him." Mikhailov returned to reading his papers.

"Is there anything else?" asked Walker. Mikhailov looked up frostily. "Right," said Walker and backed out of the room.

Within 24 hours Fortescue was at Moscow's Sheremetyevo airport. There was no embassy car. Instead, a black limousine took him straight to Mikhailov's office. He was ushered in.

Mikhailov sent out all his aides. He motioned Fortescue to a comfortable chair.

"You know all about Nautilus?" said Mikhailov almost as a statement of fact. Fortescue was giving nothing away. "I shall tell you," continued the Russian. He described the Nautilus in great detail, how it worked, what it was capable of, the power of its nuclear device. Fortescue sat unmoved, unblinking.

"What would be your reaction," asked Mikhailov, "if I were to tell you that several of these weapons are deployed right at the centre of some of the major cities of the world?" Fortescue took a cigarette from a box on the table in front of him.

"May I?" he asked and lit one. "I understand I was asked here as a messenger. What is the message?"

Mikhailov laughed. "You British. Stiff upper lip, eh? What is the message?" He leaned forward, picked up the cigarette box and banged it on the glass tabletop. "The message is clear," he snapped. "We have you by the short and curlies." He stared into Fortescue's blue eyes, studying what appeared to be a sea of incomprehension. "We have got you by the balls," he repeated. Fortescue drew on his cigarette.

"Do you mean you are threatening to let one of these things off?"

"We want one small concession from the West. That's the only reason we have deployed Nautilus. One small concession which will even save you money. That is, the abandonment of the Strategic Defence Initiative, Star Wars. The Soviet Union is against the militarisation of space, it's against the escalation of the arms race up an ever-increasing spiral." Mikhailov leaned forward with horrible intimacy. "I'll be frank with you. We can't afford it. Our industry and our agriculture are hopelessly behind and here we are about to spend billions on another tango in the arms race. We both know it's crazy." Mikhailov stood up and his angular frame lurched to the window. "Will you help us, Mr Fortescue, will you help rid the world of this madness?"

"I'll report this conversation faithfully to my superiors, yes." Mikhailov didn't want to let this Englishman go. The more he talked to him the more virtuous and reasonable he felt. Fortescue spoke: "Tell me, Mr Mikhailov, if this blackmail of yours succeeds, I mean without bloodshed, what will you do with Nautilus? Will it be included in any disarmament deal or will you maintain it as a deterrent?" Mikhailov laughed.

"Ah, my dear, you are much too clever. I have no illusions about that. Nautilus is too vulnerable to foreign intelligence. Within six months or even less I predict they would be hounded out of the water, by you or the Americans. That's why we have so little time." Mikhailov's black form was silhouetted in the window. "But one thing will remain, even after Nautilus is consigned to the scrapheap of history. The fear. The fear that any city, anywhere in the world, is vulnerable to a similar device. We Russians can live with that. Sverdlovsk, Semipalatinsk, who has heard of them? But Peterborough, Shrewsbury, Tulsa, Minneapolis - they're a different matter. In your society every corner, every household must be defended or democracy has lost its meaning."

"Our politicians may think like that," countered Fortescue, rising a little to Mikhailov's bait, "but we don't necessarily."

"When the time comes, we can let your politicians know." Mikhailov rang for some tea, a thick sweet brew which came immediately. He sat down again opposite Fortescue. "In our business there are always great adversaries, great opposites. I consider Brand a worthy opponent. He is shrewd, he has great powers of deduction. It was he, no doubt, who directed the operation in Zurich. You know about Zurich, of course; perhaps you were even there. A brilliant man. Every Holmes has his Moriarty, every George Smiley has his Carla - yes, we read those books too. They are nonsense of course but great fun. Brand, I would like to meet him some day." Fortescue chuckled invisibly. Everyone on his own side knew Brand was an ass, an example of the Peter Principle at work. But if Mikhailov chose to canonize him why should he be stopped? It proved he wasn't right about everything, Fortescue drew comfort from that. He got up to go.

"I have a plane to catch," he said.

"Sit down," said Mikhailov. "Tell Brand from me. We want an undertaking from him that Britain will veto the Star Wars project when Mrs Thatcher goes to New York on October 24th or there will be a nuclear calamity somewhere in Britain. And if he tries to find where we have hidden the Nautilus, that's also against the rules."

"Who is making these threats, you or the Soviet Union?"

"You can take it from me; this is an ultimatum from the most powerful members of the Politburo. Not Gorbachev - he's the new acceptable face of communism and it would be dangerous for him to know; it would weaken his negotiating position. But we're going right now to see Marshall Ustinov: that might convince you." They walked down followed by two bodyguards to the first floor of the same building and were shown into Ustinov's vast office.

"He speaks very little English," whispered Mikhailov, "but I imagine you speak Russian." Fortescue nodded. A short conversation convinced him that Ustinov was serious - about Nautilus and about the deadline. He left Moscow that afternoon and reported to Brand the next morning.

VULKAN

CHAPTER TWENTY

London

Brand listened to his tale, shaking with rage, unable even to make a steady pull on his cigarette. There were five days to go before Thatcher visited New York. As far as he could see there were three possible courses of action. First, to ignore the threat entirely; second, to inform Thatcher and her inner cabinet, after which it would be out of his hands; third, to go all out to find Nautilus and neutralize it, remembering the second Russian threat.

"Personally," said Brand to his own inner cabinet, "I can't see the Russians carrying this out. They want to scare us but if they detonate this thing what have they achieved? The antagonism of the entire human race. And they would face British and American retaliation. They say they're against war but that would be asking for it left right and centre." Miles Liesching, his 40-year-old deputy, was not so sure:

"It's not clear we're dealing with the Russians. All we have is the threats of two lunatics in the Ministry of Defence. I think we should confront Gorbachev with the whole thing and throw the ball back in his court."

"And if he denies all knowledge?" asked Ross, the political expert.

"We're back to square one," said Brand. "It seems to me we've got no choice. We've got to find this thing and neutralize it in five days."

"There's one thing in our favour," said Fortescue. "This isn't a KGB operation. I think this man Zilin, or his successor, is alone. And his lines of communication are poor. If he uses radio or any of the usual channels we'll be onto him immediately. So he can't phone home, or rather he can only do so once."

"We're assuming there's only one of these things in Britain, are we?" said Liesching.

"That's a risk we have to take," said Fortescue, looking at Brand. Brand nodded.

Richards had been flown to the RAF burns unit at Wroughton in Wiltshire. Fortescue went to see him. In low voices they discussed the project. Richards had one piece of advice:

"Go and see Pike. He'll have some ideas." Fortescue called Pike and they had dinner at a restaurant near Henley. Pike drove down in his 1953 Bentley, which he kept in a garage and used occasionally at weekends. Fortescue took a table in a quiet alcove and they ate early. Pike told him in detail about Laszlo's operation.

"Should we bring Laszlo in now?" asked Fortescue.

"Maybe, but remember what happened to that young student. Laszlo's network is useful but it has leaks."

"We need the police, the army, as many people as possible sweeping the river," said Fortescue. "I can probably arrange all that."

"We'd be reading about it in the newspapers within a day. It has to be a bit more surreptitious than that. What we really need to do is drain the Thames and leave the Nautilus stranded high and dry like a flounder."

"If you were Zilin, where would you take your submarine?"

"He still needs a power source to keep his batteries charged," said Pike. "My theory is he had somewhere set up all along and when things got hot he just jumped into his Nautilus and sailed there."

"Maybe Demirkan did the same."

"Let's assume that it's upriver of Wapping," said Pike. "According to the marks it left in the mud, Nautilus was moved when the tide was in flood. I imagine it's difficult to sail those things against the tide."

"Could be a bluff," said Fortescue.

"I doubt he was in a bluffing mood." Fortescue planned to get a team of frogmen and ten boats ready for Monday. Maybe with sonar and infra-red equipment they would be able to spot the Nautilus. Some radiation must be coming from the nuclear device - maybe sensitive X-ray plates could pick that up.

Pike left for home. As he drove through the night, he considered the zany possibility that he had mentioned at lunch. Suppose they could drain the Thames. Not completely: it was a mighty river. But if they could make the low tide lower. Since May 1984 the Thames barrier had been in operation. It was designed to function only when extreme high tides and winds threatened to flood London. At such a time huge barriers lying flat on the riverbed at Woolwich were raised, holding back the tide. Now if these were used at a time of very low tide, and water kept flowing down the Thames, then it stood to reason the water would get lower. Large tracts of the Thames by the City of London would be more exposed than they had ever been.

It would work even better, he thought, if we could co-ordinate it with the locks upriver. If all the sluices were opened as the tide was running out then at low tide all the flow from upriver would be blocked off. You could have an almost dry Thames. Brilliant. Pike slapped his thigh. He trod on the accelerator, pushing the Bentley to 100 miles an hour. He slowed down again as he considered the bureaucracy involved. There was the Port of London Authority, the Thames Water Authority and the Home Office. It would have to be cleared with all of them. That probably needed a ministerial decree. And what about the lock-keepers?

Once home, he called Fortescue. They arranged a meeting for early the next day. Sunday.

At the safe house in Barnes at 10am, Pike met Fortescue and two divers from the Royal Marines' special boat section. Pike outlined his plan. The divers were sceptical: they didn't think the barrier would prevent much water coming back up the Thames. It wasn't designed to stop the tide but only to act as a brake. Likewise the locks upriver couldn't stop the flow, only reduce it. The net fall of the Thames from Richmond to the barrier was only about nine metres. But it was worth a try. Anything which might make their job easier was worth a try. They congratulated Pike for thinking of it.

The plan was to use ten inflatable boats and 20 divers to comb the twenty miles of river between Richmond and the Woolwich barrier. The boats would operate in pairs, one on each side of the river, and each supporting two divers. Each team of four divers should be able to cover about four miles of river in the two hours around low tide.

"What do we do if we actually find this thing?" asked one of the divers, introduced as Fred. Fortescue deferred to Pike.

"You go for its aerial," said Pike. "Anything that looks like an external antenna. If you can snap it, the chances are it won't detonate."

"Then do we sit on it and wait for the cavalry to arrive?" asked the other diver, Jim.

"You'll have your radio," said Fortescue, "and failing that you'll each be fitted with a homing device. Don't worry; we'll be onto you in a flash."

"I don't think this thing will be manned," said Pike. "It will just be resting on the mud, waiting to be picked up, like an iron bedstead or a supermarket trolley."

Fortescue's biggest problem was to get the barrier raised and the lock sluices shut. He needed a ministerial chit. The Defence Secretary, Heseltine, was too suspicious, and too career conscious to give such a bizarre order without consulting the Prime Minister - and that had to be avoided at all costs. The Home Secretary, Douglas Hurd, was equally unpredictable, but Fortescue thought of the Environment Secretary, Kenneth Baker, a quiet, reasonable man, who might do it without trying to make political capital. What's more, Brand had been at school with him. Fortescue telephoned Brand; Brand telephoned the minister and went to see him. Within an hour the answer came back. The order would be given, but it would be up to the permanent under-secretary, a civil servant, to carry it out. The meeting broke up. Fortescue went to see the under-secretary at his home in Sussex. Pike drove back into town.

The telephone woke Dimock soon after 10am: it was Anna.

"I was lonely," she said. "I thought maybe if you weren't doing anything..."

"Hell," he said, "I'd love to see you, but I'm not sure it's a good idea, is it?"

"I've missed you." She blew down the telephone. It sounded like thunder.

"If I'm not with you in an hour, I won't be coming."

"We could go to Holland Park."

"Just like the old days." The old days were only a year ago. He put down the telephone and looked outside. The sun was burning through a layer of high mist; it was going to be a fine autumn day. On the far side of the street sat a car with a driver. He looked obvious. He looked threatening. It's the Bulgarians again, Dimock thought.

He had prepared for this moment. He dressed and shaved, packed a few belongings in a bag and went down to the basement. There was a door leading to the back garden. After the usual fashion of London terraces, the back gardens of houses in Dimock's street and the neighbouring street formed an enclosure. There were no exits except through other houses, apart from one alleyway which led down the side of a house opposite. Dimock had spotted it in a moment of foresight and stored the knowledge for future use. Such as now.

He leapt over the low garden walls, raising not a murmur from the insular, Sunday-morning neighbours, and slipped into the next street. Dimock walked through Bayswater into the quiet streets of Kensington. He liked the thick white paintwork of the buildings, the black railings and the well-kept trees. The leaves were beginning to turn autumnal but there was still a summer warmth and vibrancy in the air. Dimock appreciated the parts of Kensington which were middle-class ghettos, the Georgian terraced houses, constantly improved, refurbished, repainted, sold, extended, without ever altering their façades. It was a process of inner cleansing, like Buddhist meditation, but it cost thousands of pounds. He came to Anna's front door. What had once seemed a fortress, designed to keep him out, now looked welcoming. He rang the bell.

"I'd just about given you up," said Anna. She'd washed her hair and still smelled of hot bath and soap. "Are you coming to stay?" she asked as she saw his bag.

"I'm on the run," he said. "I might have to hole up here for a few days, if you don't mind. It's the Bulgarians again."

"Won't they follow you here?"

"I don't think so. I hope they think I'm spending Sunday at home. Anyway, why should they be interested in me? I'm out of it now. I was never anything more than a very small piece in the jigsaw. And the jigsaw's got much bigger." He sank into an armchair.

"What are you up to?" asked Anna.

"I don't think I'd better tell you."

"I'll wheedle it out of you," she said, joining him in the armchair.

"I shouldn't. For your own good and your own safety."

"Then why have you come here? To tantalize me with secrets?" She curled her tongue into his ear.

"You said you were lonely, remember?"

"Well, I'm not any longer." Anna got up. "I've made some delicious soup," she said. "I was just about to have some."

"Where's Penny?" asked Dimock, looking around

"Dorset. She'll be back this evening." They drank soup and a glass or two of wine with some cheese and French bread.

"Shall I make some coffee?" asked Anna.

"No, later." They took their wine into the bedroom and Anna drew the curtains. They prepared to make love, first rubbing the chill off their bodies under the down-filled duvet. Dimock was relaxed, almost indifferent, as he lay feeling the eager warmth of Anna's body. He let her knead his organ into stiffness and play with it like a joystick. Only when she drew him into her and enclosed him to the hilt with her warmth did he feel the urgency and power in him overtake his calm, forcing his body like a steam engine into long piston bursts. They became a single train racing towards a tunnel which finally plunged into blackness, where it stayed, silenced by its own roar. Dimock slept until Anna had to free her aching limbs.

"That was wonderful," she said. "I don't know how we remembered after so long." She made coffee and they drank it in bed, reading the Sunday papers.

"Listen to this," said Dimock, "'As far as I know, no one has yet made a study of men and their socks'. I don't know why we bother to read this rubbish."

"Let's go to the park," said Anna. They dressed and walked arm in arm to the park. They talked to the peacocks, smiled at children in pushchairs, watched the tennis players and a family at football after a heavy lunch. Anna's face had a serene smile. Her body moved and responded to Dimock's in a way that seemed to say: "I am yours." Dimock wished he could preserve that moment.

Later that afternoon they had tea and crumpets in Anna's flat. Penny came back from Dorset. Dimock said he would slip out and buy some wine. He walked to a supermarket close to South Kensington tube station and bought two bottles of Beaune. On his way back, almost on impulse, he stepped into a telephone kiosk. In the weak, yellow light Dimock opened the E-K telephone directory and looked for a number. Miraculously the page was intact. He began to dial, but never finished. The door of the kiosk was flung open. Dimock threw up his hands to protect his head, sweeping the wine bottles to the ground. One bullet planted itself accurately and almost silently into his forehead, another into his heart. Gloved hands reached for the two open pages of the telephone book and tore them out. Blood and Burgundy spilled onto the pavement.

The under-secretary was having trouble with the Port of London Authority. The PLA controls everything to do with the Thames from the estuary where it is 15 miles wide, past the docks, the Woolwich barrier, and eighteen bridges to Richmond lock where the width has dwindled to a mere 50 yards. The hydrographic officer of the PLA said the draining could technically be done. Not all the water would be cleared from the Thames but for a few hours the level above London Bridge could be lowered significantly. But there was a risk. There was a risk of permanent damage to the navigation channels in the Thames, structures which are largely built of mud held up by water. The engineer couldn't take responsibility for what would happen if those mud channels were burst by water gushing from water tables each side of the Thames.

"You could jeopardize traffic on the Thames for days or months," he said.

"I'm not empowered to tell you why the minister wants to do this," said the under-secretary, "but the jeopardy of river traffic would be a small price to pay if the operation were successful. If it isn't, there won't be any river traffic anyway."

"Very well," said the engineer. "Then let me give you some advice. If you really want a good job done, we'll do it in three stages. First we open the locks above Richmond and let down as much water as we can. Of course you're aware that it's low tide at Richmond three hours after low tide at the Woolwich Barrier. When it's low tide at Woolwich we raise the barrier and close the lock and the sluices at Richmond. Then we wait while all the water at Richmond sloshes down to the Woolwich barrier. That stretch of the Thames is no longer tidal; it's become like a reservoir blocked off at both ends, but the water level is still too high. So we wait until it's low tide again below the Woolwich barrier, then we drop the barrier and let more water out. We can go on doing that until the locks at Richmond and above can hold back no more water. We're lucky that it has been a dry autumn."

"How much lower will that make the water?"

"On the upper reaches, quite a bit lower, maybe five or six metres. Down near Woolwich there won't be much difference, I'm afraid."

"Let's hope the fish swam upstream," said the undersecretary under his breath.

CHAPTER TWENTY-ONE

Breconshire, South Wales

Zilin flicked his line over the mountain pool. The stream, in this dry autumn, slipped lazily over the rounded rocks. No fish were rising but Zilin didn't care. He was basking in the stillness of the evening in this corner of Wales, putting off the time when he would drive back to London. Since Saturday morning he had seen no one. He made camp again as he had a month earlier, across high fields at the end of a forgotten farm track, right by the stream. On Saturday he strode over hills, crashing through forests and glissading down hillsides of shale, leaping streams and charging up mountainsides, his lungs fighting for air. Supper was an onion, rice and a slice of pork cooked over a wood fire, with a half-bottle of wine. Then he lay under the stars hearing the distant roar of the forest and the occasional spot of dew on his sleeping bag.

On Sunday he took his fishing rod and caught a fat trout for breakfast. His limbs were still aching after yesterday's exertions but he forced himself to take a short run that morning, with fits of sprinting which took him close to delirium. Back at camp he bathed in the river then opened a bottle of wine and sipped it thoughtfully through the afternoon, tugging mouthfuls from a French loaf, followed by pieces of camembert. Now, a last fish in the stream, putting off the journey back to the city.

Zilin drove his van across the high fields, opening and closing gates like airlocks between the free world and London, where he could easily die. Cart track gave way to narrow road, narrow road to highway and he was soon back in the throng of traffic on the motorway to London. Zilin had no home to go to. He lived in his van. He sought the company of the Australians on the South Bank where he had bought the van. They strummed guitars, made tea, accepted him as a bum with money who was resting in London before taking off for the warmer climes of southern Europe and North Africa. Zilin liked the transience that they offered; every few days the turnover was complete, except for him and a man called Sam who was staying all winter. Sam was in business, import-export: "A little bit of this and a little bit of that," and had decided this was the cheapest way to live in London. "No rent, no rates, no landlord breathing down your neck." He had an office across the river and a portable cellular telephone; what more did he need? "I've doubled my profits in less than a year," said Sam.

Zilin played chess with Sam. It was the time of the battle in Moscow between world champion Anatoly Karpov and his challenger, the Armenian Jew from Baku, Gary Kasparov. Zilin bought the papers every day, following with bewilderment and anger the defeats of his hero Karpov. Sam was a Kasparov supporter, admiring his quick flashes of brilliance, particularly his queen sacrifice in the eleventh game which quickly brought Karpov to his knees. Zilin beat Sam quite easily, but he enjoyed the open face of his opponent - the brows kitted in concentration - and the spasms of pain which swept over it when he saw he'd made an unforced error. Zilin liked to let him win. This Sunday evening was no exception. They sipped cans of Swan lager and played late into the night.

But Zilin had work to do. Every fourteen days he needed to visit the submerged Nautilus and check that all systems were functioning. It was a two-hour programme of checks. If he left it any later he would be caught by daylight. At around three o'clock he said goodnight to Sam.

"I'm going to see my girlfriend," he said and winked.

"Don't do anything I wouldn't," said Sam. Zilin returned to his van, put on his wet suit with a track suit over it and drove to Battersea Park. He parked the van in Albert Bridge Road and ran round the park to Chelsea Bridge. The run helped to warm him in the chill, still night air. When the path seemed clear he leapt the fence into the park and padded down the side of Chelsea Bridge to the water's edge. He looked at his watch. It was approaching 4am. Low tide at London Bridge had been at 00:19 Greenwich mean time - 01:19 British summer time. Add an hour and ten minutes for low tide to reach Battersea: 02.30. The tide should now be flowing in quite strongly to help him on his 400-metre paddle up to Nautilus. He stripped off his tracksuit and stuffed it into his waterproof bag, fitted the aqualung and slid into the water, waiting for the current to take him upriver. But there was no current.

There was no tide!

Zilin trod water. His head broke the surface in alarm. The river surface was as still as a pond, as it should only have been an hour and a half before. He looked at his watch. Digital watches didn't gain time like that, and he'd checked the tide table only this evening. Zilin felt weak with nervousness. He swam to the shallows and lay resting in the mud, his mind racing through possibilities.

Had they closed the Woolwich barrier against a freak high tide? Unlikely. It wasn't the time for spring tides and there was no easterly wind to whip up the water. Were they testing the barrier? That was possible. They tested it once or twice a month but at published times. He'd checked those recently; a test wasn't due until November 14 at 19.45. So what were they doing? Emergency repairs? Perhaps they were doing some dock repairs that needed artificially low water. Whatever it was, it frightened him. He couldn't rule out the possibility that they were searching for something, something hidden in the water, like Nautilus. Should he move it and seek the deep water down river? If he moved it now he would be detectable. Sonar, if they were using sonar, would pick him up just like that. At least Nautilus, where it was, was virtually invisible to sonar, well embedded in the mud between the legs of the pier. His best plan was to stay put.

Zilin slid under the surface again and swam to Nautilus. Soon he was inside its familiar cabin carrying out the programme of checks: the electrics, pressure valves, telephone link, the state of the nuclear charge. After an hour he was quite satisfied. The depth indicator told him there was still about two metres of water overhead. But the water wasn't getting any higher.

It would soon be daylight. Zilin left the Nautilus and swam back to Chelsea Bridge. He pulled on his tracksuit and ran to the van, put on dry clothes and checked the tide tables. It was close to six o'clock, five o'clock GMT. According to the table it should be high water again at Battersea in two hours. But it was nothing like high tide. He decided to drive to Woolwich and see what the hell was going on.

At Woolwich it was an hour to high tide. The great barriers, eight of them, each close to 70 metres long, were holding up nearly four metres of boiling salty sea. There was some slippage through a 20-centimetre gap at the foot of each gate that let water back into the Thames at an average of 25 centimetres an hour. There were also the tributary rivers which ran through the City of London into the Thames, the Bow and the Fleet, but the Bow had been blocked off by an old flood gate, still operational but made redundant by the new Thames barrier. The next stage would be at low tide at midday when the barrier would open again, and a great stretch of the Thames would be emptier than it had ever been.

The calculations were simple. Since the bed of the Thames slopes upward from Woolwich to Richmond there would be a point where low water at Woolwich would be level with the river bed farther up. That point was expected to be Hammersmith, about 17 miles upriver. The six miles above that to Richmond Lock would be completely dry. Four miles below, at Battersea, the river bed, even at its deepest point, would be under only about 1.5 metres of water.

Fortescue and his team were betting that the Nautilus had fled upriver rather than down. They were on the river at dawn, pin-pointing places where they would search most intensively: anywhere where cables or street lights were close to the river, near to houseboats and jetties which could be harbouring this intruder underneath them, or nearby. They pried into disused docks and warehouses, pulled out many old wires and cables dangling in the water. The search proper would begin after midday when the residual water was released.

Ten rubber boats were scouting the river, twenty divers fully kitted sat with binoculars as they bounced along, scouring the water's edge for signs of disturbance, pieces of rope, old bits of wire. It was an operation conspicuous enough to excite the Bulgarians. Two days before, they had received orders to obstruct any kind of search operation on the river. They didn't know what the search was for, but they prepared to hinder it as far as possible.

At around midday, when the ebbing tide had fallen below the level of the Thames, the Woolwich barrier was lowered. In this final emptying operation tons of residual water was drained from the Port of London. Those great landmarks on the Thames, HMS Belfast and HMS President, started to heel over on the mud. There was a cracking as water from the sodden banks of the river sloshed into the central channel. All normal river traffic ceased. River buses hastened to deeper water downstream. Floating jetties sloped down almost vertically as they tried to track the vanishing water level. Monday-morning drivers crossing the bridges stopped their cars and gaped. It looked as though it would soon be possible to walk from one side of the Thames to the other, leaping only a narrow stream in the middle. Great shoulders of mud were revealed, black barnacled wooden piles gleamed in the sun. The very bones of the Thames were being laid bare.

Zilin was at Woolwich. He saw the water dumping itself beyond the barrier but he couldn't decide what to do. Should he race back to Nautilus and try to navigate to deeper water downstream, risking detection by frogmen or sonar? Or should he save his own skin by vanishing completely, perhaps go back to Wales? He couldn't tear himself away from the action, through a sense of duty, or perhaps curiosity. He got into his van and drove back to Battersea, parked in a car park near the jetty and leaned over the river wall, trying to judge the height of the water and whether Nautilus was still covered.

Fortescue was in one of the rubber boats, directing operations. They were by Blackfriars Bridge, approaching the Tower of London. It was a sunny day with only a slight breeze ruffling patches of the unusually calm river. Two frogmen swam behind the boat dragging the narrow channel, listening and feeling. Ahead of Fortescue three men in a launch from the Port of London Authority were taking sonar readings, trying to sort out the shadows and blips on the screen. Behind him maybe half a mile away was a second rubber boat also trailing two frogmen. He was in radio contact with all nine boats on the 24-mile stretch of river.

The helmsman of number four boat just behind Fortescue felt a bullet rip through his shoulder. The next one hit him in the head. One of the following frogmen heard something smack the water. He surfaced and a bullet smashed his face mask, taking off the side of his cheek. The second frogman heard the yell. He surfaced, pulled his wounded colleague onto the dinghy and radioed Fortescue. But he didn't get far. Two more shots left three dead men in the boat.

Fortescue saw the carnage through his binoculars. He guessed it was a sniper in one of the empty buildings on the south bank. But he could see nothing. They hadn't reckoned with any opposition.

Fortescue radioed the control vehicle at Chelsea. He asked for a team from the anti-terrorist squad to search those buildings, and for police to stand by along the entire stretch of river. He warned the other boats. "Look out for snipers, but the search goes on."

When the anti-terrorists searched the crumbling red-brick building on the south bank they were looking for cartridge cases and cigarette ends. But they found a man with a single bullet in his back, dead.

Along the 20 miles of river the frogmen were on the watch for snipers, but they had no protection. "Who the hell are they?" mused Fortescue. "I thought this wasn't a KGB operation."

Laszlo had eight men on the track of the Bulgarians. They were too late to stop the sniper before he struck, but they had spotted two other known Bulgarian cars by the river, one at Vauxhall and one at Battersea Park. There were three Bulgarians in Battersea Park, there were two Hungarians and there was Zilin.

Zilin stared at the shining snake of water winding through the mud. Afraid to show too much interest, he glanced only occasionally at the wooden piers. The water hung flat and still between the legs. There was no sign of the Nautilus; it was deep and safely buried in the mud. Then Zilin saw the rubber boats, two of them, nosing downstream. In each of them, a man sat in the bows, scanning the river banks with binoculars, and another sat in the stern, guiding the outboard motor at low revs. Two black shapes trailed each boat making the occasional splash with a flipper. "This is it," thought Zilin, "they're looking for Nautilus." What would he do if they found it? He couldn't scupper it; he couldn't detonate it, even if he had the orders from Moscow. He was rooted to the spot as if mesmerized by the snaking river. Across the narrow stream on Chelsea embankment stood Pike. He had strolled from his flat to watch the operation. He saw the boats nosing downstream. Through his binoculars he recognized Williams in the first boat, Murdoch in the second.

Williams's boat approached Battersea Pier. It circled the huge timber piles. He examined the wires leading from the two lights on the eastern pier. He let out a shout and alerted the divers. They prepared to dive to the foot of the pier.

Pike saw Williams fall into the bottom of the boat. He saw one of the divers rear out of the water in agony. They must be silent weapons, he thought and raised his binoculars to the flood wall at Battersea Park. There were two men who might have been firing. From behind them a man clad in a dark tracksuit ran forward. He appeared to be shouting. He sprang over the flood wall and landed on the Thames mud below, collapsed for a moment then ran down the mud bank and dived into the water.

"Zilin!" exclaimed Pike. On the flood wall he saw a bloody battle ensue. The two men shot all four of Williams's team and kept the second boat at bay. The men on the flood wall were also attacked from behind. One of them fell. The Nautilus was down there and Zilin was trying to move it, thought Pike. Had Fortescue reckoned with that? Did he have nets to stretch across the river? Pike felt helpless. He couldn't contact Fortescue. But he saw a police car and ran into the road to stop it. The policemen were angry.

"Do you realize you might have caused a serious accident?" said one.

"Never mind that," said Pike, "this is a matter of life and death."

"Now then, sir, calm down and tell us what would appear to be the trouble." To humour him they contacted Fortescue's office. After ten precious minutes he was able to talk to Fortescue on the radio.

"Yes, we're heading for Battersea," said Fortescue.

"I think I saw Zilin jump into the water," said Pike. "He must be trying to move Nautilus, and that has to be downstream. Have you got some nets or something?"

"Get off the bloody air!" yelled Fortescue. Pike suddenly realized they were using police radio; the whole of London could hear.

"Finished, sir?" asked one of the policemen.

"I suggest you go and help clear up the mess in Battersea Park," said Pike. Ambulances, police cars and army Land Rovers were already there.   A helicopter wheeled overhead. The helicopter scooted downriver dipping a microphone into the water at the end of a long wire. A police launch lifted three bodies out of the water and took them to Cadogan Pier on the Chelsea side. Along the Embankment there was a traffic jam as car drivers stopped to look. Pike walked over Chelsea Bridge into the park. There were two dead Bulgarians and a wounded Hungarian. "I wish they'd go somewhere else to settle their arguments," said an ambulance man. Pike judged it unwise to talk to the wounded Hungarian but a little way off he saw

Laszlo in a cashmere coat, exercising a small dog. Pike walked over to him.

"Bloody shambles," said Laszlo. "We didn't know the Bulgars were going to open up in broad daylight."

"Had you spotted Zilin?"

"No, he came out of the blue. Otherwise we'd have dropped him first."

"I suppose we've lost him now."

"Nothing we can do, my friend," said Laszlo. "Now it's up to the British army."

The British army deployed itself along the river. BBC radio described the manoeuvre as a territorial army exercise simulating a waterborne invasion. It was called Dutch Courage in memory of the Dutch naval expedition which sailed up the Thames in 1667 and wrecked the English fleet. "There must be no panic," ordered Fortescue. "Either this bomb goes up or it doesn't. There's nothing we can do to protect Joe Public." Nets were brought up and strung across the bridges at Battersea, Vauxhall and Blackfriars. But there was no telling where Nautilus had gone. The Port of London Authority's launch worked its way upriver investigating every inch with its sonar. Surely the Nautilus couldn't get through such defences.

Zilin felt the antenna and the power line snap as he gave Nautilus full throttle. He had to head downstream although he knew that was playing into their hands. The water was too shallow above Battersea. He reckoned he had 15 to 20 minutes before a full search began. The Nautilus was proofed against sonar, with a soft rubber coating on its hull. That had certainly beaten the Swedes and the best Soviet sonar devices. But maybe the British had something more sensitive. He would have to find a bolt hole.

Zilin took the midstream. He decided to head for Vauxhall Bridge. It was wide; it carried three-lane traffic in each direction. Once the tide started flowing, and they couldn't hold back the Thames for ever, Vauxhall Bridge would be a turmoil of swirls and eddies. But 20 minutes wasn't enough to get there. He decided to find the bottom in midstream, dig in and listen for action around him. Zilin waited. He heard the buzzing of an outboard motor approach and then recede again. He thought he heard the thwack of a helicopter hovering above him. That disappeared. In the distance there was the thud of an explosion, then another, then another, coming closer each time. It was like giant footsteps coming towards him, until each footfall shook the Nautilus and compressed Zilin's eardrums. It must be a helicopter dropping depth charges, he thought.

One explosion squeezed the hull of the Nautilus like a hand on a tin can. There was a sound of buckling metal but the hull survived. Zilin waited for the next charge, bracing himself for the death that he had always expected from this mission. But the charges receded. Zilin launched the Nautilus downstream again. He could navigate only by guesswork but judged that he would soon be near Vauxhall Bridge. At least they would think twice about dropping depth charges there. For the last half-kilometre he needed to use the periscope once. That was the moment of greatest danger. He cut way on the Nautilus to almost nothing. As far as he remembered there was a light breeze which should disguise any disturbance the tiny periscope would make on the surface. He raised it for half a second and lowered it again. The bridge was 200 metres away. Once again he headed for the bottom, to a depth of about three metres. He felt the thud of another depth charge. Perhaps they'd spotted the periscope, but their aim was bad. Zilin sat tight and waited for 10 minutes then inched his craft gently along the bottom towards the bridge. He should be able to tell when he'd reached it, because it should get darker. Another depth charge thudded, farther away.

There was a noticeable darkening outside the forward porthole. Zilin stopped the Nautilus. He wanted to position his craft at a point where the ebb tide hit one of the piers. He bedded Nautilus into the mud and prepared for a wait. It was 1600 GMT and it would be dark in an hour. The search seemed to slacken. There were no more explosions. Zilin saw daylight fade in the portholes until he sat in complete darkness. At around 2100 GMT a torrent of water began to wash around Nautilus, gathering strength. It was flowing downstream. They must have opened the locks again, thought Zilin. Did that mean they were preparing for another onslaught tomorrow? Zilin was scared now. He felt isolated from both sides in the conflict, a feeling enhanced by sensory deprivation - no light, no sound, no company. The ghost of Cynthia began to haunt him, an unnecessary death. Covering his tracks hadn't helped him an iota.

Zilin saw no future in staying in Nautilus. Tomorrow it would probably be found, and there was always the risk that his masters would seek to detonate it, with him inside. He prepared to abandon ship. He had no wet suit, but there was a small aqualung on board. Still in his soggy tracksuit he climbed into the airlock and filled it with water, releasing the air slowly, thankful that the water was gurgling past at a fair pace. Leaving the hatch and bolting it firmly he cast himself loose into the current. After 30 metres he hit a submarine net. It must have triggered an alarm, he thought as he struggled to slide underneath it. Thank God he hadn't tried to take Nautilus any farther.

Zilin found a way through and kicked out again into the current. He was aiming to swim two kilometres, under two more bridges. The water was cold, but, he told himself, it could have been colder this late in the year. After several minutes of drifting he dared to raise his head above the surface, but ducked immediately. A searchlight was sweeping the water. Zilin felt a piece of driftwood bump into him, a large sodden log eighty-per-cent under water, and he decided to drift down with it, rising occasionally above the surface to gauge his progress. The searchlight swept the water regularly. It found the log and dwelt on it for a moment. Zilin heard an impact on the water and the zing of a ricocheting bullet. Then a direct hit made the log dip and tremble. Target practice, thought Zilin, and he dived and fled.

Lambeth Bridge loomed ahead. He surfaced in its shelter and watched the log drift on. So there was no net, at least not on the surface. Zilin was cold; his limbs were beginning to go numb. He estimated he might last another five minutes in the water. But if he got out and couldn't get dry he would be just as badly off. Zilin set off again under water, staying close to the south shore of the river. Beyond Westminster Bridge there were some steps. He was aiming for those. After three minutes he dared to surface briefly. The bridge still seemed a long way off. To his left the Houses of Parliament stood floodlit, dominated by the tower of Big Ben. Zilin was now aching with cold and exhaustion. He lay and floated on his back. If they wanted to shoot him, that was fine. With only his snout above the surface he floated with the current like a corpse, under Westminster Bridge and past the tall building of County Hall. Zilin saw the steps. He hauled himself onto the mud and lay for a while, unable to shiver. Then he dragged himself to the steps - no searchlight, no crackle of machine-gun fire. In the deep shadow of the steps he fought to do what he knew he must to survive. He dragged off his tracksuit and squeezed it dry, twisting it between his clenched teeth and his numb hands. It stank of Thames mud. The night air stung his bare body as evaporation whipped the water from it. Then he shrugged the moist garments back on, tied on his sodden shoes and listened, his teeth chattering. A train rattled over Hungerford Bridge, the wind slapped halyards against the flagpoles of the Shell building. But there were no searchlights and there was no shouting. Zilin slid over a low gateway onto the waterfront promenade. In the distance there were people leaving concerts and theatres on the South Bank. There was a small traffic jam at the end of Belvedere Road. Life went on - the whole of London wasn't hunting him. Zilin stepped into Belvedere Road. Lights shone in some of the camper vans parked there. Zilin selected one van and knocked on the window. Sam looked through the curtain and at once opened the door.

"Hey, Alex, good to see you. Have you come for a game?"

"Yes." But Zilin didn't move.

"You get caught in the rain?" Sam looked around. The ground was dry, he looked at Zilin. "Christ, mate, you look done in. You need to get out of those clothes." Zilin looked around.

"No van," he said.

"You'd better come inside," said Sam. "What the hell have you been up to?" Sam threw him a towel. "Get out of those clothes, don't mind me. I'll find you something to put on." Sam lit a gas fire and soon the place was steaming up nicely. Zilin sat in a towel, shivering, and sipping brandy.

"I was hoping you'd show up. I thought you might know what the hell's been going on up and down the river. We've had the police, we've had helicopters, we've had explosions and boats with searchlights. The territorial army driving up and down in Land Rovers with their lights blazing."

"What does the radio say?"

"Exercise Dutch Courage," said Sam. "But it's not an exercise. They wouldn't do it in the middle of London, not without warning. The traffic's been absolute chaos. And the explosions in the river; those were real depth charges. They've been ruining the banks of the Thames." Zilin was thinking fast.

"Maybe they were looking for my van," he said.

"You mean in the river? Is that why you're wet through," Sam roared with laughter. "Pardon my laughter, but how the hell did you manage that?"

"Very easy," said Zilin, not smiling. "It was pushed in by some yobs, and I was inside it."

"I don't believe it. Where did this happen?"

"At Putney, by the boathouses. You know, there's a ramp down to the water's edge. Well, I was having a quiet supper, ready to turn in after a hard day, when I heard some very loud singing. I looked through the curtains and saw about six or eight youths peering at me through the window and laughing. They began to rock the car from side to side. I locked all the doors and windows and tried to climb into the front to drive away. But those bastards lifted the back wheels, they must have been supermen, and marched the car down to the water's edge. Then they pushed it out into the river like a boat, with me inside."

"Didn't anybody see? Didn't somebody call the police?"

"Obviously not," said Zilin angrily.

"Didn't you wave and shout?"

"I was stuck inside the bloody thing. The battery shorted, so the horn and the lights were dead. I didn't dare open the window in case the thing sank like a stone."

"What an amazing story."

"The amazing thing is, it didn't sink. Not for ages. It just carried on downstream like a beer bottle, leaning slightly to one side. And slowly the water seeped in from the back, where the engine is. I've read about escaping from sinking cars so I waited for half an hour until it was right under water. When the water was up to my neck I opened the door. By that time I was nearly at the Houses of Parliament. Then I swam for it."

"And fetched up with your old friend Sam! That was bloody convenient. Christ, man - you might have been killed. Those yobbos should be brought to justice. I'll call the police." Sam picked up his radio telephone.

"No, don't," said Zilin. "I don't want any trouble."

"You've had trouble, mate. You've lost a van, you've damn near been killed, what more do you want?"

"I mean I don't want any trouble with the police," said Zilin, "for personal reasons."

"I suppose the car wasn't taxed," suggested Sam.

"Something like that," Zilin smiled for the first time. "You're a real friend, Sam. I can trust you. The truth is; I'm not supposed to be in this country. I'm from Czechoslovakia and I was given political asylum in France in 1968. So if they catch me I have to go back to France."

"What's wrong with France?"

"Marital problems. I've been charged with deserting my wife. She's a real French bitch, and her family are blood-suckers."

"Poor old Alex. Women are all the same. You'd better stay with me until you can sort yourself out. It's not much of a place I'm afraid."

"Tomorrow I'll buy myself a new van," said Zilin. "One thing I'm not short of is money." Sam suddenly reached into a drawer, pulled out his chessboard and poured the wooden pieces onto it.

"Right. Set 'em up," he said.

CHAPTER TWENTY-TWO

At dawn the search for the Nautilus began again in earnest. It was high tide east of Woolwich but the barrier was up again and the lock was closed at Richmond. Listening microphones were planted at intervals between Battersea and Woolwich. Launches equipped with sonar plied the river. For the second day running there was no other river traffic. At street level, apart from a small military presence on the embankments, the rest of London was running normally.

It was increasingly difficult for the Bulgarians to disrupt the search, although Laszlo had been forced to pull his men off their tail. SAS units in plain clothes were patrolling the riverside.

Around midday, one of the sonar launches detected something at Vauxhall Bridge: not the hull of Nautilus itself but one of the grappling anchors which wasn't very well buried. This time there was no commotion or jubilation. Fortescue sent a frogman down to investigate.

In the murk and gloom the frogman felt the shape of Nautilus. It was unmistakably an aquatic shape, smooth and rubbery, with a hatch at the top. He fitted a homing device, and a small charge, in case the craft had to be blown up at short notice. But he couldn't open the hatch, so it was impossible to tell if Zilin was inside. After 20 minutes the frogman returned to base 300 metres upriver.

"What do we do now?" he asked.

"We must fit a cradle round it," said Fortescue, "and the disposal squad will go in and try to disarm it." Even at this stage they had no proof that it wasn't an elaborate Soviet hoax. Perhaps when they finally opened it they would find a letter inside saying: "You've been had." But this was no time to take risks. A screen of radio noise was put up in that part of London, in case, as Pike suspected, the bomb could be detonated by radio telephone.

At 2pm the disposal squad went in but were unable to penetrate the Nautilus. The best they could do was feed more interference down the antenna socket and hope for the best until nightfall.

Fortescue didn't want to move the Nautilus until it was dark. The plan then was to lift it by helicopter to a destroyer in the Channel for further tests.

At 7pm a Chinook helicopter with two big rotors swung close to Vauxhall Bridge. It lowered two cables into the water which were hooked onto strong rope netting. The Chinook rose again into the sky hauling a dripping monster from the deep. The Nautilus, trailing its four grappling anchors, looked like a horned reptile caught in a hunting net. But few citizens of London were close enough to see it. The helicopter tilted down the Thames to the estuary and the open sea.

On board the Type 22 destroyer *Glasgow*, a veteran of the Falklands war, the Nautilus was examined under searchlights. The hatch was blown and the nuclear weapon disarmed. The disposal officer popped his head out of the hatchway.

"That was a Hiroshima-size bomb," he said.

It was now Ministry of Defence property. Fortescue and his boss Brand were concentrating on the next problem: was there another Nautilus in Britain? If so, where was it? Fortescue called Pike at three in the morning.

"I think we should concentrate on Zilin; he's the only lead we have," said Pike, "unless we can get hold of Tikov."

"Tikov's been retired, according to our people in Moscow. He's under house arrest."

"Can't we get to him?"

"What would he tell us?"

"The scale of this project," said Pike. Fortescue recalled his conversation with Mikhailov in Moscow.

"I think the scale has slightly outgrown Tikov," he said. "I've got another idea."

"Go on."

"A peculiarity of Mikhailov. He expressed an extraordinary reverence for Brand."

"Brand? I always thought he was a bit pedestrian?"

"Not in Mikhailov's book. We could set something up. A special meeting between Mikhailov and Brand. With any luck we'll be able to draw some more out of him. The man's brilliant but exceedingly vain."

Pike found it impossible to get back to sleep. He'd been sleeping badly for the last three days since the news of Dimock's murder. Anna had said it was the Bulgarians, but how did she know? He had a more sinister theory, based on the pages which had been ripped out of the telephone directory. On one of those two pages would have been the telephone number of Greenpeace. Had Dimock been about to spill the beans to them? If so, and that was the response he got, what price would they put on Pike's own skin? These thoughts revolved in his mind as he shuffled around his shabby basement sipping Ovaltine laced with whisky, his remedy for insomnia.

The Ministry of Defence proceeded on a need-to-know basis. Margaret Thatcher was in Barbados winding up a Commonwealth conference. Her defence advisers in London decided she should be told nothing before her meeting with Ronald Reagan in New York, scheduled for the next day. They feared what they called the 'Falklands factor'. Maggie was not one to keep cards up her sleeve. She played them all at once with guns blazing. If she had such positive proof of Soviet aggression on British soil there was no knowing where her righteous indignation might lead. This time there was no chance her belligerence would be confined to a small corner of the South Atlantic.

Reagan's Pentagon advisers reached the same decision, on less information. They knew a little about Nautilus and were looking for one in US territory. But they didn't suspect nuclear weaponry, and they didn't know the one in London had been found. That was a closely guarded British secret. Why?

It had little to do with Britain's defence strategy and more to do with the embarrassing position of MI5 at the time. That was because of a scandal in Cyprus which was about to blow up in their faces. Seven British servicemen employed in intelligence-gathering in Cyprus were on trial at the Old Bailey charged with selling secrets in exchange for sexual favours. During the 12 weeks of the trial now coming to a close, the case for the prosecution had been torn to shreds and was about to be thrown out of court. In this most expensive spy trial in British history there was no evidence of any orgies, let alone the leaking of secrets. Worst of all for MI5, having admitted to the loss of substantial intelligence material, they could no longer claim that the leak had been plugged. These men were innocent. If there was a leak then it had to be somewhere else.

Given this extreme embarrassment MI5 didn't feel like telling the Americans anything. They held off, in fear of disbelief and ridicule, and did virtually nothing besides extending the search to other parts of Britain.

When Thatcher met Reagan her chief objective was to win as much business as possible out of the Star Wars programme for British contractors. There was none of the hesitation and aloofness that the Soviets had hoped for and expected. She was totally committed, Mikhailov noted with fury.

At the UN General Assembly the next day Reagan reaffirmed US commitment to Star Wars, and Thatcher lashed out against international terrorism. The Soviets' secret plan to undermine Western belligerence had failed, or rather, it had been ignored.

VULKAN

CHAPTER TWENTY-THREE

Moscow

In the first snow of the winter, Mikhailov drove through the suburbs to the south-eastern forests where Tikov sat in his dacha. Mikhailov's car was accompanied by two armed motorcyclists wrapped against the cold. At the dark, wooden dacha nestling among pines Mikhailov refused to come in but asked Tikov to step outside. The two men walked on the thin layer of snow to the lakeside. Mikhailov was trying to be friendly.

"I owe you an apology," he said. "It seems you aren't the treacherous bastard we took you for."

"What makes you think that?"

"Things might have worked better if you were." Two moorhens were fussing in the reeds at the edge of the lake. The motorcyclists stood at a respectful distance. Mikhailov continued: "We told the British about the Nautilus in London. They found it and neutralized it."

"And Zilin?"

"Still on the run. The British have Nautilus but as far as we can see they're not passing a thing on to the Americans."

"Isn't that good? We wanted to split NATO."

"It means the Yanks aren't afraid. Reagan used his UN speech as a platform for his Star Wars programme. He'll sail into the summit next month and win on points, just through sheer ignorance."

"Foreign secretary Shultz is coming over in a few days. Can't you scare him?"

"That's too official; it's the wrong channel. Besides, he's coming too late. No, I want you to do something for me." Tikov felt the long, claw-like hand, clothed in its black glove, rest on his shoulder.

"Ring your friend in America - Tom Stafford," said Mikhailov. "Tell him all about Nautilus, anything you like, as long as you make sure the information gets to the right people."

"But that will blow the whole programme apart; they'll pick up Irena in a matter of hours."

"No, my dear Boris Alexeivich, you're a bit out of touch. We have three Nautiluses in the United States now and we've changed the New York location to the other side of Manhattan, near Wall Street, and the UN. It's much better. Irena had to be replaced. We felt she was too susceptible to male charms. So, we want you to call Stafford and mention one Nautilus in particular which we're planting in Florida as a decoy."

"Who's the pilot?" asked Tikov.

"Lebedyev. We pulled him out of Zurich."

"That's a big sacrifice. I suppose he'll have a chance to escape."

"Of course, of course," snapped Mikhailov, "but remember he's blown his cover anyway. He's no use to us elsewhere."

"What reason do I give Stafford for telling him all this?"

"Tell him you want to prevent war. You want to warn the Americans before it's too late."

"Why can't you do that yourself?" Mikhailov laughed with forced joviality. "My dear Boris," he said, "you understand so little about diplomacy, or rather marketing: I think that's what they call it in the West. To sell an idea you have to use subtlety, and the right vehicle. You are the vehicle. And you are against war, are you not?"

"Mindless war, yes."

"Then you will do it. Of course you're being used. We're all being used by the state. But it's nice when that use coincides with our own convictions, isn't it, comrade?"

Tikov felt a powerful slap on the back. Across the lake it was getting dark. He had enjoyed this sojourn in exile with his family. But he had been growing tetchy. Having been used to a certain flow of information he was nervous without it. Now it was being held out to him again he grasped it eagerly, as Mikhailov knew he would.

"I'll have to see Stafford face to face," said Tikov.

"I'm sure a telephone call will do it," said Mikhailov.

"It's the only way. His wife betrayed me. It's the only way he's going to believe we're not playing our own dirty tricks."

"Where?"

"It doesn't matter. Helsinki, Rome, Vienna. We can meet at an airport."

"Will he come?" It was Tikov's turn to laugh. "He'll come. He's like me." They walked back to Mikhailov's car.

"I feel sorry for Zilin," said Tikov, "being hunted down in England like one of their foxes. He's so hopelessly Russian that he'll never survive." Mikahilov linked his arm with Tikov's.

"You and I," he said, "we are cosmopolitan. We can survive anywhere, from the Amazon to the Elysée Palace." He kissed Tikov fiercely on both cheeks. As he entered the car he warned: "Don't get any ideas about defecting to the West. You'll have plenty of bodyguards with instructions to shoot."

Tikov called Stafford that evening. He knew that every syllable of their conversation would be scrutinized by both sides.

"Tom, can we meet?" he said. "It's very important for the peace of both our countries. I've had an official request to contact you from my side."

"Where are you, Boris?"

"At my home outside Moscow."

"Can I call you back in 10 minutes?" Stafford was taking no chances this time, with his wife or anyone else. He wrote down Tikov's number then contacted NASA security, who contacted the CIA. When Stafford called back, the line was bristling with surveillance.

"Hi, Boris. Where would you like to meet?"

"Can I suggest Helsinki, Rome or Vienna?"

"I like Rome."

"Can I see you there in two days, that's Sunday? St Peter's Square, 7am."

"Fine."

"You can bring whoever you like, but my condition is that we talk in total privacy for ten minutes, just you and me. Agreed?"

"I'll have to call you back on that one, Boris. Oh, just a minute. OK, it's agreed." Stafford was overcome by the moment. "God bless you, Boris my old friend."

"See you, Tom." Stafford rang off. At moments like this, thought Tikov, Americans couldn't control their waterworks. It was the result of watching too many B movies. The telephone rang almost immediately; it was Mikhailov.

"What's this about ten minutes?" he asked. "That smells of conspiracy."

"Ten minutes or I don't go."

"Very well," said Mikhailov. He assumed there would still be ways of tapping into their conversation; he would get his aides to work on it. "I don't like Italy much."

"I had to offer him somewhere comfortable. I knew he wouldn't accept the other two."

"They're Western capitals too."

"A bit different, Ivan Petrovich, wouldn't you agree? Anyway I thought you liked to be cosmopolitan. Rome is a great international city."

Rome

Two days later at 7am, St Peter's Square was quite empty. A few figures scurried into the basilica for early mass. The windows of the papal palace looked blindly onto the cobblestones and the vast circular colonnade. At one side several grey-suited men were huddled round two black limousines. In the middle in more casual clothes were the Americans with what looked like a television crew. In fact it was high-resolution surveillance equipment including directional microphones and a powerful telephoto camera, for lip-reading. Stafford and Tikov met halfway between these two groups. Stafford's nerves were tight. Apart from everything else he had stage fright, although he had been on camera many times. This was different, and he felt out of his element. The two men greeted each other rather woodenly.

"I feel a bit like a Christian being fed to the lions," said Stafford. Tikov pressed his head close.

"You know this is a fit-up, Tom. I would never have called you cold from Moscow. I would never have forced you into something like this."

"That's OK, Boris. You know it is. Anything to help a friend in a tight spot." Stafford brought his head closer. "In fact, we've laid on a little free transport if it's of any use to you." Tikov smiled.

"I've been warned. Anything like that and they'll shoot me down like a dog, probably you as well. So forget it." Tikov put on a serious face. "We haven't much time," he continued. "I'll tell you what I've been told." He outlined the Nautilus project, the Swedish experiments, the Zurich disaster and the London ultimatum. "We, that is, my masters are worried that your CIA have heard nothing of this. Lines of communication which we were relying on to spread the word seem to have broken down. That's why they picked on me, to tell you. An independent source who they think can take it right to the top."

"I think they overestimate my influence at the White House."

"I don't think so. Tom, I'm not bullshitting. I've been involved in this project since day one. It began as exploration, a new challenge for my underemployed cosmonauts. Now it's been perverted into one of the most evil weapons on earth, capable of terrorism on a mass scale."

"Is that what you were trying to tell me before?"

"Shh, Tom. I'm supposed to give you the location of one of these submarines, off Miami, Florida. You must find it to convince yourselves of our sincerity. You know who's piloting it? Lebedyev. Remember him? You never met a more peace-loving man. We all love peace, Tom." Stafford did not feel good; he had always told himself he was a military man, OK, but not a button-pusher. "Are you a religious man, Tom?"

"Mary is. I seem to have lost religion on the way. Maybe it's all that vastness of space. The idea of a god doesn't seem big enough to fit round all that."

"Let's go and pray." Tikov turned round and made pantomime gestures first to the Russians, then to the Americans. He pointed to the steps of the basilica and clasped his hands together, then took Stafford's arm and began to walk towards the church. If they were going to cut him down it would be now. They walked up the steps and into the long, dark nave. Giant cupids the size of grown men squinted down at them. They passed Michelangelo's

Pietà, the broken body of Christ held in his mother's arms. From somewhere in the depths of the choir a single voice sang the mass. Tikov and Stafford sat themselves near the transept, by the great twisted bronze columns of Bernini's altar-piece. There was a scuffle behind them as the two super-power support teams jostled for position.

"I hope this has been cleared with the Vatican," muttered Stafford.

"I think I might surrender myself to a Swiss guard," replied Tikov.

"Now, cut the crap, Boris, is this really what you've come to talk to me about?"

"I was never more serious in my life. The only thing is, I have limited information. I was placed under house arrest two months ago, as soon as I got back from America. At that time there was only one Nautilus in New York. Now Mikhailov, that's the madman who's running the project, tells me they have three in the US, and they've moved the one in New York. So I'm as much in the dark as you. I've told you all I know. But talk to the British; they've tracked down two of the things."

"When you came to see us in Texas, you mentioned all those weird things about loving your country. Was this what you were hinting at?"

"Yes. But I didn't imagine it would be like this. Promise me that if ever I offer you more accurate information, if I call you and say 'Do this for the sake of humanity,' you will do it without question."

"How do I know they won't have a pistol at your head?"

"You'll know. Just promise!" Tikov gripped Stafford's hand fiercely. Suddenly the two spacemen were aware of being hustled by kneeling figures - their bodyguards. It was time to go.

The word spread like fire through the upper levels of the US defence and intelligence agencies. CIA chief Bill Casey telephoned Brand's boss on the scrambler and gave him an earful, accusing MI5 of endangering the security of the entire Western world. It was surely a time when every shred of information about the Evil Empire (Reagan's celebrated epithet for the Soviet bloc) should be pooled and shared.

At a meeting of NATO defence ministers in Brussels two days later, US defence secretary Caspar Weinberger called for unity against a new Soviet threat, although only a handful of people knew what that threat was. He offered the British and other allies a chance to participate in Star Wars development contracts. And in his public speech he reeled off a list of Soviet violations of the various treaties on nuclear weapons. But he only hinted at the latest and most serious violation.

The effect on America and its allies had been patently the reverse of Mikhailov's predictions. NATO secretary-general Lord Carrington, not usually known for his hawkishness, affirmed that NATO was solidly behind Reagan and his Star Wars programme.

Moscow

Mikhailov had Tikov collected from his dacha and brought in handcuffs to the Kremlin.

"What did you say to that man?" he yelled at Tikov. "Did you tell him the Nautilus was a toothless tiger?"

"I told him exactly what you asked. Perhaps the Americans are convinced we're a soft, peace-loving nation even when we put a bomb in their back yard." Mikhailov spat with rage at this comment. He hobbled up and down the room in fury, darting glances at the relaxed, handcuffed Tikov.

"What they need is another Pearl Harbour. That's the only way to shift those complacent Yanks," muttered Mikhailov.

"Pearl Harbour certainly did that," said Tikov, "but it didn't do the Japanese much good in the long run." Mikhailov spun round.

"You're in league with them. I always knew you were in love with Uncle Sam." Mikhailov paced along the gallery of tall windows, incongruous grandeur for this stronghold of totalitarianism. "Do you think your friend Mr Reagan will be happy to sit back and watch two or three cities burn before he gives up his mad science-fiction ideas?"

"Perhaps he doesn't know about Nautilus yet. The news has probably only spread as far as those cynics in the CIA. They'd let fifteen cities burn if they thought it would help them win." Mikhailov liked that idea. He ran his walking stick along an ancient radiator.

"We have to get to Reagan," said Mikhailov. "This is a political conflict. It's no longer a war game."

"Difficult," said Tikov. "He's protected from all sorts of information. Anything that might be dangerous for him to know. Intelligence is read for him, digested, summarized and served up in comic-strip form. That's the only way he understands it." Tikov risked a delicate question. "Does the General Secretary, Comrade Gorbachev, know about Nautilus?" Mikhailov hardly hesitated. He waved his stick in an emphatic gesture:

"He knows everything. He sees everything. Nothing escapes his attention."

"Then Comrade Gorbachev could inform Mr Reagan at the summit, with the help of illustrations if necessary." Mikhailov turned.

"At the summit it will already be too late. We want to control the summit, we must dominate it. Nothing can be left to chance. Look at those proposals we made in Geneva. A 50% reduction of warheads if they stop their Star Wars programme, two decades of military expenditure, blood, sweat and tears thrown out of the window. My god, we must look desperate."

"Or peace-loving."

"Why did we begin the Nautilus project? Because we hate the arms race, because we want to end expenditure on weaponry no one will dare use and concentrate on reforming our economy. That's what we saw five years ago, and that's why, after a power struggle which killed two presidents, Gorbachev was elected General-Secretary. Then what do Gorbachev and his friends do? With one noble gesture, they throw away our biggest bargaining counter, our nuclear overkill in Europe."

"Surely that show of humanity will score us points all round the world."

"Humanity! They don't want humanity from us, the Russian bear. They wouldn't recognize it if they saw it. The Western world has cast us as the villains and expects us to be villainous, even if we throw away every nuclear weapon. Fear is the only thing it understands. We need to appear strong and unpredictable, especially going to this summit."

"You mean we need to frighten the world."

"Precisely." Tikov's mind was racing. He had never been a political animal, had never studied closely which burrows of intrigue linked with which in this rabbit-warren of the Kremlin. He had identified Nautilus with Mikhailov and with the veteran defence chief Ustinov, but he had never looked further into its political background. Who was for it, who against, who even knew about it. Suddenly he saw Nautilus as a project kicked into an appendix and forgotten, a weapon conceived and developed in darkness, the thunderbolts of Zeus forged in a nether world by Vulkan, kept by Vulkan for his own use. Vulkan's allies were the dark forces who had defended this country during the Nazi invasion and the Cold War, before the age of enlightenment. Now with one throw they were gambling on a return to power, either for themselves or for what they believed was the future of the Soviet system.

"I've had a message from Brand," said Mikhailov eagerly. "He wants to see me."

"Who's Brand?"

"Brand is my shadow, my alter ego. Britain's grand spymaster. The Americans are a schoolboy rabble by comparison. Brand is my only noble opponent."

"What does he want to see you about?" Mikhailov ignored the question. "I must pick an appropriate meeting place. You're a man of the world, Boris Alexeivich; where would you suggest?"

"I found Rome very suitable."

"No, somewhere else, somewhere special."

"Perhaps the Reichenbach Falls, where Sherlock Holmes met his arch-enemy Moriarty."

"I want a city - romantic buildings, cathedrals, restaurants."

"Leningrad, Prague, Venice, Istanbul."

"Excellent, Venice."

Tikov was driven back to his dacha. He was still under house arrest but found the security had been reduced; only two guards round the clock and no guard-post at the head of the road. Two days later a black Zil saloon and two motorcyclists called for him again.

"Another summons from the palace," said the driver. Tikov put on his coat, hat and overshoes and stepped into the car. Sharing the back seat was an official he had never seen before. The car set off through the wooded country. It missed the Moscow turning. Tikov assumed he was being taken to Stupino military airfield. Did that mean he was back on the project or being sent to Siberia? The official hadn't said a word. Perhaps he was KGB.

"I assume this isn't a long trip," volunteered Tikov, "otherwise you would have told me to pack a toothbrush."

"Don't assume," said the official. There was something about his accent; it wasn't Russian. They passed the turning for Stupino. He knew there was a road check in fifteen kilometres, at the Voronezh turn-off. Perhaps he would learn something there. But before the road-check the little convoy took a track deep into the woods. A sign at the turning was covered with sludge and snow, illegible. The car stopped in a clearing. The driver walked round to the boot and took out a travelling bag.

"Brigadier Tikov, we'd like you to wear these." Tikov unzipped the bag. Inside were some casual clothes of good quality by Russian standards. Tikov looked at the label on the jacket: Made in Hungary. His first clue. He turned to the official.

"You're Hungarian." The official nodded. "I know you Hungarians are great hustlers. Is this an elaborate way of telling me I've been kidnapped?"

"Da."

"And you're trying to get me out of the country."

"That's the idea. We hope you will co-operate."

"Why should I want to do that?"

"Because you don't like what's going on here. At least that's what we've been told."

"You've been told wrong. I dislike some things, yes. But I'm a loyal Soviet citizen. I'm not a defector."

"Admirable qualities," said the official. "You were under house arrest. Why?" Tikov was silent. "We have gone to a great deal of trouble to get you out. Once they know you've done a bunk the whole country will be on the lookout for you. If we let you go now they'd probably shoot you anyway." Tikov laughed.

"You Hungarians. You think this is still a Stalinist state."

"If you won't co-operate we will have to be more persuasive. In fifteen minutes a bus will come down this road. It is carrying 30 Hungarian engineers back home.

They were going home at Christmas but they've miraculously over-performed on their project and have been sent off early. You will be one of them and these are your papers. There's no need to speak Hungarian, you can talk to any officials in bad Russian, as far as the Hungarian border. After that we'll take care of you and get you to Vienna." Tikov suddenly saw the path ahead of him. He would be a free man. Tom would find him a job and he could indulge that great lust he had for Western luxuries until he was sick of them.

"And my family?" he asked.

"We can arrange to have your wife and children brought out, if that's what you want. But you should think very carefully about that. If they leave too, you have no lifeline, no path of repentance should you ever wish to come back. Without them you can always claim later that you were abducted and brainwashed."

"I *am* being abducted, dammit." The official smiled.

"We know you, Tikov. We know your heart is in the right place."

"What do you want me for? I know nothing. I'm worth nothing to you or anyone in the West. I'm a simple soldier who's been kicked aside."

"Our friends in London say you're important." The official signalled to the motorcyclists. They entered the car and held Tikov down while the official injected him in the leg. "I hoped we wouldn't have to do this. It's a harmless anaesthetic. Maybe later you'll see things our way." The drowsy Tikov was helped out of his Russian clothes into the Hungarian outfit. "Look, we even gave you a toothbrush," said the official. But no flicker of amusement crossed Tikov's face. A blue Ikarus bus drew up at the slushy clearing. When the door was opened, raucous song and the stink of alcohol floated out. Tikov was bundled aboard and the bus drove on in the gathering darkness.

254

CHAPTER TWENTY-FOUR

Zilin had been in Scotland for over a week. As far as he was concerned the trail had gone cold. He had a new VW van. On his way out of London he raided a car dump and unscrewed the number plates of an abandoned car. Farther north he found a disused barn and spent a day carefully respraying the van camouflage grey. He fitted the spare number plates and buried the old ones. Now he was enjoying a second vacation. The Highland glens were shot with the red and gold of autumn leaves and dying bracken. The lone tourist was no more conspicuous than a thousand other admirers of the Scottish landscape.

In London the trail was hotting up. Zilin's first van, abandoned in Battersea Park, was picked up by Special Branch. There was nothing Zilin could have done about that - the police examined all vehicles at the scene of the Battersea shooting. They found a wet suit and a book of tide tables - that was enough to connect the van with Zilin. But the police weren't interested in finding Zilin; they were more anxious to pin charges on Bulgarian diplomats and the wounded Hungarian.

Fortescue's team took over the van and examined it for any clues that might lead to Zilin. Among other things they found some blond hair in the bedclothes, and a broken gold chain carefully hidden in a jar of talcum powder. There was a large black tarpaulin and a spade, both washed clean.

The van's previous owners were traced to Australia. They described where and how they had sold it, although they had little to add about Zilin. One of Fortescue's men, Preston, visited the Belvedere Road on the chance that someone remembered the van. At this time of year there were only a handful of vans parked there. Numbers had been further reduced by one of the traffic wardens' periodic raids.

"Try Sam, he's been here longest. He'll be back in the evening. Want to buy a van?" said one helpful owner. That was Preston's lucky break. He called on Sam in the evening.

"Do you know a man called Zilin?" he asked. "Dark, clean-shaven, about five foot nine."

"Come in," said Sam," and close the bloody door. It's freezing out there. Would you like a beer?" Preston climbed in and accepted a beer.

"Can't say I know anyone by that name," said Sam.

"He bought a van here about two months back, PGL 754X. I thought he might have stuck around for a while."

"Wait a minute." Sam hooted with laughter. "As far as I know that van's at the bottom of the Thames. You're not the law, are you?"

"Not exactly."

"I don't want to get this man into trouble. He's a nice guy and all he wants is a little peace and quiet."

"You know him, then?"

"Knew him. He's vanished. Did a bunk about a week ago, wouldn't say where he was going. He bought himself a new van and vanished. 'I'll send you a postcard, Sam,' he said. It was a terrible business with those yobboes though. I suppose you've fished the van out and want to know who owns the bloody thing."

"We didn't fish it out. It was abandoned in Battersea Park."

"Someone else must have fished it out then."

"Listen Sam, nobody fished it out. This guy wasn't telling you the truth. He's called Zilin and he's extremely dangerous. He's a spy. Now forget about this van-in-the-Thames story and tell me exactly what you know. I think you could be a great help."

"Are you MI5 or something?"

"Something like that." Sam was able to fill in details of Zilin's last night in London, of some of his nocturnal habits and his interest in chess. But he couldn't say who had sold Zilin his new van.

"At least we know what he's driving," said Fortescue. "It also means he's still likely to be in this country. If he'd planned to leave he wouldn't have bought a car with UK number plates."

"How do you know they're UK plates?" said Preston.

"You're right. We don't. Damn and blast!"

In the meantime the police were investigating the disappearance of a girl from West Norwood. Her girlfriends mentioned a dark foreigner with a motorbike. Enquiries among the biking community revealed that the bike was a new 750 cc Kawasaki. Kawasaki owners were investigated until the police stumbled on the mystery of the Kawasaki bike abandoned at Wapping. Neighbours explained that it had belonged to a previous tenant at Gun Wharf, a quiet foreigner. The link was established with Zilin.

Fortescue received a call from Special Branch: "I wonder if we could re-examine the van which belonged to Mr Zilin. We're trying to trace a missing telephonist. You've probably read about it in the papers. It's just routine."

Forensic tests on the van revealed more than just a blond hair and a broken gold chain. There were fingerprints, even a broken fingernail which matched the missing girl. It looked like an abduction. Sam couldn't remember seeing Zilin with any girlfriends although he had mentioned them. "I thought he was like me, just bragging about women but not really having any," said Sam, "so I didn't enquire too deeply."

The police decided to launch a full-scale murder hunt.

They called the news media and released a photograph of Zilin. If he was still in Britain, things would soon get hot for him.

Venice

The water taxi glided through the arsenal of the once glorious Venetian navy. On each side were great humped boathouses overgrown with weeds. Some housed a few modern grey-clad patrol boats, and from the gloomy interiors came the flashes of welding lamps. The towers and domes of Venice behind were bleached by mist.

As the taxi shot through the northern entrance of the Arsenal into the Lagoon, Brand reluctantly put away his guide books, his Ruskin and his Hugh Honour, and concentrated on the job in hand. Of course he was flattered by the suggestion that he should meet Mikhailov. Fortescue had prepared the ground well. Mikhailov's choice of venue had excited not only Brand but his wife Hilary who had decided this morning to see the paintings at the Accademia.

Brand's water taxi was bound for Torcello, a small island half an hour to the north, past the cemetery island of San Michele, and Murano, famous for its glassworks (Hilary had made him promise to buy some glass on the way back). Apart from an eleventh century cathedral with some fine Byzantine mosaics, Torcello is famous for one thing, the Locanda Cipriani. It was the lure of good food and not old stones which had prompted Mikhailov to choose this setting for what he saw as a historic meeting. He was there already, having taken the public vaporetto, and was pacing up and down, unsure which table to choose. It was too cold to sit outside on this early November day and the restaurant was empty, apart from three waiters and a family talking quietly in one corner.

Mikhailov was accompanied by three agents. They had arrived the day before to check the arrangements and they stood at the three exits of the room eyeing the waiters with contempt. The contempt was mutual; yesterday the three Russians had eaten a sumptuous meal at the restaurant and in accordance with Soviet custom left no tip. The service had not been of the usual high standard, perhaps because two of the waiters had only rudimentary catering skills; they were, in fact, British agents. Not even Brand was aware of that : Fortescue had felt it might cramp his style.

For Brand it was something of a triumphal progress to Torcello. After all he, or his department, had thwarted Mikhailov's efforts to split the Western alliance. The Nautilus had been found before it could disrupt the Western summit in New York. With that, and the Zurich fiasco, Britain had won two rounds. Brand felt he would be able to negotiate a deal from a position of strength: perhaps the disbanding of Nautilus in return for certain concessions on Cruise missiles. If they worked out an agreement in principle the details could still be settled in time for signing at the Geneva summit. For Brand that could mean an OBE and even, he dared to think, a discreet knighthood after retirement. Hilary had made it clear she expected a title to compensate for years of stilted pillow talk.

Brand's water taxi nosed down a narrow canal almost as far as the restaurant. He got out, glanced at the cathedral looming in the mist, and ducked into Cipriani's. He recognized Mikhailov from a bad photograph on file in London. Mikhailov rose on his stick to greet him and they chose a table close to the garden and its vine-hung terrace.

"A small aperitif, Mr Brand?" suggested Mikhailov. Brand ordered a Campari and soda; Mikhailov had nothing.

"Who are those people over there?" asked Brand indicating the three Russians.

"They are my bodyguards. Now that you've arrived and haven't ambushed me I can send them away." He clicked his fingers and they shuffled through a door. "You came alone?"

"I thought that was the arrangement," said Brand tetchily. Mikhailov laughed.

"Maybe after this meeting we shall trust each other more. Since you invited me out of the blue I was naturally a little suspicious." Brand sipped his Campari nervously. "Why have you brought me here?" asked Mikhailov angrily. "Have you anything new to say?"

"Today is the second of November. Ten days ago, according to your schedule, the centre of London should have been ripped apart by a nuclear bomb. What went wrong?"

"You are confusing ends with means. The intention wasn't to blow up London; it was to make you see the futility of developing sophisticated long-range weapons. You were sent running about like angry bees, not because an army was advancing, or because two hundred warheads were pointing at you from east of Berlin, but because of a little barrel in your own backyard. Your ally Mr Reagan is trying to prove the futility of war by developing an impenetrable defence network. We have proved the futility of war by showing that there is always a way round."

"You've proved nothing. It didn't work, did it? All you proved was that Soviet technology is inferior. When it comes to the crunch it doesn't deliver."

"We could have detonated that weapon at any time. We chose not to. It was a demonstration for the benefit of our friends the British. We would like to save you money by dissuading your leaders from committing billions of dollars to defence research. You don't have to. We've done all the research. You now have in your hands a prototype for one of the cheapest defence systems in the world. And of course with British technology you should be able to improve on it a hundred times."

"I don't get it," said Brand. "Are you suggesting we should now adopt Russian methods and develop one of these despicable weapons ourselves?"

"It could be the new fashion. Wouldn't you like to be in at the start?"

"I'd like to remind you that we have a commitment to our own programmes. As for Star Wars, it's not likely to be that expensive for us; the Americans are paying for most of it."

"So it won't even be your system. They'll pick your brains and let you build little bits of it, but never allow you to sit at the controls. Never before has the term client state been so well applied to one of America's allies."

"What about the Warsaw Pact?"

"That cannot be compared with the Western alliance," said Mikhailov. "It's in a political and economic mess, I admit. If the West could see the extent of the mess it would realize the Soviet Union cannot possibly have aggressive ambitions in the rest of the world."

"I suppose you would have said that before you invaded Hungary, Czechoslovakia, Cuba, Angola." Brand was getting excited now. "What about Afghanistan?" Mikhailov loathed this simplistic hurling of names. He had expected better things from Brand.

"Shall we order?" he said. Brand had come here to draw the Russian out and to get an idea of the Soviets' next move, but he was losing his cool. He looked down the handwritten Italian menu, trying to fix his mind on food while Mikhailov chose lobster followed by spaghetti and then swordfish. "It won't be as good as the Black Sea variety," he said, "but I have to admit few Georgian wines can match a good Barolo."

"I'll have the same," said Brand impatiently. "Let's get to the point. You would like to see the whole world patrolled by these nuclear squibs so that if anyone steps out of line he has to reckon with someone, somewhere pressing a little button which will blow him and half his country sky high."

"President Reagan has signalled the end of the inter-continental ballistic missile as a deterrent. I - we - are simply trying to re-establish the status quo, the nuclear balance of power."

"Have you offered one of these things to the Americans?"

"Not yet, but I will." The first course arrived, and the Barolo. The two men drank each other's health. "You know, Mr Brand," continued Mikhailov, "I had a completely different view of you - the brains behind British intelligence; the sharp wit, the inexorable brilliance of the chess-player."

"Bridge is my game, actually."

"I was completely wrong. You hide your intellect in the traditional British way, behind a camouflage of mental flabbiness and emotional armour-plating."

"That sounds like a thinly-veiled insult," said Brand. "But I don't mind, as long as it keeps you happy." His shoulders shrugged with forced mirth.

"On the contrary," said Mikhailov, "it probably shows that our agents tend to over-estimate the opposition."

"The fact that I got a double first at Cambridge cuts no ice with you, I suppose."

"You are in the wrong profession, Mr Brand."

"I wanted to be a theatre-critic."

"But since, unlike boxers or chess-players, we cannot choose who our opponents are I want to discuss a compromise with you. The English like compromises." Mikhailov sucked fiercely at a crayfish claw.

"I think you'll find we drive a pretty hard bargain," said Brand.

"We Russians have enormous respect for the British. Not the average British socialist - he's a spineless individual. They're an embarrassment when they come to Moscow, whining about brotherhood and human rights. No, I mean the British ruling class. They have somehow managed to hoodwink the masses into believing they live in a democracy, when you and I know that it is the world's most advanced form of repression. You're accountable only if you get caught. We shoot embezzlers and economic criminals; you give them knighthoods."

"The Soviet system wouldn't survive without corruption, privilege and a black economy, and you know it."

"Precisely, Mr Brand. But you are the masters, the PhDs in this business; we are merely apprentices. The City and Parliament are the fountainhead of tyranny and institutionalized crime."

"Very pretty. But what are you leading up to?"

"A wind of change is blowing through the Soviet Union. The old cobwebs of Marxism and Leninism, all that claptrap which clutters the brains of the Euro-communists, is being blown away. To go through this great change the Soviet Union needs support from its neighbours, and a guarantee of peace. We are prepared to buy that peace at almost any price. But we don't believe the Americans have the mentality to accept such an idea. Their president is an old gunfighter. The British on the other hand are a pragmatic people. Even Margaret Thatcher, beneath that mask of bigotry, is an intelligent woman, interested in political survival." Mikhailov put his hand on Brand's. "The Soviet Union needs Britain. The influence that your country could wield in helping to shape the new Soviet Union is inestimable. The benefits in terms of trade and technology transfer should make your head spin, Mr Brand. The greatest mercantile and scientific nation in history would find itself with a new partner, and a new lease of life. Our two peoples are closer than you think."

"What's the price?"

"What do you mean?"

"For all this sudden display of friendship. We'd be crucified by the Americans and our European allies, not to mention the Japanese." Mikhailov laughed. He deftly twisted his fork and shovelled in a bunch of spaghetti.

"No one is expecting you to be Christian martyrs. But think of the value to your government and the way it spends its revenues if you knew the world was a safe place. All the high-tech development could be directed to economic goals instead of military ones. Of course you would still need a small conventional force to fight your Falklands wars, but…"

"Exports of such arms to you would more than pay for their development, is that what you're saying? I don't think you've taken into account my country's deep hatred of totalitarian regimes. That's what World War Two, the Korean War and the Cold War were all about."

"Passing fashions. In terms of human history such phases are as short-lived as the miniskirt or Dixieland jazz. Anyway, the dynamics should appeal to you. After all, we're talking about a reform of the Soviet system towards more Western models." Mikhailov took a gulp of wine. "You stretched out the hand of friendship to the Chinese after 1978."

"Within limits."

"Why not to us?"

"We've had enough trouble persuading the British public to give Botha a chance to reform South Africa, and we're supposed to be on their side."

"But the difference here is that there will be tangible results; orders for British steel, coal, oil, ships, microchips, cars." Brand's mouth began to water. If there was one thing Conservative governments knew how to reward it was services to industry. Maybe Hilary would have her knight in shining armour after all. He imagined what the French would do if the Soviets made them such an offer - take it like a shot.

"Why haven't you asked the French? They're much more pragmatic in this way than we are."

"Alastair," said Mikhailov, "may I call you Alastair? It's a question of culture and pedigree. We Russians are terrible snobs. In the last analysis do you choose the flashy Citroën or the Rolls-Royce?"

"I imagine you pick the one you can afford."

"We can afford the Rolls-Royce." Mikhailov looked deeply into Brand's eyes as if to ask: "Do you understand me?" Brand wasn't sure. He looked into the bottom of his glass. The civil service pension wasn't the stuff dreams are made of - not mink coats and holidays in the Bahamas. However, he reminded himself, Cambridge had suffered enough as a breeding ground of Soviet moles and fellow-travellers; he wasn't going to add to its woes. But the knighthood...

"Suppose I were to agree with you," said Brand, "and had this great urge, as you do, to convert the Soviet Union. What are you expecting me to do?"

"You're a very influential man, Mr Brand. I think a word from you would have an enormous effect on the policy of your country towards us."

"You flatter me." Mikhailov waved his hand impatiently.

"I don't mean in terms of summits and state visits, but behind the scenes. A gradual veering away from confrontation. The end of petty embargoes on information and technology. Co-operation at the most secret level on defence, for our mutual economic benefit and safety."

"It sounds too good to be true." It is, and you are a fool, thought Mikhailov. I would very much like to sever your head from your body with one blow of the patriotic sickle. He smiled as the swordfish arrived, smoking on a bed of rice. Brand had no appetite now, his stomach churning with the possibilities crowding into his dull, frustrated life. Quickly he rummaged in his jacket pocket and crammed an indigestion pill into his mouth. "No more wine," he said, "just mineral water."

Outside, the winter evening was already drawing in. They ordered coffee and Mikhailov a Sambuca which arrived aflame, in a narrow glass.

They shared Brand's water taxi across the lagoon to Venice. As they approached the Grand Canal, Brand thought of his wife waiting at the Gritti Palace. He remembered his promise to buy some glass and swore inwardly.

As they parted on the quay Mikhailov handed him a package.

"For Mrs Brand," he said. "I know she has excellent taste." Brand knew she had execrable taste.

Hilary was delighted with her owl made of Murano glass, weighing about a kilogramme. That night, as Brand lay awake, he thought about that brilliant young Russian risking his career, working on the other side - just as he was - for a safer world.

CHAPTER TWENTY-FIVE

It was now November 4, fifteen days before the summit. It was the day the Dutch government signed an agreement to allow Cruise missiles into Holland. It was the start of US Secretary of State George Shultz's two-day visit to Moscow.

Mikhailov, fresh back from Venice, received two members of Shultz's entourage, minor CIA officials.

"Have you come to talk about Jewish emigrants?" asked Mikhailov. "That's all you Americans seem to be interested in. I, myself, am a Jew."

"No," said Lovell, one of the Americans, "we've come to discuss violations of the nuclear non-proliferation treaty to which your country is a signatory."

"Anything specific?"

"It concerns what you call Nautilus. We have information that there are three of these weapons in American territory."

"Brigadier Tikov told you so."

"We have been slow to respond only because there are limited channels open to us."

"Why doesn't your secretary of state raise the matter with Mr Shevardnadze?"

"That's impossible. Between us, he doesn't know about it." Mikhailov smiled to himself. He knew Shevardnadze didn't know, either.

"Does this mean," asked Mikhailov, "that you are choosing to ignore the threat, hoping it will go away?"

"On the contrary: we are empowered to warn you that if one of these weapons is found on American territory the Pentagon will retaliate in the strongest way, that is, with a nuclear strike on a Soviet city of more than 100,000 population."

"Your allies the British didn't respond in this way."

"The British are in a funk. But we know how to handle super-power aggression."

"You realize that could mean total nuclear war."

"It's a risk we have to take. Our intelligence tells us that the last thing Gorbachev wants right now is any kind of war to disturb his economic reforms. He's looking for a deal on Afghanistan."

"Who is Gorbachev when it comes to total war?" asked Mikhailov. "That's when the defenders of Mother Russia take over."

"The defenders of Mother Russia are dying of old age."

"Don't count on it." Mikhailov began to pace up and down the room. "So, this is the American response to what we regard as a weapon of peace. It's a device which could reduce the scale of an army to one small sentinel in the enemy camp. You talk of deterrents; this is the ultimate deterrent - something that cannot possibly be used except in an act of desperation that would bring a nuclear holocaust thundering on our heads. But you Americans misread the rules of the game - you treat the simple presence of these things as an act of war. It is not. You will come to understand that it is a gift of friendship."

"Yeah. Like the Trojan Horse was a gift of friendship."

"We can even give you one. Put it in Odessa, or Leningrad, wherever you like and feel free to press the button if you think it will give you a strategic advantage. Look, Tikov told you there is one lying off Florida right now. Take it and use it yourselves."

The two Americans looked at each other. Lovell was beginning to understand that this project wasn't part of overall Soviet defence strategy - it was the product of a single sick mind. When he got home he would recommend the assassination of Mikhailov.

"We'll think about what you say," said Lovell, and the Americans left.

VULKAN

CHAPTER TWENTY-SIX

The city of Tokyo has turned its back on the water which laps its south-western side. The waterfront has become a convenient wasteland on which to dump railway lines, subways, highways, monorail viaducts and other necessary mass-transport systems. It is ugly and functional. Yet for the waterborne explorer there is a labyrinth of canals and channels around Tokyo Harbour reaching deep into the city, in some places within a kilometre of the Imperial Palace itself.

These canals can be sealed by great floodgates if the water in Tokyo Bay rises too high, but normally there is no obstacle for small boats to nose in and moor close to the heart of the city. There are also many houses backing onto the canals, and many of them have crude jetties or landing stages jutting into the water.

Hatchobori is a district of no particular interest except that it has one of these canals, and is next door to the city's smartest shopping street and the stock exchange. In London or Paris that would mean tall mansions, high railings and smart pavements but Hatchobori, like most of earthquake-prone Tokyo, is a jumble of two storey houses built right on the street, strung together by a network of narrow alleys and a spider's web of power and telephone cables.

A coded message down one of those tangled telephone wires would have had the power to blow up a large section of inner Tokyo, leaving it much like the pictures of Hiroshima and Nagasaki, an image already burned into the memory of most Japanese, and creating another generation of maimed and suffering victims. For in Hatchobori there was a Nautilus.

Close to a dog-leg in the canal and not far from Tokyo's Holiday Inn Hotel, a small three-storey house with a wooden jetty at the rear had been smartened up and made into the offices of Engineering Research International Consultants. The company had been set up a year ago by a bright young European, Pete Garski. True, the office was in an odd corner of Tokyo, he admitted, but the rent was cheap and it was close to the subway, the Holiday Inn and Tokyo City Air Terminal. To prove his faith in the place he lived on the premises. And he ran the Nautilus.

About once a fortnight, on a dark night, Garski put on a wet suit and breathing equipment and quietly let himself into the canal from his private jetty. He swam down to examine Nautilus and test its systems, particularly the health of its nuclear device. Apart from his hair-raising journey bringing the Nautilus in through Tokyo Harbour, there had been no scares and no hitches. His only contact with Moscow was a monthly call from some part of the world, always a different one, to check the telephone link.

Garski avoided contact with other East Europeans. He held a Dutch passport. He avoided most foreigners altogether, apart from the occasional bout of business entertainment. The Soviet Embassy and KGB were unaware of his existence.

It was ironic then that a KGB scare should have led to problems for Garski. In July, Tokyo's Metropolitan Police Department hauled in the Tass news agency correspondent for questioning. Konstantine Preobrazhenski was suspected of working for the KGB, running a Chinese agent and collecting information on China and Japan. The questioning was friendly since the espionage didn't appear defence-related and Preobrazhenski was allowed to spend the night at home. He lost no time, however, in catching the next Aeroflot flight to Moscow.

There were red faces in Japan's Public Security Intelligence Agency. Since one suspect had got away, they needed another. The Metropolitan Police Department was asked to run a check on all Soviet bloc diplomatic and commercial staff operating in Tokyo. The MPD found it easier for its computer to run through its entire register of foreign names, picking out the funny, Russian-sounding ones. The computer threw up around two hundred odd-sounding names, but Takeshi Yamada, the PSIA's director-general, wanted something odd-ball, not the conventional embassy or trade mission intelligence officer.

"Garski, Engineering Research International Consultants. What does he do, I wonder. We can probably accuse him of a little harmless industrial espionage, something to keep our masters happy." The PSIA began a quiet watch on the house in Hatchobori. When that yielded nothing two agents were sent in at the weekend to search the premises. They were looking for papers and drawings but also any special equipment. They searched the flat upstairs and found Garski's wet suit and breathing apparatus, also some charts of Tokyo Harbour. Did this man go diving for pleasure in Tokyo Harbour? One of the agents, Miyabe, visited the back of the house to see if there were any signs of a boat. There was nothing. But he noticed a cable, carefully hidden and painted with creosote leading into the water. He put his hand in, but the cable extended beyond his reach. Was Garski pirating electricity from another source? Unlikely. Was it a secret telephone link with the Soviet embassy? It would have to be investigated.

Garski was arrested when he returned on Sunday night. Under extreme interrogation methods, Garski revealed the full horror of his mission. Yamada informed the Japan Staff Council. They spent 48 hours deliberating what should be done. Were there more of these things dotted about Japan, were there more in other countries? Did those other countries know about them? It was a brilliant and horrifying idea. It infringed all the disarmament and non-proliferation treaties known to man. It brought a new degree of horror to the balance of forces between nations, and it was a potential terrorist tool of unprecedented power. The Staff Council were fascinated as well as horrified. They had lived through the nightmare of Hiroshima and Nagasaki. Here was another one on their doorstep.

"I suggest we do nothing," proposed Yamada, "apart from disarming the nuclear device. If they think this one is working they're less likely to deploy others." The director-general won his argument.

Garski was re-installed at ERIC, but made aware of the consequences if he tried to step out of line, or pass any message to Moscow. It would not be a quick death, he was told. That was in September.

In late October the Japanese Prime Minister, Yasuhiro Nakasone, joined NATO leaders in New York to discuss the defence policy of the free industrial world, as a curtain-raiser to the November summit. Unlike his colleagues he knew about Nautilus but he had no reason to tell them so. They didn't mention it. He wasn't bound by any defence pact, since Japan was outside NATO. He also had no qualms about the thousands of American troops protecting Japanese territory. After all, Japan had the situation under control and had neutralized Nautilus, as far as it knew. Japan sat on its secret.

CHAPTER TWENTY-SEVEN

Budapest

Tikov reached Budapest with the busload of friendly Hungarians. By that time he was no longer a kidnap victim but a willing defector ready to make his way to Western Europe and perhaps the United States. He felt that with his inside knowledge he could blow the Nautilus project apart.

From Budapest he sailed up the Danube on a tourist hydrofoil to Vienna. He had a Cypriot passport in the name of Madig Petrossian, an Armenian engineer. With the money he carried he would be accepted anywhere.. This was a new experience for him: out of the military, beyond the oppressive grip of the Soviet Union. To start with he was determined to have a good time. Vienna held no attractions for him; it was too close to home, so he flew to Paris and spent three days eating, drinking and collapsing in nightclubs, but not whoring. He had a highly developed fear of AIDS, the decadent Western disease. Sated and tender-livered he proceeded to London.

Laszlo's right-hand man Janos met him at the airport, and within an hour he was at Albion Mews talking to Laszlo.

"Drink?" suggested Laszlo.

"No, thanks."

"We had a job keeping track of you in Paris." Laszlo studied him with his clear, humane eyes. "You are with us, aren't you?"

"Yes."

"You can do your Yurchenko performance when Nautilus is in pieces." Vitaly Yurchenko was a KGB agent who disappeared from Rome in August 1984, turning up later in Washington as a defector. But on November 4 1985, without warning he walked out of a Georgetown restaurant where he was dining with one of his CIA minders and turned up at the Soviet embassy in Washington, claiming to have been abducted, brainwashed and forced to defect. For a week or so the Yurchenko affair was a cause célèbre and an obvious propaganda coup for the Soviets so close to the summit meeting.

"Yurchenko?" said Tikov. "The poor man is only trying to save his skin and keep his family together."

"We have a job for you," said Laszlo." "We'd like you to tell the British what you know about the Nautilus project."

"I'm out of date, you realize that? I've been out of circulation for two months and apparently they've put three Nautiluses into the United States. I knew of only one."

"Can you help us find that one?"

"I can't even do that. The location's been changed."

"What about Sweden, France, Japan?"

"I can tell you a little about those."

"What about your loyalty to the Soviet Union?"

"I remain loyal to my country, and to the principles which guided my career as a cosmonaut and a military man.

But I feel no loyalty to those who have made Nautilus a terrorist weapon for their own ends."

"Who are they?"

"Mikhailov, Ustinov."

"Can we get rid of Mikhailov?"

"He's well guarded, but it's possible."

Tikov saw Fortescue and Richards. He learned about Mikhailov's trip to Venice and the meeting with Brand.

"Why didn't you get Mikhailov then?" he asked.

"At that stage we didn't know the score," said Fortescue. Tikov also learned about the hunt for Zilin and the murder charge hanging over him.

"Poor Zilin. He hasn't much imagination, but he's a good operator," said Tikov. "You'll have a job to find him."

Argyllshire, Scotland

Zilin heard about the hunt for him on the radio news. He dyed his hair. He bought a baby's push-chair and a carrycot and surrounded his van with the trappings of family life. But the van was too obvious; they would be looking for VW vans. After a few days he bought a long wheel-base Land Rover and dumped the van in a loch. He bought some stencils and white paint. On the sides of the Land Rover he painted carefully *Park School Mountainering Club* and piled up the back with cheap, multi-coloured sleeping bags. Few locals would be suspicious of a worried schoolmaster driving around the countryside looking for lost groups of schoolchildren. At night he pitched three tents close together and filled them with sleeping gear. This disguise also allowed him to drive into towns and stock up with rations for hungry boys. His only task was to keep on the move, never stay in one place long enough for the lack of children to be noticed. He was careful to avoid the police and behave strictly according to traffic regulations.

Zilin couldn't resist fishing, but he didn't like to apply for fishing permits. So he would fish always well away from his parked Land Rover. If there was trouble he would simply vanish into the highland mist. Once or twice he was shouted at by distant keepers. But one keeper wasn't satisfied with shouting. He was new, young and anxious to prove his mettle. He followed Zilin for a whole morning, watched him climb a ridge, walk through a forest and double back through rough heather to a hill road where his Land Rover was parked. The keeper got close enough to read the number and the writing on the side, noticing that 'Mountainering' was misspelt. He told the head keeper on the estate about the illegal fisherman.

"If he's a teacher he should know better. We'll make an example of him." The head keeper contacted the chief constable of the district. The police checked the number. The new owner hadn't been registered yet but the computer turned up a previous owner in Dumfriesshire. He knew nothing of Park School Mountaineering Club.

It took a day of police time to check with all the Park Schools in the country and confirm that none had a mountaineering club which owned or had owned a Land Rover.

"Either the number plates are false or the sign is false," said the chief constable.

"Perhaps it was painted for a film or something on the telly," volunteered a detective.

"We'll have to check it out," said the senior policeman. "Find me that Land Rover and the schoolmaster, whoever he is."

The game-keeper gave a description of the man and so did the Dumfries vendor. The police considered the possibility that the schoolmaster could be on the run. Otherwise why go to all that trouble to create a disguise? Perhaps he was a child molester. The police computer turned up three possibilities, and it turned up Zilin.

Fortescue learned of the possible lead in Scotland and used all his influence to gain control of the search. He didn't want Zilin scared off by some half-hearted police attempt at an arrest - if it really was Zilin.

"All we want is a sighting of the car," Fortescue told the commissioner of police. "After that we'll take over." Tikov was consulted: "It's his sort of place. It's his style," he said.

Fortescue flew to Glasgow with Tikov and four men, two of them to guard Tikov. They drove to Inveraray and checked into a hotel. The Land Rover hadn't been seen for two days then was sighted on the southern shore of Loch Etive in Argyllshire. It was a narrow road and the unmarked police car was able to pass slowly, observing the Land Rover and three tents beside it, not a soul in sight.

Fortescue and his men piled into a Range Rover hired locally. They ordered a police road block at one end of the loch, "but your job is to block the road, not to chase him," said Fortescue. At the other end of the loch two of Fortescue's men got out of the Range Rover and began a sweep of the hills. The Range Rover proceeded to within a mile of Zilin's camp. One man stayed with it to pursue Zilin's Land Rover if necessary. Fortescue, Tikov and little Mad Mitch, who had been on the Zurich expedition, covered the last mile on foot. Fortescue and Mitch carried rifles, not to shoot Zilin but to look as if they were stalking deer. The rough heather underfoot reminded Tikov of another occasion and another stalk on the Swedish foreshore where they had shot the Englishman. Was that how Nautilus had been discovered? Maybe later he would ask Fortescue.

The three men worked their way through heather, dying bracken and a jungle of dwarf oak. It was impossible to move quietly, but the secret was to imitate the irregular passage of deer, and avoid sounding like men on the march.

Zilin was standing by his Land Rover, eating sardines from a tin. His acute hearing picked up the sound of the approaching Range Rover. When the noise of the engine died and a car failed to appear on the road below he thought he had better check it out.

He took his binoculars and climbed the first shoulder of hill in the direction of the sound. That gave him a view of the next valley running down to the lake, but no car. Whoever it was must be safely beyond the next ridge. He sat down to think. Was that enough grounds to strike camp and move on? He was nervous since being chased by that keeper. He hadn't seen him turn back.

Zilin's speculation ended there. He saw a movement on the ridge, and a head move through the dense oak wood. Then on the left there was another movement and farther up yet another. Great heavens, how many were there? One man crossed an open patch 500 metres away. Zilin got the binoculars on him for a second and saw a deerstalker hat and a rifle. Maybe they're just hunting he thought. He decided to retreat in case he was separated from his Land Rover. He would sit near the Land Rover and keep watch. If they showed more interest in the vehicle than in the surrounding vermin then he would take flight and put some distance between him and them before abandoning it. He didn't like the idea of being hunted on foot at such close quarters, though he was supremely fit. He was confident he could cover great distances faster than any pursuers, and even relished the prospect.

Zilin struck camp in one minute, bundling the three tents into the back of the Land Rover. He took his binoculars and hid himself in a clump of oak. By crouching low he had a good view of the ridge he had just retreated from. He waited five minutes, ten minutes. There was no sign of the stalkers. Then for a moment high up the mountainside he saw a figure advance over the skyline and disappear. That was followed by another several degrees to the left. It can't have been the same party of deerstalkers. They could never have got so high and then come back over the skyline. Every clue now pointed to a man hunt. They certainly weren't hunting deer, since they were moving downwind.

Zilin paused for a moment like a panther preparing to spring, then rose and walked to the Land Rover. He swung into the driving seat turned the ignition and sent the car bumping downhill with the engine ticking over, joining a rough track which led to the lakeside road. At the road he turned right, leaving the unseen car behind him, though he expected it to be following soon. Up the mountainside his occasional glances could discover no movement and no human shapes. A false alarm perhaps but it was best to take no chances. In two hours he could be fifty or sixty miles away in fresh terrain.

He drove fast but not recklessly to the end of the lake, keeping an eye on his rear mirror. He could see no sign of pursuit. But a few hundred metres from the road junction he saw a sight which hit him right in the stomach; a car at the roadside, two men inside and two standing nearby. They may not have been in uniform but they stood like policemen. That was enough for Zilin. It was a saloon car so he knew his best chance was across country. He had noted a track half a kilometre back. Zilin put the Land Rover into a clumsy three-point turn, expecting at any moment to be shot at. But neither the car nor the men moved. When he glanced back in his mirror they were standing in exactly the same positon. Are they playing with me, wondered Zilin.

He plunged his car up the mountain track, threw it into four-wheel drive and gave it full throttle. He would drive until he got over the mountain or was stopped by sheer rock. There were many things he feared - a cordon of troops, other vehicles in pursuit, helicopters or even planes raking the hillside with rockets. But he was convinced this was his best bet. After two minutes on the track he glanced back and saw a Range Rover in hot pursuit just turning off the tarred road. That was the confirmation he needed; they were after him alright.

He hurled the car up the rough and rutted road, with the engine screaming in low gear. He smelled burning oil and felt shattering blows through the aluminium frame but he needed every second of advantage against the superior, smoother car below.

A five-bar gate lay ahead, enclosing a fir plantation. Zilin hesitated for a moment, but the gate was padlocked anyway, so he drove through, wrenching the gate from its hinges and carrying it twenty metres up the track. He reversed then drove over the gate, cursing the loss of time, and the thought that it was one obstacle less for the Range Rover. He looked around for ways to get his revenge. There was nothing. But the plantation was criss-crossed with rides; perhaps he could lose his pursuer. One thing was sure: if he continued on the main track the Range Rover would catch him.

Zilin saw a grassy ride going uphill. He turned up it, stopped after 20 metres and ran back to cover his tracks. It was a gamble. He was relying on his pursuer to drive on past. Zilin drove out of sight of the main track and cut the engine. He listened to the scream of the Range Rover as it sped past. Zilin waited a minute then gunned the Land Rover uphill again knowing that his ruse would soon be discovered. At the most he would have clawed his lead back to two minutes.

The grassy ride narrowed to little more than a footpath then, to his dismay, was completely blocked by a fallen tree. He could abandon the vehicle or he could venture into the plantation itself. That was risky. The trees were densely packed and even if he could weave his way through, it would be at little more than walking pace. There was another thing. A Land Rover is wider than a Range Rover by one inch. So he would have to work harder to squeeze it through.

Zilin threw the Land Rover over a drainage ditch and into the forest. Immediately he saw the enormity of the problem, every gap in the trees had to be sought out and negotiated. There was a great risk of becoming wedged between two trunks. Every move was accompanied by the shrieking and scratching of branches as if the forest were a hostile, violent rabble. He found another path and followed it for a hundred or so metres then plunged into the forest again to avoid a tree trunk. After five minutes he shut off the engine and got out. Below him he heard the angry whine of the Range Rover and the snapping of branches. It was well into the forest and after him.

He had been working uphill, hoping that he would suddenly burst from the forest onto open hillside again with a head start. He thought he saw daylight beyond the trees but time and again it proved a false horizon. Suddenly Zilin came to some high netting, with a narrow strip of forest beyond, a ditch and then rocks and heather. It was impossible to drive through the fence. Zilin stopped the Land Rover and listened. The Range Rover was still screaming below him, but farther away, he thought. Zilin dived into the toolbox below the passenger seat and pulled out pliers and a hatchet. He hacked at the wire and snapped some joints with the pliers. Very quickly he had a hole big enough to force the vehicle through. Already picking his line uphill he charged the fence then burst through the band of trees into a new hazard, heather pitted with rocks, rocks big enough to strand the Land Rover on its chassis. Zilin advanced cautiously, wildly looking for a track to follow. He saw a mountain footpath to the right and headed for it, banging the sump guard continually on hidden rocks. Downhill he saw the Range Rover buzzing angrily along the fence trying to find an opening. Zilin hammered on; perhaps he now had a three-minute lead. There was a smash of glass. He turned round to find a side-window had shattered. Another impact smacked into the side of the hull. Someone's shooting at me, he thought. Zilin saw the driver of the Range Rover standing beside it with a rifle. He screamed with fear and fury and drove on, but was pleased that the man was wasting time. Soon he saw why. The footpath fell away into a gully cut by a stream. No vehicle could get through there. Zilin threw the Land Rover into the gully to get away from the shooting. He reached behind his seat for his survival pack and began running, up the gully, towards the bare mountainside.

He reasoned that he could beat any pursuers to the ridge. That would give him twenty or thirty kilometres of country to vanish into on the other side. If he ran back into the forest, the cordon would close on him fast. If they had a wide cordon, or a helicopter he was sunk; but there was no evidence of that so far. Who are these people, he thought. They have rifles, a Range Rover, but no air support. There are a minimum of six people, but five have been left far behind unless they're mountain goats. Then there are the police, apparently neutral, driving me back into the hunting ground. They're playing with me. Zilin bent himself to the job of reaching the ridge. Even for a fit man it was a tough vertical grind and no fun with the threat of a bullet in the back.

Mitch was a mountain goat. When he, Fortescue and Tikov heard the Land Rover he was dispatched to head for the highest ground and guard the south side of the lake. The two men who had crossed the ridge climbed it again and dropped down behind, as a reception party for Zilin. Once Zilin had ditched the Land Rover, the Range Rover driver was ordered round by road to the southern side of the range. Unless things went wrong they would have Zilin by nightfall, but they wanted him alive.

Fortescue and Tikov followed Mitch. They were less fit. Fortescue had spent too much time in smoke-filled rooms and Tikov too long under house arrest and travelling in cramped conditions. The fresh air hurt their lungs.

Zilin was relying on brute strength and stamina to carry him through. He stormed up a vertical distance of 300 metres in twelve minutes then lengthened his stride towards the ridge. Mitch was on the same ridge but two kilometres away. Tikov and Fortescue were a kilometre beyond that as the crow flies. They were hopelessly spread out. Their only hope was the two men on the southern slopes but they too were well to the west. All Zilin had to do was continue eastward and he would outrun them all. But he was suspicious of the police on the eastern side. His plan was to take a straight line down to the road. He felt that if he could cross that road he was safely in another sector and his pursuers would be back to square one. They could never outpace him. When it came to endurance he would astound them all, like Napoleon or Xenophon with some of their great marches.

Zilin charged down the scree in a noisy glissade, yelling at his own death-defying speed. Deer started up in front of him and scattered. He plunged into forest but that slowed him down so he traversed to the bare mountain again. Sweat stung his eyes and each stride jarred his aching head as he fought for speed over the uneven, falling ground. He saw the road below him, thin and deserted; beyond it a wilderness of hills and forests. If he screwed up his eyes he could see his native steppe stretching as far as the eye could see, pale and beckoning.

He looked at the road again. Behind a stone sheepfold was the tail of a Range Rover plain as daylight and beside it a man with binoculars. Was it the same Range Rover? Was it another? Were there more surrounding him at intervals? The binoculars were looking right at him, unflinching. He estimated that the man was about 1,500 metres away. There was little cover, only a small stream running down a gully about 500 metres to the left. Zilin decided to head for it anyway; at least it was dead ground and would keep the man guessing. It also meant he couldn't be shot at. Above him, the two men on the upper slopes had rounded the top of the forest a good two kilometres back.

In two minutes, Zilin had reached the gully. He saw the Range Rover turn behind the sheepfold and drive to where the road crossed the gully. Tears of fury sprung into his eyes. He glanced up at the high ridge and cursed the height he had lost glissading down. He'd have to climb it again, outpacing the two men on his left and outsmarting whoever lurked behind the ridge. At least they were on foot. Zilin ran up the gully, bending low. He heard the zing of bullet on rock and the crack of a rifle below him, but he felt reasonably safe - it was a long way to shoot at a moving target. His heart pounded, his legs ached. Wouldn't it be better to hide and rest, he thought, to vanish into the rough grass and heather? His greatest fury was at not being allowed to outpace these people in a fair race. They had cheated him.

He had to watch his footwork in the narrow gully, looking up at intervals to check on his pursuers. Raising his eyes to the ridge he suddenly saw Mitch ahead of him, standing with his rifle at the ready, waiting. The only escape was to the right but that was useless, open hillside. Once he came out of the gully he would be picked off like a fly. Zilin looked around. Perhaps he could melt into the ground, bury himself as he had buried Cynthia. He crouched out of sight and waited for the inevitable. There were two men to his left, one above and one below; it was only a matter of time before they dug him, cowering, out of his hidey-hole. And then what - torture, interrogation, death? Better to have gone in the Thames, taking half a city with him, than to be hanged as a murderer or shot as a spy. Did they still hang people in Britain?

Zilin reclined on the grass with his head resting on his clasped hands. He daydreamed for half-an-hour while the sweat dried on him, leaving him cold and clear-headed. Surely they must have missed him and moved on by now; but he didn't feel like raising his head. Looming over him, against the glare of the sky, he saw a man's shape. It was Tikov. Had his ghost come to visit him? He wouldn't have been surprised.

"Boris Alexeivich. Have you come to tell me to make my peace with God? I always knew you were a closet Christian."

"No, Comrade Zilin. I've come to rescue you from the British police and the consequences of your filthy crimes."

"You've gone over to them; you've defected, you crafty whore." Zilin said with admiration not anger. "And you led them straight to me."

"The rules of the game have changed, as you'll discover when we've had a chance to talk." Zilin stood up. He was surrounded by his six pursuers. They marched down to the Range Rover and drove straight to London. Fortescue telephoned the police and told them they had lost their man. The hunt must go on, he said.

Zilin spent three days at the safe house in Barnes. Fortescue's people threatened him with fifteen years in an English prison unless he co-operated. He must tell them everything about the Nautilus, about the number deployed in Britain and elsewhere.

He must tell them who gave him his orders. Tikov was brought in to work on his conscience, to shame him for his perverse, sexual crime. Tikov had never liked Zilin; to him he was a different breed, an animal that ate other food, and hung close in the affections of the loathsome Mikhailov. Tikov had some pleasure in making Zilin squirm, pleading pathetically for his life.

Finally they offered Zilin a deal. It was the kind of deal he couldn't refuse because there was no alternative but death. Nobody knew him; nobody would come looking for him six foot down in the English earth. He wept for Cynthia and he wept for himself.

Then he was set free three miles from Dundee, a port where Russian ships often call and Russian sailors explore the local taverns. Zilin had no trouble inviting himself aboard a freighter bound for Riga. The captain was happy to take him, on the understanding he would give himself up on arrival.

CHAPTER TWENTY-EIGHT

Sombrero Beach, Florida Keys

A gentle Caribbean swell washed the Florida shore, sculpting fresh ribs in the white sand. Dawn was pulsing in the east; soon those grey shapes on the shore would take on the vibrant tones of a warm November day.

A grey shape lay rocking in the six-inch breakers, a dull rubbery form like a large porpoise or a small whale. A man lay 20 metres up the beach, reclining on one arm, watching the sunrise but frequently allowing his eyes to rest on the grey shape, lovingly, as on the corpse of a favourite dog.

Lebedyev couldn't move. He should have slunk inland under cover of darkness immediately after beaching the Nautilus, but a huge weariness, enhanced by his own disbelief, kept him sprawled on the sand. Disbelief because they told him he wouldn't stand a chance. He had penetrated one of the most heavily patrolled stretches of ocean in the world, between Cuba and the United States, doing much of his journey on the surface in broad daylight. US customs boats had churned within a mile of him hastening about their business.

They were meant to catch him, dammit! That was the whole point of the exercise. But he didn't see why he should make it easy for them. What should he have done? Stood up and waved at them, saying here it is, the Soviet Union's most secret weapon trying to sneak into the playground of America's superrich? They had been tipped off about the threat; surely that was enough?

Lebedyev waited for a coastguard or a police patrol to pick him up. A beachcomber shuffled along the line of breakers, picking things up and discarding them, hardly noticing the grey hull until he almost stumbled on it. He proceeded without curiosity but occasionally glanced back at the thing riding in the breakers.

Then came the joggers from nearby condominiums. One was a former army colonel. He looked at the Nautilus, pushed it and shoved it, saw some stencils in Russian and ran back home.

A small crowd gathered round the Nautilus. They examined it but couldn't open the hatch. Lebedyev felt this was his cue. He strolled across the sand and began to address the crowd.

"Ladies and gentlemen, my name is Sergei Lebedyev, the former Soviet cosmonaut and this is my miniature submarine Nautilus. As you can see it is a remarkable machine and has managed to penetrate through all your fabulous military defences. It is not only a machine it is a bomb, a lightweight plutonium bomb which can be detonated at any moment by a signal from the Kremlin." There were a few shrieks and some people started to run until they realized that running would achieve nothing. They stood and listened.

"Of course it won't go off," said Lebedyev. "It's just a warning, a present from the Soviet Union, bringing a message of peace and goodwill to you American people."

"Are you some kind of nut?" asked one.

"No, I'm not a kind of nut. I'm deadly serious. This weapon is as powerful as the bombs you Americans dropped on Hiroshima and Nagasaki. It's a gift for you. We have others, but we are certain that with your co-operation they will never be used."

The crowd began to mutter. "He's crazy." "The guy's out of his mind." And some of them shuffled off. But one was more credulous. "Can I see inside your machine?" he asked. Lebedyev climbed onto the hull and began to open the hatch. But the sound of sirens came from the road. Three jeeps from the military police drove onto the sand with lights flashing. At the same moment a helicopter swooped down and scattered the sand. The curious people were shepherded away, Lebedyev was bundled into the helicopter and six men were left to guard the Nautilus. Three minutes later a bigger helicopter arrived and hovered above the Nautilus while a sling was fixed beneath it. The Nautilus was skylifted to a destroyer twenty miles offshore.

Lebedyev was already there. In an interrogation room three officers, one naval, one from the CIA and the other from NASA, plied him with questions and coffee. He was perfectly prepared to answer since he had been told this was a peace offering. As the Americans had agreed to share their Star Wars technology with the Soviets, so the Soviets had delivered their own sacrificial lamb: that was how Lebedyev saw it.

"This man has a touching innocence," observed the CIA man.

"With astronauts that's standard issue," commented the NASA man. "They need pure faith to risk their lives in little capsules."

"Major Lebedyev," asked the CIA man, "do you think we are as naive as you? Are we likely to believe that a bomb which can take the lives of 200,000 people is a gesture of goodwill?"

"I don't think you understand," said Lebedyev. "It's no worse than pointing 20,000-kilotonne warheads at distant towns from five thousand kilometres away. But it's more real."

"It sounds totally unreal to me," said the CIA man.

"The idea of a hostage is older than war itself. With one Nautilus we take a town hostage, or part of a town, yet those townspeople are able to go about their lives as usual. They aren't in prison. There's no occupying power. They are free."

"Free?" the CIA man burst into laughter. "Yeah, insofar as you can be free with a 20-kilotonne bomb underneath you that can go off at any minute. Would you feel free in those circumstances?"

"I wouldn't know about it. Any more than I know which Pershing missile is pointing at me, with my name on it. It's a secret agreement between the superpowers. We take one of your towns hostage, you take one of ours. Then it would need a quite ruthless general to push the button."

"There are plenty of those around," said the naval man under his breath.

"Look Sergei," said the NASA man, "we like you very much but we think your plan is bullshit. We won't buy it."

"Besides which," said the CIA man, "have you thought what this weapon could do if it fell into the hands of a terrorist organisation like the PLO? They wouldn't just be killing a few innocent people at an airport; they would be holding whole cities to ransom. No, no, this Nautilus is far worse than any conventional nuclear weapon. It should be outlawed by every nation on earth."

"How much do you know about Mikhailov?" asked the CIA man.

"I've seen him about three times since Brigadier Tikov was arrested. Before then I took my orders from Tikov."

"Tikov has defected, did you know that? In fact we've arranged for him to come and see you."

"Why?"

"He might knock some sense into you."

"Why did he defect?"

"Because he came to understand what Nautilus is. It's not part of Soviet defence strategy, it's been hi-jacked by Mikhailov for his power games in the Kremlin. You, Tikov, Demirkan, Zilin, you were all hi-jacked. And Tikov realized it. Let's hope he wasn't too late."

"But we had orders from the very top, from Ustinov and the General Secretary."

"You thought you had orders. In fact you're right about Ustinov, but he's a rubber stamp; he sacrificed his brain at the siege of Leningrad. Mikhailov knew how to use him."

"But you can't do that in the Soviet Union. I refuse to believe it. You have kidnapped Tikov and brainwashed him as you kidnapped Yurchenko."

"Soon enough you'll be able to judge for yourself," the CIA man smiled kindly. Lebedyev was locked in cell on board the *USS Briscoe*. It wasn't uncomfortable. They had given him plenty of books to read and the food was good. He settled down to re-read Catch 22 -. Meanwhile the technicians outside had disarmed the Nautilus. The *Briscoe* headed for Norfolk, Virginia.

The time had come to tell the President about Nautilus. He was spending the weekend at Camp David being briefed for the impending summit. CIA chief Bill Casey paid him a call.

"Why in hell's name didn't you tell me sooner?" demanded Reagan. "OK," he said, softening, "you probably had a reason. But what does this mean? Can we beat the shit out of Gorbachev at the summit?"

"Not exactly, Mr President."

"If we've captured one of these things on sovereign US territory we've got him by the balls."

"The problem is, there may be more of them on US territory. We've been told of three."

"Then we'd better find them before next Tuesday."

"Easier said than done."

"Holy shit!" Reagan wasn't given to swearing, except in strict privacy. "What's your advice, Bill? Maybe we should have Don and Caspar in on this."

"They've already been briefed."

"I see. I'm the dummy who gets to know the plot right at the end of the movie, when everyone's gone home." Casey greeted that remark with frosty silence. "OK, OK," continued Reagan, "just give me the script and I'll say what you want me to say. But I'm telling you this; I want nothing on earth to screw up this summit meeting. Jesus, I think I detect a glint of humanity in those commie bastards for the first time since the October Revolution. I really think they want peace. This could be a turning point in world history."

"We have to make another gesture," said Casey. "They may want peace but they're fighting and winning a propaganda war."

"What do you suggest?"

"They've offered to cut their obsolete warheads by 50%. I think we should say we'll freeze Cruise and Pershing."

"But that's the whole of our defence programme up the spout, apart from Star Wars."

"I'm saying we should offer a freeze. No one expects us to carry it out."

"OK, OK, tell them in Geneva. Meanwhile," Reagan's voice became softer, sending a chill down the CIA chief's spine, "we have to get even with them on this Neptune thing. We need to show those bastards that you can't monkey around with the great American people. Even that pipsqueak Kennedy turned them back from Cuba. After this summit we'll zap 'em, won't we, Bill?" He put a scaly hand on Casey's shoulder as he ushered him to the door.

The US navy and coastguard began intensive searches of the water around Manhattan, Washington, Los Angeles and San Francisco. Every metre of shoreline was to be scrutinized.

Lebedyev left his comfortable cabin on *USS Briscoe* and was installed in a country house in Virginia, still under heavy guard. His hosts said little but were polite and kind. One evening a helicopter came to collect him. In it were a man from the State Department and an interpreter. After an hour's flight, Lebedyev saw lights below.

"That's Washington," said the man from the State Department.

"Last time I was in Washington I met your President, Mr Ford," said Lebedyev.

"You might meet him again."

"You mean Gerald Ford?"

"No, Ronald Reagan." The helicopter came down on a floodlit lawn near the centre of the city. "This is the British Embassy," he added. The men got out, and waited on the lawn as the rotor blades swung to a halt. More rotor noise and another helicopter plunged into the glare of the floodlights. Lebedyev stared as three men got out. One of them was Tikov, free, unguarded, obviously trusted. Tikov walked straight to Lebedyev. They faced each other in silence.

"You have defected, Boris Alexeivich," said Lebedyev. Tikov had expected a certain coldness.

"Embrace me, Sergei," he said. Reluctantly Lebedyev obliged. "The rules of the game have changed," continued Tikov. "It's no longer the job of a loyal Soviet citizen to support the Nautilus project. Mikhailov has turned it into a mutinous weapon of his own. He has to be stopped."

"How has he done that? Who let him?"

"There's no chain of command. Mikhailov has had Ustinov and his successor eating out of his hand."

"But surely our all-seeing General Secretary can put a stop to that?" Lebedyev had been brooding on this for some days. He couldn't believe the Soviet leadership could be so blind.

"Everything suggests Gorbachev knows nothing about Nautilus, or anyway its real purpose."

"Then can't he be told?"

"He will be, by the only people who have access to him, the Americans, in Geneva in two days' time." One of the embassy staff came up.

"Mr Tikov, shall we go inside?" he said. He led them through French windows into a drawing room with a fire crackling in the hearth. Coffee and brandy were served although the evening was warm. The others kept their distance from the two Russians as if afraid to interrupt a delicate chemical process.

"The Americans will spill the beans, but they need help," said Tikov. "They need a propaganda weapon."

"And what is that?"

"You." Lebedyev smiled.

"What am I supposed to do?"

"You star in a television show."

"Like Dallas?"

"A special show for Mr Gorbachev, recorded here and flown out to Geneva. You tell him about Nautilus, you tell him the truth, and with deep regret you warn him about Comrade Mikhailov."

"You're so clever and photogenic, Boris Alexeivich, why don't you do it?"

"I'm a defector, remember, I ran away. I've probably been brainwashed. But they've only had you for a couple of days. You'll be filmed here, with the British ambassador - what greater proof will they want of fair play?"

"And you've written my script, am I right?"

"You can say what you like," Tikov reached into his jacket, "but I've written down a few things here to help you. You might get tongue-tied."

"Boris Alexeivich, you're a son of a bitch," said Lebedyev, "but I'd follow you to hell and back." There were tears in his eyes, partly of love for this man, and partly from thinking that he might not see his Mother Russia again.

VULKAN

CHAPTER TWENTY-NINE

Geneva, Switzerland

November 19 dawned cold and grey. Light flurries of snow danced over the lawns of the Maison Fleur d'Eau and vanished into the ruffled waters of Lac Léman. Lights had burned in the lakeside mansion though the night, guards with dogs patrolled the grounds. This was the venue of the first superpower summit since 1979. Nothing must be left to chance; no surprises must be slipped into the carefully prepared programme.

At 8.55am precisely the motorcade of the US president would sweep up the gravel drive. Two minutes later it was the turn of the Soviet leader. The two men would hover pleasantly on the steps of the building, for photographs, then with the studied casualness of the Hollywood actor President Reagan would suggest a walk down to the lakeside. As if by chance, the two men would find a little summer house by the shore with a warming fire already crackling in the grate. Accompanied only by their interpreters the superpower leaders would launch into small talk. If they could keep the conversation going for more than a quarter of an hour the summit was already on the road to success; both men knew this. Both were aware of the enormous propaganda benefits that fireside chat could bring.

But behind the ritualized puppet-play the two negotiating teams, the Pentagon strategists and the Soviet ballistics chiefs, were in turmoil. The night before, the Soviets had dropped a bombshell. The Pentagon bosses received a message direct from the Kremlin, in one of their own codes.

"In the interests of a lasting world peace we request you to make a firm undertaking that the United States of America will cease all work on its strategic defence initiative, the infamous Star Wars. Failure to make such an undertaking at the summit meeting will result in detonation of a 20-kilotonne nuclear device, of which you are well aware, in the New York area. The deadline is 2100 GMT Wednesday November 20. Signed, Dmitri Ustinov, Supreme Commander, Soviet Armed Forces.

The American response to the Soviet negotiators in Geneva was clear and unambiguous: "We regard such a threat to the lives of innocent citizens as a casus belli. Unless it is withdrawn immediately the United States of America will consider itself at war with the Union of Soviet Socialist Republics."

To which the Soviet negotiators responded: "What threat?"

"It's signed by Ustinov in the Kremlin."

"We know of no such threat. We are horrified by such an ultimatum."

"Will you check with Ustinov?" The Soviet delegation asked the Kremlin for confirmation that the threat was spurious. The Kremlin and Ustinov himself said it was. They knew of no such threat.

"Ustinov denies he sent a message," the Soviet delegation told the Americans. "You must ignore it. We know of no device hidden in New York or anywhere else.

We are signatories of the 1970 nuclear non-proliferation treaty which forbids such duplicity. And we abhor any suggestions that the Soviet Union is employing the tactics of terrorism."

"We know about the Soviet Nautilus programme, and we have evidence that such weapons exist. In fact we have captured one; so have the British."

"The Nautilus programme is a peaceful scientific research project."

"Not according to our information, or that of the British or the Swedes."

"Are you still complaining about our accident in Sweden?"

"A series of accidents." The Americans tried another tack. "Who has been running your Nautilus project?"

"Ustinov and his chief adviser, Mikhailov."

"Military men, engaged in a peaceful scientific project?"

"It's a question of funding and the training of personnel. It's no different from our space programme - or yours for that matter."

"Are there any checks and balances to control what Ustinov and Mikhailov have been doing?"

"You mean are those two officials conducting their own private campaign? Impossible."

"Have you checked with Mikhailov?"

"What is there to check? He is a Soviet official doing his duty."

"Where does this ultimatum come from?"

"We don't know."

"Are you aware that one of your Nautilus submarines was captured four weeks ago in the Thames, loaded with an armed nuclear bomb equivalent to 20 kilotonnes of TNT? And that another was found beached near Miami with a similar payload."

"We're hearing this for the first time." Either the Soviets were bluffing or they were truly ignorant of the use to which Nautilus had been diverted.

"We suggest you check with Mikhailov. Ask him point blank if his Nautilus carries a nuclear payload." The Soviet delegation referred to Mikhailov and brought back their answer.

"He says the idea is absurd and not even feasible. The Nautilus has no nuclear payload."

"In the last two months Mikhailov has even told Western intelligence experts to their faces that he has deployed nuclear-armed Nautiluses in Britain, the US and Japan. We have captured two. And yet his own side appears to know nothing about it. We think you should arrest Mikhailov immediately and Ustinov too." The Americans offered to fly two Soviet defence delegates to Portland, England, to inspect one of the captured Nautiluses. The Soviets indignantly refused, beginning to suspect an elaborate hoax. They were careful not to bother their leader Gorbachev with news of these exchanges, fearing it might affect his performance at the summit the next day.

The American delegation received another coded message from the Kremlin:

"Don't take the risk of ignoring this warning. Despite the lies and protests of the Soviet delegation the deadline is unchanged. We, the Soviet people and you, the United States, understand each other."

The Americans showed the message to the Soviet delegation but got little reaction. The Soviet attitude had become entrenched. They were even more convinced that this was an American hoax. The Americans had one more card to play, the videotape of Lebedyev. But it was now 12.30 at night, too late to hope to change the Soviet view. Besides, the Lebedyev tape was addressed to Gorbachev. They had nearly 48 hours until the deadline so, in Geneva, they decided to sleep on it.

In New York, the hunt for the hidden Nautilus was intensified. In Moscow, Hungarian agents were making preparations to ensure that a certain Soviet citizen carried out his task on arrival in the capital.

Reagan and Gorbachev braved the icy wind and strolled arm in arm for a time by the lakeside. It was phoney, thought Gorbachev; this played-out movie actor is banal, but I'm doing this for the lives of our children. The eyes of the world are on us.

"You and I are very similar," said Reagan. "We come from a simple background, we are family men, we love peace." Gorbachev smiled to himself. Wasn't this the man who only 10 months ago had referred to the Soviet Union as the Evil Empire? He was an impressive actor and a remarkable hypocrite.

Reagan was fascinated by the birthmark on Gorbachev's forehead. How could a man with such a disfigurement rise to the highest office in the land? The thought intrigued him. It was quite clear that television didn't play a role in selecting politicians over there. And Reagan forgot his carefully prepared lines. His interpreter steered him towards the summer house where a fire was crackling in the grate. The two men stood before it and warmed their hands.

The room was simply furnished but it wasn't empty. One corner was dominated by a large television screen and beneath it a video-recorder. Unprompted, the American interpreter walked to the recorder and loaded in a tape. Before the two leaders could protest, a picture leapt onto the screen and a voice began in Russian.

"My name is Sergei Lebedyev. I am a Soviet cosmonaut and graduate from the Nakhimov School in Leningrad ....". Gorbachev looked round hastily and started to object, then stood still and listened. Reagan settled into an armchair and followed the subtitles. The tape showed pictures of the Nautilus, the Russian lettering, and, inside, offered a glimpse of the nuclear device. "Comrade General Secretary," continued Lebedyev on the tape, "I am a loyal Soviet citizen and was engaged on the Nautilus project for two years. At the outset I was told it was a purely scientific project which required skilled cosmonauts to pilot the craft. Of course, we were always aware of the potential for espionage and reconnaissance in foreign territorial waters. But it was only when I was sent on a mission to Switzerland that I learned the craft would carry a nuclear payload. I asked to be taken off the project but was told that the order, and my selection, came from the highest authority, from the very top. I was expected to serve and to obey.

"Now, of course I'm aware that this development was nothing more than a plot by reactionary elements within the Kremlin. I have been told that you yourself know nothing of Nautilus's sinister purpose. It's quite clear to me now that if you had known anything you would have put an end to it immediately. But unfortunately things have reached a very advanced stage. It will be very difficult to act against the traitors within the Kremlin. The mind of military commander Ustinov has been completely perverted by his adviser. I am talking to you knowing that since I bear all the outward signs of having betrayed my country my words will carry little weight. But I assure you that I, like yourself, have the higher objective of world peace in mind, and I beg you to do everything in your power to avert disaster." The tape ended, leaving Gorbachev in stunned silence.

"He has a good delivery," said Reagan, commenting on Lebedyev's television technique.

"How long have you known about this, Mr Reagan?" asked Gorbachev.

"About a week."

"And you said nothing?"

"We said plenty last night, when we got the ultimatum."

"What ultimatum?"

"The ultimatum from your man Mikhailov, which he then denied, saying if we didn't backtrack on Star Wars he would blow up New York."

"Has he the power to blow up New York?"

"So we understand. A big part of New York anyway, depending on where this Nautilus thing is. We can't locate it at the moment."

"I'll order his arrest immediately and put an end to this affair. It's outrageous." Gorbachev paced up and down. Grabbing the nearest telephone he shouted over his shoulder, "We may be against your Star Wars but we're not madmen."

"Hold on, Mr Gorbachev. Don't be too trigger-happy. Our information is that these guys will resist arrest. Any more and they'll bring forward the deadline."

"When is the deadline?"

"Tomorrow night, around 10 o'clock." Gorbachev was incensed by the American's apparent calm, and by his own ignorance.

"Is this some kind of cowboy joke?" he challenged.

"Now really, Mr Gorbachev. You have a very uncharitable view of us Americans."

"Answer me, answer me," yelled Gorbachev. His shrill voice carried down the telephone to his nest of advisers.

"Yes, Comrade General Secretary," came a humble reply.

"Now listen to me," said Gorbachev down the telephone. "You've been keeping me in the dark about this catastrophic development. I want an explanation and I want action. Arrest Ustinov and Mikhailov, and disarm this weapon immediately."

"They deny any part in it, comrade chairman. We didn't want to trouble you with such a vicious American hoax."

"Open your eyes, man, it can hardly be a hoax. Give me Venkov." Venkov came to the telephone. "Now listen

Vassily, you will do everything in your power to contain those criminals in Moscow. If you fail, God have mercy on your grandchildren." Gorbachev turned to Reagan; his healthy glow had sunk to an ashen pallour. "Listen, my good friend, the Soviet Union will do everything it can to end this nightmare. I beg you for your co-operation. That co-operation might mean that temporarily, only temporarily, we may ask you to make a public statement that you renounce the Star Wars programme." Reagan pondered this for some time.

"I'm sorry, Mr Gorbachev, we just can't do that."

CHAPTER THIRTY

Moscow

At 10.30pm two Soviet officers walked through the high gates of the Kremlin. Their papers were in order and they proceeded to the second checkpoint. Across Red Square a driver was watching through infra-red glasses.

"Good luck, my friends," he said under his breath.

The two officers were well wrapped against the November frost. They walked across an inner courtyard past the black shapes of official cars. At the second checkpoint they declared their business.

"We have a situation report for Marshall Ustinov to be delivered by hand," said one. The telephonist checked with Ustinov's office but the call was intercepted. Mikhailov's orders were to monitor all unusual traffic into the Kremlin. He was informed about the two officers.

"Where are they from?"

"Missile reserve," said the telephonist.

"Search them. I want them stripped." The two officers were led at gunpoint to a guardroom. Under their warm winter wrapping they were sweating profusely.

"I'm sorry, Captain Scholyabin, but our orders are to search you." Scholyabin knew what they would find. Beneath his uniform was a bullet-proof vest, made in Kansas. How would he explain that?

He decided to duck the problem and launched himself at one of the guards, taking him by surprise. He bulldozed the man out into the courtyard before the second guard had time to react, disabling him with a blow to the neck. Then he ran through glass doors into the labyrinth of the Kremlin.

The second officer leapt on the remaining guard but both men were felled by a hail of bullets. Scholyabin was on his own. He had one objective - to get to Mikhailov and kill him. He had a powerful sense of invincibility as he pounded down the Kremlin corridor in his billowing fur coat. But it was short-lived. A pistol shot wounded him in the foot.

He spun round and emptied half a magazine at three figures running after him. One went down, the others continued. With blood gushing from his foot, signposting every move he made, Scholyabin had little chance left as an assassin. He decided to fight his way out of the building instead.

He turned and aimed carefully at the foremost of the running figures. A direct hit in the stomach. The third man dived to the ground and he only winged him. Scholyabin hopped to a window giving onto the courtyard: he was on the ground floor so it wasn't far to jump. He leapt onto the ledge, but a shot pierced the glass and hit him in the shoulder. He crashed through the window frame, a desperate, bleeding figure and ran towards the high gateway, crouching behind the parked cars. Whoever had shot at him was waiting for him to re-appear, reluctant to damage too many black Zil saloons. Scholyabin made a final dash for it, emptying his magazine at the guards. He got through the gateway and began to run across Red Square. A car was heading straight for him. When they met, a man leapt out and began to bundle Scholyabin into the back. But another volley of bullets eliminated all signs of life and left the car in flames in the middle of Red Square.

"What was all that shooting?" asked Mikhailov.

"Those officers turned out to be hostile," said the telephonist.

"Are they dead?"

"Yes."

"Examine everything they were carrying. I want to know who sent them." said Mikhailov.

Langley, Virginia

Two hours later news of the failure came through to CIA headquarters..

"Another Desert One," commented Spiro McLeod, head of foreign operations. Desert One was a secret landing strip in Iran where a US helicopter collided with a C130 transporter in 1980, ending a bid to free 50 American hostages from Tehran.

Tikov was in New York, assisting the US navy in its frantic search for Nautilus. He advised them on the locations he knew Irena had explored, but he also knew that it was fruitless. Irena had been taken off the project and a new man, one of Mikhailov's own operators like Zilin, had been put in her place.

At 4.30 that morning they had learned of the deadline: 1500 hours Eastern Standard Time. The most sophisticated magnetic, electronic and visual equipment in the world was scanning the seaboard of Manhattan Island exploring every creek and disused jetty, the shipwrecks where a Nautilus might lurk, masked by tons of rusting metal.

"Not even a shrimp could move down there without us tracking it," said a confident marine lieutenant who drove Tikov uptown to the 79th Street marina.

"Wait for me here," said Tikov. Across the huddle of expensive yachts battened down for the winter he saw the sad hulk of the Mary Jane. She was down in the water. That meant no one had been pumping the bilges. Tikov walked down and tried the cabin hatch. It wasn't locked. He stepped inside. Water was just showing about the floorboards, and the woodwork was beginning to smell of mould.

"You want to buy her?" Tikov looked up to see a young face in the hatchway. "The owner was down here yesterday; she wants to sell." Tikov's mind raced. Irena! She must still be in New York. Even if she was off the project she might know something about the new operator.

"Did she leave an address?"

"She's dealing through us."

"But you have her telephone number."

"I do, but -"

"I'll give you three hundred dollars for that number."

"Wait a minute, I can't do this," protested the young man. Tikov pulled a wad of notes out of his pocket and was counting.

"Dammit, here's two hundred and seventy. It's all I have," said Tikov. He stuffed the bills into the man's pocket and followed him back to the office. The man looked up the number. Tikov could hardly believe it; it was the old number at the apartment in 74th Street. She hadn't moved and she hadn't covered her tracks in any way. Maybe she was still on the project. He ran to the lieutenant's car.

"139 West 74th Street," yelled Tikov. It wasn't far and they were there in three minutes. "Wait here," said Tikov to the baffled marine.

The apartment was on the first floor. Tikov wasn't sure what kind of reception he'd get from Irena, but in theory she was a dropout like him. He took the stairs and listened outside the door. There was a movement inside, there was laughter. The laughter stung him. He rang the doorbell, and the laughter died immediately.

"Irena," he said in a stage whisper. He heard someone come to the door.

"Irena, this is Boris." Irena laughed wildly. Were they drinking in there? It was only midday.

"Boris is dead. Try somebody else." Tikov threw his weight at the door; he knew the lock was weak. On the second charge it flew open. Tikov found himself faced by a colt automatic held not by Irena, but by a man in a bathrobe. Tikov could smell the whisky and judged the man might be slow. He launched himself at the gun arm and chopped the weapon away, then went for the man's testicles. He felt a couple of blows hammer on his back but rammed the man against the bookcase. He went down immediately. It was hardly a contest and Tikov, who had been keyed up for a fight, was furious at the lack of resistance.

"Who is this man?" he asked. Irena laughed.

"My successor. Yorgi Petrov."

"Why can't these Muscovites hold their liquor?"

"He's terrified 24 hours a day. That his little bomb's going to go off."

"Maybe he's right. Listen, there's no time to lose. What's the new location of the Nautilus?"

"You think that pig would tell me? He may be drunk, but he's loyal to that cripple in Moscow."

"Are you?"

"What?"

"Loyal to Mikhailov."

"Not him exactly."

"Mikhailov has gone berserk. He's threatened to detonate the Nautilus here in New York an hour. He delivered an ultimatum in Geneva."

"You're crazy."

"We have to stop him. We have to get to Nautilus and disarm it." Irena was shaking with laughter again.

"Borushka, first I see a ghost, and then this ghost comes and tells me the end of the world is coming. Let's feel if you're flesh and blood." She curled herself around Tikov. "The Borushka smell. My God, I've missed you. Let's see if ghosts can fuck."

"Irena! Do you want 200,000 people to die?" She tore at his trousers. It was more than drink; Tikov suspected some kind of drug - heroin, cocaine. "Later," he said, "just tell me where this drunken bastard lives."

"Why don't you ask him?" Petrov was lying full-length on the floor, snoring heavily. Tikov raised his head and slapped his cheeks, but he slept on. Tikov saw some clothes on the bedroom floor, searched them but found nothing. He noticed a leather coat slung across a chair. In it was a wallet containing a passport, credit cards and business cards, all in the name of Michael Parker, photographer. There was a set of keys.

Tikov took the coat, the wallet and the keys and raced for the door. The marine was on his way up.

"I thought something might have happened," he said.

"It did. Lieutenant, there's a man in there, asleep. Get him to a doctor and a Russian-speaking interrogator. He's the only one who knows where the Nautilus is. They have an hour to make him talk."

"Where are you going?"

"His apartment; there may be some clues." Tikov burst into the street and looked for Petrov's car. After three tries the key opened the door of a squat Porsche. "Where did Petrov get that kind of money?" thought Tikov as he searched the glove compartment and under the bonnet. There were some more business cards and some photographic paper but no hint of submarine equipment. Tikov jumped into the driver's seat and gunned the engine into life. On another occasion he would have thrilled to the decadent Western power under his toes but that sensation lasted only a moment. He had to get downtown fast to Petrov's apartment on the Lower East Side. Luckily, that was against the tide of midday traffic.

The Porsche blazed through red lights onto the West Side Highway. Tikov was touching ninety miles an hour as he tried to beat the sequence of lights changing from amber to red. It wasn't long before there was a police car on his tail, then another. It would be difficult to stop and explain, he thought, so he put his foot down hoping they wouldn't alert more cars ahead. Didn't New York cops shoot and ask questions afterwards? Tikov wasn't used to this kind of driving: Moscow traffic was a sedate affair. This was more like piloting a jet plane at zero altitude. He'd done that before, but not through a screen of cars. The chase continued to the tip of Manhattan. Passing the World Trade Center Tikov swung left up Liberty Street and into the heart of the financial district. One police car wasn't far behind and in front of Tikov was a security truck crawling down a narrow street. Tikov took a chance and mounted the pavement scraping the low hull of the Porsche. He squeezed past the security truck and left the sirens and the blue and red lights flashing behind. After three more blocks he was at Petrov's apartment. All was quiet. He parked the Porsche soberly and took the lift to the fifth floor. It was an old and cracking apartment building in a district crowded with Dickensian offices. Tikov let himself into the apartment. What was he looking for?

The apartment stank of stale takeaway food. On the dining table was a pile of papers and an ashtray heaped with cigarette ends. There was an empty can of beer and the remains of a pizza. Tikov took the papers and riffled through them. He went into the bedroom and searched the cupboard, finding a wetsuit and the tell-tale midget aqualung. But none of this helped. He returned to the papers and examined them one by one. Something caught his attention near the bottom of the pile. Literature from NYNEX Mobile Communications. That was it! If he could find the number he was halfway there. Tikov looked at his watch. It was 2.32 - 28 minutes to the deadline.

Petrov came round. A soft, friendly voice was talking to him in Russian. He opened his eyes and saw a man in naval uniform, a Soviet second lieutenant.

"You're safe now, comrade," the officer said. "You've been out for several days."

"Where am I?"

"The naval infirmary at Riga. Congratulations. The bomb went off but we were able to get you out."

"How?"

"Comrade Tikov rescued you."

"He laid me out cold." Petrov still felt the pain in the back of his head.

"It was the only way," said the lieutenant. "Now, to business," he continued, drawing out a folder. "I have to make a report for our bomb experts. Aerial photographs have shown the extent of the devastation but for a full understanding of the blast they have to know where the Nautilus was, depth, distance from land, etcetera." Petrov pondered for some time.

"That's top secret information," he said. The sub-lieutenant laughed.

"Very correct, comrade," he said, "but an explosion like that can hardly be kept from the public eye. The Nautilus has blown its cover. All our scientists want to know is, where exactly it was."

"Right now, immediately? The moment I wake up? I doubt if it's that important."

"The explosion wasn't as destructive as they anticipated and they want to know why, as soon as possible. There are Nautiluses in other countries and we want to deploy them with maximum efficiency."

"What's the matter? Didn't we kill enough innocent Americans?"

"The explosion did most damage to Staten Island."

"But it wasn't anywhere near there."

"Where was it near?" asked the lieutenant.

Petrov laughed weakly: "A neat trap lieutenant. I have orders to talk only to those who sent me on my mission."

"Do you think they will be pleased to hear about your conduct during that mission? Tikov found you drunk at midday, in Manhattan, in a woman's apartment."

"Where should I have been? What difference did it make? We Russians aren't Buddhists, or Muslims."

"I was just indicating that we could make things very unpleasant for you, Comrade Petrov. You're endangering Soviet security by refusing to answer my questions."

"What are your credentials?" said Petrov grinning wildly. His head was throbbing. "How do I know you're not a spy? How do I know I'm in Riga? Did the Nautilus even explode? Last time I was conscious I was in New York, fighting Tikov." The lieutenant pressed a buzzer and a doctor came in.

"You need more sleep," said the lieutenant. "We'll try again tomorrow." He left the room. The doctor gave him an injection. Petrov didn't like injections. He turned his head and put a hand over his eyes. When the injection was over he ran his hand over his face. He was still clean-shaven. Would they have bothered to shave him? There was another test. He felt his genitals. The pubic hair was still damp and tropical from making love with Irena. For a moment he relived their drunken, fierce union. It can only have been a matter of minutes, not days, since he blacked out. These men weren't Russians, they were Americans. Petrov stumbled out of bed and struggled for the door, but fell unconscious again. The doctors put him on the bed, and the lieutenant was recalled.

"Now we can try the truth game," he said. He went through the same routine of questions with Petrov. But Petrov, even in his drugged state, was on his guard.

"Damn," said the lieutenant, "we're running out of time."

London

Pike was a worrier. He was with Fortescue in Whitehall when the news came that the Russians had given an ultimatum and were threatening to blow up New York.

"Don't tell a bloody soul," said Fortescue. "We know nothing about it. There's nothing we can do except pray that our American friends are as lucky as us and find the Nautilus."

"Can't they evacuate New York?"

"It's too late for that, I imagine." Pike padded up and down, frustrated by his own helplessness. He craved innocent, uninformed company.

"Fancy a drink at the pub round the corner?" he asked.

"Sorry old boy, I can't let you out of my sight. You might do something silly like ring up NBC." Pike gasped. "I wouldn't do a thing like that." But he admitted to himself that he might. "Surely they can find this thing. It's got a telephone wire sticking out of it. Unless of course it has a radio telephone." Pike thought to himself that even then it would have an aerial. He stood by the window staring across Horse Guards Parade and St James's Park, where only a handful of leaves hung on the trees. In twenty minutes, he thought, the pulse would go out from Moscow, digits would click across the international exchanges, beamed by satellite into New York and…"My god!" he said aloud. "The exchange! We can stop all traffic through the exchange and the message won't get through." Pike was dancing up and down. "They didn't think of that, did they, the bastards."

"I wonder if the Americans have," said Fortescue. He picked up a telephone. "You think that would do it?" he asked Pike.

"If it's a radio telephone they probably only have a couple of exchanges covering the New York area. It's like our Cellnet."

"Get me Spiro at Langley," said Fortescue.

CHAPTER THIRTY-ONE

Moscow

Zilin was on the last leg of his journey. A fall of snow had covered Red Square. Muscovites shuffled across it in heavy clothing unaware of the threat to the world made in the name of the Soviet Union. Venkov in Geneva had tried to mobilise troops in Moscow to take over Mikhailov's stronghold in the Kremlin. But communications between Moscow and Geneva were dead - not an unusual occurrence. Ustinov and his loyal followers were poised to take over Moscow and Leningrad, peacefully if possible, but by force if their ultimatum failed to bring the United States into line. They needed a propaganda victory on which to base their bid for power.

Zilin was Mikhailov's old national service friend. They had messed from the same tin, frozen in the same tent, even shat together. Now Zilin was home, humiliated by his failure in England, but eager to get back into harness. Two hours ago he had telephoned Mikhailov's office wanting to report to his commander. Mikhailov welcomed the voice of an old friend as a diversion from his global war of nerves. He needed Zilin's calm grin and his evil humour.

"Send him in. He has priority clearance," Mikhailov told the guard at the outer gate. Zilin had no trouble entering the inner sanctum of the Kremlin. He wasn't searched. He entered the long gallery that was Mikhailov's office. At the end sat Mikhailov at a desk crowded with telephones.

"Here it is," said Mikhailov pointing to one of them. "The telephone that may trigger World War Three. Do you think Uncle Sam is scared? Do you think his nerve is cracking?"

Zilin's task, the bargain with which he had bought his life, was to neutralize Mikhailov at the earliest opportunity. Failure would mean immediate death outside the Kremlin at the hands of Hungarian agents. Yet here he was, faced by a madman, and fascinated by the sight of evil enhanced by power. Mikhailov was the snake, he told himself, and he was the rabbit. So it had always been, even when Mikhailov had been half dead with cold and hunger on the steppe and Zilin had to carry his backpack. Mikhailov had fought him for the last scrap of food and won. That was the power he had.

"In seven minutes," said Mikhailov, "unless I get a message on that screen there, or on this television here which is showing one of the American channels, I shall dial a certain number in New York. It will take fifteen or twenty seconds to make the connection. Once the connection is made I press the button on this tape recorder and deliver a coded message. Goodbye Manhattan." Zilin laughed softly, and eyed the distance between himself and the tape recorder. While Mikhailov was dialling he would tear the recorder from the desk and destroy the tape.

"How did you escape from England, Alexei?"

"I took one of our own ships from Dundee. It was easy."

"Too easy. Have they brainwashed you and sent you as a spy," asked Mikhailov, "or as an assassin?"

"My brain is too filthy to wash," said Zilin sadly. Mikhailov exploded with laughter.

"Listen, Igor Alexeivich. You and I will be kings when this is over. After the necessary purges there will be a new era of revolution at home and ascendancy abroad. This country survives on distrust in the world, distrust of us by our enemies and distrust between our enemies of themselves. Whether this crazy Nautilus blows up or not is immaterial; we shall have won. Terror at home, chaos abroad; that is the key to the advancement of the Soviet system over all others. Gorbachev, Shevardnadze - they're flabby salesmen. Stalin, Ustinov - they are the men of steel."

Zilin's heart was pounding. He felt the sweat break on his forehead and glue his shirt to his body. Sweat invaded his socks and shoes. But he could not move.

In Geneva a banquet given by President Reagan and his wife Nancy was coming to a close. The meal was notable for the numbers of messengers sliding apologetically to the side of Mikhail Gorbachev to give him the latest news - no contact with Moscow.

Gorbachev and his wife Raisa faced the television cameras. He made his expected speech urging a reduction of arms and the growth of detente. He was even a little aggressive, warning the Americans that their pursuit of the iniquitous Star Wars could only end in disaster. Only a small section of his audience knew how real that warning was. Gorbachev meant what he said, but he was talking in a vacuum. He was no longer leader of the second greatest power on earth but a king in exile in Geneva with only his small entourage. Would he and Raisa ever get back to Moscow? Only in chains, he thought.

For Reagan the problem was different. Could he justify his refusal to be blackmailed if 100,000 New Yorkers died? An explosion in Manhattan would rip the heart out of the greatest financial centre in the world which was also the heart of the American economy. As a modern-day Nero he would never be forgiven for banqueting in Geneva while Manhattan burned. Reagan looked at his watch; there were four minutes to the deadline. He turned to his closest political adviser of the day, White House Chief of Staff Don Regan, and whispered: "I'm going to back down."

"I already have the speech here, Mr President," said Regan heavily. This was an occasion where the future had been too important to leave to an ageing president. After the CIA's failure in Moscow, an emergency council including Pentagon bosses and CIA chief Bill Casey had decided to act independently and have a message, however spurious, put out to the news agencies. A word to the army of reporters massed in Geneva, but barred from the conference itself, was enough. If Reagan had not turned to his aide in the next two minutes, that speech would have gone out anyway.

Reagan read the speech quickly. He laughed.

"Not bad, Don. That's exactly my style. Send it out." Reagan turned to the trembling Gorbachev who had just finished his speech.

"You have a way with words, Mr Gorbachev," said Reagan. "I can tell that, even though I don't understand Russian. Now I have something to tell you privately, in English." Reagan bent very close to Gorbachev. "The United States of America has agreed to renounce its iniquitous Star Wars programme in response to an unprecedented act of terrorism. You have 24 hours to get that guy out of the Kremlin and disarm all your Nautilus subs around the world." Gorbachev's face worked with emotion.

"You won't regret this act of humanity, Mr President. You have saved thousands of lives and also my political career. When I get back to Moscow you will see how far detente can go, you will see." He looked at his watch. "But you must send a message to Moscow via Washington. Our delegation is cut off."

"That's all taken care of," said Reagan, "now relax and enjoy yourself."

The news agencies flashed the message across the world: "Reagan renounces Star Wars." It was short, sensational and phoney.

VULKAN

CHAPTER THIRTY-TWO

The Reuters monitor in Mikhailov's office showed the message. It was unambiguous. Mikhailov picked up a telephone.

"Is Tass showing the same thing?" he asked. "Good." He looked at Zilin with an impish gleam in his eye. "The Americans are lying, and besides, their message came too late." He began to dial New York.

Tikov was also dialling. From the NYNEX exchange he had learned the number of Michael Parker's mobile telephone. His plan was simple. If he dialled the number and kept it ringing, no one else could dial in: Mikhailov wouldn't get the coded message through - and there would be no explosion.

He dialled the number, and heard it ring. Somewhere at the bottom of the East River, in a miniature submarine primed with a 20-kilotonne bomb, a telephone was ringing. The ringing stopped, and there was a hiss, which after half-a-minute switched to an engaged signal. Tikov dialled again. Obviously the radiophone cut unintelligible calls after a certain time. He looked at his watch. There were two minutes to go: it was worth a try. He dialled a number in Texas.

"Tom. It's Boris. Take down this number: 212 835 0015. Have you got that? Now for the sake of humanity dial it and dial again when you get the engaged signal. Do you have two lines in the house?"

"We have a car phone."

"Get Mary to call your friends or NASA. Get them all dialling that number. It's to stop a message getting through from Moscow. Otherwise boom, do you read me?"

"I read you."

"Goodbye, Tom." Tikov dialled the same number himself. He looked at his watch - there were fifteen seconds to go. If the number rang for half a minute before aborting the call, that should take him over the deadline. He hoped Mikhailov's watch was accurate.

At CIA headquarters in Langley, Virginia, Spiro McLeod was watching the seconds tick by. Since the call from Fortescue he had been trying to get clearance to shut down the NYNEX mobile telephone switching office in Jersey City. That was the office which controlled all mobile telephone calls in the Manhattan area. NYNEX were uncooperative. They hated CIA interference since the image of spooks and phone-tapping wasn't popular with customers. McLeod took it to the top, to the chairman of NYNEX Mobile and the New Jersey Police Department. They laughed at him.

"So, the CIA wants to run us out of business," said NYNEX chief William Hunter III. "The answer is a reluctant no."

McLeod was already formulating an alternative plan but it would take time. He made some more telephone calls. By three o'clock Eastern Standard Time a carload of CIA professionals was within a mile of the switching office in Jersey City, but McLeod knew they were already too late.

Mikhailov listed to the digits click through the exchanges at the speed of light, like a safe-cracker reading a combination lock. Zilin watched his face, powerless to intervene. The death of so many women and children was no longer important. We all have to die, he thought; why not sooner rather than later. It saves us the agony of existence; my own has been miserable and short. Mikhailov and I are fit for each other. Yes, he even felt a peculiar love for this man hunched over the telephone. At least he was positive; at least he was a doer!

Mikhailov's face turned black.

"The line is busy," he said. His eyes darted to Zilin. "Does that mean the international lines are busy or the number itself is busy?" He dialled again. "Busy," he said patiently. And again. "Busy." He dialled furiously. "You dial," he said to Zilin, pointing to another telephone.

Zilin read the number and dialled. "I'll get the international operator," said Mikhailov. After a minute he got the operator. "I'm trying to dial a number in New York," he said., "It's top priority. Will you check whether there's a fault on the line?"

Suddenly, Zilin heard a new tone. The number was ringing. It was a terrible shock and his pulse raced. For a moment he listened in dread, then hung up.

"Busy," he said and dialled again.

"Hello, this is the New York operator," an American voice told Mikhailov. "There's no fault on the line; would you like me to connect you?"

"Please," said Mikhailov, "it's extremely urgent." The operator tried the number.

"There does appear to be a fault now, sir. The line's dead." Mikhailov hurled the telephone across the room. He was speechless with rage.

In Jersey City the CIA professionals had burst into the switching office, killing one security guard. They began to rip out all the wires they could see.

"What the hell are you doing?" shouted an employee, with his hands above his head.

"We have to cut off all mobile telephone calls in this area," said a CIA man continuing his destructive path. "We're the CIA."

"Will you allow me?" said the employee. He turned round and flicked three switches. "There," he said.

Tikov dialled the number again. Instead of an engaged signal he got a high-pitched whine. He dialled again, same result. Had the thing gone off? Surely he would have heard, or been vaporised. What was the time lag between the detonation and the blast? Surely he would have been burned by now. It must be miles away, up by Long Island or Staten.

Tikov decided to risk a look out of the window. There were people alive in the street, and there was a police car. He heard steps outside on the landing, and the doorbell rang. Tikov froze.

"Open up, police." Tikov didn't move. "Okay, we know you're in there, Mr Parker, you've been talking on the phone." Tikov suspected they were bluffing; but there was a thud and a crack of splitting wood.

"There he is, there's the son-of-a-bitch," said one policeman.

"Mr Parker?" asked another, more formally.

"No," said Tikov.

"You fancy yourself some kind of racing driver, doing the Indianapolis five hundred down West Side Highway?" said the aggressive one.

"Gentlemen," pleaded Tikov, "I'm not Michael Parker, but everything will be explained. Please can I make one telephone call?"

"You have the number?"

"Marine headquarters on Governor's Island, Commander Dittrich."

"OK smart-arse, let's go."

"Where?"

"Down to the precinct, to make a statement. Nobody plays chicken with Sergeant Howard P Bradfield."

It was true, thought Tikov, what *Pravda* said about the New York Police.

On the East River normal water traffic was at a standstill. Divers scoured the seabed. Gunboats hung in the water dangling sensitive sonar and acoustic equipment. During one of the passive listening periods, when all activity ceased and the acoustics experts scanned the depths, they picked up something.

"It was a buzzing, sir," said a corporal on one of the gunboats. "Sounded like a telephone ringing."

"Underwater, Jones?" asked the gunboat captain, Commander Bancroft.

"Had to be, sir."

"Maybe it was a radio telephone on a yacht."

"I got a depth reading of around 30 feet." Bancroft was sceptical; but he checked with the control room on Governor's Island.

"Commander Dittrich, this sounds crazy but I have a man here who says he heard a telephone ringing 30 feet underwater."

"When was that?"

"About a minute, minute and a half ago."

"Is it ringing now?"

"No." Commander Dittrich felt a thrill of excitement.

"You may have something there boys, did you get a bearing?"

"Affirmative."

"Give me your exact position and the bearing. We'll send in the recovery team. Meanwhile keep listening. If you hear the telephone again, tell me immediately. Good work."

The source of the ringing was pinpointed 60 feet offshore on the east side of Manhattan, between the United Nations building and Wall Street. A fast launch was over the spot within five minutes. Nothing showed up on the sonar, but that was expected. Two divers, bomb disposal experts, were sent down. They found the Nautilus and ripped out the antenna. One diver followed the aerial wire. The first few yards were buried in the east river mud, then rose from a weight on the bottom. It was a hair-thin wire attached to a float on the surface.

The protrusion above the surface was so fine that someone five yards away with his eyes at sea level might have failed to spot it.

A message was flashed to all ships and personnel to call off the search. The Nautilus had been found.

"Your idea seems to have worked," said Fortescue turning to Pike who was chewing his fingernails. "The exchange was shut down 20 minutes ago."

"But have they found Nautilus?" asked Pike, "It may be programmed to go off if interfered with."

"Not according to our knowledge of Nautilus. It doesn't have any equipment like that on board. The Russians were probably too afraid it might be triggered by mistake. Anyway, there hasn't been an explosion yet. Shall we go and have that drink? You deserve it."

The telephone rang. Fortescue answered, with one arm already in his coat.

"Mikhailov has made fresh demands," said Spiro's voice from Langley, Virginia. "They're beyond our control." His voice trembled a little. "This time it's Japan - right in the middle of Tokyo."

"What does he want?"

"This is the crazy bit. He wants the West to make a nuclear strike on Peking and Shanghai. Nothing spectacular, just a couple of 40-kilotonne warheads. He's completely insane."

"What are you going to do about it?"

"The Japs want us to nuke the Chinese."

"You won't do that, will you?" asked Fortescue.

"We have a mutual defence pact with Japan as you know."

"Then you must retaliate against the aggressor, not the innocent Chinese." There was a pause the other end.

"I'd like to agree with you, Charles. But you know, and I know, what a nuclear strike against the Soviet Union would mean." Fortescue knew it would most likely mean total nuclear war, with Europe as the main theatre. The Soviets' first move would be to pre-empt Cruise missile launches from Britain and West Germany. It was a nightmare worse than any alternative.

"Okay, so you nuke the Chinese," said Fortescue. "What then?"

"A thousand million people. What's a couple of million more or less?" said Spiro. "It might upset Sino-American relations for a bit. The open door will close again for a couple of decades, but we'll say we're sorry.

"You're prepared to trade a few million Chinese for a couple of hundred thousand Japanese?"

"We figure the Japanese need a break. It was them last time round."

"I'm beginning to wonder who's mad," said Fortescue, "Mikhailov or the CIA."

"It's pretty macabre, isn't it?"

"What's the deadline?"

"There isn't one yet. He's just waiting for our reply."

"Listen," said Fortescue, "we have a man in there with Mikhailov. When he left Britain he agreed to get access to Mikhailov and kill him."

"What went wrong? The bastard's still alive."

"I don't know, but there's a chance he'll still get to him. All I'm saying is we should play for time. Maybe something will show up. Are the Japanese searching for a Nautilus in Tokyo Harbour?"

"Yes. But they've refused our help. They say it's a question of internal security."

"Then why don't you just walk away from the whole problem. Let them sort it out."

"You don't understand Japanese-American relations. They go back a long way."

"Yes. All the way to Pearl Harbour," said Fortescue, and slammed down the receiver. Then he picked it up again and dialled a London number.

"Laszlo," he said, "where the hell is our man Zilin?"

"Our latest information is that he's with Mikhailov in the Kremlin."

"But Mikhailov's still alive."

"Maybe he killed Zilin first."

"Maybe Zilin changed his mind."

"Then we kill him when he comes out. He knows that," said Laszlo.

"Can anyone else get into the Kremlin?"

"We thought of mortars, but Mikhailov's office is well protected."

"What about a plane?"

"Even if we had a suicide pilot, it would be impossible to organize in time."

"I thought you Hungarians could hustle your way in anywhere."

"The Kremlin has no revolving doors," said Laszlo sadly.

President Reagan was called away from the banquet by an aide.

"Mr President, it's Mr Nakasone on the line from Japan. He wants to know what you've decided." Reagan picked up the telephone.

"I can do nothing. This man is an international pirate. He's an enemy of the entire planet. If my good friend Mr Gorbachev could do anything he would. We will not bow to pressure from tyrants and terrorists."

"Then America will once again be responsible for a nuclear atrocity in Japan."

"Mr Nakasone, if you like to view it that way, go ahead. But my country will not raise its hand against an innocent people to appease a third party. Of course we are deeply concerned at the threat to Tokyo. I remind you that we've offered assistance which you have refused. Naturally if the worst happens you can count on us to provide all the relief assistance we can."

"Are you on nuclear alert?"

"No. The only conceivable threat to us can be from the Soviet Union and at the moment I'm with the Soviet leader at dinner. God be with you and the Japanese people at this time." Reagan hung up.

VULKAN

CHAPTER THIRTY-THREE

Moscow

Mikhailov and Zilin sat in armchairs each side of a low table. Between them lay a tray of bread and sausage half-eaten and coffee half-drunk, and beside it a chessboard. They were well into the middle game - Mikhailov black, Zilin white. Zilin had the advantage. His rooks, one behind the other, dominated the queen's bishop's file. Both knights were poised to inflict severe damage on black's rear line. Yet his own defence was intact with his king neatly tucked on the knight's square, and the rook's pawn advanced.

Mikhailov wanted to break that defence. He had exchanged a knight for a bishop in the early game and was a pawn down. The thought of revenge drove him to attack and send his queen's bishop against that defensive wall. Zilin devoured it, and the knight which followed soon after, hoping to fork the white rook and the white queen. Mikhailov went for the slaughter, exchanging rook for rook and exposing his scattered pawns. Zilin gobbled them up, and offered his queen - a sacrifice which plunged Mikhailov into thought for twenty minutes. Mikhailov took the queen and laid his rear line open to an inexorable assault of pawns. On they came, dying on his ragged battlements, until one of them was crowned queen. Now it was Zilin's turn to patrol the board mopping up survivors of the black army until almost reluctantly he pinned its king to one, fatal square. Mikhailov swept his king off the board.

"You have a lot on your mind, Misha," said Zilin. "You used to beat me hollow."

"Games become unreal when reality has become a game. Four of my pieces have been taken - Zurich, London, New York and Florida, a sacrifice. Now I shall play the darkest, most powerful piece of all, my black samurai." Mikhailov leapt up and lurched off to his desk. He opened a drawer and pulled out a heavy black revolver which he stroked against his head.

"The game is set up. If I lose I shall, you see, eliminate myself from the board." He laid the revolver in front of him on the desk.

Mikhailov picked up the telephone. He dialled a number in the United States.

"Is that you Spiro?" he said, "Have you decided which piece should be sacrificed?"

"The United States will not play your evil game," said the CIA man. "If you detonate this thing it will have been the single most inhuman, unprovoked piece of barbarism in the history of mankind. That may not cut much ice with you, but think of the generations of Russian children who will feel shame for what you have done."

"Do Americans feel shame for Hiroshima and Nagasaki?"

"That was different."

"My only aim has been to put an end to all ambitions of war. To show mankind the ultimate evil. The spread of such weapons to every corner of the earth is a thought so horrible that after this that everyone will agree to outlaw them for ever. I offered you collaboration. You refused. Now you are reaping the reward."

"No one is denying that this is the most horrible weapon on earth. Since we're agreed on that, do we need a live demonstration? Surely the panic you've caused in London and New York and Tokyo is enough."

"Man is a forgetful animal. He needs something to be burned on his memory, otherwise he never learns."

"The answer is, Mikhailov, we're calling your bluff. You failed in London, you failed in New York. The chances are you'll fail in Japan too."

"Then you must take the consequences." The United States administration, that is, the few who knew about the crisis, braced themselves for a blackout and seismic irregularities in Japan. There wasn't time to warn the US ambassador. But plans were prepared to put US troops in Japan on massive relief duty if an explosion occurred.

Mikhailov put down the receiver then picked it up again.

He dialled twelve digits. As they clicked through the exchanges he began to finger the tape recorder on his desk. He checked it was fully rewound. He checked the connection to the base of the telephone then lifted his eyes to Zilin with a penetrating stare.

Zilin felt dizzy. It was as though Mikhailov, who sat two metres away, was on the other side of the room, or at the end of a long tube. The desk lamp etched Mikhailov's features finely but minutely. Mikhailov might have been a fly or a mouse dialling at the end of a tunnel. He wasn't real, he couldn't be taken seriously.

"Japan," said Mikhailov loudly. Zilin started. Mikhailov held out the receiver and Zilin could hear the double purr as the telephone rang deep underwater on the other side of the world. There was a click and a receptive hiss. The Nautilus was waiting for orders to blow itself sky high.

Mikhailov kept his eyes on Zilin and pressed the play button on the tape recorder. There was a squirt of sound, then a sudden whining from the telephone. Mikhailov replaced the receiver. In his imagination twenty kilotonnes of TNT had burst over Tokyo's banking district, uprooting high-rise buildings, turning trees, cars and people to uniform ash - a clean death at the epicentre, a dirty, lingering, sickening end at the periphery. Poor Garski, he thought. He was one of the best. Loyal to the end. Mikhailov felt a tear in the corner of his eye. One hand rose to wipe it away. The gesture broke the spell on Zilin.

"It's done," said Mikhailov. Zilin walked behind the desk and seized him by the throat. He lifted Mikhailov bodily from his chair and by his neck carried him to one of the tall windows. He wanted to show Mikhailov the world outside the window, which he had just denied. Even more, he wanted to strangle him as he had strangled Cynthia. He kneeled against the puny body and stretched the neck away from him towards the window and the blackness outside. Something snapped, but Mikhailov had already ceased to struggle. Zilin flung him away as one might a dead rat, over the sumptuous Kazak carpet, towards the chessboard where the black king already lay dead on the floor.

Then Zilin walked to the desk. He sat in Mikhailov's chair, which to his disgust was still warm, and looked down from the throne of evil. He picked up the revolver and spun the chamber, held the muzzle to his head and scratched the cold steel against the stubble on his chin and his close-cropped hair. Then he pulled the trigger. There was a click. He pulled a second time. A bullet ripped through his skull. Zilin slumped forward and blood bubbled over the desk.

The Reuters screen near the remains of his head showed the first news report from Tokyo:

"Good morning. Trading on the Tokyo Stock exchange made a brisk start this morning on overnight news of improved yield on 30-year US government bonds. The Nikkei Average firmed after a fall yesterday of 93.04 to 12,607.27. Short term domestic interest rates have kept rising under Central Bank guidance and are set to move higher as the three long-term credit banks are planning to raise their prime lending rates from December 2."

VULKAN

CHAPTER THIRTY-FOUR

Ogasawara Islands, Japan

The rocky shore sloped steeply into the sea, emerald green oak trees clinging to rotting crags which at every earthquake left another scar of torn rubble and broken boughs on their career into the ocean.

Garski sipped at his second can of Kirin beer and gazed at the featureless sea. Sweat clung to his back. It was early December yet it was warm, like summer in Leningrad. Life could be worse. He had five minutes before a second submersion test at 100 metres. There was trouble with the Japanese version of the air filter system and until they got it right they wouldn't risk a Japanese pilot at that depth. Garski had to go. A far cry from the days of World War Two kamikaze pilots, thought Garski - Japanese lives are more precious now.

"Very interesting problem," said Hiro Yasuda, planting himself next to the Russian. "It's peculiar how only the Hungarians could get this right."

"Good engineers, the Hungarians," said Garski, "we couldn't make filters to the same specifications and neither can you."

"We'd have to build a whole new factory to do it, and that would make tongues wag all over Japan."

From the sea, little could be seen of this most secret of Japan's military research projects, beyond a few prefabricated huts and a brace of fishing boats. The coast was uninhabited for miles on each side. There was little flat ground, and fresh water was scarce. Defence engineers had to blast a ledge for the huts and build a jetty for the boats. The original Russian Nautilus and its Japanese copy, the Notiru, were housed in a steel tube within a natural cave. Because of earthquakes no one knew how long the cave would exist.

"Let's go," said Garski. He stretched, freeing the sodden shirt from his back. They walked down wooden steps to the mouth of the cave and clambered over rock fragments to a steel door. Inside the steel tube bright
lights shone on the team of white-coated technicians preparing their prototype for a fresh experiment. The Notiru was obviously a descendant of the Nautilus, but it was smaller, a triumph of Japanese micro-technology. Garski buttoned his overall and squeezed himself through the hatchway. The cabin, surprisingly, was about the same size and the controls were much the same. His Japanese masters swore to him that Notiru was being developed only for passive reconnaissance, not for a nuclear payload, but there was the same ominous housing the size of a suitcase in the centre of the cabin around which Garski had to fit himself. He wasn't that bothered. What the hell, he thought; if we do it, why shouldn't they?

Garski filled the ballast tanks to negative buoyancy and took the craft gently towards the mouth of the tube. A steel door slid open. He continued out to sea at periscope depth followed by one of the fishing boats. Their destination was a bank of white sand several miles out.

The Notiru and the fishing boat were connected by an umbilical wire, not radio, in case signals were picked up by shore observers or even spy satellites.

At the testing ground Garski nosed the craft into a shallow dive. He would take it slowly. He wanted to observe every change as pressure squeezed the hull. He didn't trust the Japanese; he thought they might have skimped on the structure to save weight and reduce sonar profile. It didn't pay, as the Russians had found to their cost in early prototypes..

The Notiru circled downward. Garski relayed information in English to the fishing boat above. Through the portlights he could see bright fishes and the pale ribs of sand below. This was a holiday. He began to feel light-headed, a little dizzied by the thrill of being suspended in a third dimension gliding with the fishes. Then he realized why. The air filter system. The delicate mechanism which squeezed and scrubbed carbon dioxide and other poisonous gases from the compressed air mixture was fouling up. To stay inside would be lethal. He remembered what happened to Karpov back in 1984. Garski prepared to abandon ship. He couldn't bring it to the surface for security reasons and they could easily pick it up again from the sandy bottom. He snapped on his aqualung and blew ballast from the tanks so that the Notiru would land gently. Then he squeezed himself into the airlock and escaped into the warm pacific. His Japanese masters wouldn't be pleased, but at least he was alive.

CHAPTER THIRTY-FIVE

London

It was a bitter February morning in Hyde Park. Pike's brogues scrunched on a thin layer of snow and his breath billowed in front of him, some of it freezing on his moustache. His stride was eager, impatient, even though he had chosen to walk rather than take the car. Laszlo's message had intrigued him: "It concerns Captain Nemo."

As far as Pike was concerned Captain Nemo was dead. The Nautilus project had been cancelled and a secret agreement between Moscow and Washington stipulated that no such weapon would be developed in future, for fear, not so much of another Mikhailov, but that one might fall in to the hands of terrorists - Muslim extremists, for example, or the IRA.

So what had Laszlo dug up? Pike rapped the door knocker at 7 Albion Mews. Laszlo opened the door, still in dressing gown and slippers, with a scarf round his throat.

"Come in, dear friend," he said. "I hope my voice doesn't give out on me." It was hoarse with laryngitis. Laszlo's wife brought coffee and cakes then disappeared.

"My friend the engineer in Budapest, at great personal risk, has sent a copy of an aircraft weigh bill." Laszlo reverently unfolded a piece of paper and handed it to Pike. It was a faint photocopy of a weigh bill from the national Hungarian airline Malev, a delivery from Budapest to Tokyo. Pike couldn't read much of it but he thought he could make out a few words.

"Air filters?" he said. "Are these the same filters that were supplied for Nautilus?"

"My friend doesn't say so, but that's the implication. Eight air filters."

"My god. Does that mean the Japanese…there must have been a Nautilus in Tokyo after all."

"Precisely - and they're being typically Japanese. Another piece of superb industrial espionage. But somehow they couldn't quite achieve the perfection of these Hungarian air filters." Pike laughed.

"Only a Hungarian would have come to that very modest conclusion." Then Pike stopped smiling. "Do you really think that's it?" Laszlo opened a box of pills and put one in his mouth.

"There are two possibilities. One, they found this toy in their backyard and now they're reproducing it purely for ocean research and maybe a little quiet espionage. Or two, having recovered from the shock of a nuclear threat they're building a nuclear weapon of their own."

"Who could blame them?"

"No one, except that it's in violation of their defence agreements with the United States."

"Who can blame them for having lost faith in the American umbrella?" said Pike. He poured himself another cup of coffee. "Let's assume the worst. That the Japanese are developing a Nautilus with a nuclear capability. What will they do with it?"

"I suspect they wouldn't deploy them as the Russians did. Japanese ships have the run of the entire free world and most of the communist world too. It would be much cleverer to store say seven or eight of these things permanently on board Japanese tankers, or freighters, or whalers, ready to be deployed only in an emergency."

"What about a clandestine arms industry?" said Pike. "Age has made me increasingly cynical about man's compulsion to buy and sell instruments of death. Don't you think they might be tempted to sell them under the counter to subversive groups around the world - to Colonel Gaddafi, perhaps or Israel, for the right price?"

"They don't have the nuclear capability."

"They might well have by now."

"Why would they want to put these things into the hands of madmen?"

"Perhaps they've worked out a way of detecting them. That's what the Americans are working on right now." Laszlo sighed and stretched back in his armchair.

"Anyway," he said, "I'm sharing this information with you because I don't know what the hell to do with it. I'm taking the risk that you might go running to your friends at MI5, but I hope you won't without thinking it over. I'm not sure that would be the right thing. There's enough paranoia in the world without us adding to it. Maybe it's best that the Japanese have Nautilus - after all, it's a weapon which is primarily defensive. You can't get into a Nautilus and conquer the world. Moreover, I'm suspicious of this superpower ban on Nautilus. Such bans never work. If the Russians or the Americans or the British are still developing Nautilus then it might be useful to have someone else with the same or even superior technology, and perhaps a means of combatting it."

"That's a very old argument." Pike felt sad. The ability of man to go back on every pact, every article of trust struck with his neighbour, even with his brother, was a constant source of disappointment to him, despite his age and experience. "I won't do anything without discussing it with you first," he said, wondering whether he would keep his word.

"I have to go," he continued. "I'm lunching with Mother." He wrapped himself up and ventured into the cold air again. It was another long walk to his mother's flat in Pimlico but he fancied it would do him good.

EPILOGUE

October 2014

For six days the Swedish navy kept up its relentless search. Minesweepers, helicopters and soldiers on foot crisscrossed the thousands of islands that make up the Stockholm archipelago. A search for what? An unidentified vessel had been spotted carving a wake somewhere in Kanholms Fjord then had disappeared, presumably underwater. Was it a Russian submarine?

Tensions at the time in Ukraine and on the Turkish-Syrian border had pitted Russia against the Western alliance in ways not seen since the 1980s. Sweden's new prime minister, Stefan Löfven, was determined to show the world that his country would not tolerate any intrusion, whether it was the Russians or, as some bizarrely speculated, the Dutch.

Why would Moscow be flexing its muscles now? Other evidence also seemed to point to Russia. An intercepted wireless signal suggested that a Russian submarine was in trouble somewhere in Swedish waters. The transmission in clear text on an emergency frequency was followed by an encrypted reply from Kaliningrad, the Baltic base for Russian submarines. But there was no international appeal for help as there had been in 2005 when a Russian sub snagged itself on cables deep under water in the Pacific Ocean. On that occasion a British submersible came to the rescue and cut it free, saving the crew of seven.

This time, if there was an emergency, the Russians were handling it alone or, for the sake of secrecy, consigning the crew to a watery grave.

For William Pike, convalescing after heart surgery at the age of 85, this item on the television news excited him more than anything had done for nigh on thirty years.

"It's Nautilus," he shouted as he saw video footage of the Swedish navy conducting its search operations.

"Alright, we're not deaf," said a fellow patient in the television room.

"It's Nautilus," said Pike more softly.

Later in his private room he pulled out a box file from under the bed. In it there were drawings and photographs: among them a snapshot of a rocky Nordic shore with a dark shape wallowing in the breakers like a beached whale. There was another of a rubber boat on the same shore. The firm jaw of the man in the bows was recognisable even with such poor resolution. Boris Tikov.

Pike scrolled back thirty years to 1984. Despite the more open policy of Soviet leader Mikhail Gorbachev the Iron Curtain had still been the world's biggest fault-line, with the Cold War costing both sides billions a year. Very few people had imagined that within five years the Berlin Wall would be down, to be followed by the rapid dissolution of the Soviet empire.

Pike fumbled with his mobile phone and finally dialled the number he wanted.

"Hello?" a voice answered.

"Fortescue?"

"Good lord, is that Pike? I thought you'd been put out to grass."

"Well I have, sort of. Can we meet? We can't talk about this on the phone."

Fortescue had long since retired from the service.

"About what?" he asked wearily.

Pike whispered into the phone: "Nautilus."

"Of course we can talk about Nautilus."

"Shhh!"

"No one listens to old farts like us."

"Please. Indulge an old man."

They met for tea in the garden. It was a beautiful day during one of the warmest Octobers on record. Pike was in his dressing-gown. Fortescue, a fit-looking sixty-five, now had white hair.

"What do you think they're playing at?" asked Pike.

"The Russians?"

"I don't think it's them," said Pike. "I believe the worst has happened."

"What's that?"

"If they can fly planes into the twin towers they can certainly turn other forms of transport into lethal weapons."

"Interesting thought, but I suspect you're in a minority of one," said Fortescue. Pike seized him by the arm impatiently.

"We know that the technology was passed to the Japanese. Then for years the trail went cold. I've been piecing things together. It's amazing what you can find on the web if you dig hard enough."

"Such as?"

Pike was ready for this and got out his iPad. "Remember the Flying Finn? Here she is, after a refit, cruising in the Baltic a year ago, renamed Swordfish. Registered in Panama."

"What does that prove?"

"Nothing. But if you look back at her history, she was shipped out of Switzerland by a Saudi company, and laid up for nearly fifteen years in Yemen. A year ago she reappears. Why?"

"You just love conspiracy theories, don't you, William?"

"It's what keeps me alive."

www.ingramcontent.com/pod-product-compliance
Lightning Source LLC
Chambersburg PA
CBHW060933120726
47910CB00002B/317